PEOPLE AND STORIES THAT SHOULD NOT BE FORGOTTEN

ADVENTURES

ADVENTURES

PEOPLE AND STORIES THAT SHOULD NOT BE FORGOTTEN

Fall 2024

WWW.ADVENTURESBOOKZINE.COM

ADVENTURES

PEOPLE AND STORIES THAT SHOULD NOT BE FORGOTTEN

FALL 2024 **ISSUE #13**

WHAT

WHERE

Editor's Note

FALL IS A TIME WHEN WE'RE STARTING TO SETTLE IN FOR COLDER WEATHER, and with the change of wardrobe comes the change of reading material. The light summer reading is past, and it's time to read a bit more seriously, to read those tales while you curl up in that oversized armchair next to the fireplace, blanket on your lap, cup of steaming hot coffee off to the side. (I have a very specific idea of reading comfortably!)

In this new edition of *Adventures* you'll find some stories that fit this bill.

For starters, we have *Flappers and Philosophers* by F. Scott Fitzgerald. This classic isn't as serious as *The Great Gatsby*, but the short stories in the collection are perfect for cozy reading.

Once you're finished with *Flappers and Philosophers*, we have *A Rebours* (Against The Grain) by Joris-Karl Huysmans, an original story *The Raven Messenger* by Teel James Glenn—and a good story for Halloween time, the disconcerting tale *The Most Dangerous Game* by Richard Connell. (You might recall that this one was a "Simpsons" parody.)

Of course, this being *Adventures*, we also take you on the usual fan favorite journeys: We have a Pretty Sinister Books review, Southwest Scenarios with Darryle Purcell, a fun page, and more. So go ahead and settle in and get comfortable, and enjoy this fall edition.

We will see you in the winter!

Thank you!

Michael Brian

Letters to the editor:

Comments/Questions are accepted. Put *Letter to Editor* in Subject and send to: OffBeatReads@pm.me *Email content could be published in future *Adventures To Go*.

The following stories may contain words or language some consider offensive. *Adventures* treats its readers as mature and discerning, and will always publish works as originally written by the author.

FLAPPERS AND PHILOSOPHERS

F. SCOTT FITZGERALD

To Zelda.

CONTENTS

THE OFFSHORE PIRATE

I

This unlikely story begins on a sea that was a blue dream, as colorful as blue-silk stockings, and beneath a sky as blue as the irises of children's eyes. From the western half of the sky the sun was shying little golden disks at the sea—if you gazed intently enough you could see them skip from wave tip to wave tip until they joined a broad collar of golden coin that was collecting half a mile out and would eventually be a dazzling sunset. About half-way between the Florida shore and the golden collar a white steam-yacht, very young and graceful, was riding at anchor and under a blue-and-white awning aft a yellow-haired girl reclined in a wicker settee reading The Revolt of the Angels, by Anatole France.

She was about nineteen, slender and supple, with a spoiled alluring mouth and quick gray eyes full of a radiant curiosity. Her feet, stockingless, and adorned rather than clad in blue-satin slippers which swung nonchalantly from her toes, were perched on the arm of a settee adjoining the one she occupied. And as she read she intermittently regaled herself by a faint application to her tongue of a half-lemon that she held in her hand. The other half, sucked dry, lay on the deck at her feet and rocked very gently to and fro at the almost imperceptible motion of the tide.

The second half-lemon was well-nigh pulpless and the golden collar had grown astonishing in width, when suddenly the drowsy silence which enveloped the yacht was broken by the sound of heavy footsteps and an elderly man topped with orderly gray hair and clad in a white-flannel suit appeared at the head of the companionway. There he paused for a moment until his eyes became accustomed to the sun, and then seeing the girl under the awning he uttered a long even grunt of disapproval.

If he had intended thereby to obtain a rise of any sort he was doomed to disappointment. The girl calmly turned over two pages, turned back one, raised the lemon mechanically to tasting distance, and then very faintly but quite unmistakably yawned.

"Ardita!" said the gray-haired man sternly.

Ardita uttered a small sound indicating nothing.

"Ardita!" he repeated. "Ardita!"

Ardita raised the lemon languidly, allowing three words to slip out before it reached her tongue.

"Oh, shut up."

"Ardita!"

"What?"

"Will you listen to me—or will I have to get a servant to hold you while I talk to you?"

The lemon descended very slowly and scornfully.

"Put it in writing."

"Will you have the decency to close that abominable book and discard that damn lemon for two minutes?"

"Oh, can't you lemme alone for a second?"

"Ardita, I have just received a telephone message from the shore——"

"Telephone?" She showed for the first time a faint interest.

"Yes, it was——"

"Do you mean to say," she interrupted wonderingly, "'at they let you run a wire out here?"

"Yes, and just now——"

"Won't other boats bump into it?"

"No. It's run along the bottom. Five min——"

"Well, I'll be darned! Gosh! Science is golden or something—isn't it?"

"Will you let me say what I started to?"

"Shoot!"

"Well it seems—well, I am up here——" He paused and swallowed several times distractedly. "Oh, yes. Young woman, Colonel Moreland has called up again to ask me to be sure to bring you in to dinner. His son Toby has come all the way from New York to meet you and he's invited several other young people. For the last time, will you——"

"No," said Ardita shortly, "I won't. I came along on this darn cruise with the one idea of going to Palm Beach, and you knew it, and I absolutely refuse to meet any darn old colonel or any darn young Toby or any darn old young people or to set foot in any other darn old town in this crazy state. So you either take me to Palm Beach or else shut up and go away."

"Very well. This is the last straw. In your infatuation for this man.—a man who is notorious for his excesses—a man your father would not have allowed to so much as mention your name—you have rejected the demi-monde rather than the circles in which you have presumably grown up. From now on——"

"I know," interrupted Ardita ironically, "from now on you go your way and I go mine. I've heard that story before. You know I'd like nothing better."

"From now on," he announced grandiloquently, "you are no niece of mine. I——"

"O-o-o-oh!" The cry was wrung from Ardita with the agony of a lost soul. "Will you stop boring me! Will you go 'way! Will you jump overboard and drown! Do you want me to throw this book at you!"

"If you dare do any——"

Smack! The Revolt of the Angels sailed through the air, missed its target by the length of a short nose, and bumped cheerfully down the companionway.

The gray-haired man made an instinctive step backward and then two cautious steps forward. Ardita jumped to her five feet four and stared at him defiantly, her gray eyes blazing.

"Keep off!"

"How dare you!" he cried.

"Because I darn please!"

"You've grown unbearable! Your disposition——"

"You've made me that way! No child ever has a bad disposition unless it's her fancy's fault! Whatever I am, you did it."

Muttering something under his breath her uncle turned and, walking forward called in a loud voice for the launch. Then he returned to the awning, where Ardita had again seated herself and resumed her attention to the lemon.

"I am going ashore," he said slowly. "I will be out again at nine o'clock to-night. When I return we start back to New York, wither I shall turn you over to your aunt for the rest of your natural, or rather unnatural, life." He paused and looked at her, and then all at once something in the utter childness of her beauty seemed to puncture his anger like an inflated tire, and render him helpless, uncertain, utterly fatuous.

"Ardita," he said not unkindly, "I'm no fool. I've been round. I know men. And, child, confirmed libertines don't reform until they're tired—and then they're not themselves—they're husks of themselves." He looked at her as if expecting agreement, but receiving no sight or sound of it he continued. "Perhaps the man loves you—that's possible. He's loved many women and he'll love many more. Less than a month ago, one month, Ardita, he was involved in a notorious affair with that red-haired woman, Mimi Merril; promised to give her the diamond bracelet that the Czar of Russia gave his mother. You know—you read the papers."

"Thrilling scandals by an anxious uncle," yawned Ardita. "Have it filmed. Wicked clubman making eyes at virtuous flapper. Virtuous flapper conclusively vamped by his lurid past. Plans to meet him at Palm Beach. Foiled by anxious uncle."

"Will you tell me why the devil you want to marry him?"

"I'm sure I couldn't say," said Audits shortly. "Maybe because he's the only man I know, good or bad, who has an imagination and the courage of his convictions. Maybe it's to get away from the young fools that spend their vacuous hours pursuing me around the country. But as for the famous Russian bracelet, you can set your mind at rest on that score. He's going to give it to me at Palm Beach—if you'll show a little intelligence."

"How about the—red-haired woman?"

"He hasn't seen her for six months," she said angrily. "Don't you suppose I have enough pride to see to that? Don't you know by this time that I can do any darn thing with any darn man I want to?"

She put her chin in the air like the statue of France Aroused, and then spoiled the pose somewhat by raising the lemon for action.

"Is it the Russian bracelet that fascinates you?"

"No, I'm merely trying to give you the sort of argument that would appeal to your intelligence. And I wish you'd go 'way," she said, her temper rising again. "You know I never change my mind. You've been boring me for three days until I'm about to go crazy. I won't go ashore! Won't! Do you hear? Won't!"

"Very well," he said, "and you won't go to Palm Beach either. Of all the selfish, spoiled, uncontrolled disagreeable, impossible girl I have———"

Splush! The half-lemon caught him in the neck. Simultaneously came a hail from over the side.

"The launch is ready, Mr. Farnam."

Too full of words and rage to speak, Mr. Farnam cast one utterly condemning glance at his niece and, turning, ran swiftly down the ladder.

II

FIVE O'CLOCK ROBED DOWN FROM THE SUN AND PLUMPED SOUNDLESSLY INTO the sea. The golden collar widened into a glittering island; and a faint breeze that had been playing with the edges of the awning and swaying one of the dangling blue slippers became suddenly freighted with song. It was a chorus of men in close harmony and in perfect rhythm to an accompanying sound of oars dealing the blue writers. Ardita lifted her head and listened.

"Carrots and Peas,
Beans on their knees,
Pigs in the seas,
Lucky fellows!
Blow us a breeze,
Blow us a breeze,

Blow us a breeze,
With your bellows."

Ardita's brow wrinkled in astonishment. Sitting very still she listened eagerly as the chorus took up a second verse.

"Onions and beans,
Marshalls and Deans,
Goldbergs and Greens
And Costellos.
Blow us a breeze,
Blow us a breeze,
Blow us a breeze,
With your bellows."

With an exclamation she tossed her book to the desk, where it sprawled at a straddle, and hurried to the rail. Fifty feet away a large rowboat was approaching containing seven men, six of them rowing and one standing up in the stern keeping time to their song with an orchestra leader's baton.

"Oysters and Rocks,
Sawdust and socks,
Who could make clocks
Out of cellos?——"

The leader's eyes suddenly rested on Ardita, who was leaning over the rail spellbound with curiosity. He made a quick movement with his baton and the singing instantly ceased. She saw that he was the only white man in the boat—the six rowers were negroes.

"Narcissus ahoy!" he called politely.

"What's the idea of all the discord?" demanded Ardita cheerfully. "Is this the varsity crew from the county nut farm?"

By this time the boat was scraping the side of the yacht and a great bulking negro in the bow turned round and grasped the ladder. Thereupon the leader left his position in the stern and before Ardita had realized his intention he ran up the ladder and stood breathless before her on the deck.

"The women and children will be spared!" he said briskly. "All crying babies will be immediately drowned and all males put in double irons!" Digging her hands excitedly down into the pockets of her dress Ardita stared at him, speechless with astonishment. He was a young man with a scornful mouth and the bright blue eyes of a healthy baby set in a dark sensitive face. His hair was pitch black, damp and curly—the hair of a Grecian statue gone brunette. He was trimly built, trimly dressed, and graceful as an agile quarter-back.

"Well, I'll be a son of a gun!" she said dazedly.

They eyed each other coolly.

"Do you surrender the ship?"

"Is this an outburst of wit?" demanded Ardita. "Are you an idiot—or just being initiated to some fraternity?"

"I asked you if you surrendered the ship."

"I thought the country was dry," said Ardita disdainfully. "Have you been drinking finger-nail enamel? You better get off this yacht!"

"What?" the young man's voice expressed incredulity.

"Get off the yacht! You heard me!"

He looked at her for a moment as if considering what she had said.

"No," said his scornful mouth slowly; "No, I won't get off the yacht. You can get off if you wish."

Going to the rail be gave a curt command and immediately the crew of the rowboat scrambled up the ladder and ranged themselves in line before him, a coal-black and burly darky at one end and a miniature mulatto of four feet nine at to other. They seemed to be uniformly dressed in some sort of blue costume ornamented with dust, mud, and tatters; over the shoulder of each was slung a small, heavy-looking white sack, and under their arms they carried large black cases apparently containing musical instruments.

""Ten-shun!" commanded the young man, snapping his own heels together crisply. "Right driss! Front! Step out here, Babe!"

The smallest Negro took a quick step forward and saluted.

"Take command, go down below, catch the crew and tie 'em up—all except the engineer. Bring him up to me. Oh, and pile those bags by the rail there."

"Yas-suh!"

Babe saluted again and wheeling about motioned for the five others to gather about him. Then after a short whispered consultation they all filed noiselessly down the companionway.

"Now," said the young man cheerfully to Ardita, who had witnessed this last scene in withering silence, "if you will swear on your honor as a flapper—which probably isn't worth much—that you'll keep that spoiled little mouth of yours tight shut for forty-eight hours, you can row yourself ashore in our rowboat."

"Otherwise what?"

"Otherwise you're going to sea in a ship."

With a little sigh as for a crisis well passed, the young man sank into the settee Ardita had lately vacated and stretched his arms lazily. The corners of his mouth relaxed appreciatively as he looked round at the rich striped awning, the polished brass, and the luxurious fittings of the deck. His eye felt on the book, and then on the exhausted lemon.

"Hm," he said, "Stonewall Jackson claimed that lemon-juice cleared his head. Your head feel pretty clear?"

Ardita disdained to answer.

"Because inside of five minutes you'll have to make a clear decision whether it's go or stay."

He picked up the book and opened it curiously.

"The Revolt of the Angels. Sounds pretty good. French, eh?" He stared at her with new interest "You French?"

"No."

"What's your name?"

"Farnam."

"Farnam what?"

"Ardita Farnam."

"Well Ardita, no use standing up there and chewing out the insides of your mouth. You ought to break those nervous habits while you're young. Come over here and sit down."

Ardita took a carved jade case from her pocket, extracted a cigarette and lit it with a conscious coolness, though she knew her hand was trembling a little; then she crossed over with her supple, swinging walk, and sitting down in the other settee blew a mouthful of smoke at the awning.

"You can't get me off this yacht," she raid steadily; "and you haven't got very much sense if you think you'll get far with it. My uncle'll have wirelesses zigzagging all over this ocean by half past six."

"Hm."

She looked quickly at his face, caught anxiety stamped there plainly in the faintest depression of the mouth's corners.

"It's all the same to me," she said, shrugging her shoulders. "'Tisn't my yacht. I don't mind going for a coupla hours' cruise. I'll even lend you that book so you'll have something to read on the revenue boat that takes you up to Sing-Sing."

He laughed scornfully.

"If that's advice you needn't bother. This is part of a plan arranged before I ever knew this yacht existed. If it hadn't been this one it'd have been the next one we passed anchored along the coast."

"Who are you?" demanded Ardita suddenly. "And what are you?"

"You've decided not to go ashore?"

"I never even faintly considered it."

"We're generally known," he said "all seven of us, as Curtis Carlyle and his Six Black Buddies late of the Winter Garden and the Midnight Frolic."

"You're singers?"

"We were until to-day. At present, due to those white bags you see there we're fugitives from justice and if the reward offered for our capture hasn't by this time reached twenty thousand dollars I miss my guess."

"What's in the bags?" asked Ardita curiously.

"Well," he said "for the present we'll call it—mud—Florida mud."

III

Within ten minutes after Curtis Carlyle's interview with a very frightened engineer the yacht Narcissus was under way, steaming south through a balmy tropical twilight. The little mulatto, Babe, who seems to have Carlyle's implicit confidence, took full command of the situation. Mr. Farnam's valet and the chef, the only members of the crew on board except the engineer, having shown fight, were now reconsidering, strapped securely to their bunks below. Trombone Mose, the biggest negro, was set busy with a can of paint obliterating the name Narcissus from the bow, and substituting the name Hula Hula, and the others congregated aft and became intently involved in a game of craps.

Having given order for a meal to be prepared and served on deck at seven-thirty, Carlyle rejoined Ardita, and, sinking back into his settee, half closed his eyes and fell into a state of profound abstraction.

Ardita scrutinized him carefully—and classed him immediately as a romantic figure. He gave the effect of towering self-confidence erected on a slight foundation—just under the surface of each of his decisions she discerned a hesitancy that was in decided contrast to the arrogant curl of his lips.

"He's not like me," she thought "There's a difference somewhere." Being a supreme egotist Ardita frequently thought about herself; never having had her egotism disputed she did it entirely naturally and with no detraction from her unquestioned charm. Though she was nineteen she gave the effect of a high-spirited precocious child, and in the present glow of her youth and beauty all the men and women she had known were but driftwood on the ripples of her temperament. She had met other egotists—in fact she found that selfish people bored her rather less than unselfish people—but as yet there had not been one she had not eventually defeated and brought to her feet.

But though she recognized an egotist in the settee, she felt none of that usual shutting of doors in her mind which meant clearing ship for action; on the contrary her instinct told her that this man was somehow completely pregnable and quite defenseless. When Ardita defied convention—and of late it had been her chief amusement—it was from an intense desire to be herself, and she felt that this man, on the contrary, was preoccupied with his own defiance.

She was much more interested in him than she was in her own situation, which affected her as the prospect of a matineé might affect a ten-year-old child. She had implicit confidence in her ability to take care of herself under any and all circumstances.

The night deepened. A pale new moon smiled misty-eyed upon the sea, and as the shore faded dimly out and dark clouds were blown like leaves along the far horizon a great haze of moonshine suddenly bathed the yacht and spread an avenue of glittering mail in her swift path. From time to time there was the bright flare of a match as one of them lighted a cigarette, but except for the low under-tone of the throbbing engines and the even wash of the waves about the stern the yacht was quiet as a dream boat star-bound through the heavens. Round them bowed the smell of the night sea, bringing with it an infinite languor.

Carlyle broke the silence at last.

"Lucky girl," he sighed "I've always wanted to be rich—and buy all this beauty."

Ardita yawned.

"I'd rather be you," she said frankly.

"You would—for about a day. But you do seem to possess a lot of nerve for a flapper."

"I wish you wouldn't call me that."

"Beg your pardon."

"As to nerve," she continued slowly, "it's my one redeemiug feature. I'm not afraid of anything in heaven or earth."

"Hm, I am."

"To be afraid," said Ardita, "a person has either to be very great and strong—or else a coward. I'm neither." She paused for a moment, and eagerness crept into her tone. "But I want to talk about you. What on earth have you done—and how did you do it?"

"Why?" he demanded cynically. "Going to write a movie, about me?"

"Go on," she urged. "Lie to me by the moonlight. Do a fabulous story."

A negro appeared, switched on a string of small lights under the awning, and began setting the wicker table for supper. And while they ate cold sliced chicken, salad, artichokes and strawberry jam from the plentiful larder below, Carlyle began to talk, hesitatingly at first, but eagerly as he saw she was interested. Ardita scarcely touched her food as she watched his dark young face—handsome, ironic faintly ineffectual.

He began life as a poor kid in a Tennessee town, he said, so poor that his people were the only white family in their street. He never remembered any white children—but there were inevitably a dozen pickaninnies streaming in his trail, passionate admirers whom he kept in tow by the vividness of his imagination and the amount of trouble he was always getting them in and out of. And it seemed that this association diverted a rather unusual musical gift into a strange channel.

There had been a colored woman named Belle Pope Calhoun who played the piano at parties given for white children—nice white children that would have passed Curtis Carlyle with a sniff. But the ragged little "poh white" used to sit beside her piano by the hour and try to get in an alto with one of those kazoos that boys hum through. Before he was thirteen he was picking up a living teasing ragtime out of a battered violin in little cafés round Nashville. Eight years later the ragtime craze hit the country, and he took six darkies on the Orpheum circuit. Five of them were boys he had grown up with; the other was the little mulatto, Babe Divine, who was a wharf nigger round New York, and long before that a plantation hand in Bermuda, until he stuck an eight-inch stiletto in his master's back. Almost before Carlyle realized his good fortune he was on Broadway, with offers of engagements on all sides, and more money than he had ever dreamed of.

It was about then that a change began in his whole attitude, a rather curious, embittering change. It was when he realized that he was spending the golden years of his life gibbering round a stage with a lot of black men. His act was good of its kind—three trombones, three saxaphones, and Carlyle's flute—and it was his own peculiar sense of rhythm that made all the difference; but he began to grow strangely sensitive about it, began to hate the thought of appearing, dreaded it from day to day.

They were making money—each contract he signed called for more— but when he went to managers and told them that he wanted to separate from his sextet and go on as a regular pianist, they laughed at him and told him he was crazy—it would be an artistic suicide. He used to laugh afterward at the phrase "artistic suicide." They all used it.

Half a dozen times they played at private dances at three thousand dollars a night, and it seemed as if these crystallized all his distaste for his mode of livlihood. They took place in clubs and houses that he couldn't have gone into in the daytime. After all, he was merely playing to rôle of the eternal monkey, a sort of sublimated chorus man. He was sick of the very smell of the theatre, of powder and rouge and the chatter of the greenroom, and the patronizing approval of the boxes. He couldn't put his heart into it any more. The idea of a slow approach to the luxury of leisure drove him wild. He was, of course, progressing toward it, but, like a child, eating his ice-cream so slowly that he couldn't taste it at all.

He wanted to have a lot of money and time and opportunity to read and play, and the sort of men and women round him that he could never have—the kind who, if they thought of him at all, would have considered him rather contemptible; in short he wanted all those things which he was beginning to lump under the general head of aristocracy, an aristocracy which it seemed almost any money could buy except money made as he was making it. He was twenty-five then, without family or education or any promise that he would succeed in a business career. He began speculating wildly, and within three weeks he had lost every cent he had saved.

Then the war came. He went to Plattsburg, and even there his profession followed him. A brigadier-general called him up to headquarters and told him he could serve his country better as a band leader—so he spent the war entertaining celebrities behind the line with a headquarters band. It was not so bad—except that when the infantry came limping back from the trenches he wanted to be one of them. The sweat and mud they wore seemed only one of those ineffable symbols of aristocracy that were forever eluding him.

"It was the private dances that did it. After I came back from the war the old routine started. We had an offer from a syndicate of Florida hotels. It was only a question of time then."

He broke off and Ardita looked at him expectantly, but he shook his head.

"No," he said, "I'm going to tell you about it. I'm enjoying it too much, and I'm afraid I'd lose a little of that enjoyment if I shared it with anyone else. I want to hang on to those few breathless, heroic moments when I stood out before them all and let them know I was more than a damn bobbing, squawking clown."

From up forward came suddenly the low sound of singing. The negroes had gathered together on the deck and their voices rose together in a haunting melody that soared in poignant harmonics toward the moon. And Ardita listens in enchantment.

"Oh down——

oh down,

Mammy wanna take me down milky way,

Oh down,

oh down,

Pappy say to-morra-a-a-ah

But mammy say to-day,

Yes—mammy say to-day!"

Carlyle sighed and was silent for a moment looking up at the gathered host of stars blinking like arc-lights in the warm sky. The negroes' song had died away to a plaintive humming and it seemed as if minute by minute the brightness and the great silence were increasing until he could almost hear the midnight toilet of the mermaids as they combed their silver dripping curls under the moon and gossiped to each other of the fine wrecks they lived on the green opalescent avenues below.

"You see," said Carlyle softly, "this is the beauty I want. Beauty has got to be astonishing, astounding—it's got to burst in on you like a dream, like the exquisite eyes of a girl."

He turned to her, but she was silent.

"You see, don't you, Anita—I mean, Ardita?"

Again she made no answer. She had been sound asleep for some time.

IV

IN THE DENSE SUN-FLOODED NOON OF NEXT DAY A SPOT IN THE SEA BEFORE them resolved casually into a green-and-gray islet, apparently composed of a great granite cliff at its northern end which slanted south through a mile of vivid coppice and grass to a sandy beach melting lazily into the surf. When Ardita, reading in her favorite seat, came to the last page of The Revolt of the Angels, and slamming the book shut looked up and saw it, she gave a little cry of delight, and called to Carlyle, who was standing moodily by the rail.

"Is this it? Is this where you're going?"

Carlyle shrugged his shoulders carelessly.

"You've got me." He raised his voice and called up to the acting skipper: "Oh, Babe, is this your island?"

The mulatto's miniature head appeared from round the corner of the deck-house.

"Yas-suh! This yeah's it."

Carlyle joined Ardita.

"Looks sort of sporting, doesn't it?"

"Yes," she agreed; "but it doesn't look big enough to be much of a hiding-place."

"You still putting your faith in those wirelesses your uncle was going to have zigzagging round?"

"No," said Ardita frankly. "I'm all for you. I'd really like to see you make a get-away."

He laughed.

"You're our Lady Luck. Guess we'll have to keep you with us as a mascot—for the present anyway."

"You couldn't very well ask me to swim back," she said coolly. "If you do I'm going to start writing dime novels founded on that interminable history of your life you gave me last night."

He flushed and stiffened slightly.

"I'm very sorry I bored you."

"Oh, you didn't—until just at the end with some story about how furious you were because you couldn't dance with the ladies you played music for."

He rose angrily.

"You have got a darn mean little tongue."

"Excuse me," she said melting into laughter, "but I'm not used to having men regale me with the story of their life ambitions—especially if they've lived such deathly platonic lives."

"Why? What do men usually regale you with?"

"Oh, they talk about me," she yawned. "They tell me I'm the spirit of youth and beauty."

"What do you tell them?"

"Oh, I agree quietly."

"Does every man you meet tell you he loves you?"

Ardita nodded.

"Why shouldn't he? All life is just a progression toward, and then a recession from, one phrase—'I love you.'"

Carlyle laughed and sat down.

"That's very true. That's—that's not bad. Did you make that up?"

"Yes—or rather I found it out. It doesn't mean anything especially. It's just clever."

"It's the sort of remark," he said gravely, "that's typical of your class."

"Oh," she interrupted impatiently, "don't start that lecture on aristocracy again! I distrust people who can be intense at this hour in the morning. It's a mild form of insanity—a sort of breakfast-food jag. Morning's the time to sleep, swim, and be careless."

Ten minutes later they had swung round in a wide circle as if to approach the island from the north.

"There's a trick somewhere," commented Ardita thoughtfully. "He can't mean just to anchor up against this cliff."

They were heading straight in now toward the solid rock, which must have been well over a hundred feet tall, and not until they were within fifty yards of it did Ardita see their objective. Then she clapped her hands in delight. There was a break in the cliff entirely hidden by a curious overlapping of rock, and through this break the yacht entered and very slowly traversed a narrow channel of crystal-clear water between high gray walls. Then they were riding at anchor in a miniature world of green and gold, a gilded bay smooth as glass and set round with tiny palms, the whole resembling the mirror lakes and twig trees that children set up in sand piles.

"Not so darned bad!" cried Carlyle excitedly.

"I guess that little coon knows his way round this corner of the Atlantic."

His exuberance was contagious, and Ardita became quite jubilant.

"It's an absolutely sure-fire hiding-place!"

"Lordy, yes! It's the sort of island you read about."

The rowboat was lowered into the golden lake and they pulled to shore.

"Come on," said Carlyle as they landed in the slushy sand, "we'll go exploring."

The fringe of palms was in turn ringed in by a round mile of flat, sandy country. They followed it south and brushing through a farther rim of tropical vegetation came out on a pearl-gray virgin beach where Ardita kicked of her brown golf shoes—she seemed to have permanently abandoned stockings—and went wading. Then they sauntered back to the yacht, where the indefatigable Babe had luncheon ready for them. He had posted a lookout on the high cliff to the north to watch the sea on both sides, though he doubted if the entrance to the cliff was generally known— he had never even seen a map on which the island was marked.

"What's its name," asked Ardita—"the island, I mean?"

"No name 'tall," chuckled Babe. "Reckin she jus' island, 'at's all."

In the late afternoon they sat with their backs against great boulders on the highest part of the cliff and Carlyle sketched for her his vague plans. He was sure they were hot after him by this time. The total proceeds of the coup he had pulled off and concerning which he still refused to enlighten her, he estimated as just under a million dollars. He counted on lying up here several weeks and then setting off southward, keeping well outside the usual channels of travel rounding the Horn and heading for Callao, in Peru. The details of coaling and provisioning he was leaving entirely to Babe who, it seemed, had sailed these seas in every capacity from cabin-boy aboard a coffee trader to virtual first mate on a Brazillian pirate craft, whose skipper had long since been hung.

"If he'd been white he'd have been king of South America long ago," said Carlyle emphatically. "When it comes to intelligence he makes Booker T. Washington look like a moron. He's got the guile of every race and nationality whose blood is in his veins, and that's half a dozen or I'm a liar. He worships me because I'm the only man in the world who can play better ragtime than he can. We used to sit together on the wharfs down on the New York water-front, he with a bassoon and me with an oboe, and we'd blend minor keys in African harmonics a thousand years old until the rats would crawl up the posts and sit round groaning and squeaking like dogs will in front of a phonograph."

Ardita roared.

"How you can tell 'em!"

Carlyle grinned.

"I swear that's the gos——"

"What you going to do when you get to Callao?" she interrupted.

"Take ship for India. I want to be a rajah. I mean it. My idea is to go up into Afghanistan somewhere, buy up a palace and a reputation, and then after about five years appear in England with a foreign accent and a mysterious past. But India first. Do you know, they say that all the gold in the world drifts very gradually back to India. Something fascinating about that to me. And I want leisure to read—an immense amount."

"How about after that?"

"Then," he answered defiantly, "comes aristocracy. Laugh if you want to—but at least you'll have to admit that I know what I want—which I imagine is more than you do."

"On the contrary," contradicted Ardita, reaching in her pocket for her cigarette case, "when I met you I was in the midst of a great uproar of all my friends and relatives because I did know what I wanted."

"What was it?"

"A man."

He started.

"You mean you were engaged?"

"After a fashion. If you hadn't come aboard I had every intention of slipping ashore yesterday evening—how long ago it seems—and meeting him in Palm Beach. He's waiting there for me with a bracelet that once belonged to Catherine of Russia. Now don't mutter anything about aristocracy," she put in quickly. "I liked him simply because he had had an imagination and the utter courage of his convictions."

"But your family disapproved, eh?"

"What there is of it—only a silly uncle and a sillier aunt. It seems he got into some scandal with a red-haired woman name Mimi something—it was frightfully exaggerated, he said, and men don't lie to me—and anyway I didn't care what he'd done; it was the future that counted. And I'd see to that. When a man's in love with me he doesn't care for other amusements. I told him to drop her like a hot cake, and he did."

"I feel rather jealous," said Carlyle, frowning—and then he laughed. "I guess I'll just keep you along with us until we get to Callao. Then I'll lend you enough money to get back to the States. By that time you'll have had a chance to think that gentleman over a little more."

"Don't talk to me like that!" fired up Ardita. "I won't tolerate the parental attitude from anybody! Do you understand me?" He chuckled and then stopped, rather abashed, as her cold anger seemed to fold him about and chill him.

"I'm sorry," he offered uncertainly.

"Oh, don't apologize! I can't stand men who say 'I'm sorry' in that manly, reserved tone. Just shut up!"

A pause ensued, a pause which Carlyle found rather awkward, but which Ardita seemed not to notice at all as she sat contentedly enjoying her cigarette and gazing out at the shining sea. After a minute she crawled out on the rock and lay with her face over the edge looking down. Carlyle, watching her, reflected how it seemed impossible for her to assume an ungraceful attitude.

"Oh, look," she cried. "There's a lot of sort of ledges down there. Wide ones of all different heights."

"We'll go swimming to-night!" she said excitedly. "By moonlight."

"Wouldn't you rather go in at the beach on the other end?"

"Not a chance. I like to dive. You can use my uncle's bathing suit, only it'll fit you like a gunny sack, because he's a very flabby man. I've got a one-piece that's shocked the natives all along the Atlantic coast from Biddeford Pool to St. Augustine."

"I suppose you're a shark."

"Yes, I'm pretty good. And I look cute too. A sculptor up at Rye last summer told me my calves are worth five hundred dollars."

There didn't seem to be any answer to this, so Carlyle was silent, permitting himself only a discreet interior smile.

V

When the night crept down in shadowy blue and silver they threaded the shimmering channel in the rowboat and, tying it to a jutting rock, began climbing the cliff together. The first shelf was ten feet up, wide, and furnishing a natural diving platform. There they sat down in the bright moonlight and watched the faint incessant surge of the waters almost stilled now as the tide set seaward.

"Are you happy?" he asked suddenly.

She nodded.

"Always happy near the sea. You know," she went on, "I've been thinking all day that you and I are somewhat alike. We're both rebels—only for different reasons. Two years ago, when I was just eighteen and you were——"

"Twenty-five."

"——well, we were both conventional successes. I was an utterly devastating débutante and you were a prosperous musician just commissioned in the army——"

"Gentleman by act of Congress," he put in ironically.

"Well, at any rate, we both fitted. If our corners were not rubbed off they were at least pulled in. But deep in us both was something that made us require more for happiness. I didn't know what I wanted. I went from man to man, restless, impatient, month by month getting less acquiescent and more dissatisfied. I used to sit sometimes chewing at the insides of my mouth and thinking I was going crazy—I had a frightful sense of transiency. I wanted things now—now—now! Here I was—beautiful—I am, aren't I?"

"Yes," agreed Carlyle tentatively.

Ardita rose suddenly.

"Wait a second. I want to try this delightful-looking sea."

She walked to the end of the ledge and shot out over the sea, doubling up in mid-air and then straightening out and entering to water straight as a blade in a perfect jack-knife dive.

In a minute her voice floated up to him.

"You see, I used to read all day and most of the night. I began to resent society——"

"Come on up here," he interrupted. "What on earth are you doing?"

"Just floating round on my back. I'll be up in a minute. Let me tell you. The only thing I enjoyed was shocking people; wearing something quite impossible and quite charming to a fancy-dress party, going round with the fastest men in New York, and getting into some of the most hellish scrapes imaginable."

The sounds of splashing mingled with her words, and then he heard her hurried breathing as she began climbing up side to the ledge.

"Go on in!" she called

Obediently he rose and dived. When he emerged, dripping, and made the climb he found that she was no longer on the ledge, but after a second frightened he heard her light laughter from another shelf ten feet up. There he joined her and they both sat quietly for a moment, their arms clasped round their knees, panting a little from the climb.

"The family were wild," she said suddenly. "They tried to marry me off. And then when I'd begun to feel that after all life was scarcely worth living I found something"—her eyes went skyward exultantly——"I found something!"

Carlyle waited and her words came with a rush.

"Courage—just that; courage as a rule of life, and something to cling to always. I began to build up this enormous faith in myself. I began to see that in all my idols in the past some manifestation of courage had unconsciously been the thing that attracted me. I began separating courage from the other things of life. All sorts of courage—the beaten, bloody prize-fighter coming up for more—I used to make men take me to prize-fights; the déclassé woman sailing through a nest of cats and looking at them as if they were mud under her feet; the liking what you like always; the utter disregard for other people's opinions—just to live as I liked always and to die in my own way— Did you bring up the cigarettes?"

He handed one over and held a match for her gently.

"Still," Ardita continued, "the men kept gathering—old men and young men, my mental and physical inferiors, most of them, but all intensely desiring to have me—to own this rather magnificent proud tradition I'd built up round me. Do you see?"

"Sort of. You never were beaten and you never apologized."

"Never!"

She sprang to the edge, poised for a moment like a crucified figure against the sky; then describing a dark parabola plunked without a slash between two silver ripples twenty feet below.

Her voice floated up to him again.

"And courage to me meant ploughing through that dull gray mist that comes down on life—not only overriding people and circumstances but overriding the bleakness of living. A sort of insistence on the value of life and the worth of transient things."

She was climbing up now, and at her last words her head, with the damp yellow hair slicked symmetrically back appeared on his level.

"All very well," objected Carlyle. "You can call it courage, but your courage is really built, after all, on a pride of birth. You were bred to that defiant attitude. On my gray days even courage is one of the things that's gray and lifeless."

She was sitting near the edge, hugging her knees and gazing abstractedly at the white moon; he was farther back, crammed like a grotesque god into a niche in the rock.

"I don't want to sound like Pollyanna," she began, "but you haven't grasped me yet. My courage is faith—faith in the eternal resilience of me—that joy'll come back, and hope and spontaneity. And I feel that till it does I've got to keep my lips shut and my chin high, and my eyes wide—not necessarily any silly smiling. Oh, I've been through hell without a whine quite often—and the female hell is deadlier than the male."

"But supposing," suggested Carlyle, "that before joy and hope and all that came back the curtain was drawn on you for good?"

Ardita rose, and going to the wall climbed with some difficulty to the next ledge, another ten or fifteen feet above.

"Why," she called back "then I'd have won!"

He edged out till he could see her.

"Better not dive from there! You'll break your back," he said quickly.

She laughed.

"Not I!"

Slowly she spread her arms and stood there swan-like, radiating a pride in her young perfection that lit a warm glow in Carlyle's heart.

"We're going through the black air with our arms wide and our feet straight out behind like a dolphin's tail, and we're going to think we'll never hit the silver down there till suddenly it'll be all warm round us and full of little kissing, caressing waves."

Then she was in the air, and Carlyle involuntarily held his breath. He had not realized that the dive was nearly forty feet. It seemed an eternity before he heard the swift compact sound as she reached the sea.

And it was with his glad sigh of relief when her light watery laughter curled up the side of the cliff and into his anxious ears that he knew he loved her.

VI

Time, having no axe to grind, showered down upon them three days of afternoons. When the sun cleared the port-hole of Ardita's cabin an hour after dawn she rose cheerily, donned her bathing-suit, and went up on deck. The negroes would leave their work when they saw her, and crowd, chuckling and chattering, to the rail as she floated, an agile minnow, on and under the surface of the clear water. Again in the cool of the afternoon she would swim—and loll and smoke with Carlyle upon the cliff; or else they would lie on their sides in the sands of the southern beach, talking little, but watching the day fade colorfully and tragically into the infinite langour of a tropical evening.

And with the long, sunny hours Ardita's idea of the episode as incidental, madcap, a sprig of romance in a desert of reality, gradually left her. She dreaded the time when he would strike off southward; she dreaded all the eventualities that presented themselves to her; thoughts were suddenly troublesome and decisions odious. Had prayers found place in the pagan rituals of her soul she would have asked of life only to be unmolested for a while, lazily acquiescent to the ready, naïf flow of Carlyle's ideas, his vivid boyish imagination, and the vein of monomania that seemed to run crosswise through his temperament and colored his every action.

But this is not a story of two on an island, nor concerned primarily with love bred of isolation. It is merely the presentation of two personalities, and its idyllic setting among the palms of the Gulf Stream is quite incidental. Most of us are content to exist and breed and fight for the right to do both, and the dominant idea, the foredoomed attest to control one's destiny, is reserved for the fortunate or unfortunate few. To me the interesting thing about Ardita is the courage that will tarnish with her beauty and youth.

"Take me with you," she said late one night as they sat lazily in the grass under the shadowy spreading palms. The negroes had brought ashore their musical instruments, and the sound of weird ragtime was drifting softly over on the warm breath of the night. "I'd love to reappear in ten years, as a fabulously wealthy high-caste Indian lady," she continued.

Carlyle looked at her quickly.

"You can, you know."

She laughed.

"Is it a proposal of marriage? Extra! Ardita Farnam becomes pirate's bride. Society girl kidnapped by ragtime bank robber."

"It wasn't a bank."

"What was it? Why won't you tell me?"

"I don't want to break down your illusions."

"My dear man, I have no illusions about you."

"I mean your illusions about yourself."

She looked up in surprise.

"About myself! What on earth have I got to do with whatever stray felonies you've committed?"

"That remains to be seen."

She reached over and patted his hand.

"Dear Mr. Curtis Carlyle," she said softly, "are you in love with me?"

"As if it mattered."

"But it does—because I think I'm in love with you."

He looked at her ironically.

"Thus swelling your January total to half a dozen," he suggested. "Suppose I call your bluff and ask you to come to India with me?"

"Shall I?"

He shrugged his shoulders.

"We can get married in Callao."

"What sort of life can you offer me? I don't mean that unkindly, but seriously; what would become of me if the people who want that twenty-thousand-dollar reward ever catch up with you?"

"I thought you weren't afraid."

"I never am—but I won't throw my life away just to show one man I'm not."

"I wish you'd been poor. Just a little poor girl dreaming over a fence in a warm cow country."

"Wouldn't it have been nice?"

"I'd have enjoyed astonishing you—watching your eyes open on things. If you only wanted things! Don't you see?"

"I know—like girls who stare into the windows of jewelry-stores."

"Yes—and want the big oblong watch that's platinum and has diamonds all round the edge. Only you'd decide it was too expensive and choose one of white gold for a hundred dollar. Then I'd say: 'Expensive? I should say not!' And we'd go into the store and pretty soon the platinum one would be gleaming on your wrist."

"That sounds so nice and vulgar—and fun, doesn't it?" murmured Ardita.

"Doesn't it? Can't you see us travelling round and spending money right and left, and being worshipped by bell-boys and waiters? Oh, blessed are the simple rich for they inherit the earth!"

"I honestly wish we were that way."

"I love you, Ardita," he said gently.

Her face lost its childish look for moment and became oddly grave.

"I love to be with you," she said, "more than with any man I've ever met. And I like your looks and your dark old hair, and the way you go over the side of the rail when we come ashore. In fact, Curtis Carlyle, I like all the things you do when you're perfectly natural. I think you've got nerve and you know how I feel about that. Sometimes when you're around I've been tempted to kiss you suddenly and tell you that you were just an idealistic boy with a lot of caste nonsense in his head. Perhaps if I were just a little bit older and a little more bored I'd go with you. As it is, I think I'll go back and marry—that other man."

Over across the silver lake the figures of the negroes writhed and squirmed in the moonlight like acrobats who, having been too long inactive, must go through their tacks from sheer surplus energy. In single file they marched, weaving in concentric circles, now with their heads thrown back, now bent over their instruments like piping fauns. And from trombone and saxaphone ceaselessly whined a blended melody, sometimes riotous and jubilant, sometimes haunting and plaintive as a death-dance from the Congo's heart.

"Let's dance," cried Ardita. "I can't sit still with that perfect jazz going on."

Taking her hand he led her out into a broad stretch of hard sandy soil that the moon flooded with great splendor. They floated out like drifting moths under the rich hazy light, and as the fantastic symphony wept and exulted and wavered and despaired Ardita's last sense of reality dropped away, and she abandoned her imagination to the dreamy summer scents of tropical flowers and the infinite starry spaces overhead, feeling that if she opened her eyes it would be to find herself dancing with a ghost in a land created by her own fancy.

"This is what I should call an exclusive private dance," he whispered.

"I feel quite mad—but delightfully mad!"

"We're enchanted. The shades of unnumbered generations of cannibals are watching us from high up on the side of the cliff there."

"And I'll bet the cannibal women are saying that we dance too close, and that it was immodest of me to come without my nose-ring."

They both laughed softly—and then their laughter died as over across the lake they heard the trombones stop in the middle of a bar, and the saxaphones give a startled moan and fade out.

"What's the matter?" called Carlyle.

After a moment's silence they made out the dark figure of a man rounding the silver lake at a run. As he came closer they saw it was Babe in a state of unusual excitement. He drew up before them and gasped out his news in a breath.

"Ship stan'in' off sho' 'bout half a mile suh. Mose, he uz on watch, he say look's if she's done ancho'd."

"A ship—what kind of a ship?" demanded Carlyle anxiously.

Dismay was in his voice, and Ardita's heart gave a sudden wrench as she saw his whole face suddenly droop.

"He say he don't know, suh."

"Are they landing a boat?"

"No, suh."

"We'll go up," said Carlyle.

They ascended the hill in silence, Ardita's hand still resting in Carlyle's as it had when they finished dancing. She felt it clinch nervously from time to time as though he were unaware of the contact, but though he hurt her she made no attempt to remove it. It seemed an hour's climb before they reached the top and crept cautiously across the silhouetted plateau to the edge of the cliff. After one short look Carlyle involuntarily gave a little cry. It was a revenue boat with six-inch guns mounted fore and aft.

"They know!" he said with a short intake of breath. "They know! They picked up the trail somewhere."

"Are you sure they know about the channel? They may be only standing by to take a look at the island in the morning. From where they are they couldn't see the opening in the cliff."

"They could with field-glasses," he said hopelessly. He looked at his wrist-watch. "It's nearly two now. They won't do anything until dawn, that's certain. Of course there's always the faint possibility that they're waiting for some other ship to join; or for a coaler."

"I suppose we may as well stay right here."

The hour passed and they lay there side by side, very silently, their chins in their hands like dreaming children. In back of them squatted the negroes, patient, resigned, acquiescent, announcing now and then with sonorous snores that not even the presence of danger could subdue their unconquerable African craving for sleep.

Just before five o'clock Babe approached Carlyle. There were half a dozen rifles aboard the Narcissus he said. Had it been decided to offer no resistance?

A pretty good fight might be made, he thought, if they worked out some plan.

Carlyle laughed and shook his head.

"That isn't a Spic army out there, Babe. That's a revenue boat. It'd be like a bow and arrow trying to fight a machine-gun. If you want to bury those bags somewhere and take a chance on recovering them later, go on and do it. But it won't work—they'd dig this island over from one end to the other. It's a lost battle all round, Babe."

Babe inclined his head silently and turned away, and Carlyle's voice was husky as he turned to Ardita.

"There's the best friend I ever had. He'd die for me, and be proud to, if I'd let him."

"You've given up?"

"I've no choice. Of course there's always one way out—the sure way—but that can wait. I wouldn't miss my trial for anything—it'll be an interesting experiment in notoriety. 'Miss Farnam testifies that the pirate's attitude to her was at all times that of a gentleman.'"

"Don't!" she said. "I'm awfully sorry."

When the color faded from the sky and lustreless blue changed to leaden gray a commotion was visible on the ship's deck, and they made out a group of officers clad in white duck, gathered near the rail. They had field-glasses in their hands and were attentively examining the islet.

"It's all up," said Carlyle grimly.

"Damn," whispered Ardita. She felt tears gathering in her eyes "We'll go back to the yacht," he said. "I prefer that to being hunted out up here like a 'possum."

Leaving the plateau they descended the hill, and reaching the lake were rowed out to the yacht by the silent negroes. Then, pale and weary, they sank into the settees and waited.

Half an hour later in the dim gray light the nose of the revenue boat appeared in the channel and stopped, evidently fearing that the bay might be too shallow. From the peaceful look of the yacht, the man and the girl in the settees, and the negroes lounging curiously against the rail, they evidently judged that there would be no resistance, for two boats were lowered casually over the side, one containing an officer and six bluejackets, and the other, four rowers and in the stern two gray-haired men in yachting flannels. Ardita and Carlyle stood up, and half unconsciously started toward each other.

Then he paused and putting his hand suddenly into his pocket he pulled out a round, glittering object and held it out to her.

"What is it?" she asked wonderingly.

"I'm not positive, but I think from the Russian inscription inside that it's your promised bracelet."

"Where—where on earth——"

"It came out of one of those bags. You see, Curtis Carlyle and his Six Black Buddies, in the middle of their performance in the tea-room of the hotel at Palm Beach, suddenly changed their instruments for automatics and held up the crowd. I took this bracelet from a pretty, overrouged woman with red hair."

Ardita frowned and then smiled.

"So that's what you did! You have got nerve!"

He bowed.

"A well-known bourgeois quality," he said.

And then dawn slanted dynamically across the deck and flung the shadows reeling into gray corners. The dew rose and turned to golden mist, thin as a dream, enveloping them until they seemed gossamer relics of the late night, infinitely transient and already fading. For a moment sea and sky were breathless, and dawn held a pink hand over the young mouth of life—then from out in the lake came the complaint of a rowboat and the swish of oars.

Suddenly against the golden furnace low in the east their two graceful figures melted into one, and he was kissing her spoiled young mouth.

"It's a sort of glory," he murmured after a second.

She smiled up at him.

"Happy, are you?"

Her sigh was a benediction—an ecstatic surety that she was youth and beauty now as much as she would ever know. For another instant life was radiant and time a phantom and their strength eternal—then there was a bumping, scraping sound as the rowboat scraped alongside.

Up the ladder scrambled the two gray-haired men, the officer and two of the sailors with their hands on their revolvers. Mr. Farnam folded his arms and stood looking at his niece.

"So," he said nodding his head slowly.

With a sigh her arms unwound from Carlyle's neck, and her eyes, transfigured and far away, fell upon the boarding party. Her uncle saw her upper lip slowly swell into that arrogant pout he knew so well.

"So," he repeated savagely. "So this is your idea of—of romance. A runaway affair, with a high-seas pirate."

Ardita glanced at him carelessly.

"What an old fool you are!" she said quietly.

"Is that the best you can say for yourself?"

"No," she said as if considering. "No, there's something else. There's that well-known phrase with which I have ended most of our conversations for the past few years—'Shut up!'"

And with that she turned, included the two old men, the officer, and the two sailors in a curt glance of contempt, and walked proudly down the companionway.

But had she waited an instant longer she would have heard a sound from her uncle quite unfamiliar in most of their interviews. He gave vent to a whole-hearted amused chuckle, in which the second old man joined.

The latter turned briskly to Carlyle, who had been regarding this scene with an air of cryptic amusement.

"Well Toby," he said genially, "you incurable, hare-brained romantic chaser of rainbows, did you find that she was the person you wanted?"

Carlyle smiled confidently.

"Why—naturally," he said "I've been perfectly sure ever since I first heard tell of her wild career. That'd why I had Babe send up the rocket last night."

"I'm glad you did," said Colonel Moreland gravely. "We've been keeping pretty close to you in case you should have trouble with those six strange niggers. And we hoped we'd find you two in some such compromising position," he sighed. "Well, set a crank to catch a crank!"

"Your father and I sat up all night hoping for the best—or perhaps it's the worst. Lord knows you're welcome to her, my boy. She's run me crazy. Did you give her the Russian bracelet my detective got from that Mimi woman?"

Carlyle nodded.

"Sh!" he said. "She's coming on deck."

Ardita appeared at the head of the companionway and gave a quick involuntary glance at Carlyle's wrists. A puzzled look passed across her face. Back aft the negroes had begun to sing, and the cool lake, fresh with dawn, echoed serenely to their low voices.

"Ardita," said Carlyle unsteadily.

She swayed a step toward him.

"Ardita," he repeated breathlessly, "I've got to tell you the—the truth. It was all a plant, Ardita. My name isn't Carlyle. It's Moreland, Toby Moreland. The story was invented, Ardita, invented out of thin Florida air."

She stared at him, bewildered, amazement, disbelief, and anger flowing in quick waves across her face. The three men held their breaths. Moreland, Senior, took a step toward her; Mr. Farnam's mouth dropped a little open as he waited, panic-stricken, for the expected crash.

But it did not come. Ardita's face became suddenly radiant, and with a little laugh she went swiftly to young Moreland and looked up at him without a trace of wrath in her gray eyes.

"Will you swear," she said quietly "That it was entirely a product of your own brain?"

"I swear," said young Moreland eagerly.

She drew his head down and kissed him gently.

"What an imagination!" she said softly and almost enviously. "I want you to lie to me just as sweetly as you know how for the rest of my life."

The negroes' voices floated drowsily back, mingled in an air that she had heard them singing before.

"Time is a thief;
Gladness and grief
Cling to the leaf
As it yellows———"

"What was in the bags?" she asked softly.

"Florida mud," he answered. "That was one of the two true things I told you."

"Perhaps I can guess the other one," she said; and reaching up on her tiptoes she kissed him softly in the illustration.

THE ICE PALACE

I

The sunlight dripped over the house like golden paint over an art jar, and the freckling shadows here and there only intensified the rigor of the bath of light. The Butterworth and Larkin houses flanking were entrenched behind great stodgy trees; only the Happer house took the full sun, and all day long faced the dusty road-street with a tolerant kindly patience. This was the city of Tarleton in southernmost Georgia, September afternoon.

Up in her bedroom window Sally Carrol Happer rested her nineteen-year-old chin on a fifty-two-year-old sill and watched Clark Darrow's ancient Ford turn the corner. The car was hot—being partly metallic it retained all the heat it absorbed or evolved—and Clark Darrow sitting bolt upright at the wheel wore a pained, strained expression as though he considered himself a spare part, and rather likely to break. He laboriously crossed two dust ruts, the wheels squeaking indignantly at the encounter, and then with a terrifying expression he gave the steering-gear a final wrench and deposited self and car approximately in front of the Happer steps. There was a heaving sound, a death-rattle, followed by a short silence; and then the air was rent by a startling whistle.

Sally Carrol gazed down sleepily. She started to yawn, but finding this quite impossible unless she raised her chin from the window-sill, changed her mind and continued silently to regard the car, whose owner sat brilliantly if perfunctorily at attention as he waited for an answer to his signal. After a moment the whistle once more split the dusty air.

"Good mawnin'."

With difficulty Clark twisted his tall body round and bent a distorted glance on the window.

"'Tain't mawnin', Sally Carrol."

"Isn't it, sure enough?"

"What you doin'?"

"Eatin' 'n apple."

"Come on go swimmin'—want to?"

"Reckon so."

"How 'bout hurryin' up?"

"Sure enough."

Sally Carrol sighed voluminously and raised herself with profound inertia from the floor where she had been occupied in alternately destroyed parts of a green apple and painting paper dolls for her younger sister. She approached a mirror, regarded her expression with a pleased and pleasant languor, dabbed two spots of rouge on her lips and a grain of powder on her nose, and covered her bobbed corn-colored hair with a rose-littered sunbonnet. Then she kicked over the painting water, said, "Oh, damn!"— but let it lay—and left the room.

"How you, Clark?" she inquired a minute later as she slipped nimbly over the side of the car.

"Mighty fine, Sally Carrol."

"Where we go swimmin'?"

"Out to Walley's Pool. Told Marylyn we'd call by an' get her an' Joe Ewing."

Clark was dark and lean, and when on foot was rather inclined to stoop. His eyes were ominous and his expression somewhat petulant except when startlingly illuminated by one of his frequent smiles. Clark had "a income"—just enough to keep himself in ease and his car in gasolene—

and he had spent the two years since he graduated from Georgia Tech in dozing round the lazy streets of his home town, discussing how he could best invest his capital for an immediate fortune.

Hanging round he found not at all difficult; a crowd of little girls had grown up beautifully, the amazing Sally Carrol foremost among them; and they enjoyed being swum with and danced with and made love to in the flower-filled summery evenings—and they all liked Clark immensely. When feminine company palled there were half a dozen other youths who were always just about to do something, and meanwhile were quite willing to join him in a few holes of golf, or a game of billiards, or the consumption of a quart of "hard yella licker." Every once in a while one of these contemporaries made a farewell round of calls before going up to New York or Philadelphia or Pittsburgh to go into business, but mostly they just stayed round in this languid paradise of dreamy skies and firefly evenings and noisy nigger street fairs—and especially of gracious, soft-voiced girls, who were brought up on memories instead of money.

The Ford having been excited into a sort of restless resentful life Clark and Sally Carrol rolled and rattled down Valley Avenue into Jefferson Street, where the dust road became a pavement; along opiate Millicent Place, where there were half a dozen prosperous, substantial mansions; and on into the down-town section. Driving was perilous here, for it was shopping time; the population idled casually across the streets and a drove of low-moaning oxen were being urged along in front of a placid street-car; even the shops seemed only yawning their doors and blinking their windows in the sunshine before retiring into a state of utter and finite coma.

"Sally Carrol," said Clark suddenly, "it a fact that you're engaged?"

She looked at him quickly.

"Where'd you hear that?"

"Sure enough, you engaged?"

"'At's a nice question!"

"Girl told me you were engaged to a Yankee you met up in Asheville last summer."

Sally Carrol sighed.

"Never saw such an old town for rumors."

"Don't marry a Yankee, Sally Carrol. We need you round here."

Sally Carrol was silent a moment.

"Clark," she demanded suddenly, "who on earth shall I marry?"

"I offer my services."

"Honey, you couldn't support a wife," she answered cheerfully. "Anyway, I know you too well to fall in love with you."

"'At doesn't mean you ought to marry a Yankee," he persisted.

"S'pose I love him?"

He shook his head.

"You couldn't. He'd be a lot different from us, every way."

He broke off as he halted the car in front of a rambling, dilapidated house. Marylyn Wade and Joe Ewing appeared in the doorway.

"'Lo Sally Carrol."

"Hi!"

"How you-all?"

"Sally Carrol," demanded Marylyn as they started of again, "you engaged?"

"Lawdy, where'd all this start? Can't I look at a man 'thout everybody in town engagin' me to him?"

Clark stared straight in front of him at a bolt on the clattering wind-shield.

"Sally Carrol," he said with a curious intensity, "don't you 'like us?"

"What?"

"Us down here?"

"Why, Clark, you know I do. I adore all you boys."

"Then why you gettin' engaged to a Yankee?"

"Clark, I don't know. I'm not sure what I'll do, but—well, I want to go places and see people. I want my mind to grow. I want to live where things happen on a big scale."

"What you mean?"

"Oh, Clark, I love you, and I love Joe here and Ben Arrot, and you-all, but you'll—you'll——"

"We'll all be failures?"

"Yes. I don't mean only money failures, but just sort of—of ineffectual and sad, and—oh, how can I tell you?"

"You mean because we stay here in Tarleton?"

"Yes, Clark; and because you like it and never want to change things or think or go ahead."

He nodded and she reached over and pressed his hand.

"Clark," she said softly, "I wouldn't change you for the world. You're sweet the way you are. The things that'll make you fail I'll love always—the living in the past, the lazy days and nights you have, and all your carelessness and generosity."

"But you're goin' away?"

"Yes—because I couldn't ever marry you. You've a place in my heart no one else ever could have, but tied down here I'd get restless. I'd feel I was—wastin' myself. There's two sides to me, you see. There's the sleepy old side you love an' there's a sort of energy—the feeling that makes me do wild things. That's the part of me that may be useful somewhere, that'll last when I'm not beautiful any more."

She broke of with characteristic suddenness and sighed, "Oh, sweet cooky!" as her mood changed.

Half closing her eyes and tipping back her head till it rested on the seat-back she let the savory breeze fan her eyes and ripple the fluffy curls of her bobbed hair. They were in the country now, hurrying between tangled growths of bright-green coppice and grass and tall trees that sent sprays of foliage to hang a cool welcome over the road. Here and there they passed a battered negro cabin, its oldest white-haired inhabitant smoking a corncob pipe beside the door, and half a dozen scantily clothed pickaninnies parading tattered dolls on the wild-grown grass in front. Farther out were lazy cotton-fields where even the workers seemed intangible shadows lent by the sun to the earth, not for toil, but to while away some age-old tradition in the golden September fields. And round the drowsy picturesqueness, over the trees and shacks and muddy rivers, flowed the heat, never hostile, only comforting, like a great warm nourishing bosom for the infant earth.

"Sally Carrol, we're here!"

"Poor chile's soun' asleep."

"Honey, you dead at last outa sheer laziness?"

"Water, Sally Carrol! Cool water waitin' for you!"

Her eyes opened sleepily.

"Hi!" she murmured, smiling.

II

In November Harry Bellamy, tall, broad, and brisk, came down from his Northern city to spend four days. His intention was to settle a matter that had been hanging fire since he and Sally Carrol had met in Asheville, North Carolina, in midsummer. The settlement took only a quiet afternoon and an evening in front of a glowing open fire, for Harry Bellamy had everything she wanted; and, beside, she loved him—loved him with that side of her she kept especially for loving. Sally Carrol had several rather clearly defined sides.

On his last afternoon they walked, and she found their steps tending half-unconsciously toward one of her favorite haunts, the cemetery. When it came in sight, gray-white and golden-green under the cheerful late sun, she paused, irresolute, by the iron gate.

"Are you mournful by nature, Harry?" she asked with a faint smile.

"Mournful? Not I."

"Then let's go in here. It depresses some folks, but I like it."

They passed through the gateway and followed a path that led through a wavy valley of graves—dusty-gray and mouldy for the fifties; quaintly carved with flowers and jars for the seventies; ornate and hideous for the nineties, with fat marble cherubs lying in sodden sleep on stone pillows, and great impossible growths of nameless granite flowers.

Occasionally they saw a kneeling figure with tributary flowers, but over most of the graves lay silence and withered leaves with only the fragrance that their own shadowy memories could waken in living minds.

They reached the top of a hill where they were fronted by a tall, round head-stone, freckled with dark spots of damp and half grown over with vines.

"Margery Lee," she read; "1844-1873. Wasn't she nice? She died when she was twenty-nine. Dear Margery Lee," she added softly. "Can't you see her, Harry?"

"Yes, Sally Carrol."

He felt a little hand insert itself into his.

"She was dark, I think; and she always wore her hair with a ribbon in it, and gorgeous hoop-skirts of Alice blue and old rose."

"Yes."

"Oh, she was sweet, Harry! And she was the sort of girl born to stand on a wide, pillared porch and welcome folks in. I think perhaps a lot of men went away to war meanin' to come back to her; but maybe none of 'em ever did."

He stooped down close to the stone, hunting for any record of marriage.

"There's nothing here to show."

"Of course not. How could there be anything there better than just 'Margery Lee,' and that eloquent date?"

She drew close to him and an unexpected lump came into his throat as her yellow hair brushed his cheek.

"You see how she was, don't you Harry?"

"I see," he agreed gently. "I see through your precious eyes. You're beautiful now, so I know she must have been."

Silent and close they stood, and he could feel her shoulders trembling a little. An ambling breeze swept up the hill and stirred the brim of her floppidy hat.

"Let's go down there!"

She was pointing to a flat stretch on the other side of the hill where along the green turf were a thousand grayish-white crosses stretching in endless, ordered rows like the stacked arms of a battalion.

"Those are the Confederate dead," said Sally Carrol simply.

They walked along and read the inscriptions, always only a name and a date, sometimes quite indecipherable.

"The last row is the saddest—see, 'way over there. Every cross has just a date on it and the word 'Unknown.'"

She looked at him and her eyes brimmed with tears.

"I can't tell you how real it is to me, darling—if you don't know."

"How you feel about it is beautiful to me."

"No, no, it's not me, it's them—that old time that I've tried to have live in me. These were just men, unimportant evidently or they wouldn't have been 'unknown'; but they died for the most beautiful thing in the world— the dead South. You see," she continued, her voice still husky, her eyes glistening with tears, "people have these dreams they fasten onto things, and I've always grown up with that dream. It was so easy because it was all dead and there weren't any disillusions comin' to me. I've tried in a way to live up to those past standards of noblesse oblige—there's just the last remnants of it, you know, like the roses of an old garden dying all round us—streaks of strange courtliness and chivalry in some of these boys an' stories I used to hear from a Confederate soldier who lived next door, and a few old darkies. Oh, Harry, there was something, there was something! I couldn't ever make you understand but it was there."

"I understand," he assured her again quietly.

Sally Carol smiled and dried her eyes on the tip of a handkerchief protruding from his breast pocket.

"You don't feel depressed, do you, lover? Even when I cry I'm happy here, and I get a sort of strength from it."

Hand in hand they turned and walked slowly away. Finding soft grass she drew him down to a seat beside her with their backs against the remnants of a low broken wall.

"Wish those three old women would clear out," he complained. "I want to kiss you, Sally Carrol."

"Me, too."

They waited impatiently for the three bent figures to move off, and then she kissed him until the sky seemed to fade out and all her smiles and tears to vanish in an ecstasy of eternal seconds.

Afterward they walked slowly back together, while on the corners twilight played at somnolent black-and-white checkers with the end of day.

"You'll be up about mid-January," he said, "and you've got to stay a month at least. It'll be slick. There's a winter carnival on, and if you've never really seen snow it'll be like fairy-land to you. There'll be skating and skiing and tobogganing and sleigh-riding, and all sorts of torchlight parades on snow-shoes. They haven't had one for years, so they're gong to make it a knock-out."

"Will I be cold, Harry?" she asked suddenly.

"You certainly won't. You may freeze your nose, but you won't be shivery cold. It's hard and dry, you know."

"I guess I'm a summer child. I don't like any cold I've ever seen."

She broke off and they were both silent for a minute.

"Sally Carol," he said very slowly, "what do you say to—March?"

"I say I love you."

"March?"

"March, Harry."

III

ALL NIGHT IN THE PULLMAN IT WAS VERY COLD. SHE RANG FOR THE PORTER TO ask for another blanket, and when he couldn't give her one she tried vainly, by squeezing down into the bottom of her berth and doubling back the bedclothes, to snatch a few hours' sleep. She wanted to look her best in the morning.

She rose at six and sliding uncomfortably into her clothes stumbled up to the diner for a cup of coffee. The snow had filtered into the vestibules and covered the door with a slippery coating. It was intriguing this cold, it crept in everywhere. Her breath was quite visible and she blew into the air with a naïve enjoyment. Seated in the diner she stared out the window at white hills and valleys and scattered pines whose every branch was a green platter for a cold feast of snow. Sometimes a solitary farmhouse would fly by, ugly and bleak and lone on the white waste; and with each one she had an instant of chill compassion for the souls shut in there waiting for spring.

As she left the diner and swayed back into the Pullman she experienced a surging rush of energy and wondered if she was feeling the bracing air of which Harry had spoken. This was the North, the North—her land now!

"Then blow, ye winds, heighho!

A-roving I will go,"

she chanted exultantly to herself.

"What's 'at?" inquired the porter politely.

"I said: 'Brush me off.'"

The long wires of the telegraph poles doubled, two tracks ran up beside the train—three—four; came a succession of white-roofed houses, a glimpse of a trolley-car with frosted windows, streets—more streets—the city.

She stood for a dazed moment in the frosty station before she saw three fur-bundled figures descending upon her.

"There she is!"

"Oh, Sally Carrol!"

Sally Carrol dropped her bag.

"Hi!"

A faintly familiar icy-cold face kissed her, and then she was in a group of faces all apparently emitting great clouds of heavy smoke; she was shaking hands. There were Gordon, a short, eager man of thirty who looked like an amateur knocked-about model for Harry, and his wife, Myra, a listless lady with flaxen hair under a fur automobile cap. Almost immediately Sally Carrol thought of her as vaguely Scandinavian. A cheerful chauffeur adopted her bag, and amid ricochets of half-phrases, exclamations and perfunctory listless "my dears" from Myra, they swept each other from the station.

Then they were in a sedan bound through a crooked succession of snowy streets where dozens of little boys were hitching sleds behind grocery wagons and automobiles.

"Oh," cried Sally Carrol, "I want to do that! Can we Harry?"

"That's for kids. But we might——"

"It looks like such a circus!" she said regretfully.

Home was a rambling frame house set on a white lap of snow, and there she met a big, gray-haired man of whom she approved, and a lady who was like an egg, and who kissed her—these were Harry's parents. There was a breathless indescribable hour crammed full of self-sentences, hot water, bacon and eggs and confusion; and after that she was alone with Harry in the library, asking him if she dared smoke.

It was a large room with a Madonna over the fireplace and rows upon rows of books in covers of light gold and dark gold and shiny red. All the chairs had little lace squares where one's head should rest, the couch was just comfortable, the books looked as if they had been read—some—and Sally Carrol had an instantaneous vision of the battered old library at home, with her father's huge medical books, and the oil-paintings of her three great-uncles, and the old couch that had been mended up for forty-five years and was still luxurious to dream in. This room struck her as being neither attractive nor particularly otherwise. It was simply a room with a lot of fairly expensive things in it that all looked about fifteen years old.

"What do you think of it up here?" demanded Harry eagerly. "Does it surprise you? Is it what you expected I mean?"

"You are, Harry," she said quietly, and reached out her arms to him.

But after a brief kiss he seemed to extort enthusiasm from her.

"The town, I mean. Do you like it? Can you feel the pep in the air?"

"Oh, Harry," she laughed, "you'll have to give me time. You can't just fling questions at me."

She puffed at her cigarette with a sigh of contentment.

"One thing I want to ask you," he began rather apologetically; "you Southerners put quite an emphasis on family, and all that—not that it isn't quite all right, but you'll find it a little different here. I mean—you'll notice a lot of things that'll seem to you sort of vulgar display at first, Sally Carrol; but just remember that this is a three-generation town. Everybody has a father, and about half of us have grandfathers. Back of that we don't go."

"Of course," she murmured.

"Our grandfathers, you see, founded the place, and a lot of them had to take some pretty queer jobs while they were doing the founding. For instance there's one woman who at present is about the social model for the town; well, her father was the first public ash man—things like that."

"Why," said Sally Carol, puzzled, "did you s'pose I was goin' to make remarks about people?"

"Not at all," interrupted Harry, "and I'm not apologizing for any one either. It's just that—well, a Southern girl came up here last summer and said some unfortunate things, and—oh, I just thought I'd tell you."

Sally Carrol felt suddenly indignant—as though she had been unjustly spanked—but Harry evidently considered the subject closed, for he went on with a great surge of enthusiasm.

"It's carnival time, you know. First in ten years. And there's an ice palace they're building new that's the first they've had since eighty-five. Built out of blocks of the clearest ice they could find—on a tremendous scale."

She rose and walking to the window pushed aside the heavy Turkish portières and looked out.

"Oh!" she cried suddenly. "There's two little boys makin' a snow man! Harry, do you reckon I can go out an' help 'em?"

"You dream! Come here and kiss me."

She left the window rather reluctantly.

"I don't guess this is a very kissable climate, is it? I mean, it makes you so you don't want to sit round, doesn't it?"

"We're not going to. I've got a vacation for the first week you're here, and there's a dinner-dance to-night."

"Oh, Harry," she confessed, subsiding in a heap, half in his lap, half in the pillows, "I sure do feel confused. I haven't got an idea whether I'll like it or not, an' I don't know what people expect, or anythin'. You'll have to tell me, honey."

"I'll tell you," he said softly, "if you'll just tell me you're glad to be here."

"Glad—just awful glad!" she whispered, insinuating herself into his arms in her own peculiar way. "Where you are is home for me, Harry."

And as she said this she had the feeling for almost the first time in her life that she was acting a part.

That night, amid the gleaming candles of a dinner-party, where the men seemed to do most of the talking while the girls sat in a haughty and expensive aloofness, even Harry's presence on her left failed to make her feel at home.

"They're a good-looking crowd, don't you think?" he demanded. "Just look round. There's Spud Hubbard, tackle at Princeton last year, and Junie Morton—he and the red-haired fellow next to him were both Yale hockey captains; Junie was in my class. Why, the best athletes in the world come from these States round here. This is a man's country, I tell you. Look at John J. Fishburn!"

"Who's he?" asked Sally Carrol innocently.

"Don't you know?"

"I've heard the name."

"Greatest wheat man in the Northwest, and one of the greatest financiers in the country."

She turned suddenly to a voice on her right.

"I guess they forget to introduce us. My name's Roger Patton."

"My name is Sally Carrol Happer," she said graciously.

"Yes, I know. Harry told me you were coming."

"You a relative?"

"No, I'm a professor."

"Oh," she laughed.

"At the university. You're from the South, aren't you?"

"Yes; Tarleton, Georgia."

She liked him immediately—a reddish-brown mustache under watery blue eyes that had something in them that these other eyes lacked, some quality of appreciation. They exchanged stray sentences through dinner, and she made up her mind to see him again.

After coffee she was introduced to numerous good-looking young men who danced with conscious precision and seemed to take it for granted that she wanted to talk about nothing except Harry.

"Heavens," she thought, "They talk as if my being engaged made me older than they are—as if I'd tell their mothers on them!"

In the South an engaged girl, even a young married woman, expected the same amount of half-affectionate badinage and flattery that would be accorded a débutante, but here all that seemed banned. One young man after getting well started on the subject of Sally Carrol's eyes and, how they had allured him ever since she entered the room, went into a violent convulsion when he found she was visiting the Bellamys—was Harry's fiancée. He seemed to feel as though he had made some risqué and inexcusable blunder, became immediately formal and left her at the first opportunity.

She was rather glad when Roger Patton cut in on her and suggested that they sit out a while.

"Well," he inquired, blinking cheerily, "how's Carmen from the South?"

"Mighty fine. How's—how's Dangerous Dan McGrew? Sorry, but he's the only Northerner I know much about."

He seemed to enjoy that.

"Of course," he confessed, "as a professor of literature I'm not supposed to have read Dangerous Dan McGrew."

"Are you a native?"

"No, I'm a Philadelphian. Imported from Harvard to teach French. But I've been here ten years."

"Nine years, three hundred an' sixty-four days longer than me."

"Like it here?"

"Uh-huh. Sure do!"

"Really?"

"Well, why not? Don't I look as if I were havin' a good time?"

"I saw you look out the window a minute ago—and shiver."

"Just my imagination," laughed Sally Carroll "I'm used to havin' everythin' quiet outside an' sometimes I look out an' see a flurry of snow an' it's just as if somethin' dead was movin'.''

He nodded appreciatively.

"Ever been North before?"

"Spent two Julys in Asheville, North Carolina."

"Nice-looking crowd aren't they?" suggested Patton, indicating the swirling floor.

Sally Carrol started. This had been Harry's remark.

"Sure are! They're—canine."

"What?"

She flushed.

"I'm sorry; that sounded worse than I meant it. You see I always think of people as feline or canine, irrespective of sex."

"Which are you?"

"I'm feline. So are you. So are most Southern men an' most of these girls here."

"What's Harry?"

"Harry's canine distinctly. All the men I've to-night seem to be canine."

"What does canine imply? A certain conscious masculinity as opposed to subtlety?"

"Reckon so. I never analyzed it—only I just look at people an' say 'canine' or 'feline' right off. It's right absurd I guess."

"Not at all. I'm interested. I used to have a theory about these people. I think they're freezing up."

"What?"

"Well, they're growing' like Swedes—Ibsenesque, you know. Very gradually getting gloomy and melancholy. It's these long winters. Ever read Ibsen?"

She shook her head.

"Well, you find in his characters a certain brooding rigidity. They're righteous, narrow, and cheerless, without infinite possibilities for great sorrow or joy."

"Without smiles or tears?"

"Exactly. That's my theory. You see there are thousands of Swedes up here. They come, I imagine, because the climate is very much like their own, and there's been a gradual mingling. There're probably not half a dozen here to-night, but—we've had four Swedish governors. Am I boring you?"

"I'm mighty interested."

"Your future sister-in-law is half Swedish. Personally I like her, but my theory is that Swedes react rather badly on us as a whole. Scandinavians, you know, have the largest suicide rate in the world."

"Why do you live here if it's so depressing?"

"Oh, it doesn't get me. I'm pretty well cloistered, and I suppose books mean more than people to me anyway."

"But writers all speak about the South being tragic. You know—Spanish señoritas, black hair and daggers an' haunting music."

He shook his head.

"No, the Northern races are the tragic races—they don't indulge in the cheering luxury of tears."

Sally Carrol thought of her graveyard. She supposed that that was vaguely what she had meant when she said it didn't depress her.

"The Italians are about the gayest people in the world—but it's a dull subject," he broke off. "Anyway, I want to tell you you're marrying a pretty fine man."

Sally Carrol was moved by an impulse of confidence.

"I know. I'm the sort of person who wants to be taken care of after a certain point, and I feel sure I will be."

"Shall we dance? You know," he continued as they rose, "it's encouraging to find a girl who knows what she's marrying for. Nine-tenths of them think of it as a sort of walking into a moving-picture sunset."

She laughed and liked him immensely.

Two hours later on the way home she nestled near Harry in the back seat.

"Oh, Harry," she whispered "it's so co-old!"

"But it's warm in here, daring girl."

"But outside it's cold; and oh, that howling wind!"

She buried her face deep in his fur coat and trembled involuntarily as his cold lips kissed the tip of her ear.

IV

THE FIRST WEEK OF HER VISIT PASSED IN A WHIRL. SHE HAD HER PROMISED toboggan-ride at the back of an automobile through a chill January twilight. Swathed in furs she put in a morning tobogganing on the country-club hill; even tried skiing, to sail through the air for a glorious moment and then land in a tangled laughing bundle on a soft snow-drift. She liked all the winter sports, except an afternoon spent snow-shoeing over a glaring plain under pale yellow sunshine, but she soon realized that these things were for children—that she was being humored and that the enjoyment round her was only a reflection of her own.

At first the Bellamy family puzzled her. The men were reliable and she liked them; to Mr. Bellamy especially, with his iron-gray hair and energetic dignity, she took an immediate fancy, once she found that he was born in Kentucky; this made of him a link between the old life and the new. But toward the women she felt a definite hostility. Myra, her future sister-in-law, seemed the essence of spiritless conversationality. Her conversation was so utterly devoid of personality that Sally Carrol, who came from a country where a certain amount of charm and assurance could be taken for granted in the women, was inclined to despise her.

"If those women aren't beautiful," she thought, "they're nothing. They just fade out when you look at them. They're glorified domestics. Men are the centre of every mixed group."

Lastly there was Mrs. Bellamy, whom Sally Carrol detested. The first day's impression of an egg had been confirmed—an egg with a cracked, veiny voice and such an ungracious dumpiness of carriage that Sally Carrol felt that if she once fell she would surely scramble. In addition, Mrs. Bellamy seemed to typify the town in being innately hostile to strangers. She called Sally Carrol "Sally," and could not be persuaded that the double name was anything more than a tedious ridiculous nickname. To Sally Carrol this shortening of her name was presenting her to the public half clothed. She loved "Sally Carrol"; she loathed "Sally." She knew also that Harry's mother disapproved of her bobbed hair; and she had never dared smoke down-stairs after that first day when Mrs. Bellamy had come into the library sniffing violently.

Of all the men she met she preferred Roger Patton, who was a frequent visitor at the house. He never again alluded to the Ibsenesque tendency of the populace, but when he came in one day and found her curled upon the sofa bent over "Peer Gynt" he laughed and told her to forget what he'd said—that it was all rot.

They had been walking homeward between mounds of high-piled snow and under a sun which Sally Carrol scarcely recognized. They passed a little girl done up in gray wool until she resembled a small Teddy bear, and Sally Carrol could not resist a gasp of maternal appreciation.

"Look! Harry!"

"What?"

"That little girl—did you see her face?"

"Yes, why?"

"It was red as a little strawberry. Oh, she was cute!"

"Why, your own face is almost as red as that already! Everybody's healthy here. We're out in the cold as soon as we're old enough to walk. Wonderful climate!"

She looked at him and had to agree. He was mighty healthy-looking; so was his brother. And she had noticed the new red in her own cheeks that very morning.

Suddenly their glances were caught and held, and they stared for a moment at the street-corner ahead of them. A man was standing there, his knees bent, his eyes gazing upward with a tense expression as though he were about to make a leap toward the chilly sky. And then they both exploded into a shout of laughter, for coming closer they discovered it had been a ludicrous momentary illusion produced by the extreme bagginess of the man's trousers.

"Reckon that's one on us," she laughed.

"He must be Southerner, judging by those trousers," suggested Harry mischievously.

"Why, Harry!"

Her surprised look must have irritated him.

"Those damn Southerners!"

Sally Carrol's eyes flashed.

"Don't call 'em that."

"I'm sorry, dear," said Harry, malignantly apologetic, "but you know what I think of them. They're sort of—sort of degenerates—not at all like the old Southerners. They've lived so long down there with all the colored people that they've gotten lazy and shiftless."

"Hush your mouth, Harry!" she cried angrily. "They're not! They may be lazy—anybody would be in that climate—but they're my best friends, an' I don't want to hear 'em criticised in any such sweepin' way. Some of 'em are the finest men in the world."

"Oh, I know. They're all right when they come North to college, but of all the hangdog, ill-dressed, slovenly lot I ever saw, a bunch of small-town Southerners are the worst!"

Sally Carrol was clinching her gloved hands and biting her lip furiously.

"Why," continued Harry, "if there was one in my class at New Haven, and we all thought that at last we'd found the true type of Southern aristocrat, but it turned out that he wasn't an aristocrat at all—just the son of a Northern carpetbagger, who owned about all the cotton round Mobile."

"A Southerner wouldn't talk the way you're talking now," she said evenly.

"They haven't the energy!"

"Or the somethin' else."

"I'm sorry Sally Carrol, but I've heard you say yourself that you'd never marry——"

"That's quite different. I told you I wouldn't want to tie my life to any of the boys that are round Tarleton now, but I never made any sweepin' generalities."

They walked along in silence.

"I probably spread it on a bit thick Sally Carrol. I'm sorry."

She nodded but made no answer. Five minutes later as they stood in the hallway she suddenly threw her arms round him.

"Oh, Harry," she cried, her eyes brimming with tears; "let's get married next week. I'm afraid of having fusses like that. I'm afraid, Harry. It wouldn't be that way if we were married."

But Harry, being in the wrong, was still irritated.

"That'd be idiotic. We decided on March."

The tears in Sally Carrol's eyes faded; her expression hardened slightly.

"Very well—I suppose I shouldn't have said that."

Harry melted.

"Dear little nut!" he cried. "Come and kiss me and let's forget." That very night at the end of a vaudeville performance the orchestra played "Dixie" and Sally Carrol felt something stronger and more enduring than her tears and smiles of the day brim up inside her. She leaned forward gripping the arms of her chair until her face grew crimson.

"Sort of get you dear?" whispered Harry.

But she did not hear him. To the limited throb of the violins and the inspiring beat of the kettle-drums her own old ghosts were marching by and on into the darkness, and as fifes whistled and sighed in the low encore they seemed so nearly out of sight that she could have waved good-by.

"Away, Away,

Away down South in Dixie!

Away, away,

Away down South in Dixie!"

V

IT WAS A PARTICULARLY COLD NIGHT. A SUDDEN THAW HAD NEARLY CLEARED the streets the day before, but now they were traversed again with a powdery wraith of loose snow that travelled in wavy lines before the feet of the wind, and filled the lower air with a fine-particled mist. There was no sky—only a dark, ominous tent that draped in the tops of the streets and was in reality a vast approaching army of snowflakes—while over it all, chilling away the comfort from the brown-and-green glow of lighted windows and muffling the steady trot of the horse pulling their sleigh, interminably washed the north wind. It was a dismal town after all, she though, dismal.

Sometimes at night it had seemed to her as though no one lived here—they had all gone long ago—leaving lighted houses to be covered in time by tombing heaps of sleet. Oh, if there should be snow on her grave! To be beneath great piles of it all winter long, where even her headstone would be a light shadow against light shadows. Her grave—a grave that should be flower-strewn and washed with sun and rain.

She thought again of those isolated country houses that her train had passed, and of the life there the long winter through—the ceaseless glare through the windows, the crust forming on the soft drifts of snow, finally the slow cheerless melting and the harsh spring of which Roger Patton had told her. Her spring—to lose it forever—with its lilacs and the lazy sweetness it stirred in her heart. She was laying away that spring—afterward she would lay away that sweetness.

With a gradual insistence the storm broke. Sally Carrol felt a film of flakes melt quickly on her eyelashes, and Harry reached over a furry arm and drew down her complicated flannel cap. Then the small flakes came in skirmish-line, and the horse bent his neck patiently as a transparency of white appeared momentarily on his coat.

"Oh, he's cold, Harry," she said quickly.

"Who? The horse? Oh, no, he isn't. He likes it!"

After another ten minutes they turned a corner and came in sight of their destination. On a tall hill outlined in vivid glaring green against the wintry sky stood the ice palace. It was three stories in the air, with battlements and embrasures and narrow icicled windows, and the innumerable electric lights inside made a gorgeous transparency of the great central hall. Sally Carrol clutched Harry's hand under the fur robe.

"It's beautiful!" he cried excitedly. "My golly, it's beautiful, isn't it! They haven't had one here since eighty-five!"

Somehow the notion of there not having been one since eighty-five oppressed her. Ice was a ghost, and this mansion of it was surely peopled by those shades of the eighties, with pale faces and blurred snow-filled hair.

"Come on, dear," said Harry.

She followed him out of the sleigh and waited while he hitched the horse. A party of four—Gordon, Myra, Roger Patton, and another girl—drew up beside them with a mighty jingle of bells. There were quite a crowd already, bundled in fur or sheepskin, shouting and calling to each other as they moved through the snow, which was now so thick that people could scarcely be distinguished a few yards away.

"It's a hundred and seventy feet tall," Harry was saying to a muffled figure beside him as they trudged toward the entrance; "covers six thousand square yards."

She caught snatches of conversation: "One main hall"—"walls twenty to forty inches thick"—"and the ice cave has almost a mile of—"—"this Canuck who built it——"

They found their way inside, and dazed by the magic of the great crystal walls Sally Carrol found herself repeating over and over two lines from "Kubla Khan":

"It was a miracle of rare device,

A sunny pleasure-dome with caves of ice!"

In the great glittering cavern with the dark shut out she took a seat on a wooded bench and the evening's oppression lifted. Harry was right—it was beautiful; and her gaze travelled the smooth surface of the walls, the blocks for which had been selected for their purity and dearness to obtain this opalescent, translucent effect.

"Look! Here we go—oh, boy!" cried Harry.

A band in a far corner struck up "Hail, Hail, the Gang's All Here!" which echoed over to them in wild muddled acoustics, and then the lights suddenly went out; silence seemed to flow down the icy sides and sweep over them. Sally Carrol could still see her white breath in the darkness, and a dim row of pale faces over on the other side.

The music eased to a sighing complaint, and from outside drifted in the full-throated remnant chant of the marching clubs. It grew louder like some pæan of a viking tribe traversing an ancient wild; it swelled—they were coming nearer; then a row of torches appeared, and another and another, and keeping time with their moccasined feet a long column of gray-mackinawed figures swept in, snow-shoes slung at their shoulders, torches soaring and flickering as their voice rose along the great walls.

The gray column ended and another followed, the light streaming luridly this time over red toboggan caps and flaming crimson mackinaws, and as they entered they took up the refrain; then came a long platoon of blue and white, of green, of white, of brown and yellow.

"Those white ones are the Wacouta Club," whispered Harry eagerly. "Those are the men you've met round at dances."

The volume of the voices grew; the great cavern was a phantasmagoria of torches waving in great banks of fire, of colors and the rhythm of soft-leather steps. The leading column turned and halted, platoon deploys in front of platoon until the whole procession made a solid flag of flame, and then from thousands of voices burst a mighty shout that filled the air like a crash of thunder, and sent the torches wavering. It was magnificent, it was tremendous! To Sally Carol it was the North offering sacrifice on some mighty altar to the gray pagan God of Snow. As the shout died the band struck up again and there came more singing, and then long reverberating cheers by each club. She sat very quiet listening while the staccato cries rent the stillness; and then she started, for there was a volley of explosion, and great clouds of smoke went up here and there through the cavern—the flash-light photographers at work—and the council was over. With the band at their head the clubs formed in column once more, took up their chant, and began to march out.

"Come on!" shouted Harry. "We want to see the labyrinths down-stairs before they turn the lights off!"

They all rose and started toward the chute—Harry and Sally Carrol in the lead, her little mitten buried in his big fur gantlet. At the bottom of the chute was a long empty room of ice, with the ceiling so low that they had to stoop—and their hands were parted. Before she realized what he intended Harry had darted down one of the half-dozen glittering passages that opened into the room and was only a vague receding blot against the green shimmer.

"Harry!" she called.

"Come on!" he cried back.

She looked round the empty chamber; the rest of the party had evidently decided to go home, were already outside somewhere in the blundering snow. She hesitated and then darted in after Harry.

"Harry!" she shouted.

She had reached a turning-point thirty feet down; she heard a faint muffled answer far to the left, and with a touch of panic fled toward it. She passed another turning, two more yawning alleys.

"Harry!"

No answer. She started to run straight forward, and then turned like lightning and sped back the way she had come, enveloped in a sudden icy terror.

She reached a turn—was it here?—took the left and came to what should have been the outlet into the long, low room, but it was only another glittering passage with darkness at the end. She called again, but the walls gave back a flat, lifeless echo with no reverberations. Retracing her steps she turned another corner, this time following a wide passage. It was like the green lane between the parted water of the Red Sea, like a damp vault connecting empty tombs.

She slipped a little now as she walked, for ice had formed on the bottom of her overshoes; she had to run her gloves along the half-slippery, half-sticky walls to keep her balance.

"Harry!"

Still no answer. The sound she made bounced mockingly down to the end of the passage.

Then on an instant the lights went out, and she was in complete darkness. She gave a small, frightened cry, and sank down into a cold little heap on the ice. She felt her left knee do something as she fell, but she scarcely noticed it as some deep terror far greater than any fear of being lost settled upon her. She was alone with this presence that came out of the North, the dreary loneliness that rose from ice-bound whalers in the Arctic seas, from smokeless, trackless wastes where were strewn the whitened bones of adventure. It was an icy breath of death; it was rolling down low across the land to clutch at her.

With a furious, despairing energy she rose again and started blindly down the darkness. She must get out. She might be lost in here for days, freeze to death and lie embedded in the ice like corpses she had read of, kept perfectly preserved until the melting of a glacier. Harry probably thought she had left with the others—he had gone by now; no one would know until next day. She reached pitifully for the wall. Forty inches thick, they had said—forty inches thick!

On both sides of her along the walls she felt things creeping, damp souls that haunted this palace, this town, this North.

"Oh, send somebody—send somebody!" she cried aloud.

Clark Darrow—he would understand; or Joe Ewing; she couldn't be left here to wander forever—to be frozen, heart, body, and soul. This her—this Sally Carrol! Why, she was a happy thing. She was a happy little girl. She liked warmth and summer and Dixie. These things were foreign—foreign.

"You're not crying," something said aloud. "You'll never cry any more. Your tears would just freeze; all tears freeze up here!"

She sprawled full length on the ice.

"Oh, God!" she faltered.

A long single file of minutes went by, and with a great weariness she felt her eyes dosing. Then some one seemed to sit down near her and take her face in warm, soft hands. She looked up gratefully.

"Why it's Margery Lee," she crooned softly to herself. "I knew you'd come." It really was Margery Lee, and she was just as Sally Carrol had known she would be, with a young, white brow, and wide welcoming eyes, and a hoop-skirt of some soft material that was quite comforting to rest on.

"Margery Lee."

It was getting darker now and darker—all those tombstones ought to be repainted sure enough, only that would spoil 'em, of course. Still, you ought to be able to see 'em.

Then after a succession of moments that went fast and then slow, but seemed to be ultimately resolving themselves into a multitude of blurred rays converging toward a pale-yellow sun, she heard a great cracking noise break her new-found stillness.

It was the sun, it was a light; a torch, and a torch beyond that, and another one, and voices; a face took flesh below the torch, heavy arms raised her and she felt something on her cheek—it felt wet. Some one had seized her and was rubbing her face with snow. How ridiculous—with snow!

"Sally Carrol! Sally Carrol!"

It was Dangerous Dan McGrew; and two other faces she didn't know. "Child, child! We've been looking for you two hours! Harry's half-crazy!"

Things came rushing back into place—the singing, the torches, the great shout of the marching clubs. She squirmed in Patton's arms and gave a long low cry.

"Oh, I want to get out of here! I'm going back home. Take me home"——her voice rose to a scream that sent a chill to Harry's heart as he came racing down the next passage—"to-morrow!" she cried with delirious, unstrained passion—"To-morrow! To-morrow! To-morrow!"

VI

THE WEALTH OF GOLDEN SUNLIGHT POURED A QUITE ENERVATING YET ODDLY comforting heat over the house where day long it faced the dusty stretch of road. Two birds were making a great to-do in a cool spot found among the branches of a tree next door, and down the street a colored woman was announcing herself melodiously as a purveyor of strawberries. It was April afternoon.

Sally Carrol Happer, resting her chin on her arm, and her arm on an old window-seat, gazed sleepily down over the spangled dust whence the heat waves were rising for the first time this spring. She was watching a very ancient Ford turn a perilous corner and rattle and groan to a jolting stop at the end of the walk. See made no sound and in a minute a strident familiar whistle rent the air. Sally Carrol smiled and blinked.

"Good mawnin'."

A head appeared tortuously from under the car-top below.

"Tain't mawnin', Sally Carrol."

"Sure enough!" she said in affected surprise. "I guess maybe not."

"What you doin'?"

"Eatin' a green peach. 'Spect to die any minute."

Clark twisted himself a last impossible notch to get a view of her face.

"Water's warm as a kettla steam, Sally Carol. Wanta go swimmin'?"

"Hate to move," sighed Sally Carol lazily, "but I reckon so."

HEAD AND SHOULDERS

I

In 1915 Horace Tarbox was thirteen years old. In that year he took the examinations for entrance to Princeton University and received the Grade A—excellent—in Cæsar, Cicero, Vergil, Xenophon, Homer, Algebra, Plane Geometry, Solid Geometry, and Chemistry.

Two years later while George M. Cohan was composing "Over There," Horace was leading the sophomore class by several lengths and digging out theses on "The Syllogism as an Obsolete Scholastic Form," and during the battle of Château-Thierry he was sitting at his desk deciding whether or not to wait until his seventeenth birthday before beginning his series of essays on "The Pragmatic Bias of the New Realists."

After a while some newsboy told him that the war was over, and he was glad, because it meant that Peat Brothers, publishers, would get out their new edition of "Spinoza's Improvement of the Understanding." Wars were all very well in their way, made young men self-reliant or something but Horace felt that he could never forgive the President for allowing a brass band to play under his window the night of the false armistice, causing him to leave three important sentences out of his thesis on "German Idealism."

The next year he went up to Yale to take his degree as Master of Arts.

He was seventeen then, tall and slender, with near-sighted gray eyes and an air of keeping himself utterly detached from the mere words he let drop.

"I never feel as though I'm talking to him," expostulated Professor Dillinger to a sympathetic colleague. "He makes me feel as though I were talking to his representative. I always expect him to say: 'Well, I'll ask myself and find out.'"

And then, just as nonchalantly as though Horace Tarbox had been Mr. Beef the butcher or Mr. Hat the haberdasher, life reached in, seized him, handled him, stretched him, and unrolled him like a piece of Irish lace on a Saturday-afternoon bargain-counter.

To move in the literary fashion I should say that this was all because when way back in colonial days the hardy pioneers had come to a bald place in Connecticut and asked of each other, "Now, what shall we build here?" the hardiest one among 'em had answered: "Let's build a town where theatrical managers can try out musical comedies!" How afterward they founded Yale College there, to try the musical comedies on, is a story every one knows. At any rate one December, "Home James" opened at the Shubert, and all the students encored Marcia Meadow, who sang a song about the Blundering Blimp in the first act and did a shaky, shivery, celebrated dance in the last.

Marcia was nineteen. She didn't have wings, but audiences agreed generally that she didn't need them. She was a blonde by natural pigment, and she wore no paint on the streets at high noon. Outside of that she was no better than most women.

It was Charlie Moon who promised her five thousand Pall Malls if she would pay a call on Horace Tarbox, prodigy extraordinary. Charlie was a senior in Sheffield, and he and Horace were first cousins. They liked and pitied each other.

Horace had been particularly busy that night. The failure of the Frenchman Laurier to appreciate the significance of the new realists was preying on his mind. In fact, his only reaction to a low, clear-cut rap at his study was to make him speculate as to whether any rap would have actual existence without an ear there to hear it. He fancied he was verging more and more toward pragmatism. But at that moment, though he did not know it, he was verging with astounding rapidity toward something quite different.

The rap sounded—three seconds leaked by—the rap sounded.

"Come in," muttered Horace automatically.

He heard the door open and then close, but, bent over his book in the big armchair before the fire, he did not look up.

"Leave it on the bed in the other room," he said absently.

"Leave what on the bed in the other room?"

Marcia Meadow had to talk her songs, but her speaking voice was like byplay on a harp.

"The laundry."

"I can't."

Horace stirred impatiently in his chair.

"Why can't you?"

"Why, because I haven't got it."

"Hm!" he replied testily. "Suppose you go back and get it."

Across the fire from Horace was another easychair. He was accustomed to change to it in the course of an evening by way of exercise and variety. One chair he called Berkeley, the other he called Hume. He suddenly heard a sound as of a rustling, diaphanous form sinking into Hume. He glanced up.

"Well," said Marcia with the sweet smile she used in Act Two ("Oh, so the Duke liked my dancing!") "Well, Omar Khayyam, here I am beside you singing in the wilderness."

Horace stared at her dazedly. The momentary suspicion came to him that she existed there only as a phantom of his imagination. Women didn't come into men's rooms and sink into men's Humes. Women brought laundry and took your seat in the street-car and married you later on when you were old enough to know fetters.

This woman had clearly materialized out of Hume. The very froth of her brown gauzy dress was art emanation from Hume's leather arm there! If he looked long enough he would see Hume right through her and then he would be alone again in the room. He passed his fist across his eyes. He really must take up those trapeze exercises again.

"For Pete's sake, don't look so critical!" objected the emanation pleasantly. "I feel as if you were going to wish me away with that patent dome of yours. And then there wouldn't be anything left of me except my shadow in your eyes."

Horace coughed. Coughing was one of his two gestures. When he talked you forgot he had a body at all. It was like hearing a phonograph record by a singer who had been dead a long time.

"What do you want?" he asked.

"I want them letters," whined Marcia melodramatically—"them letters of mine you bought from my grandsire in 1881."

Horace considered.

"I haven't got your letters," he said evenly. "I am only seventeen years old. My father was not born until March 3, 1879. You evidently have me confused with some one else."

"You're only seventeen?" repeated March suspiciously.

"Only seventeen."

"I knew a girl," said Marcia reminiscently, "who went on the ten-twenty-thirty when she was sixteen. She was so stuck on herself that she could never say 'sixteen' without putting the 'only' before it. We got to calling her 'Only Jessie.' And she's just where she was when she started—only worse. 'Only' is a bad habit, Omar—it sounds like an alibi."

"My name is not Omar."

"I know," agreed Marcia, nodding—"your name's Horace. I just call you Omar because you remind me of a smoked cigarette."

"And I haven't your letters. I doubt if I've ever met your grandfather. In fact, I think it very improbable that you yourself were alive in 1881."

Marcia stared at him in wonder.

"Me—1881? Why sure! I was second-line stuff when the Florodora Sextette was still in the convent. I was the original nurse to Mrs. Sol Smith's Juliette. Why, Omar, I was a canteen singer during the War of 1812."

Horace's mind made a sudden successful leap, and he grinned.

"Did Charlie Moon put you up to this?"

Marcia regarded him inscrutably.

"Who's Charlie Moon?"

"Small—wide nostrils—big ears."

She grew several inches and sniffed.

"I'm not in the habit of noticing my friends' nostrils.

"Then it was Charlie?"

Marcia bit her lip—and then yawned. "Oh, let's change the subject, Omar. I'll pull a snore in this chair in a minute."

"Yes," replied Horace gravely, "Hume has often been considered soporific——"

"Who's your friend—and will he die?"

Then of a sudden Horace Tarbox rose slenderly and began to pace the room with his hands in his pockets. This was his other gesture.

"I don't care for this," he said as if he were talking to himself—"at all. Not that I mind your being here—I don't. You're quite a pretty little thing, but I don't like Charlie Moon's sending you up here. Am I a laboratory experiment on which the janitors as well as the chemists can make experiments? Is my intellectual development humorous in any way? Do I look like the pictures of the little Boston boy in the comic magazines? Has that callow ass, Moon, with his eternal tales about his week in Paris, any right to——"

"No," interrupted Marcia emphatically. "And you're a sweet boy. Come here and kiss me."

Horace stopped quickly in front of her.

"Why do you want me to kiss you?" he asked intently, "Do you just go round kissing people?"

"Why, yes," admitted Marcia, unruffled. "'At's all life is. Just going round kissing people."

"Well," replied Horace emphatically, "I must say your ideas are horribly garbled! In the first place life isn't just that, and in the second place. I won't kiss you. It might get to be a habit and I can't get rid of habits. This year I've got in the habit of lolling in bed until seven-thirty——"

Marcia nodded understandingly.

"Do you ever have any fun?" she asked.

"What do you mean by fun?"

"See here," said Marcia sternly, "I like you, Omar, but I wish you'd talk as if you had a line on what you were saying. You sound as if you were gargling a lot of words in your mouth and lost a bet every time you spilled a few. I asked you if you ever had any fun."

Horace shook his head.

"Later, perhaps," he answered. "You see I'm a plan. I'm an experiment. I don't say that I don't get tired of it sometimes—I do. Yet—oh, I can't explain! But what you and Charlie Moon call fun wouldn't be fun to me."

"Please explain."

Horace stared at her, started to speak and then, changing his mind, resumed his walk. After an unsuccessful attempt to determine whether or not he was looking at her Marcia smiled at him.

"Please explain."

Horace turned.

"If I do, will you promise to tell Charlie Moon that I wasn't in?"

"Uh-uh."

"Very well, then. Here's my history: I was a 'why' child. I wanted to see the wheels go round. My father was a young economics professor at Princeton. He brought me up on the system of answering every question I asked him to the best of his ability. My response to that gave him the idea of making an experiment in precocity. To aid in the massacre I had ear trouble—seven operations between the age of nine and twelve. Of course this kept me apart from other boys and made me ripe for forcing. Anyway, while my generation was laboring through Uncle Remus I was honestly enjoying Catullus in the original.

"I passed off my college examinations when I was thirteen because I couldn't help it. My chief associates were professors, and I took a tremendous pride in knowing that I had a fine intelligence, for though I was unusually gifted I was not abnormal in other ways. When I was sixteen I got tired of being a freak; I decided that some one had made a bad mistake. Still as I'd gone that far I concluded to finish it up by taking my degree of Master of Arts. My chief interest in life is the study of modern philosophy. I am a realist of the School of Anton Laurier—with Bergsonian trimmings—and I'll be eighteen years old in two months. That's all."

"Whew!" exclaimed Marcia. "That's enough! You do a neat job with the parts of speech."

"Satisfied?"

"No, you haven't kissed me."

"It's not in my programme," demurred Horace. "Understand that I don't pretend to be above physical things. They have their place, but——"

"Oh, don't be so darned reasonable!"

"I can't help it."

"I hate these slot-machine people."

"I assure you I——" began Horace.

"Oh shut up!"

"My own rationality——"

"I didn't say anything about your nationality. You're Amuricun, ar'n't you?"

"Yes."

"Well, that's O.K. with me. I got a notion I want to see you do something that isn't in your highbrow programme. I want to see if a what-ch-call-em with Brazilian trimmings—that thing you said you were—can be a little human."

Horace shook his head again.

"I won't kiss you."

"My life is blighted," muttered Marcia tragically. "I'm a beaten woman. I'll go through life without ever having a kiss with Brazilian trimmings." She sighed. "Anyways, Omar, will you come and see my show?"

"What show?"

"I'm a wicked actress from 'Home James'!"

"Light opera?"

"Yes—at a stretch. One of the characters is a Brazilian rice-planter. That might interest you."

"I saw 'The Bohemian Girl' once," reflected Horace aloud. "I enjoyed it—to some extent——"

"Then you'll come?"

"Well, I'm—I'm——"

"Oh, I know—you've got to run down to Brazil for the week-end."

"Not at all. I'd be delighted to come——"

Marcia clapped her hands.

"Goodyforyou! I'll mail you a ticket—Thursday night?"

"Why, I——"

"Good! Thursday night it is."

She stood up and walking close to him laid both hands on his shoulders.

"I like you, Omar. I'm sorry I tried to kid you. I thought you'd be sort of frozen, but you're a nice boy."

He eyed her sardonically.

"I'm several thousand generations older than you are."

"You carry your age well."

They shook hands gravely.

"My name's Marcia Meadow," she said emphatically. "'Member it—Marcia Meadow. And I won't tell Charlie Moon you were in."

An instant later as she was skimming down the last flight of stairs three at a time she heard a voice call over the upper banister: "Oh, say——"

She stopped and looked up—made out a vague form leaning over.

"Oh, say!" called the prodigy again. "Can you hear me?"

"Here's your connection Omar."

"I hope I haven't given you the impression that I consider kissing intrinsically irrational."

"Impression? Why, you didn't even give me the kiss! Never fret—so long."

Two doors near her opened curiously at the sound of a feminine voice. A tentative cough sounded from above. Gathering her skirts, Marcia dived wildly down the last flight, and was swallowed up in the murky Connecticut air outside.

Up-stairs Horace paced the floor of his study. From time to time he glanced toward Berkeley waiting there in suave dark-red reputability, an open book lying suggestively on his cushions. And then he found that his circuit of the floor was bringing him each time nearer to Hume. There was something about Hume that was strangely and inexpressibly different. The diaphanous form still seemed hovering near, and had Horace sat there he would have felt as if he were sitting on a lady's lap. And though Horace couldn't have named the quality of difference, there was such a quality—quite intangible to the speculative mind, but real, nevertheless. Hume was radiating something that in all the two hundred years of his influence he had never radiated before.

Hume was radiating attar of roses.

II

ON THURSDAY NIGHT HORACE TARBOX SAT IN AN AISLE SEAT IN THE FIFTH row and witnessed "Home James." Oddly enough he found that he was enjoying himself. The cynical students near him were annoyed at his audible appreciation of time-honored jokes in the Hammerstein tradition. But Horace was waiting with anxiety for Marcia Meadow singing her song about a Jazz-bound Blundering Blimp. When she did appear, radiant under a floppity flower-faced hat, a warm glow settled over him, and when the song was over he did not join in the storm of applause. He felt somewhat numb.

In the intermission after the second act an usher materialized beside him, demanded to know if he were Mr. Tarbox, and then handed him a note written in a round adolescent band. Horace read it in some confusion, while the usher lingered with withering patience in the aisle.

"Dear Omar: After the show I always grow an awful hunger. If you want to satisfy it for me in the Taft Grill just communicate your answer to the big-timber guide that brought this and oblige.

Your friend,

Marcia Meadow."

"Tell her,"—he coughed—"tell her that it will be quite all right. I'll meet her in front of the theatre."

The big-timber guide smiled arrogantly.

"I giss she meant for you to come roun' t' the stage door."

"Where—where is it?"

"Ou'side. Tunayulef. Down ee alley."

"What?"

"Ou'side. Turn to y' left! Down ee alley!"

The arrogant person withdrew. A freshman behind Horace snickered.

Then half an hour later, sitting in the Taft Grill opposite the hair that was yellow by natural pigment, the prodigy was saying an odd thing.

"Do you have to do that dance in the last act?" he was asking earnestly—"I mean, would they dismiss you if you refused to do it?"

Marcia grinned.

"It's fun to do it. I like to do it."

And then Horace came out with a faux pas.

"I should think you'd detest it," he remarked succinctly. "The people behind me were making remarks about your bosom."

Marcia blushed fiery red.

"I can't help that," she said quickly. "The dance to me is only a sort of acrobatic stunt. Lord, it's hard enough to do! I rub liniment into my shoulders for an hour every night."

"Do you have—fun while you're on the stage?"

"Uh-huh—sure! I got in the habit of having people look at me, Omar, and I like it."

"Hm!" Horace sank into a brownish study.

"How's the Brazilian trimmings?"

"Hm!" repeated Horace, and then after a pause: "Where does the play go from here?"

"New York."

"For how long?"

"All depends. Winter—maybe."

"Oh!"

"Coming up to lay eyes on me, Omar, or aren't you int'rested? Not as nice here, is it, as it was up in your room? I wish we was there now."

"I feel idiotic in this place," confessed Horace, looking round him nervously.

"Too bad! We got along pretty well."

At this he looked suddenly so melancholy that she changed her tone, and reaching over patted his hand.

"Ever take an actress out to supper before?"

"No," said Horace miserably, "and I never will again. I don't know why I came to-night. Here under all these lights and with all these people laughing and chattering I feel completely out of my sphere. I don't know what to talk to you about."

"We'll talk about me. We talked about you last time."

"Very well."

"Well, my name really is Meadow, but my first name isn't Marcia—it's Veronica. I'm nineteen. Question—how did the girl make her leap to the footlights? Answer—she was born in Passaic, New Jersey, and up to a year ago she got the right to breathe by pushing Nabiscoes in Marcel's tea-room in Trenton. She started going with a guy named Robbins, a singer in the Trent House cabaret, and he got her to try a song and dance with him one evening. In a month we were filling the supper-room every night. Then we went to New York with meet-my-friend letters thick as a pile of napkins.

"In two days we landed a job at Divinerries', and I learned to shimmy from a kid at the Palais Royal. We stayed at Divinerries' six months until one night Peter Boyce Wendell, the columnist, ate his milk-toast there. Next morning a poem about Marvellous Marcia came out in his newspaper, and within two days I had three vaudeville offers and a chance at the Midnight Frolic. I wrote Wendell a thank-you letter, and he printed it in his column—said that the style was like Carlyle's, only more rugged and that I ought to quit dancing and do North American literature. This got me a coupla more vaudeville offers and a chance as an ingénue in a regular show. I took it—and here I am, Omar."

When she finished they sat for a moment in silence she draping the last skeins of a Welsh rabbit on her fork and waiting for him to speak.

"Let's get out of here," he said suddenly.

Marcia's eyes hardened.

"What's the idea? Am I making you sick?"

"No, but I don't like it here. I don't like to be sitting here with you."

Without another word Marcia signalled for the waiter.

"What's the check?" she demanded briskly "My part—the rabbit and the ginger ale."

Horace watched blankly as the waiter figured it.

"See here," he began, "I intended to pay for yours too. You're my guest."

With a half-sigh Marcia rose from the table and walked from the room. Horace, his face a document in bewilderment, laid a bill down and followed her out, up the stairs and into the lobby. He overtook her in front of the elevator and they faced each other.

"See here," he repeated "You're my guest. Have I said something to offend you?"

After an instant of wonder Marcia's eyes softened.

"You're a rude fella!" she said slowly. "Don't you know you're rude?"

"I can't help it," said Horace with a directness she found quite disarming. "You know I like you."

"You said you didn't like being with me."

"I didn't like it."

"Why not?" Fire blazed suddenly from the gray forests of his eyes.

"Because I didn't. I've formed the habit of liking you. I've been thinking of nothing much else for two days."

"Well, if you——"

"Wait a minute," he interrupted. "I've got something to say. It's this: in six weeks I'll be eighteen years old. When I'm eighteen years old I'm coming up to New York to see you. Is there some place in New York where we can go and not have a lot of people in the room?"

"Sure!" smiled Marcia. "You can come up to my 'partment. Sleep on the couch if you want to."

"I can't sleep on couches," he said shortly. "But I want to talk to you."

"Why, sure," repeated Marcia, "in my 'partment."

In his excitement Horace put his hands in his pockets.

"All right—just so I can see you alone. I want to talk to you as we talked up in my room."

"Honey boy," cried Marcia, laughing, "is it that you want to kiss me?"

"Yes," Horace almost shouted. "I'll kiss you if you want me to."

The elevator man was looking at them reproachfully. Marcia edged toward the grated door.

"I'll drop you a post-card," she said.

Horace's eyes were quite wild.

"Send me a post-card! I'll come up any time after January first. I'll be eighteen then."

And as she stepped into the elevator he coughed enigmatically, yet with a vague challenge, at the calling, and walked quickly away.

III

HE WAS THERE AGAIN. SHE SAW HIM WHEN SHE TOOK HER FIRST GLANCE AT THE restless Manhattan audience—down in the front row with his head bent a bit forward and his gray eyes fixed on her. And she knew that to him they were alone together in a world where the high-rouged row of ballet faces and the massed whines of the violins were as imperceivable as powder on a marble Venus. An instinctive defiance rose within her.

"Silly boy!" she said to herself hurriedly, and she didn't take her encore.

"What do they expect for a hundred a week—perpetual motion?" she grumbled to herself in the wings.

"What's the trouble? Marcia?"

"Guy I don't like down in front."

During the last act as she waited for her specialty she had an odd attack of stage fright. She had never sent Horace the promised post-card. Last night she had pretended not to see him— had hurried from the theatre immediately after her dance to pass a sleepless night in her apartment, thinking—as she had so often in the last month—of his pale, rather intent face, his slim, boyish fore, the merciless, unworldly abstraction that made him charming to her.

And now that he had come she felt vaguely sorry—as though an unwonted responsibility was being forced on her.

"Infant prodigy!" she said aloud.

"What?" demanded the negro comedian standing beside her.

"Nothing—just talking about myself."

On the stage she felt better. This was her dance—and she always felt that the way she did it wasn't suggestive any more than to some men every pretty girl is suggestive. She made it a stunt.

"Uptown, downtown, jelly on a spoon,

After sundown shiver by the moon."

He was not watching her now. She saw that clearly. He was looking very deliberately at a castle on the back drop, wearing that expression he had worn in the Taft Grill. A wave of exasperation swept over her—he was criticising her.

"That's the vibration that thrills me,

Funny how affection fi-lls me

Uptown, downtown——"

Unconquerable revulsion seized her. She was suddenly and horribly conscious of her audience as she had never been since her first appearance. Was that a leer on a pallid face in the front row, a droop of disgust on one young girl's mouth? These shoulders of hers—these shoulders shaking— were they hers? Were they real? Surely shoulders weren't made for this!

"Then—you'll see at a glance

I'll need some funeral ushers with St. Vitus dance

At the end of the world I'll———"

The bassoon and two cellos crashed into a final chord. She paused and poised a moment on her toes with every muscle tense, her young face looking out dully at the audience in what one young girl afterward called "such a curious, puzzled look," and then without bowing rushed from the stage. Into the dressing-room she sped, kicked out of one dress and into another, and caught a taxi outside.

Her apartment was very warm—small, it was, with a row of professional pictures and sets of Kipling and O. Henry which she had bought once from a blue-eyed agent and read occasionally. And there were several chairs which matched, but were none of them comfortable, and a pink-shaded lamp with blackbirds painted on it and an atmosphere of other stifled pink throughout. There were nice things in it—nice things unrelentingly hostile to each other, offspring of a vicarious, impatient taste acting in stray moments. The worst was typified by a great picture framed in oak bark of Passaic as seen from the Erie Railroad—altogether a frantic, oddly extravagant, oddly penurious attempt to make a cheerful room. Marcia knew it was a failure.

Into this room came the prodigy and took her two hands awkwardly.

"I followed you this time," he said.

"Oh!"

"I want you to marry me," he said.

Her arms went out to him. She kissed his mouth with a sort of passionate wholesomeness.

"There!"

"I love you," he said.

She kissed him again and then with a little sigh flung herself into an armchair and half lay there, shaken with absurd laughter.

"Why, you infant prodigy!" she cried.

"Very well, call me that if you want to. I once told you that I was ten thousand years older than you—I am."

She laughed again.

"I don't like to be disapproved of."

"No one's ever going to disapprove of you again."

"Omar," she asked, "why do you want to marry me?"

The prodigy rose and put his hands in his pockets.

"Because I love you, Marcia Meadow."

And then she stopped calling him Omar.

"Dear boy," she said, "you know I sort of love you. There's something about you—I can't tell what—that just puts my heart through the wringer every time I'm round you. But honey—" She paused.

"But what?"

"But lots of things. But you're only just eighteen, and I'm nearly twenty."

"Nonsense!" he interrupted. "Put it this way—that I'm in my nineteenth year and you're nineteen. That makes us pretty close—without counting that other ten thousand years I mentioned."

Marcia laughed.

"But there are some more 'buts.' Your people——

"My people!" exclaimed the prodigy ferociously. "My people tried to make a monstrosity out of me." His face grew quite crimson at the enormity of what he was going to say. "My people can go way back and sit down!"

"My heavens!" cried Marcia in alarm. "All that? On tacks, I suppose."

"Tacks—yes," he agreed wildly—"on anything. The more I think of how they allowed me to become a little dried-up mummy——"

"What makes you thank you're that?" asked Marcia quietly—"me?"

"Yes. Every person I've met on the streets since I met you has made me jealous because they knew what love was before I did. I used to call it the 'sex impulse.' Heavens!"

"There's more 'buts,'" said Marcia

"What are they?"

"How could we live?"

"I'll make a living."

"You're in college."

"Do you think I care anything about taking a Master of Arts degree?"

"You want to be Master of Me, hey?"

"Yes! What? I mean, no!"

Marcia laughed, and crossing swiftly over sat in his lap. He put his arm round her wildly and implanted the vestige of a kiss somewhere near her neck.

"There's something white about you," mused Marcia "but it doesn't sound very logical."

"Oh, don't be so darned reasonable!"

"I can't help it," said Marcia.

"I hate these slot-machine people!"

"But we——"

"Oh, shut up!"

And as Marcia couldn't talk through her ears she had to.

IV

HORACE AND MARCIA WERE MARRIED EARLY IN FEBRUARY. THE SENSATION IN academic circles both at Yale and Princeton was tremendous. Horace Tarbox, who at fourteen had been played up in the Sunday magazines sections of metropolitan newspapers, was throwing over his career, his chance of being a world authority on American philosophy, by marrying a chorus girl—they made Marcia a chorus girl. But like all modern stories it was a four-and-a-half-day wonder.

They took a flat in Harlem. After two weeks' search, during which his idea of the value of academic knowledge faded unmercifully, Horace took a position as clerk with a South American export company—some one had told him that exporting was the coming thing. Marcia was to stay in her show for a few months—anyway until he got on his feet. He was getting a hundred and twenty-five to start with, and though of course they told him it was only a question of months until he would be earning double that, Marcia refused even to consider giving up the hundred and fifty a week that she was getting at the time.

"We'll call ourselves Head and Shoulders, dear," she said softly, "and the shoulders'll have to keep shaking a little longer until the old head gets started."

"I hate it," he objected gloomily.

"Well," she replied emphatically, "Your salary wouldn't keep us in a tenement. Don't think I want to be public—I don't. I want to be yours. But I'd be a half-wit to sit in one room and count the sunflowers on the wall-paper while I waited for you. When you pull down three hundred a month I'll quit."

And much as it hurt his pride, Horace had to admit that hers was the wiser course.

March mellowed into April. May read a gorgeous riot act to the parks and waters of Manhatten, and they were very happy. Horace, who had no habits whatsoever—he had never had time to form any—proved the most adaptable of husbands, and as Marcia entirely lacked opinions on the subjects that engrossed him there were very few jottings and bumping. Their minds moved in different spheres. Marcia acted as practical factotum, and Horace lived either in his old world of abstract ideas or in a sort of triumphantly earthy worship and adoration of his wife. She was a continual source of astonishment to him—the freshness and originality of her mind, her dynamic, clear-headed energy, and her unfailing good humor.

And Marcia's co-workers in the nine-o'clock show, whither she had transferred her talents, were impressed with her tremendous pride in her husband's mental powers. Horace they knew only as a very slim, tight-lipped, and immature-looking young man, who waited every night to take her home.

"Horace," said Marcia one evening when she met him as usual at eleven, "you looked like a ghost standing there against the street lights. You losing weight?"

He shook his head vaguely.

"I don't know. They raised me to a hundred and thirty-five dollars to-day, and——"

"I don't care," said Marcia severely. "You're killing yourself working at night. You read those big books on economy——"

"Economics," corrected Horace.

"Well, you read 'em every night long after I'm asleep. And you're getting all stooped over like you were before we were married."

"But, Marcia, I've got to——"

"No, you haven't dear. I guess I'm running this shop for the present, and I won't let my fella ruin his health and eyes. You got to get some exercise."

"I do. Every morning I——"

"Oh, I know! But those dumb-bells of yours wouldn't give a consumptive two degrees of fever. I mean real exercise. You've got to join a gymnasium. 'Member you told me you were such a trick gymnast once that they tried to get you out for the team in college and they couldn't because you had a standing date with Herb Spencer?"

"I used to enjoy it," mused Horace, "but it would take up too much time now."

"All right," said Marcia. "I'll make a bargain with you. You join a gym and I'll read one of those books from the brown row of 'em."

"'Pepys' Diary'? Why, that ought to be enjoyable. He's very light."

"Not for me—he isn't. It'll be like digesting plate glass. But you been telling me how much it'd broaden my lookout. Well, you go to a gym three nights a week and I'll take one big dose of Sammy."

Horace hesitated.

"Well——"

"Come on, now! You do some giant swings for me and I'll chase some culture for you."

So Horace finally consented, and all through a baking summer he spent three and sometimes four evenings a week experimenting on the trapeze in Skipper's Gymnasium. And in August he admitted to Marcia that it made him capable of more mental work during the day.

"Mens sana in corpore sano," he said.

"Don't believe in it," replied Marcia. "I tried one of those patent medicines once and they're all bunk. You stick to gymnastics."

One night in early September while he was going through one of his contortions on the rings in the nearly deserted room he was addressed by a meditative fat man whom he had noticed watching him for several nights.

"Say, lad, do that stunt you were doin' last night."

Horace grinned at him from his perch.

"I invented it," he said. "I got the idea from the fourth proposition of Euclid."

"What circus he with?"

"He's dead."

"Well, he must of broke his neck doin' that stunt. I set here last night thinkin' sure you was goin' to break yours."

"Like this!" said Horace, and swinging onto the trapeze he did his stunt.

"Don't it kill your neck an' shoulder muscles?"

"It did at first, but inside of a week I wrote the Quod erat demonstrandum on it."

"Hm!"

Horace swung idly on the trapeze.

"Ever think of takin' it up professionally?" asked the fat man.

"Not I."

"Good money in it if you're willin' to do stunts like 'at an' can get away with it."

"Here's another," chirped Horace eagerly, and the fat man's mouth dropped suddenly agape as he watched this pink-jerseyed Prometheus again defy the gods and Isaac Newton.

The night following this encounter Horace got home from work to find a rather pale Marcia stretched out on the sofa waiting for him.

"I fainted twice to-day," she began without preliminaries.

"What?"

"Yep. You see baby's due in four months now. Doctor says I ought to have quit dancing two weeks ago."

Horace sat down and thought it over.

"I'm glad of course," he said pensively—"I mean glad that we're going to have a baby. But this means a lot of expense."

"I've got two hundred and fifty in the bank," said Marcia hopefully, "and two weeks' pay coming."

Horace computed quickly.

"Inducing my salary, that'll give us nearly fourteen hundred for the next six months."

Marcia looked blue.

"That all? Course I can get a job singing somewhere this month. And I can go to work again in March."

"Of course nothing!" said Horace gruffly. "You'll stay right here. Let's see now—there'll be doctor's bills and a nurse, besides the maid: We've got to have some more money."

"Well," said Marcia wearily, "I don't know where it's coming from. It's up to the old head now. Shoulders is out of business."

Horace rose and pulled on his coat.

"Where are you going?"

"I've got an idea," he answered. "I'll be right back."

Ten minutes later as he headed down the street toward Skipper's Gymnasium he felt a placid wonder, quite unmixed with humor, at what he was going to do. How he would have gaped at himself a year before! How every one would have gaped! But when you opened your door at the rap of life you let in many things.

The gymnasium was brightly lit, and when his eyes became accustomed to the glare he found the meditative fat man seated on a pile of canvas mats smoking a big cigar.

"Say," began Horace directly, "were you in earnest last night when you said I could make money on my trapeze stunts?"

"Why, yes," said the fat man in surprise.

"Well, I've been thinking it over, and I believe I'd like to try it. I could work at night and on Saturday afternoons—and regularly if the pay is high enough."

The fat men looked at his watch.

"Well," he said, "Charlie Paulson's the man to see. He'll book you inside of four days, once he sees you work out. He won't be in now, but I'll get hold of him for to-morrow night."

The fat man was as good as his word. Charlie Paulson arrived next night and put in a wondrous hour watching the prodigy swap through the air in amazing parabolas, and on the night following he brought two age men with him who looked as though they had been born smoking black cigars and talking about money in low, passionate voices. Then on the succeeding Saturday Horace Tarbox's torso made its first professional appearance in a gymnastic exhibition at the Coleman Street Gardens. But though the audience numbered nearly five thousand people, Horace felt no nervousness. From his childhood he had read papers to audiences— learned that trick of detaching himself.

"Marcia," he said cheerfully later that same night, "I think we're out of the woods. Paulson thinks he can get me an opening at the Hippodrome, and that means an all-winter engagement. The Hippodrome you know, is a big——"

"Yes, I believe I've heard of it," interrupted Marcia, "but I want to know about this stunt you're doing. It isn't any spectacular suicide, is it?"

"It's nothing," said Horace quietly. "But if you can think of an nicer way of a man killing himself than taking a risk for you, why that's the way I want to die."

Marcia reached up and wound both arms tightly round his neck.

"Kiss me," she whispered, "and call me 'dear heart.' I love to hear you say 'dear heart.' And bring me a book to read to-morrow. No more Sam Pepys, but something trick and trashy. I've been wild for something to do all day. I felt like writing letters, but I didn't have anybody to write to."

"Write to me," said Horace. "I'll read them."

"I wish I could," breathed Marcia. "If I knew words enough I could write you the longest love-letter in the world—and never get tired."

But after two more months Marcia grew very tired indeed, and for a row of nights it was a very anxious, weary-looking young athlete who walked out before the Hippodrome crowd. Then there were two days when his place was taken by a young man who wore pale blue instead of white, and got very little applause. But after the two days Horace appeared again, and those who sat close to the stage remarked an expression of beatific happiness on that young acrobat's face even when he was twisting breathlessly in the air an the middle of his amazing and original shoulder swing. After that performance he laughed at the elevator man and dashed up the stairs to the flat five steps at a time—and then tiptoed very carefully into a quiet room.

"Marcia," he whispered.

"Hello!" She smiled up at him wanly. "Horace, there's something I want you to do. Look in my top bureau drawer and you'll find a big stack of paper. It's a book—sort of—Horace. I wrote it down in these last three months while I've been laid up. I wish you'd take it to that Peter Boyce Wendell who put my letter in his paper. He could tell you whether it'd be a good book. I wrote it just the way I talk, just the way I wrote that letter to him. It's just a story about a lot of things that happened to me. Will you take it to him, Horace?"

"Yes, darling."

He leaned over the bed until his head was beside her on the pillow, and began stroking back her yellow hair.

"Dearest Marcia," he said softly.

"No," she murmured, "call me what I told you to call me."

"Dear heart," he whispered passionately—"dearest heart."

"What'll we call her?"

They rested a minute in happy, drowsy content, while Horace considered.

"We'll call her Marcia Hume Tarbox," he said at length.

"Why the Hume?"

"Because he's the fellow who first introduced us."

"That so?" she murmured, sleepily surprised. "I thought his name was Moon."

Her eyes dosed, and after a moment the slow lengthening surge of the bedclothes over her breast showed that she was asleep.

Horace tiptoed over to the bureau and opening the top drawer found a heap of closely scrawled, lead-smeared pages. He looked at the first sheet:

SANDRA PEPYS, SYNCOPATED BY Marcia Tarbox

He smiled. So Samuel Pepys had made an impression on her after all. He turned a page and began to read. His smile deepened—he read on. Half an hour passed and he became aware that Marcia had waked and was watching him from the bed.

"Honey," came in a whisper.

"What Marcia?"

"Do you like it?"

Horace coughed.

"I seem to be reading on. It's bright."

"Take it to Peter Boyce Wendell. Tell him you got the highest marks in Princeton once and that you ought to know when a book's good. Tell him this one's a world beater."

"All right, Marcia," Horace said gently.

Her eyes closed again and Horace crossing over kissed her forehead—stood there for a moment with a look of tender pity. Then he left the room.

All that night the sprawly writing on the pages, the constant mistakes in spelling and grammar, and the weird punctuation danced before his eyes. He woke several times in the night, each time full of a welling chaotic sympathy for this desire of Marcia's soul to express itself in words. To him there was something infinitely pathetic about it, and for the first time in months he began to turn over in his mind his own half-forgotten dreams.

He had meant to write a series of books, to popularize the new realism as Schopenhauer had popularized pessimism and William James pragmatism.

But life hadn't come that way. Life took hold of people and forced them into flying rings. He laughed to think of that rap at his door, the diaphanous shadow in Hume, Marcia's threatened kiss.

"And it's still me," he said aloud in wonder as he lay awake in the darkness. "I'm the man who sat in Berkeley with temerity to wonder if that rap would have had actual existence had my ear not been there to hear it. I'm still that man. I could be electrocuted for the crimes he committed.

"Poor gauzy souls trying to express ourselves in something tangible. Marcia with her written book; I with my unwritten ones. Trying to choose our mediums and then taking what we get—and being glad."

V

"SANDRA PEPYS, SYNCOPATED," WITH AN INTRODUCTION BY PETER BOYCE Wendell the columnist, appeared serially in Jordan's Magazine, and came out in book form in March. From its first published instalment it attracted attention far and wide. A trite enough subject—a girl from a small New Jersey town coming to New York to go on the stage—treated simply, with a peculiar vividness of phrasing and a haunting undertone of sadness in the very inadequacy of its vocabulary, it made an irresistible appeal.

Peter Boyce Wendell, who happened at that time to be advocating the enrichment of the American language by the immediate adoption of expressive vernacular words, stood as its sponsor and thundered his indorsement over the placid bromides of the conventional reviewers.

Marcia received three hundred dollars an instalment for the serial publication, which came at an opportune time, for though Horace's monthly salary at the Hippodrome was now more than Marcia's had ever been, young Marcia was emitting shrill cries which they interpreted as a demand for country air. So early April found them installed in a bungalow in Westchester County, with a place for a lawn, a place for a garage, and a place for everything, including a sound-proof impregnable study, in which Marcia faithfully promised Mr. Jordan she would shut herself up when her daughter's demands began to be abated, and compose immortally illiterate literature.

"It's not half bad," thought Horace one night as he was on his way from the station to his house. He was considering several prospects that had opened up, a four months' vaudeville offer in five figures, a chance to go back to Princeton in charge of all gymnasium work. Odd! He had once intended to go back there in charge of all philosophic work, and now he had not even been stirred by the arrival in New York of Anton Laurier, his old idol.

The gravel crunched raucously under his heel. He saw the lights of his sitting-room gleaming and noticed a big car standing in the drive. Probably Mr. Jordan again, come to persuade Marcia to settle down' to work.

She had heard the sound of his approach and her form was silhouetted against the lighted door as she came out to meet him. "There's some Frenchman here," she whispered nervously. "I can't pronounce his name, but he sounds awful deep. You'll have to jaw with him."

"What Frenchman?"

"You can't prove it by me. He drove up an hour ago with Mr. Jordan, and said he wanted to meet Sandra Pepys, and all that sort of thing."

Two men rose from chairs as they went inside.

"Hello Tarbox," said Jordan. "I've just been bringing together two celebrities. I've brought M'sieur Laurier out with me. M'sieur Laurier, let me present Mr. Tarbox, Mrs. Tarbox's husband."

"Not Anton Laurier!" exclaimed Horace.

"But, yes. I must come. I have to come. I have read the book of Madame, and I have been charmed"—he fumbled in his pocket—"ah I have read of you too. In this newspaper which I read to-day it has your name."

He finally produced a clipping from a magazine.

"Read it!" he said eagerly. "It has about you too."

Horace's eye skipped down the page.

"A distinct contribution to American dialect literature," it said. "No attempt at literary tone; the book derives its very quality from this fact, as did 'Huckleberry Finn.'"

Horace's eyes caught a passage lower down; he became suddenly aghast—read on hurriedly:

"Marcia Tarbox's connection with the stage is not only as a spectator but as the wife of a performer. She was married last year to Horace Tarbox, who every evening delights the children at the Hippodrome with his wondrous flying performance. It is said that the young couple have dubbed themselves Head and Shoulders, referring doubtless to the fact that Mrs. Tarbox supplies the literary and mental qualities, while the supple and agile shoulder of her husband contribute their share to the family fortunes.

"Mrs. Tarbox seems to merit that much-abused title—'prodigy.' Only twenty——"

Horace stopped reading, and with a very odd expression in his eyes gazed intently at Anton Laurier.

"I want to advise you—" he began hoarsely.

"What?"

"About raps. Don't answer them! Let them alone—have a padded door."

THE CUT-GLASS BOWL

I

There was a rough stone age and a smooth stone age and a bronze age, and many years afterward a cut-glass age. In the cut-glass age, when young ladies had persuaded young men with long, curly mustaches to marry them, they sat down several months afterward and wrote thank-you notes for all sorts of cut-glass presents—punch-bowls, finger-bowls, dinner-glasses, wine-glasses, ice-cream dishes, bonbon dishes, decanters, and vases—for, though cut glass was nothing new in the nineties, it was then especially busy reflecting the dazzling light of fashion from the Back Bay to the fastnesses of the Middle West.

After the wedding the punch-bowls were arranged in the sideboard with the big bowl in the centre; the glasses were set up in the china-closet; the candlesticks were put at both ends of things—and then the struggle for existence began. The bonbon dish lost its little handle and became a pin-tray upstairs; a promenading cat knocked the little bowl off the sideboard, and the hired girl chipped the middle-sized one with the sugar-dish; then the wine-glasses succumbed to leg fractures, and even the dinner-glasses disappeared one by one like the ten little niggers, the last one ending up, scarred and maimed as a tooth-brush holder among other shabby genteels on the bathroom shelf. But by the time all this had happened the cut-glass age was over, anyway.

It was well past its first glory on the day the curious Mrs. Roger Fairboalt came to see the beautiful Mrs. Harold Piper.

"My dear," said the curious Mrs. Roger Fairboalt, "I love your house. I think it's quite artistic."

"I'm so glad," said the beautiful Mrs. Harold Piper, lights appearing in her young, dark eyes; "and you must come often. I'm almost always alone in the afternoon."

Mrs. Fairboalt would have liked to remark that she didn't believe this at all and couldn't see how she'd be expected to—it was all over town that Mr. Freddy Gedney had been dropping in on Mrs. Piper five afternoons a week for the past six months. Mrs. Fairboalt was at that ripe age where she distrusted all beautiful women——

"I love the dining-room most," she said, "all that marvellous china, and that huge cut-glass bowl."

Mrs. Piper laughed, so prettily that Mrs. Fairboalt's lingering reservations about the Freddy Gedney story quite vanished.

"Oh, that big bowl!" Mrs. Piper's mouth forming the words was a vivid rose petal. "There's a story about that bowl——"

"Oh——"

"You remember young Carleton Canby? Well, he was very attentive at one time, and the night I told him I was going to marry Harold, seven years ago in ninety-two, he drew himself way up and said: 'Evylyn, I'm going to give a present that's as hard as you are and as beautiful and as empty and as easy to see through.' He frightened me a little—his eyes were so black. I thought he was going to deed me a haunted house or something that would explode when you opened it. That bowl came, and of course it's beautiful. Its diameter or circumference or something is two and a half feet—or perhaps it's three and a half. Anyway, the sideboard is really too small for it; it sticks way out."

"My dear, wasn't that odd! And he left town about then didn't he?" Mrs. Fairboalt was scribbling italicized notes on her memory—"hard, beautiful, empty, and easy to see through."

"Yes, he went West—or South—or somewhere," answered Mrs. Piper, radiating that divine vagueness that helps to lift beauty out of time.

Mrs. Fairboalt drew on her gloves, approving the effect of largeness given by the open sweep from the spacious music-room through the library, disclosing a part of the dining-room beyond. It was really the nicest smaller house in town, and Mrs. Piper had talked of moving to a larger one on Devereaux Avenue. Harold Piper must be coining money.

As she turned into the sidewalk under the gathering autumn dusk she assumed that disapproving, faintly unpleasant expression that almost all successful women of forty wear on the street.

If _I_ were Harold Piper, she thought, I'd spend a little less time on business and a little more time at home. Some friend should speak to him.

But if Mrs. Fairboalt had considered it a successful afternoon she would have named it a triumph had she waited two minutes longer. For while she was still a black receding figure a hundred yards down the street, a very good-looking distraught young man turned up the walk to the Piper house. Mrs. Piper answered the door-bell herself, and with a rather dismayed expression led him quickly into the library.

"I had to see you," he began wildly; "your note played the devil with me. Did Harold frighten you into this?"

She shook her head.

"I'm through, Fred," she said slowly, and her lips had never looked to him so much like tearings from a rose. "He came home last night sick with it. Jessie Piper's sense of duty was to much for her, so she went down to his office and told him. He was hurt and—oh, I can't help seeing it his way, Fred. He says we've been club gossip all summer and he didn't know it, and now he understands snatches of conversation he's caught and veiled hints people have dropped about me. He's mighty angry, Fred, and he loves me and I love him—rather."

Gedney nodded slowly and half closed his eyes.

"Yes," he said "yes, my trouble's like yours. I can see other people's points of view too plainly." His gray eyes met her dark ones frankly. "The blessed thing's over. My God, Evylyn, I've been sitting down at the office all day looking at the outside of your letter, and looking at it and looking at it——"

"You've got to go, Fred," she said steadily, and the slight emphasis of hurry in her voice was a new thrust for him. "I gave him my word of honor I wouldn't see you. I know just how far I can go with Harold, and being here with you this evening is one of the things I can't do."

They were still standing, and as she spoke she made a little movement toward the door. Gedney looked at her miserably, trying, here at the end, to treasure up a last picture of her—and then suddenly both of them were stiffened into marble at the sound of steps on the walk outside. Instantly her arm reached out grasping the lapel of his coat—half urged, half swung him through the big door into the dark dining-room.

"I'll make him go up-stairs," she whispered close to his ear; "don't move till you hear him on the stairs. Then go out the front way."

Then he was alone listening as she greeted her husband in the hall.

Harold Piper was thirty-six, nine years older than his wife. He was handsome—with marginal notes: these being eyes that were too close together, and a certain woodenness when his face was in repose. His attitude toward this Gedney matter was typical of all his attitudes. He had told Evylyn that he considered the subject closed and would never reproach her nor allude to it in any form; and he told himself that this was rather a big way of looking at it—that she was not a little impressed. Yet, like all men who are preoccupied with their own broadness, he was exceptionally narrow.

He greeted Evylyn with emphasized cordiality this evening.

"You'll have to hurry and dress, Harold," she said eagerly; "we're going to the Bronsons'."

He nodded.

"It doesn't take me long to dress, dear," and, his words trailing off, he walked on into the library. Evylyn's heart clattered loudly.

"Harold——" she began, with a little catch in her voice, and followed him in. He was lighting a cigarette. "You'll have to hurry, Harold," she finished, standing in the doorway.

"Why?" he asked a trifle impatiently; "you're not dressed yourself yet, Evie."

He stretched out in a Morris chair and unfolded a newspaper. With a sinking sensation Evylyn saw that this meant at least ten minutes—and Gedney was standing breathless in the next room. Supposing Harold decided that before he went upstairs he wanted a drink from the decanter on the sideboard. Then it occurred to her to forestall this contingency by bringing him the decanter and a glass. She dreaded calling his attention to the dining-room in any way, but she couldn't risk the other chance.

But at the same moment Harold rose and, throwing his paper down, came toward her.

"Evie, dear," he said, bending and putting his arms about her, "I hope you're not thinking about last night——" She moved close to him, trembling. "I know," he continued, "it was just an imprudent friendship on your part. We all make mistakes."

Evylyn hardly heard him. She was wondering if by sheer clinging to him she could draw him out and up the stairs. She thought of playing sick, asking to be carried up—unfortunately she knew he would lay her on the couch and bring her whiskey.

Suddenly her nervous tension moved up a last impossible notch. She had heard a very faint but quite unmistakable creak from the floor of the dining room. Fred was trying to get out the back way.

Then her heart took a flying leap as a hollow ringing note like a gong echoed and re-echoed through the house. Gedney's arm had struck the big cut-glass bowl.

"What's that!" cried Harold. "Who's there?"

She clung to him but he broke away, and the room seemed to crash about her ears. She heard the pantry-door swing open, a scuffle, the rattle of a tin pan, and in wild despair she rushed into the kitchen and pulled up the gas. Her husband's arm slowly unwound from Gedney's neck, and he stood there very still, first in amazement, then with pain dawning in his face.

"My golly!" he said in bewilderment, and then repeated: "My golly!"

He turned as if to jump again at Gedney, stopped, his muscles visibly relaxed, and he gave a bitter little laugh.

"You people—you people——" Evylyn's arms were around him and her eyes were pleading with him frantically, but he pushed her away and sank dazed into a kitchen chair, his face like porcelain. "You've been doing things to me, Evylyn. Why, you little devil! You little devil!"

She had never felt so sorry for him; she had never loved him so much.

"It wasn't her fault," said Gedney rather humbly. "I just came." But Piper shook his head, and his expression when he stared up was as if some physical accident had jarred his mind into a temporary inability to function. His eyes, grown suddenly pitiful, struck a deep, unsounded chord in Evylyn—and simultaneously a furious anger surged in her. She felt her eyelids burning; she stamped her foot violently; her hands scurried nervously over the table as if searching for a weapon, and then she flung herself wildly at Gedney.

"Get out!" she screamed, dark eyes blazing, little fists beating helplessly on his outstretched arm. "You did this! Get out of here—get out—get out! get out!"

II

Concerning Mrs. Harold Piper at thirty-five, opinion was divided—women said she was still handsome; men said she was pretty no longer. And this was probably because the qualities in her beauty that women had feared and men had followed had vanished. Her eyes were still as large and as dark and as sad, but the mystery had departed; their sadness was no longer eternal, only human, and she had developed a habit, when she was startled or annoyed, of twitching her brows together and blinking several times. Her mouth also had lost: the red had receded and the faint down-turning of its corners when she smiled, that had added to the sadness of the eyes and been vaguely mocking and beautiful, was quite gone. When she smiled now the corners of her lips turned up. Back in the days when she revelled in her own beauty Evylyn had enjoyed that smile of hers—she had accentuated it. When she stopped accentuating it, it faded out and the last of her mystery with it.

Evylyn had ceased accentuating her smile within a month after the Freddy Gedney affair. Externally things had gone an very much as they had before. But in those few minutes during which she had discovered how much she loved her husband, Evylyn had realized how indelibly she had hurt him. For a month she struggled against aching silences, wild reproaches and accusations—she pled with him, made quiet, pitiful little love to him, and he laughed at her bitterly—and then she, too, slipped gradually into silence and a shadowy, impenetrable barrier dropped between them. The surge of love that had risen in her she lavished on Donald, her little boy, realizing him almost wonderingly as a part of her life.

The next year a piling up of mutual interests and responsibilities and some stray flicker from the past brought husband and wife together again—but after a rather pathetic flood of passion Evylyn realized that her great opportunity was gone. There simply wasn't anything left. She might have been youth and love for both—but that time of silence had slowly dried up the springs of affection and her own desire to drink again of them was dead.

She began for the first time to seek women friends, to prefer books she had read before, to sew a little where she could watch her two children to whom she was devoted. She worried about little things—if she saw crumbs on the dinner-table her mind drifted off the conversation: she was receding gradually into middle age.

Her thirty-fifth birthday had been an exceptionally busy one, for they were entertaining on short notice that night, as she stood in her bedroom window in the late afternoon she discovered that she was quite tired. Ten years before she would have lain down and slept, but now she had a feeling that things needed watching: maids were cleaning down-stairs, bric-à-brac was all over the floor, and there were sure to be grocery-men that had to be talked to imperatively—and then there was a letter to write Donald, who was fourteen and in his first year away at school.

She had nearly decided to lie down, nevertheless, when she heard a sudden familiar signal from little Julie down-stairs. She compressed her lips, her brows twitched together, and she blinked.

"Julie!" she called.

"Ah-h-h-ow!" prolonged Julie plaintively. Then the voice of Hilda, the second maid, floated up the stairs.

"She cut herself a little, Mis' Piper."

Evylyn flew to her sewing-basket, rummaged until she found a torn handkerchief, and hurried downstairs. In a moment Julie was crying in her arms as she searched for the cut, faint, disparaging evidences of which appeared on Julie's dress.

"My thu-umb!" explained Julie. "Oh-h-h-h, t'urts."

"It was the bowl here, the he one," said Hilda apologetically. "It was waitin' on the floor while I polished the sideboard, and Julie come along an' went to foolin' with it. She yust scratch herself."

Evylyn frowned heavily at Hilda, and twisting Julie decisively in her lap, began tearing strips of the handkerchief.

"Now—let's see it, dear."

Julie held it up and Evelyn pounced.

"There!"

Julie surveyed her swathed thumb doubtfully. She crooked it; it waggled. A pleased, interested look appeared in her tear-stained face. She sniffled and waggled it again.

"You precious!" cried Evylyn and kissed her, but before she left the room she levelled another frown at Hilda. Careless! Servants all that way nowadays. If she could get a good Irishwoman—but you couldn't any more—and these Swedes——

At five o'clock Harold arrived and, coming up to her room, threatened in a suspiciously jovial tone to kiss her thirty-five times for her birthday. Evylyn resisted.

"You've been drinking," she said shortly, and then added qualitatively, "a little. You know I loathe the smell of it."

"Evie," he said after a pause, seating himself in a chair by the window, "I can tell you something now. I guess you've known things haven't beep going quite right down-town."

She was standing at the window combing her hair, but at these words she turned and looked at him.

"How do you mean? You've always said there was room for more than one wholesale hardware house in town." Her voice expressed some alarm.

"There was," said Harold significantly, "but this Clarence Ahearn is a smart man."

"I was surprised when you said he was coming to dinner."

"Evie," he went on, with another slap at his knee, "after January first 'The Clarence Ahearn Company' becomes 'The Ahearn, Piper Company'—and 'Piper Brothers' as a company ceases to exist."

Evylyn was startled. The sound of his name in second place was somehow hostile to her; still he appeared jubilant.

"I don't understand, Harold."

"Well, Evie, Ahearn has been fooling around with Marx. If those two had combined we'd have been the little fellow, struggling along, picking up smaller orders, hanging back on risks. It's a question of capital, Evie, and 'Ahearn and Marx' would have had the business just like 'Ahearn and Piper' is going to now." He paused and coughed and a little cloud of whiskey floated up to her nostrils. "Tell you the truth, Evie, I've suspected that Ahearn's wife had something to do with it. Ambitious little lady, I'm told. Guess she knew the Marxes couldn't help her much here."

"Is she—common?" asked Evie.

"Never met her, I'm sure—but I don't doubt it. Clarence Ahearn's name's been up at the Country Club five months—no action taken." He waved his hand disparagingly. "Ahearn and I had lunch together to-day and just about clinched it, so I thought it'd be nice to have him and his wife up to-night—just have nine, mostly family. After all, it's a big thing for me, and of course we'll have to see something of them, Evie."

"Yes," said Evie thoughtfully, "I suppose we will."

Evylyn was not disturbed over the social end of it—but the idea of "Piper Brothers" becoming "The Ahearn, Piper Company" startled her. It seemed like going down in the world.

Half an hour later, as she began to dress for dinner, she heard his voice from down-stairs.

"Oh, Evie, come down!"

She went out into the hall and called over the banister:

"What is it?"

"I want you to help me make some of that punch before dinner."

Hurriedly rehooking her dress, she descended the stairs and found him grouping the essentials on the dining-room table. She went to the sideboard and, lifting one of the bowls, carried it over.

"Oh, no," he protested, "let's use the big one. There'll be Ahearn and his wife and you and I and Milton, that's five, and Tom and Jessie, that's seven: and your sister and Joe Ambler, that's nine. You don't know how quick that stuff goes when you make it."

"We'll use this bowl," she insisted. "It'll hold plenty. You know how Tom is."

Tom Lowrie, husband to Jessie, Harold's first cousin, was rather inclined to finish anything in a liquid way that he began.

Harold shook his head.

"Don't be foolish. That one holds only about three quarts and there's nine of us, and the servants'll want some—and it isn't strong punch. It's so much more cheerful to have a lot, Evie; we don't have to drink all of it."

"I say the small one."

Again he shook his head obstinately.

"No; be reasonable."

"I am reasonable," she said shortly. "I don't want any drunken men in the house."

"Who said you did?"

"Then use the small bowl."

"Now, Evie——"

He grasped the smaller bowl to lift it back. Instantly her hands were on it, holding it down. There was a momentary struggle, and then, with a little exasperated grunt, he raised his side, slipped it from her fingers, and carried it to the sideboard.

She looked at him and tried to make her expression contemptuous, but he only laughed. Acknowledging her defeat but disclaiming all future interest in the punch, she left the room.

III

At seven-thirty, her cheeks glowing and her high-piled hair gleaming with a suspicion of brilliantine, Evylyn descended the stairs. Mrs. Ahearn, a little woman concealing a slight nervousness under red hair and an extreme Empire gown, greeted her volubly. Evelyn disliked her on the spot, but the husband she rather approved of. He had keen blue eyes and a natural gift of pleasing people that might have made him, socially, had he not so obviously committed the blunder of marrying too early in his career.

"I'm glad to know Piper's wife," he said simply. "It looks as though your husband and I are going to see a lot of each other in the future."

She bowed, smiled graciously, and turned to greet the others: Milton Piper, Harold's quiet, unassertive younger brother; the two Lowries, Jessie and Tom; Irene, her own unmarried sister; and finally Joe Ambler, a confirmed bachelor and Irene's perennial beau.

Harold led the way into dinner.

"We're having a punch evening," he announced jovially—Evylyn saw that he had already sampled his concoction—"so there won't be any cocktails except the punch. It's m' wife's greatest achievement, Mrs. Ahearn; she'll give you the recipe if you want it; but owing to a slight"—he caught his wife's eye and paused —"to a slight indisposition; I'm responsible for this batch. Here's how!"

All through dinner there was punch, and Evylyn, noticing that Ahearn and Milton Piper and all the women were shaking their heads negatively at the maid, knew she had been right about the bowl; it was still half full. She resolved to caution Harold directly afterward, but when the women left the table Mrs. Ahearn cornered her, and she found herself talking cities and dressmakers with a polite show of interest.

"We've moved around a lot," chattered Mrs. Ahearn, her red head nodding violently. "Oh, yes, we've never stayed so long in a town before— but I do hope we're here for good. I like it here; don't you?"

"Well, you see, I've always lived here, so, naturally——"

"Oh, that's true," said Mrs. Ahearn and laughed. Clarence always used to tell me he had to have a wife he could come home to and say: "Well, we're going to Chicago to-morrow to live, so pack up."

"I got so I never expected to live anywhere." She laughed her little laugh again; Evylyn suspected that it was her society laugh.

"Your husband is a very able man, I imagine."

"Oh, yes," Mrs. Ahearn assured her eagerly. "He's brainy, Clarence is. Ideas and enthusiasm, you know. Finds out what he wants and then goes and gets it."

Evylyn nodded. She was wondering if the men were still drinking punch back in the dining-room. Mrs. Ahearn's history kept unfolding jerkily, but Evylyn had ceased to listen. The first odor of massed cigars began to drift in. It wasn't really a large house, she reflected; on an evening like this the library sometimes grew blue with smoke, and next day one had to leave the windows open for hours to air the heavy staleness out of the curtains. Perhaps this partnership might . . . she began to speculate on a new house . . .

Mrs. Ahearn's voice drifted in on her:

"I really would like the recipe if you have it written down somewhere——"

Then there was a sound of chairs in the dining-room and the men strolled in. Evylyn saw at once that her worst fears were realized. Harold's face was flushed and his words ran together at the ends of sentences, while Tom Lowrie lurched when he walked and narrowly missed Irene's lap when he tried to sink onto the couch beside her. He sat there blinking dazedly at the company. Evylyn found herself blinking back at him, but she saw no humor in it. Joe Ambler was smiling contentedly and purring on his cigar. Only Ahearn and Milton Piper seemed unaffected.

"It's a pretty fine town, Ahearn," said Ambler, "you'll find that."

"I've found it so," said Ahearn pleasantly.

"You find it more, Ahearn," said Harold, nodding emphatically "'f I've an'thin' do 'th it."

He soared into a eulogy of the city, and Evylyn wondered uncomfortably if it bored every one as it bored her. Apparently not. They were all listening attentively. Evylyn broke in at the first gap.

"Where've you been living, Mr. Ahearn?" she asked interestedly. Then she remembered that Mrs. Ahearn had told her, but it didn't matter. Harold mustn't talk so much. He was such an ass when he'd been drinking. But he plopped directly back in.

"Tell you, Ahearn. Firs' you wanna get a house up here on the hill. Get Stearne house or Ridgeway house. Wanna have it so people say: 'There's Ahearn house.' Solid, you know, tha's effec' it gives."

Evylyn flushed. This didn't sound right at all. Still Ahearn didn't seem to notice anything amiss, only nodded gravely.

"Have you been looking——" But her words trailed off unheard as Harold's voice boomed on.

"Get house—tha's start. Then you get know people. Snobbish town first toward outsider, but not long—after know you. People like you"—he indicated Ahearn and his wife with a sweeping gesture—"all right. Cordial as an'thin' once get by first barrer-bar-barrer——" He swallowed, and then said "barrier," repeated it masterfully.

Evylyn looked appealingly at her brother-in-law, but before he could intercede a thick mumble had come crowding out of Tom Lowrie, hindered by the dead cigar which he gripped firmly with his teeth.

"Huma uma ho huma ahdy um——"

"What?" demanded Harold earnestly.

Resignedly and with difficulty Tom removed the cigar—that is, he removed part of it, and then blew the remainder with a whut sound across the room, where it landed liquidly and limply in Mrs. Ahearn's lap.

"Beg pardon," he mumbled, and rose with the vague intention of going after it. Milton's hand on his coat collapsed him in time, and Mrs. Ahearn not ungracefully flounced the tobacco from her skirt to the floor, never once looking at it.

"I was sayin'," continued Tom thickly, "'fore 'at happened,"—he waved his hand apologetically toward Mrs. Ahearn—"I was sayin' I heard all truth that Country Club matter."

Milton leaned and whispered something to him.

"Lemme 'lone," he said petulantly; "know what I'm doin'. 'Ats what they came for."

Evylyn sat there in a panic, trying to make her mouth form words. She saw her sister's sardonic expression and Mrs. Ahearn's face turning a vivid red. Ahearn was looking down at his watch-chain, fingering it.

"I heard who's been keepin' y' out, an' he's not a bit better'n you. I can fix whole damn thing up. Would've before, but I didn't know you. Harol' tol' me you felt bad about the thing———"

Milton Piper rose suddenly and awkwardly to his feet. In a second every one was standing tensely and Milton was saying something very hurriedly about having to go early, and the Ahearns were listening with eager intentness. Then Mrs. Ahearn swallowed and turned with a forced smile toward Jessie. Evylyn saw Tom lurch forward and put his hand on Ahearns shoulder—and suddenly she was listening to a new, anxious voice at her elbow, and, turning, found Hilda, the second maid.

"Please, Mis' Piper, I tank Yulie got her hand poisoned. It's all swole up and her cheeks is hot and she's moanin' an' groanin'———"

"Julie is?" Evylyn asked sharply. The party suddenly receded. She turned quickly, sought with her eyes for Mrs. Ahearn, slipped toward her.

"If you'll excuse me, Mrs.—" She had momentarily forgotten the name, but she went right on: "My little girl's been taken sick. I'll be down when I can." She turned and ran quickly up the stairs, retaining a confused picture of rays of cigar smoke and a loud discussion in the centre of the room that seemed to be developing into an argument.

Switching on the light in the nursery, she found Julie tossing feverishly and giving out odd little cries. She put her hand against the cheeks. They were burning. With an exclamation she followed the arm down under the cover until she found the hand. Hilda was right. The whole thumb was swollen to the wrist and in the centre was a little inflamed sore. Blood-poisoning! her mind cried in terror. The bandage had come off the cut and she'd gotten something in it. She'd cut it at three o'clock—it was now nearly eleven. Eight hours. Blood-poisoning couldn't possibly develop so soon.

She rushed to the 'phone.

Doctor Martin across the street was out. Doctor Foulke, their family physician, didn't answer. She racked her brains and in desperation called her throat specialist, and bit her lip furiously while he looked up the numbers of two physicians. During that interminable moment she thought she heard loud voices down-stairs—but she seemed to be in another world now. After fifteen minutes she located a physician who sounded angry and sulky at being called out of bed. She ran back to the nursery and, looking at the hand, found it was somewhat more swollen.

"Oh, God!" she cried, and kneeling beside the bed began smoothing back Julie's hair over and over. With a vague idea of getting some hot water, she rose and stared toward the door, but the lace of her dress caught in the bed-rail and she fell forward on her hands and knees. She struggled up and jerked frantically at the lace. The bed moved and Julie groaned. Then more quietly but with suddenly fumbling fingers she found the pleat in front, tore the whole pannier completely off, and rushed from the room.

Out in the hall she heard a single loud, insistent voice, but as she reached the head of the stairs it ceased and an outer door banged.

The music-room came into view. Only Harold and Milton were there, the former leaning against a chair, his face very pale, his collar open, and his mouth moving loosely.

"What's the matter?"

Milton looked at her anxiously.

"There was a little trouble——"

Then Harold saw her and, straightening up with an effort, began to speak.

"Sult m'own cousin m'own house. God damn common nouveau rish. 'Sult m'own cousin——"

"Tom had trouble with Ahearn and Harold interfered," said Milton. "My Lord Milton," cried Evylyn, "couldn't you have done something?"

"I tried; I——"

"Julie's sick," she interrupted; "she's poisoned herself. Get him to bed if you can."

Harold looked up.

"Julie sick?"

Paying no attention, Evylyn brushed by through the dining-room, catching sight, with a burst of horror, of the big punch-bowl still on the table, the liquid from melted ice in its bottom. She heard steps on the front stairs—it was Milton helping Harold up—and then a mumble: "Why, Julie's a'righ'."

"Don't let him go into the nursery!" she shouted.

The hours blurred into a nightmare. The doctor arrived just before midnight and within a half-hour had lanced the wound. He left at two after giving her the addresses of two nurses to call up and promising to return at half past six. It was blood-poisoning.

At four, leaving Hilda by the bedside, she went to her room, and slipping with a shudder out of her evening dress, kicked it into a corner. She put on a house dress and returned to the nursery while Hilda went to make coffee.

Not until noon could she bring herself to look into Harold's room, but when she did it was to find him awake and staring very miserably at the ceiling. He turned blood-shot hollow eyes upon her. For a minute she hated him, couldn't speak. A husky voice came from the bed.

"What time is it?"

"Noon."

"I made a damn fool——"

"It doesn't matter," she said sharply. "Julie's got blood-poisoning. They may"—she choked over the words—"they think she'll have to lose her hand."

"What?"

"She cut herself on that—that bowl."

"Last night?"

"Oh, what does it matter?" see cried; "she's got blood-poisoning. Can't you hear?" He looked at her bewildered—sat half-way up in bed.

"I'll get dressed," he said.

Her anger subsided and a great wave of weariness and pity for him rolled over her. After all, it was his trouble, too.

"Yes," she answered listlessly, "I suppose you'd better."

IV

IF EVYLYN'S BEAUTY HAD HESITATED AN HER EARLY THIRTIES IT CAME TO AN abrupt decision just afterward and completely left her. A tentative outlay of wrinkles on her face suddenly deepened and flesh collected rapidly on her legs and hips and arms. Her mannerism of drawing her brows together had become an expression—it was habitual when she was reading or speaking and even while she slept. She was forty-six.

As in most families whose fortunes have gone down rather than up, she and Harold had drifted into a colorless antagonism. In repose they looked at each other with the toleration they might have felt for broken old chairs; Evylyn worried a little when he was sick and did her best to be cheerful under the wearying depression of living with a disappointed man.

Family bridge was over for the evening and she sighed with relief. She had made more mistakes than usual this evening and she didn't care. Irene shouldn't have made that remark about the infantry being particularly dangerous. There had been no letter for three weeks now, and, while this was nothing out of the ordinary, it never failed to make her nervous; naturally she hadn't known how many clubs were out.

Harold had gone up-stairs, so she stepped out on the porch for a breath of fresh air. There was a bright glamour of moonlight diffusing on the sidewalks and lawns, and with a little half yawn, half laugh, she remembered one long moonlight affair of her youth. It was astonishing to think that life had once been the sum of her current love-affairs. It was now the sum of her current problems.

There was the problem of Julie—Julie was thirteen, and lately she was growing more and more sensitive about her deformity and preferred to stay always in her room reading. A few years before she had been frightened at the idea of going to school, and Evylyn could not bring herself to send her, so she grew up in her mother's shadow, a pitiful little figure with the artificial hand that she made no attempt to use but kept forlornly in her pocket. Lately she had been taking lessons in using it because Evylyn had feared she would cease to lift the arm altogether, but after the lessons, unless she made a move with it in listless obedience to her mother, the little hand would creep back to the pocket of her dress. For a while her dresses were made without pockets, but Julie had moped around the house so miserably at a loss all one month that Evylyn weakened and never tried the experiment again.

The problem of Donald had been different from the start. She had attempted vainly to keep him near her as she had tried to teach Julie to lean less on her—lately the problem of Donald had been snatched out of her hands; his division had been abroad for three months.

She yawned again—life was a thing for youth. What a happy youth she must have had! She remembered her pony, Bijou, and the trip to Europe with her mother when she was eighteen——

"Very, very complicated," she said aloud and severely to the moon, and, stepping inside, was about to close the door when she heard a noise in the library and started.

It was Martha, the middle-aged servant: they kept only one now.

"Why, Martha!" she said in surprise.

Martha turned quickly.

"Oh, I thought you was up-stairs. I was jist——"

"Is anything the matter?"

Martha hesitated.

"No; I——" She stood there fidgeting. "It was a letter, Mrs. Piper, that I put somewhere.

"A letter? Your own letter?" asked Evylyn.

"No, it was to you. 'Twas this afternoon, Mrs. Piper, in the last mail. The postman give it to me and then the back door-bell rang. I had it in my hand, so I must have stuck it somewhere. I thought I'd just slip in now and find it."

"What sort of a letter? From Mr. Donald?"

"No, it was an advertisement, maybe, or a business letter. It was a long narrow one, I remember."

They began a search through the music-room, looking on trays and mantelpieces, and then through the library, feeling on the tops of rows of books. Martha paused in despair.

"I can't think where. I went straight to the kitchen. The dining-room, maybe." She started hopefully for the dining-room, but turned suddenly at the sound of a gasp behind her. Evylyn had sat down heavily in a Morris chair, her brows drawn very close together eyes blanking furiously.

"Are you sick?"

For a minute there was no answer. Evylyn sat there very still and Martha could see the very quick rise and fall of her bosom.

"Are you sick?" she repeated.

"No," said Evylyn slowly, "but I know where the letter is. Go 'way, Martha. I know."

Wonderingly, Martha withdrew, and still Evylyn sat there, only the muscles around her eyes moving—contracting and relaxing and contracting again. She knew now where the letter was—she knew as well as if she had put it there herself. And she felt instinctively and unquestionably what the letter was. It was long and narrow like an advertisement, but up in the corner in large letters it said "War Department" and, in smaller letters below, "Official Business." She knew it lay there in the big bowl with her name in ink on the outside and her soul's death within.

Rising uncertainly, she walked toward the dining-room, feeling her way along the bookcases and through the doorway. After a moment she found the light and switched it on.

There was the bowl, reflecting the electric light in crimson squares edged with black and yellow squares edged with blue, ponderous and glittering, grotesquely and triumphantly ominous. She took a step forward and paused again; another step and she would see over the top and into the inside—another step and she would see an edge of white—another step—her hands fell on the rough, cold surface—

In a moment she was tearing it open, fumbling with an obstinate fold, holding it before her while the typewritten page glared out and struck at her. Then it fluttered like a bird to the floor. The house that had seemed whirring, buzzing a moment since, was suddenly very quiet; a breath of air crept in through the open front door carrying the noise of a passing motor; she heard faint sounds from upstairs and then a grinding racket in the pipe behind the bookcases-her husband turning of a water-tap——

And in that instant it was as if this were not, after all, Donald's hour except in so far as he was a marker in the insidious contest that had gone on in sudden surges and long, listless interludes between Evylyn and this cold, malignant thing of beauty, a gift of enmity from a man whose face she had long since forgotten. With its massive, brooding passivity it lay there in the centre of her house as it had lain for years, throwing out the ice-like beams of a thousand eyes, perverse glitterings merging each into each, never aging, never changing.

Evylyn sat down on the edge of the table and stared at it fascinated. It seemed to be smiling now, a very cruel smile, as if to say:

"You see, this time I didn't have to hurt you directly. I didn't bother. You know it was I who took your son away. You know how cold I am and how hard and how beautiful, because once you were just as cold and hard and beautiful."

The bowl seemed suddenly to turn itself over and then to distend and swell until it became a great canopy that glittered and trembled over the room, over the house, and, as the walls melted slowly into mist, Evylyn saw that it was still moving out, out and far away from her, shutting off far horizons and suns and moons and stars except as inky blots seen faintly through it. And under it walked all the people, and the light that came through to them was refracted and twisted until shadow seamed light and light seemed shadow—until the whole panoply of the world became changed and distorted under the twinkling heaven of the bowl.

Then there came a far-away, booming voice like a low, clear bell. It came from the centre of the bowl and down the great sides to the ground and then bounced toward her eagerly.

"You see, I am fate," it shouted, "and stronger than your puny plans; and I am how-things-turn-out and I am different from your little dreams, and I am the flight of time and the end of beauty and unfulfilled desire; all the accidents and imperceptions and the little minutes that shape the crucial hours are mine. I am the exception that proves no rules, the limits of your control, the condiment in the dish of life."

The booming sound stopped; the echoes rolled away over the wide land to the edge of the bowl that bounded the world and up the great sides and back to the centre where they hummed for a moment and died. Then the great walls began slowly to bear down upon her, growing smaller and smaller, coming closer and closer as if to crush her; and as she clinched her hands and waited for the swift bruise of the cold glass, the bowl gave a sudden wrench and turned over—and lay there on the side-board, shining and inscrutable, reflecting in a hundred prisms, myriad, many-colored glints and gleams and crossings and interlaces of light.

The cold wind blew in again through to front door, and with a desperate, frantic energy Evylyn stretched both her arms around the bowl. She must be quick—she must be strong. She tightened her arms until they ached, tauted the thin strips of muscle under her soft flesh, and with a mighty effort raised it and held it. She felt the wind blow cold on her back where her dress had come apart from the strain of her effort, and as she felt it she turned toward it and staggered under the great weight out through the library and on toward the front door. She must be quick—she must be strong. The blood in her arms throbbed dully and her knees kept giving way under her, but the feel of the cool glass was good.

Out the front door she tottered and over to the stone steps, and there, summoning every fibre of her soul and body for a last effort, swung herself half around—for a second, as she tried to loose her hold, her numb fingers clung to the rough surface, and in that second she slipped and, losing balance, toppled forward with a despairing cry, her arms still around the bowl . . . down . . .

Over the way lights went on; far down the block the crash was heard, and pedestrians rushed up wonderingly; up-stairs a tired man awoke from the edge of sleep and a little girl whimpered in a haunted doze. And all over the moonlit sidewalk around the still, black form, hundreds of prisms and cubes and splinters of glass reflected the light in little gleams of blue, and black edged with yellow, and yellow, and crimson edged with black.

BERNICE BOBS HER HAIR

I

After dark on Saturday night one could stand on the first tee of the golf-course and see the country-club windows as a yellow expanse over a very black and wavy ocean. The waves of this ocean, so to speak, were the heads of many curious caddies, a few of the more ingenious chauffeurs, the golf professional's deaf sister—and there were usually several stray, diffident waves who might have rolled inside had they so desired. This was the gallery.

The balcony was inside. It consisted of the circle of wicker chairs that lined the wall of the combination clubroom and ballroom. At these Saturday-night dances it was largely feminine; a great babel of middle-aged ladies with sharp eyes and icy hearts behind lorgnettes and large bosoms. The main function of the balcony was critical, it occasionally showed grudging admiration, but never approval, for it is well known among ladies over thirty-five that when the younger set dance in the summer-time it is with the very worst intentions in the world, and if they are not bombarded with stony eyes stray couples will dance weird barbaric interludes in the corners, and the more popular, more dangerous, girls will sometimes be kissed in the parked limousines of unsuspecting dowagers.

But, after all, this critical circle is not close enough to the stage to see the actors' faces and catch the subtler byplay. It can only frown and lean, ask questions and make satisfactory deductions from its set of postulates, such as the one which states that every young man with a large income leads the life of a hunted partridge. It never really appreciates the drama of the shifting, semi-cruel world of adolescence. No; boxes, orchestra-circle, principals, and chorus be represented by the medley of faces and voices that sway to the plaintive African rhythm of Dyer's dance orchestra.

From sixteen-year-old Otis Ormonde, who has two more years at Hill School, to G. Reece Stoddard, over whose bureau at home hangs a Harvard law diploma; from little Madeleine Hogue, whose hair still feels strange and uncomfortable on top of her head, to Bessie MacRae, who has been the life of the party a little too long—more than ten years—the medley is not only the centre of the stage but contains the only people capable of getting an unobstructed view of it.

With a flourish and a bang the music stops. The couples exchange artificial, effortless smiles, facetiously repeat "la-de-da-da dum-dum," and then the clatter of young feminine voices soars over the burst of clapping.

A few disappointed stags caught in midfloor as they had been about to cut in subsided listlessly back to the walls, because this was not like the riotous Christmas dances—these summer hops were considered just pleasantly warm and exciting, where even the younger marrieds rose and performed ancient waltzes and terrifying fox trots to the tolerant amusement of their younger brothers and sisters.

Warren McIntyre, who casually attended Yale, being one of the unfortunate stags, felt in his dinner-coat pocket for a cigarette and strolled out onto the wide, semidark veranda, where couples were scattered at tables, filling the lantern-hung night with vague words and hazy laughter. He nodded here and there at the less absorbed and as he passed each couple some half-forgotten fragment of a story played in his mind, for it was not a large city and every one was Who's Who to every one else's past. There, for example, were Jim Strain and Ethel Demorest, who had been privately engaged for three years. Every one knew that as soon as Jim managed to hold a job for more than two months she would marry him. Yet how bored they both looked, and how wearily Ethel regarded Jim sometimes, as if she wondered why she had trained the vines of her affection on such a wind-shaken poplar.

Warren was nineteen and rather pitying with those of his friends who hadn't gone East to college. But, like most boys, he bragged tremendously about the girls of his city when he was away from it. There was Genevieve Ormonde, who regularly made the rounds of dances, house-parties, and football games at Princeton, Yale, Williams, and Cornell; there was black-eyed Roberta Dillon, who was quite as famous to her own generation as Hiram Johnson or Ty Cobb; and, of course, there was Marjorie Harvey, who besides having a fairylike face and a dazzling, bewildering tongue was already justly celebrated for having turned five cart-wheels in succession during the last pump-and-slipper dance at New Haven.

Warren, who had grown up across the street from Marjorie, had long been "crazy about her." Sometimes she seemed to reciprocate his feeling with a faint gratitude, but she had tried him by her infallible test and informed him gravely that she did not love him. Her test was that when she was away from him she forgot him and had affairs with other boys. Warren found this discouraging, especially as Marjorie had been making little trips all summer, and for the first two or three days after each arrival home he saw great heaps of mail on the Harveys' hall table addressed to her in various masculine handwritings. To make matters worse, all during the month of August she had been visited by her cousin Bernice from Eau Claire, and it seemed impossible to see her alone. It was always necessary to hunt round and find some one to take care of Bernice. As August waned this was becoming more and more difficult.

Much as Warren worshipped Marjorie he had to admit that Cousin Bernice was sorta dopeless. She was pretty, with dark hair and high color, but she was no fun on a party. Every Saturday night he danced a long arduous duty dance with her to please Marjorie, but he had never been anything but bored in her company.

"Warren"——a soft voice at his elbow broke in upon his thoughts, and he turned to see Marjorie, flushed and radiant as usual. She laid a hand on his shoulder and a glow settled almost imperceptibly over him.

"Warren," she whispered "do something for me—dance with Bernice. She's been stuck with little Otis Ormonde for almost an hour."

Warren's glow faded.

"Why—sure," he answered half-heartedly.

"You don't mind, do you? I'll see that you don't get stuck."

"'Sall right."

Marjorie smiled—that smile that was thanks enough.

"You're an angel, and I'm obliged loads."

With a sigh the angel glanced round the veranda, but Bernice and Otis were not in sight. He wandered back inside, and there in front of the women's dressing-room he found Otis in the centre of a group of young men who were convulsed with laughter. Otis was brandishing a piece of timber he had picked up, and discoursing volubly.

"She's gone in to fix her hair," he announced wildly. "I'm waiting to dance another hour with her."

Their laughter was renewed.

"Why don't some of you cut in?" cried Otis resentfully. "She likes more variety."

"Why, Otis," suggested a friend "you've just barely got used to her."

"Why the two-by-four, Otis?" inquired Warren, smiling.

"The two-by-four? Oh, this? This is a club. When she comes out I'll hit her on the head and knock her in again."

Warren collapsed on a settee and howled with glee.

"Never mind, Otis," he articulated finally. "I'm relieving you this time."

Otis simulated a sudden fainting attack and handed the stick to Warren.

"If you need it, old man," he said hoarsely.

No matter how beautiful or brilliant a girl may be, the reputation of not being frequently cut in on makes her position at a dance unfortunate. Perhaps boys prefer her company to that of the butterflies with whom they dance a dozen times an but, youth in this jazz-nourished generation is temperamentally restless, and the idea of fox-trotting more than one full fox trot with the same girl is distasteful, not to say odious. When it comes to several dances and the intermissions between she can be quite sure that a young man, once relieved, will never tread on her wayward toes again.

Warren danced the next full dance with Bernice, and finally, thankful for the intermission, he led her to a table on the veranda. There was a moment's silence while she did unimpressive things with her fan.

"It's hotter here than in Eau Claire," she said.

Warren stifled a sigh and nodded. It might be for all he knew or cared. He wondered idly whether she was a poor conversationalist because she got no attention or got no attention because she was a poor conversationalist.

"You going to be here much longer?" he asked and then turned rather red. She might suspect his reasons for asking.

"Another week," she answered, and stared at him as if to lunge at his next remark when it left his lips.

Warren fidgeted. Then with a sudden charitable impulse he decided to try part of his line on her. He turned and looked at her eyes.

"You've got an awfully kissable mouth," he began quietly.

This was a remark that he sometimes made to girls at college proms when they were talking in just such half dark as this. Bernice distinctly jumped. She turned an ungraceful red and became clumsy with her fan. No one had ever made such a remark to her before.

"Fresh!"——the word had slipped out before she realized it, and she bit her lip. Too late she decided to be amused, and offered him a flustered smile.

Warren was annoyed. Though not accustomed to have that remark taken seriously, still it usually provoked a laugh or a paragraph of sentimental banter. And he hated to be called fresh, except in a joking way. His charitable impulse died and he switched the topic.

"Jim Strain and Ethel Demorest sitting out as usual," he commented.

This was more in Bernice's line, but a faint regret mingled with her relief as the subject changed. Men did not talk to her about kissable mouths, but she knew that they talked in some such way to other girls.

"Oh, yes," she said, and laughed. "I hear they've been mooning around for years without a red penny. Isn't it silly?"

Warren's disgust increased. Jim Strain was a close friend of his brother's, and anyway he considered it bad form to sneer at people for not having money. But Bernice had had no intention of sneering. She was merely nervous.

II

WHEN MARJORIE AND BERNICE REACHED HOME AT HALF AFTER MIDNIGHT they said good night at the top of the stairs. Though cousins, they were not intimates. As a matter of fact Marjorie had no female intimates—she considered girls stupid. Bernice on the contrary all through this parent-arranged visit had rather longed to exchange those confidences flavored with giggles and tears that she considered an indispensable factor in all feminine intercourse. But in this respect she found Marjorie rather cold; felt somehow the same difficulty in talking to her that she had in talking to men. Marjorie never giggled, was never frightened, seldom embarrassed, and in fact had very few of the qualities which Bernice considered appropriately and blessedly feminine.

As Bernice busied herself with tooth-brush and paste this night she wondered for the hundredth time why she never had any attention when she was away from home. That her family were the wealthiest in Eau Claire; that her mother entertained tremendously, gave little diners for her daughter before all dances and bought her a car of her own to drive round in, never occurred to her as factors in her home-town social success. Like most girls she had been brought up on the warm milk prepared by Annie Fellows Johnston and on novels in which the female was beloved because of certain mysterious womanly qualities, always mentioned but never displayed.

Bernice felt a vague pain that she was not at present engaged in being popular. She did not know that had it not been for Marjorie's campaigning she would have danced the entire evening with one man; but she knew that even in Eau Claire other girls with less position and less pulchritude were given a much bigger rush. She attributed this to something subtly unscrupulous in those girls. It had never worried her, and if it had her mother would have assured her that the other girls cheapened themselves and that men really respected girls like Bernice.

She turned out the light in her bathroom, and on an impulse decided to go in and chat for a moment with her aunt Josephine, whose light was still on. Her soft slippers bore her noiselessly down the carpeted hall, but hearing voices inside she stopped near the partly openers door. Then she caught her own name, and without any definite intention of eavesdropping lingered—and the thread of the conversation going on inside pierced her consciousness sharply as if it had been drawn through with a needle.

"She's absolutely hopeless!" It was Marjorie's voice. "Oh, I know what you're going to say! So many people have told you how pretty and sweet she is, and how she can cook! What of it? She has a bum time. Men don't like her."

"What's a little cheap popularity?"

Mrs. Harvey sounded annoyed.

"It's everything when you're eighteen," said Marjorie emphatically. "I've done my best. I've been polite and I've made men dance with her, but they just won't stand being bored. When I think of that gorgeous coloring wasted on such a ninny, and think what Martha Carey could do with it—oh!"

"There's no courtesy these days."

Mrs. Harvey's voice implied that modern situations were too much for her. When she was a girl all young ladies who belonged to nice families had glorious times.

"Well," said Marjorie, "no girl can permanently bolster up a lame-duck visitor, because these days it's every girl for herself. I've even tried to drop hints about clothes and things, and she's been furious—given me the funniest looks. She's sensitive enough to know she's not getting away with much, but I'll bet she consoles herself by thinking that she's very virtuous and that I'm too gay and fickle and will come to a bad end. All unpopular girls think that way. Sour grapes! Sarah Hopkins refers to Genevieve and Roberta and me as gardenia girls! I'll bet she'd give ten years of her life and her European education to be a gardenia girl and have three or four men in love with her and be cut in on every few feet at dances."

"It seems to me," interrupted Mrs. Harvey rather wearily, "that you ought to be able to do something for Bernice. I know she's not very vivacious."

Marjorie groaned.

"Vivacious! Good grief! I've never heard her say anything to a boy except that it's hot or the floor's crowded or that she's going to school in New York next year. Sometimes she asks them what kind of car they have and tells them the kind she has. Thrilling!"

There was a short silence and then Mrs. Harvey took up her refrain:

"All I know is that other girls not half so sweet and attractive get partners. Martha Carey, for instance, is stout and loud, and her mother is distinctly common. Roberta Dillon is so thin this year that she looks as though Arizona were the place for her. She's dancing herself to death."

"But, mother," objected Marjorie impatiently, "Martha is cheerful and awfully witty and an awfully slick girl, and Roberta's a marvellous dancer. She's been popular for ages!"

Mrs. Harvey yawned.

"I think it's that crazy Indian blood in Bernice," continued Marjorie. "Maybe she's a reversion to type. Indian women all just sat round and never said anything."

"Go to bed, you silly child," laughed Mrs. Harvey. "I wouldn't have told you that if I'd thought you were going to remember it. And I think most of your ideas are perfectly idiotic," she finished sleepily.

There was another silence, while Marjorie considered whether or not convincing her mother was worth the trouble. People over forty can seldom be permanently convinced of anything. At eighteen our convictions are hills from which we look; at forty-five they are caves in which we hide.

Having decided this, Marjorie said good night. When she came out into the hall it was quite empty.

III

WHILE MARJORIE WAS BREAKFASTING LATE NEXT DAY BERNICE CAME INTO THE room with a rather formal good morning, sat down opposite, stared intently over and slightly moistened her lips.

"What's on your mind?" inquired Marjorie, rather puzzled.

Bernice paused before she threw her hand-grenade.

"I heard what you said about me to your mother last night."

Marjorie was startled, but she showed only a faintly heightened color and her voice was quite even when she spoke.

"Where were you?"

"In the hall. I didn't mean to listen—at first."

After an involuntary look of contempt Marjorie dropped her eyes and became very interested in balancing a stray corn-flake on her finger.

"I guess I'd better go back to Eau Claire—if I'm such a nuisance." Bernice's lower lip was trembling violently and she continued on a wavering note: "I've tried to be nice, and—and I've been first neglected and then insulted. No one ever visited me and got such treatment."

Marjorie was silent.

"But I'm in the way, I see. I'm a drag on you. Your friends don't like me." She paused, and then remembered another one of her grievances. "Of course I was furious last week when you tried to hint to me that that dress was unbecoming. Don't you think I know how to dress myself?"

"No," murmured less than half-aloud.

"What?"

"I didn't hint anything," said Marjorie succinctly. "I said, as I remember, that it was better to wear a becoming dress three times straight than to alternate it with two frights."

"Do you think that was a very nice thing to say?"

"I wasn't trying to be nice." Then after a pause: "When do you want to go?"

Bernice drew in her breath sharply.

"Oh!" It was a little half-cry.

Marjorie looked up in surprise.

"Didn't you say you were going?"

"Yes, but——"

"Oh, you were only bluffing!"

They stared at each other across the breakfast-table for a moment. Misty waves were passing before Bernice's eyes, while Marjorie's face wore that rather hard expression that she used when slightly intoxicated undergraduate's were making love to her.

"So you were bluffing," she repeated as if it were what she might have expected.

Bernice admitted it by bursting into tears. Marjorie's eyes showed boredom.

"You're my cousin," sobbed Bernice. "I'm v-v-visiting you. I was to stay a month, and if I go home my mother will know and she'll wah-wonder——"

Marjorie waited until the shower of broken words collapsed into little sniffles.

"I'll give you my month's allowance," she said coldly, "and you can spend this last week anywhere you want. There's a very nice hotel——"

Bernice's sobs rose to a flute note, and rising of a sudden she fled from the room.

An hour later, while Marjorie was in the library absorbed in composing one of those non-committal marvelously elusive letters that only a young girl can write, Bernice reappeared, very red-eyed, and consciously calm. She cast no glance at Marjorie but took a book at random from the shelf and sat down as if to read. Marjorie seemed absorbed in her letter and continued writing. When the clock showed noon Bernice closed her book with a snap.

"I suppose I'd better get my railroad ticket."

This was not the beginning of the speech she had rehearsed upstairs, but as Marjorie was not getting her cues—wasn't urging her to be reasonable; it's an a mistake—it was the best opening she could muster.

"Just wait till I finish this letter," said Marjorie without looking round. "I want to get it off in the next mail."

After another minute, during which her pen scratched busily, she turned round and relaxed with an air of "at your service." Again Bernice had to speak.

"Do you want me to go home?"

"Well," said Marjorie, considering, "I suppose if you're not having a good time you'd better go. No use being miserable."

"Don't you think common kindness——"

"Oh, please don't quote 'Little Women'!" cried Marjorie impatiently. "That's out of style."

"You think so?"

"Heavens, yes! What modern girl could live like those inane females?"

"They were the models for our mothers."

Marjorie laughed.

"Yes, they were—not! Besides, our mothers were all very well in their way, but they know very little about their daughters' problems."

Bernice drew herself up.

"Please don't talk about my mother."

Marjorie laughed.

"I don't think I mentioned her."

Bernice felt that she was being led away from her subject.

"Do you think you've treated me very well?"

"I've done my best. You're rather hard material to work with."

The lids of Bernice's eyes reddened.

"I think you're hard and selfish, and you haven't a feminine quality in you."

"Oh, my Lord!" cried Marjorie in desperation "You little nut! Girls like you are responsible for all the tiresome colorless marriages; all those ghastly inefficiencies that pass as feminine qualities. What a blow it must be when a man with imagination marries the beautiful bundle of clothes that he's been building ideals round, and finds that she's just a weak, whining, cowardly mass of affectations!"

Bernice's mouth had slipped half open.

"The womanly woman!" continued Marjorie. "Her whole early life is occupied in whining criticisms of girls like me who really do have a good time."

Bernice's jaw descended farther as Marjorie's voice rose.

"There's some excuse for an ugly girl whining. If I'd been irretrievably ugly I'd never have forgiven my parents for bringing me into the world. But you're starting life without any handicap—" Marjorie's little fist clinched, "If you expect me to weep with you you'll be disappointed. Go or stay, just as you like." And picking up her letters she left the room.

Bernice claimed a headache and failed to appear at luncheon. They had a matinée date for the afternoon, but the headache persisting, Marjorie made explanation to a not very downcast boy. But when she returned late in the afternoon she found Bernice with a strangely set face waiting for her in her bedroom.

"I've decided," began Bernice without preliminaries, "that maybe you're right about things—possibly not. But if you'll tell me why your friends aren't—aren't interested in me I'll see if I can do what you want me to."

Marjorie was at the mirror shaking down her hair.

"Do you mean it?"

"Yes."

"Without reservations? Will you do exactly what I say?"

"Well, I——"

"Well nothing! Will you do exactly as I say?"

"If they're sensible things."

"They're not! You're no case for sensible things."

"Are you going to make—to recommend——"

"Yes, everything. If I tell you to take boxing-lessons you'll have to do it. Write home and tell your mother you're going' to stay another two weeks.

"If you'll tell me——"

"All right—I'll just give you a few examples now. First you have no ease of manner. Why? Because you're never sure about your personal appearance. When a girl feels that she's perfectly groomed and dressed she can forget that part of her. That's charm. The more parts of yourself you can afford to forget the more charm you have."

"Don't I look all right?"

"No; for instance you never take care of your eyebrows. They're black and lustrous, but by leaving them straggly they're a blemish. They'd be beautiful if you'd take care of them in one-tenth the time you take doing nothing. You're going to brush them so that they'll grow straight."

Bernice raised the brows in question.

"Do you mean to say that men notice eyebrows?"

"Yes—subconsciously. And when you go home you ought to have your teeth straightened a little. It's almost imperceptible, still——"

"But I thought," interrupted Bernice in bewilderment, "that you despised little dainty feminine things like that."

"I hate dainty minds," answered Marjorie. "But a girl has to be dainty in person. If she looks like a million dollars she can talk about Russia, ping-pong, or the League of Nations and get away with it."

"What else?"

"Oh, I'm just beginning! There's your dancing."

"Don't I dance all right?"

"No, you don't—you lean on a man; yes, you do—ever so slightly. I noticed it when we were dancing together yesterday. And you dance standing up straight instead of bending over a little. Probably some old lady on the side-line once told you that you looked so dignified that way.

But except with a very small girl it's much harder on the man, and he's the one that counts."

"Go on." Bernice's brain was reeling.

"Well, you've got to learn to be nice to men who are sad birds. You look as if you'd been insulted whenever you're thrown with any except the most popular boys. Why, Bernice, I'm cut in on every few feet—and who does most of it? Why, those very sad birds. No girl can afford to neglect them. They're the big part of any crowd. Young boys too shy to talk are the very best conversational practice. Clumsy boys are the best dancing practice. If you can follow them and yet look graceful you can follow a baby tank across a barb-wire sky-scraper."

Bernice sighed profoundly, but Marjorie was not through.

"If you go to a dance and really amuse, say, three sad birds that dance with you; if you talk so well to them that they forget they're stuck with you, you've done something. They'll come back next time, and gradually so many sad birds will dance with you that the attractive boys will see there's no danger of being stuck—then they'll dance with you."

"Yes," agreed Bernice faintly. "I think I begin to see."

"And finally," concluded Marjorie, "poise and charm will just come. You'll wake up some morning knowing you've attained it and men will know it too."

Bernice rose.

"It's been awfully kind of you—but nobody's ever talked to me like this before, and I feel sort of startled."

Marjorie made no answer but gazed pensively at her own image in the mirror.

"You're a peach to help me," continued Bernice.

Still Marjorie did not answer, and Bernice thought she had seemed too grateful.

"I know you don't like sentiment," she said timidly.

Marjorie turned to her quickly.

"Oh, I wasn't thinking about that. I was considering whether we hadn't better bob your hair."

Bernice collapsed backward upon the bed.

IV

ON THE FOLLOWING WEDNESDAY EVENING THERE WAS A DINNER-DANCE AT THE country club. When the guests strolled in Bernice found her place-card with a slight feeling of irritation. Though at her right sat G. Reece Stoddard, a most desirable and distinguished young bachelor, the all-important left held only Charley Paulson. Charley lacked height, beauty, and social shrewdness, and in her new enlightenment Bernice decided that his only qualification to be her partner was that he had never been stuck with her. But this feeling of irritation left with the last of the soup-plates, and Marjorie's specific instruction came to her. Swallowing her pride she turned to Charley Paulson and plunged.

"Do you think I ought to bob my hair, Mr. Charley Paulson?"

Charley looked up in surprise.

"Why?"

"Because I'm considering it. It's such a sure and easy way of attracting attention."

Charley smiled pleasantly. He could not know this had been rehearsed. He replied that he didn't know much about bobbed hair. But Bernice was there to tell him.

"I want to be a society vampire, you see," she announced coolly, and went on to inform him that bobbed hair was the necessary prelude. She added that she wanted to ask his advice, because she had heard he was so critical about girls.

Charley, who knew as much about the psychology of women as he did of the mental states of Buddhist contemplatives, felt vaguely flattered.

"So I've decided," she continued, her voice rising slightly, "that early next week I'm going down to the Sevier Hotel barber-shop, sit in the first chair, and get my hair bobbed." She faltered noticing that the people near her had paused in their conversation and were listening; but after a confused second Marjorie's coaching told, and she finished her paragraph to the vicinity at large. "Of course I'm charging admission, but if you'll all come down and encourage me I'll issue passes for the inside seats."

There was a ripple of appreciative laughter, and under cover of it G. Reece Stoddard leaned over quickly and said close to her ear: "I'll take a box right now."

She met his eyes and smiled as if he had said something surprisingly brilliant.

"Do you believe in bobbed hair?" asked G. Reece in the same undertone.

"I think it's unmoral," affirmed Bernice gravely. "But, of course, you've either got to amuse people or feed 'em or shock 'em." Marjorie had culled this from Oscar Wilde. It was greeted with a ripple of laughter from the men and a series of quick, intent looks from the girls. And then as though she had said nothing of wit or moment Bernice turned again to Charley and spoke confidentially in his ear.

"I want to ask you your opinion of several people. I imagine you're a wonderful judge of character."

Charley thrilled faintly—paid her a subtle compliment by overturning her water.

Two hours later, while Warren McIntyre was standing passively in the stag line abstractedly watching the dancers and wondering whither and with whom Marjorie had disappeared, an unrelated perception began to creep slowly upon him—a perception that Bernice, cousin to Marjorie, had been cut in on several times in the past five minutes. He closed his eyes, opened them and looked again. Several minutes back she had been dancing with a visiting boy, a matter easily accounted for; a visiting boy would know no better. But now she was dancing with some one else, and there was Charley Paulson headed for her with enthusiastic determination in his eye. Funny—Charley seldom danced with more than three girls an evening.

Warren was distinctly surprised when—the exchange having been effected—the man relieved proved to be none ether than G. Reece Stoddard himself. And G. Reece seemed not at all jubilant at being relieved. Next time Bernice danced near, Warren regarded her intently. Yes, she was pretty, distinctly pretty; and to-night her face seemed really vivacious. She had that look that no woman, however histrionically proficient, can successfully counterfeit—she looked as if she were having a good time. He liked the way she had her hair arranged, wondered if it was brilliantine that made it glisten so. And that dress was becoming—a dark red that set off her shadowy eyes and high coloring. He remembered that he had thought her pretty when she first came to town, before he had realized that she was dull. Too bad she was dull—dull girls unbearable—certainly pretty though.

His thoughts zigzagged back to Marjorie. This disappearance would be like other disappearances. When she reappeared he would demand where she had been—would be told emphatically that it was none of his business. What a pity she was so sure of him! She basked in the knowledge that no other girl in town interested him; she defied him to fall in love with Genevieve or Roberta.

Warren sighed. The way to Marjorie's affections was a labyrinth indeed. He looked up. Bernice was again dancing with the visiting boy. Half unconsciously he took a step out from the stag line in her direction, and hesitated. Then he said to himself that it was charity. He walked toward her—collided suddenly with G. Reece Stoddard.

"Pardon me," said Warren.

But G. Reece had not stopped to apologize. He had again cut in on Bernice.

That night at one o'clock Marjorie, with one hand on the electric-light switch in the hall, turned to take a last look at Bernice's sparkling eyes.

"So it worked?"

"Oh, Marjorie, yes!" cried Bernice.

"I saw you were having a gay time."

"I did! The only trouble was that about midnight I ran short of talk. I had to repeat myself—with different men of course. I hope they won't compare notes."

"Men don't," said Marjorie, yawning, "and it wouldn't matter if they did—they'd think you were even trickier."

She snapped out the light, and as they started up the stairs Bernice grasped the banister thankfully. For the first time in her life she had been danced tired.

"You see," said Marjorie it the top of the stairs, "one man sees another man cut in and he thinks there must be something there. Well, we'll fix up some new stuff to-morrow. Good night."

"Good night."

As Bernice took down her hair she passed the evening before her in review. She had followed instructions exactly. Even when Charley Paulson cut in for the eighth time she had simulated delight and had apparently been both interested and flattered. She had not talked about the weather or Eau Claire or automobiles or her school, but had confined her conversation to me, you, and us.

But a few minutes before she fell asleep a rebellious thought was churning drowsily in her brain—after all, it was she who had done it. Marjorie, to be sure, had given her her conversation, but then Marjorie got much of her conversation out of things she read. Bernice had bought the red dress, though she had never valued it highly before Marjorie dug it out of her trunk—and her own voice had said the words, her own lips had smiled, her own feet had danced. Marjorie nice girl—vain, though— nice evening—nice boys—like Warren—Warren—Warren—what's his name—Warren——

She fell asleep.

V

To Bernice the next week was a revelation. With the feeling that people really enjoyed looking at her and listening to her came the foundation of self-confidence. Of course there were numerous mistakes at first. She did not know, for instance, that Draycott Deyo was studying for the ministry; she was unaware that he had cut in on her because he thought she was a quiet, reserved girl. Had she known these things she would not have treated him to the line which began "Hello, Shell Shock!" and continued with the bathtub story—"It takes a frightful lot of energy to fix my hair in the summer—there's so much of it—so I always fix it first and powder my face and put on my hat; then I get into the bathtub, and dress afterward. Don't you think that's the best plan?"

Though Draycott Deyo was in the throes of difficulties concerning baptism by immersion and might possibly have seen a connection, it must be admitted that he did not. He considered feminine bathing an immoral subject, and gave her some of his ideas on the depravity of modern society.

But to offset that unfortunate occurrence Bernice had several signal successes to her credit. Little Otis Ormonde pleaded off from a trip East and elected instead to follow her with a puppylike devotion, to the amusement of his crowd and to the irritation of G. Reece Stoddard, several of whose afternoon calls Otis completely ruined by the disgusting tenderness of the glances he bent on Bernice. He even told her the story of the two-by-four and the dressing-room to show her how frightfully mistaken he and every one else had been in their first judgment of her. Bernice laughed off that incident with a slight sinking sensation.

Of all Bernice's conversation perhaps the best known and most universally approved was the line about the bobbing of her hair.

"Oh, Bernice, when you goin' to get the hair bobbed?"

"Day after to-morrow maybe," she would reply, laughing. "Will you come and see me? Because I'm counting on you, you know."

"Will we? You know! But you better hurry up."

Bernice, whose tonsorial intentions were strictly dishonorable, would laugh again.

"Pretty soon now. You'd be surprised."

But perhaps the most significant symbol of her success was the gray car of the hypercritical Warren McIntyre, parked daily in front of the Harvey house. At first the parlor-maid was distinctly startled when he asked for Bernice instead of Marjorie; after a week of it she told the cook that Miss Bernice had gotta holda Miss Marjorie's best fella.

And Miss Bernice had. Perhaps it began with Warren's desire to rouse jealousy in Marjorie; perhaps it was the familiar though unrecognized strain of Marjorie in Bernice's conversation; perhaps it was both of these and something of sincere attraction besides. But somehow the collective mind of the younger set knew within a week that Marjorie's most reliable beau had made an amazing face-about and was giving an indisputable rush to Marjorie's guest. The question of the moment was how Marjorie would take it. Warren called Bernice on the 'phone twice a day, sent her notes, and they were frequently seen together in his roadster, obviously engrossed in one of those tense, significant conversations as to whether or not he was sincere.

Marjorie on being twitted only laughed. She said she was mighty glad that Warren had at last found some one who appreciated him. So the younger set laughed, too, and guessed that Marjorie didn't care and let it go at that.

One afternoon when there were only three days left of her visit Bernice was waiting in the hall for Warren, with whom she was going to a bridge party. She was in rather a blissful mood, and when Marjorie—also bound for the party—appeared beside her and began casually to adjust her hat in the mirror, Bernice was utterly unprepared for anything in the nature of a clash. Marjorie did her work very coldly and succinctly in three sentences.

"You may as well get Warren out of your head," she said coldly.

"What?" Bernice was utterly astounded.

"You may as well stop making a fool of yourself over Warren McIntyre. He doesn't care a snap of his fingers about you."

For a tense moment they regarded each other—Marjorie scornful, aloof; Bernice astounded, half-angry, half-afraid. Then two cars drove up in front of the house and there was a riotous honking. Both of them gasped faintly, turned, and side by side hurried out.

All through the bridge party Bernice strove in vain to master a rising uneasiness. She had offended Marjorie, the sphinx of sphinxes. With the most wholesome and innocent intentions in the world she had stolen Marjorie's property. She felt suddenly and horribly guilty. After the bridge game, when they sat in an informal circle and the conversation became general, the storm gradually broke. Little Otis Ormonde inadvertently precipitated it.

"When you going back to kindergarten, Otis?" some one had asked.

"Me? Day Bernice gets her hair bobbed."

"Then your education's over," said Marjorie quickly. "That's only a bluff of hers. I should think you'd have realized."

"That a fact?" demanded Otis, giving Bernice a reproachful glance.

Bernice's ears burned as she tried to think up an effectual come-back. In the face of this direct attack her imagination was paralyzed.

"There's a lot of bluffs in the world," continued Marjorie quite pleasantly. "I should think you'd be young enough to know that, Otis."

"Well," said Otis, "maybe so. But gee! With a line like Bernice's——"

"Really?" yawned Marjorie. "What's her latest bon mot?"

No one seemed to know. In fact, Bernice, having trifled with her muse's beau, had said nothing memorable of late.

"Was that really all a line?" asked Roberta curiously.

Bernice hesitated. She felt that wit in some form was demanded of her, but under her cousin's suddenly frigid eyes she was completely incapacitated.

"I don't know," she stalled.

"Splush!" said Marjorie. "Admit it!"

Bernice saw that Warren's eyes had left a ukulele he had been tinkering with and were fixed on her questioningly.

"Oh, I don't know!" she repeated steadily. Her cheeks were glowing.

"Splush!" remarked Marjorie again.

"Come through, Bernice," urged Otis. "Tell her where to get off." Bernice looked round again—she seemed unable to get away from Warren's eyes.

"I like bobbed hair," she said hurriedly, as if he had asked her a question, "and I intend to bob mine."

"When?" demanded Marjorie.

"Any time."

"No time like the present," suggested Roberta.

Otis jumped to his feet.

"Good stuff!" he cried. "We'll have a summer bobbing party. Sevier Hotel barber-shop, I think you said."

In an instant all were on their feet. Bernice's heart throbbed violently.

"What?" she gasped.

Out of the group came Marjorie's voice, very clear and contemptuous. "Don't worry—she'll back out!"

"Come on, Bernice!" cried Otis, starting toward the door.

Four eyes—Warren's and Marjorie's—stared at her, challenged her, defied her. For another second she wavered wildly.

"All right," she said swiftly "I don't care if I do."

An eternity of minutes later, riding down-town through the late afternoon beside Warren, the others following in Roberta's car close behind, Bernice had all the sensations of Marie Antoinette bound for the guillotine in a tumbrel. Vaguely she wondered why she did not cry out that it was all a mistake. It was all she could do to keep from clutching her hair with both bands to protect it from the suddenly hostile world. Yet she did neither. Even the thought of her mother was no deterrent now. This was the test supreme of her sportsmanship; her right to walk unchallenged in the starry heaven of popular girls.

Warren was moodily silent, and when they came to the hotel he drew up at the curb and nodded to Bernice to precede him out. Roberta's car emptied a laughing crowd into the shop, which presented two bold plate-glass windows to the street.

Bernice stood on the curb and looked at the sign, Sevier Barber-Shop. It was a guillotine indeed, and the hangman was the first barber, who, attired in a white coat and smoking a cigarette, leaned nonchalantly against the first chair. He must have heard of her; he must have been waiting all week, smoking eternal cigarettes beside that portentous, too-often-mentioned first chair. Would they blind-fold her? No, but they would tie a white cloth round her neck lest any of her blood—nonsense—hair—should get on her clothes.

"All right, Bernice," said Warren quickly.

With her chin in the air she crossed the sidewalk, pushed open the swinging screen-door, and giving not a glance to the uproarious, riotous row that occupied the waiting bench, went up to the fat barber.

"I want you to bob my hair."

The first barber's mouth slid somewhat open. His cigarette dropped to the floor.

"Huh?"

"My hair—bob it!"

Refusing further preliminaries, Bernice took her seat on high. A man in the chair next to her turned on his side and gave her a glance, half lather, half amazement. One barber started and spoiled little Willy Schuneman's monthly haircut. Mr. O'Reilly in the last chair grunted and swore musically in ancient Gaelic as a razor bit into his cheek. Two bootblacks became wide-eyed and rushed for her feet. No, Bernice didn't care for a shine.

Outside a passer-by stopped and stared; a couple joined him; half a dozen small boys' nose sprang into life, flattened against the glass; and snatches of conversation borne on the summer breeze drifted in through the screen-door.

"Lookada long hair on a kid!"

"Where'd yuh get 'at stuff? 'At's a bearded lady he just finished shavin'."

But Bernice saw nothing, heard nothing. Her only living sense told her that this man in the white coat had removed one tortoise-shell comb and then another; that his fingers were fumbling clumsily with unfamiliar hairpins; that this hair, this wonderful hair of hers, was going—she would never again feel its long voluptuous pull as it hung in a dark-brown glory down her back. For a second she was near breaking down, and then the picture before her swam mechanically into her vision—Marjorie's mouth curling in a faint ironic smile as if to say:

"Give up and get down! You tried to buck me and I called your bluff. You see you haven't got a prayer."

And some last energy rose up in Bernice, for she clinched her hands under the white cloth, and there was a curious narrowing of her eyes that Marjorie remarked on to some one long afterward.

Twenty minutes later the barber swung her round to face the mirror, and she flinched at the full extent of the damage that had been wrought. Her hair was not curls and now it lay in lank lifeless blocks on both sides of her suddenly pale face. It was ugly as sin—she had known it would be ugly as sin. Her face's chief charm had been a Madonna-like simplicity. Now that was gone and she was—well frightfully mediocre—not stagy; only ridiculous, like a Greenwich Villager who had left her spectacles at home.

As she climbed down from the chair she tried to smile—failed miserably. She saw two of the girls exchange glances; noticed Marjorie's mouth curved in attenuated mockery—and that Warren's eyes were suddenly very cold.

"You see,"—her words fell into an awkward pause—"I've done it."

"Yes, you've—done it," admitted Warren.

"Do you like it?"

There was a half-hearted "Sure" from two or three voices, another awkward pause, and then Marjorie turned swiftly and with serpentlike intensity to Warren.

"Would you mind running me down to the cleaners?" she asked. "I've simply got to get a dress there before supper. Roberta's driving right home and she can take the others."

Warren stared abstractedly at some infinite speck out the window. Then for an instant his eyes rested coldly on Bernice before they turned to Marjorie.

"Be glad to," he said slowly.

VI

BERNICE DID NOT FULLY REALIZE THE OUTRAGEOUS TRAP THAT HAD BEEN SET for her until she met her aunt's amazed glance just before dinner.

"Why Bernice!"

"I've bobbed it, Aunt Josephine."

"Why, child!"

"Do you like it?"

"Why Bernice!"

"I suppose I've shocked you."

"No, but what'll Mrs. Deyo think tomorrow night? Bernice, you should have waited until after the Deyo's dance—you should have waited if you wanted to do that."

"It was sudden, Aunt Josephine. Anyway, why does it matter to Mrs. Deyo particularly?"

"Why child," cried Mrs. Harvey, "in her paper on 'The Foibles of the Younger Generation' that she read at the last meeting of the Thursday Club she devoted fifteen minutes to bobbed hair. It's her pet abomination. And the dance is for you and Marjorie!"

"I'm sorry."

"Oh, Bernice, what'll your mother say? She'll think I let you do it."

"I'm sorry."

Dinner was an agony. She had made a hasty attempt with a curling-iron, and burned her finger and much hair. She could see that her aunt was both worried and grieved, and her uncle kept saying, "Well, I'll be darned!" over and over in a hurt and faintly hostile torte. And Marjorie sat very quietly, intrenched behind a faint smile, a faintly mocking smile.

Somehow she got through the evening. Three boy's called; Marjorie disappeared with one of them, and Bernice made a listless unsuccessful attempt to entertain the two others—sighed thankfully as she climbed the stairs to her room at half past ten. What a day!

When she had undressed for the night the door opened and Marjorie came in.

"Bernice," she said "I'm awfully sorry about the Deyo dance. I'll give you my word of honor I'd forgotten all about it."

"'Sall right," said Bernice shortly. Standing before the mirror she passed her comb slowly through her short hair.

"I'll take you down-town to-morrow," continued Marjorie, "and the hairdresser'll fix it so you'll look slick. I didn't imagine you'd go through with it. I'm really mighty sorry."

"Oh, 'sall right!"

"Still it's your last night, so I suppose it won't matter much."

Then Bernice winced as Marjorie tossed her own hair over her shoulders and began to twist it slowly into two long blond braids until in her cream-colored negligée she looked like a delicate painting of some Saxon princess. Fascinated, Bernice watched the braids grow. Heavy and luxurious they were moving under the supple fingers like restive snakes—and to Bernice remained this relic and the curling-iron and a to-morrow full of eyes. She could see G. Reece Stoddard, who liked her, assuming his Harvard manner and telling his dinner partner that Bernice shouldn't have been allowed to go to the movies so much; she could see Draycott Deyo exchanging glances with his mother and then being conscientiously charitable to her. But then perhaps by to-morrow Mrs. Deyo would have heard the news; would send round an icy little note requesting that she fail to appear—and behind her back they would all laugh and know that Marjorie had made a fool of her; that her chance at beauty had been sacrificed to the jealous whim of a selfish girl. She sat down suddenly before the mirror, biting the inside of her cheek.

"I like it," she said with an effort. "I think it'll be becoming."

Marjorie smiled.

"It looks all right. For heaven's sake, don't let it worry you!"

"I won't."

"Good night Bernice."

But as the door closed something snapped within Bernice. She sprang dynamically to her feet, clinching her hands, then swiftly and noiseless crossed over to her bed and from underneath it dragged out her suitcase. Into it she tossed toilet articles and a change of clothing, Then she turned to her trunk and quickly dumped in two drawerfulls of lingerie and stammer dresses. She moved quietly, but deadly efficiency, and in three-quarters of an hour her trunk was locked and strapped and she was fully dressed in a becoming new travelling suit that Marjorie had helped her pick out.

Sitting down at her desk she wrote a short note to Mrs. Harvey, in which she briefly outlined her reasons for going. She sealed it, addressed it, and laid it on her pillow. She glanced at her watch. The train left at one, and she knew that if she walked down to the Marborough Hotel two blocks away she could easily get a taxicab.

Suddenly she drew in her breath sharply and an expression flashed into her eyes that a practiced character reader might have connected vaguely with the set look she had worn in the barber's chair—somehow a development of it. It was quite a new look for Bernice—and it carried consequences.

She went stealthily to the bureau, picked up an article that lay there, and turning out all the lights stood quietly until her eyes became accustomed to the darkness. Softly she pushed open the door to Marjorie's room. She heard the quiet, even breathing of an untroubled conscience asleep.

She was by the bedside now, very deliberate and calm. She acted swiftly. Bending over she found one of the braids of Marjorie's hair, followed it up with her hand to the point nearest the head, and then holding it a little slack so that the sleeper would feel no pull, she reached down with the shears and severed it. With the pigtail in her hand she held her breath. Marjorie had muttered something in her sleep. Bernice deftly amputated the other braid, paused for an instant, and then flitted swiftly and silently back to her own room.

Down-stairs she opened the big front door, closed it carefully behind her, and feeling oddly happy and exuberant stepped off the porch into the moonlight, swinging her heavy grip like a shopping-bag. After a minute's brisk walk she discovered that her left hand still held the two blond braids. She laughed unexpectedly—had to shut her mouth hard to keep from emitting an absolute peal. She was passing Warren's house now, and on the impulse she set down her baggage, and swinging the braids like piece of rope flung them at the wooden porch, where they landed with a slight thud. She laughed again, no longer restraining herself.

"Huh," she giggled wildly. "Scalp the selfish thing!"

Then picking up her staircase she set off at a half-run down the moonlit street.

BENEDICTION

I

The Baltimore Station was hot and crowded, so Lois was forced to stand by the telegraph desk for interminable, sticky seconds while a clerk with big front teeth counted and recounted a large lady's day message, to determine whether it contained the innocuous forty-nine words or the fatal fifty-one.

Lois, waiting, decided she wasn't quite sure of the address, so she took the letter out of her bag and ran over it again.

"Darling," it began—"I understand and I'm happier than life ever meant me to be. If I could give you the things you've always been in tune with—but I can't Lois; we can't marry and we can't lose each other and let all this glorious love end in nothing.

"Until your letter came, dear, I'd been sitting here in the half dark and thinking where I could go and ever forget you; abroad, perhaps, to drift through Italy or Spain and dream away the pain of having lost you where the crumbling ruins of older, mellower civilizations would mirror only the desolation of my heart—and then your letter came.

"Sweetest, bravest girl, if you'll wire me I'll meet you in Wilmington—till then I'll be here just waiting and hoping for every long dream of you to come true.

"Howard."

She had read the letter so many times that she knew it word by word, yet it still startled her. In it she found many faint reflections of the man who wrote it—the mingled sweetness and sadness in his dark eyes, the furtive, restless excitement she felt sometimes when he talked to her, his dreamy sensuousness that lulled her mind to sleep. Lois was nineteen and very romantic and curious and courageous.

The large lady and the clerk having compromised on fifty words, Lois took a blank and wrote her telegram. And there were no overtones to the finality of her decision.

It's just destiny—she thought—it's just the way things work out in this damn world. If cowardice is all that's been holding me back there won't be any more holding back. So we'll just let things take their course and never be sorry.

The clerk scanned her telegram:

"Arrived Baltimore today spend day with my brother meet me Wilmington three P.M. Wednesday Love

"Lois."

"Fifty-four cents," said the clerk admiringly.

And never be sorry—thought Lois—and never be sorry——

II

Trees filtering light onto dapple grass. Trees like tall, languid ladies with feather fans coquetting airily with the ugly roof of the monastery. Trees like butlers, bending courteously over placid walks and paths. Trees, trees over the hills on either side and scattering out in clumps and lines and woods all through eastern Maryland, delicate lace on the hems of many yellow fields, dark opaque backgrounds for flowered bushes or wild climbing garden.

Some of the trees were very gay and young, but the monastery trees were older than the monastery which, by true monastic standards, wasn't very old at all. And, as a matter of fact, it wasn't technically called a monastery, but only a seminary; nevertheless it shall be a monastery here despite its Victorian architecture or its Edward VII additions, or even its Woodrow Wilsonian, patented, last-a-century roofing.

Out behind was the farm where half a dozen lay brothers were sweating lustily as they moved with deadly efficiency around the vegetable-gardens. To the left, behind a row of elms, was an informal baseball diamond where three novices were being batted out by a fourth, amid great chasings and puffings and blowings. And in front as a great mellow bell boomed the half-hour a swarm of black, human leaves were blown over the checker-board of paths under the courteous trees.

Some of these black leaves were very old with cheeks furrowed like the first ripples of a splashed pool. Then there was a scattering of middle-aged leaves whose forms when viewed in profile in their revealing gowns were beginning to be faintly unsymmetrical. These carried thick volumes of Thomas Aquinas and Henry James and Cardinal Mercier and Immanuel Kant and many bulging note-books filled with lecture data.

But most numerous were the young leaves; blond boys of nineteen with very stern, conscientious expressions; men in the late twenties with a keen self-assurance from having taught out in the world for five years—several hundreds of them, from city and town and country in Maryland and Pennsylvania and Virginia and West Virginia and Delaware.

There were many Americans and some Irish and some tough Irish and a few French, and several Italians and Poles, and they walked informally arm in arm with each other in twos and threes or in long rows, almost universally distinguished by the straight mouth and the considerable chin—for this was the Society of Jesus, founded in Spain five hundred years before by a tough-minded soldier who trained men to hold a breach or a salon, preach a sermon or write a treaty, and do it and not argue . . .

Lois got out of a bus into the sunshine down by the outer gate. She was nineteen with yellow hair and eyes that people were tactful enough not to call green. When men of talent saw her in a street-car they often furtively produced little stub-pencils and backs of envelopes and tried to sum up that profile or the thing that the eyebrows did to her eyes. Later they looked at their results and usually tore them up with wondering sighs.

Though Lois was very jauntily attired in an expensively appropriate travelling affair, she did not linger to pat out the dust which covered her clothes, but started up the central walk with curious glances at either side. Her face was very eager and expectant, yet she hadn't at all that glorified expression that girls wear when they arrive for a Senior Prom at Princeton or New Haven; still, as there were no senior proms here, perhaps it didn't matter.

She was wondering what he would look like, whether she'd possibly know him from his picture. In the picture, which hung over her mother's bureau at home, he seemed very young and hollow-cheeked and rather pitiful, with only a well-developed mouth and all ill-fitting probationer's gown to show that he had already made a momentous decision about his life. Of course he had been only nineteen then and now he was thirty-six— didn't look like that at all; in recent snap-shots he was much broader and his hair had grown a little thin—but the impression of her brother she had always retained was that of the big picture. And so she had always been a little sorry for him. What a life for a man! Seventeen years of preparation and he wasn't even a priest yet—wouldn't be for another year.

Lois had an idea that this was all going to be rather solemn if she let it be. But she was going to give her very best imitation of undiluted sunshine, the imitation she could give even when her head was splitting or when her mother had a nervous breakdown or when she was particularly romantic and curious and courageous. This brother of hers undoubtedly needed cheering up, and he was going to be cheered up, whether he liked it or not.

As she drew near the great, homely front door she saw a man break suddenly away from a group and, pulling up the skirts of his gown, run toward her. He was smiling, she noticed, and he looked very big and— and reliable. She stopped and waited, knew that her heart was beating unusually fast.

"Lois!" he cried, and in a second she was in his arms. She was suddenly trembling.

"Lois!" he cried again, "why, this is wonderful! I can't tell you, Lois, how much I've looked forward to this. Why, Lois, you're beautiful!"

Lois gasped.

His voice, though restrained, was vibrant with energy and that odd sort of enveloping personality she had thought that she only of the family possessed.

"I'm mighty glad, too—Kieth."

She flushed, but not unhappily, at this first use of his name.

"Lois—Lois—Lois," he repeated in wonder. "Child, we'll go in here a minute, because I want you to meet the rector, and then we'll walk around. I have a thousand things to talk to you about."

His voice became graver. "How's mother?"

She looked at him for a moment and then said something that she had not intended to say at all, the very sort of thing she had resolved to avoid.

"Oh, Kieth—she's—she's getting worse all the time, every way."

He nodded slowly as if he understood.

"Nervous, well—you can tell me about that later. Now———"

She was in a small study with a large desk, saying something to a little, jovial, white-haired priest who retained her hand for some seconds.

"So this is Lois!"

He said it as if he had heard of her for years.

He entreated her to sit down.

Two other priests arrived enthusiastically and shook hands with her and addressed her as "Kieth's little sister," which she found she didn't mind a bit.

How assured they seemed; she had expected a certain shyness, reserve at least. There were several jokes unintelligible to her, which seemed to delight every one, and the little Father Rector referred to the trio of them as "dim old monks," which she appreciated, because of course they weren't monks at all. She had a lightning impression that they were especially fond of Kieth—the Father Rector had called him "Kieth" and one of the others had kept a hand on his shoulder all through the conversation. Then she was shaking hands again and promising to come back a little later for some ice-cream, and smiling and smiling and being rather absurdly happy . . . she told herself that it was because Kieth was so delighted in showing her off.

Then she and Kieth were strolling along a path, arm in arm, and he was informing her what an absolute jewel the Father Rector was.

"Lois," he broke off suddenly, "I want to tell you before we go any farther how much it means to me to have you come up here. I think it was—mighty sweet of you. I know what a gay time you've been having."

Lois gasped. She was not prepared for this. At first when she had conceived the plan of taking the hot journey down to Baltimore staying the night with a friend and then coming out to see her brother, she had felt rather consciously virtuous, hoped he wouldn't be priggish or resentful about her not having come before—but walking here with him under the trees seemed such a little thing, and surprisingly a happy thing.

"Why, Kieth," she said quickly, "you know I couldn't have waited a day longer. I saw you when I was five, but of course I didn't remember, and how could I have gone on without practically ever having seen my only brother?"

"It was mighty sweet of you, Lois," he repeated.

Lois blushed—he did have personality.

"I want you to tell me all about yourself," he said after a pause. "Of course I have a general idea what you and mother did in Europe those fourteen years, and then we were all so worried, Lois, when you had pneumonia and couldn't come down with mother—let's see that was two years ago—and then, well, I've seen your name in the papers, but it's all been so unsatisfactory. I haven't known you, Lois."

She found herself analyzing his personality as she analyzed the personality of every man she met. She wondered if the effect of—of intimacy that he gave was bred by his constant repetition of her name. He said it as if he loved the word, as if it had an inherent meaning to him.

"Then you were at school," he continued.

"Yes, at Farmington. Mother wanted me to go to a convent—but I didn't want to."

She cast a side glance at him to see if he would resent this.

But he only nodded slowly.

"Had enough convents abroad, eh?"

"Yes—and Kieth, convents are different there anyway. Here even in the nicest ones there are so many common girls."

He nodded again.

"Yes," he agreed, "I suppose there are, and I know how you feel about it. It grated on me here, at first, Lois, though I wouldn't say that to any one but you; we're rather sensitive, you and I, to things like this."

"You mean the men here?"

"Yes, some of them of course were fine, the sort of men I'd always been thrown with, but there were others; a man named Regan, for instance—I hated the fellow, and now he's about the best friend I have. A wonderful character, Lois; you'll meet him later. Sort of man you'd like to have with you in a fight."

Lois was thinking that Kieth was the sort of man she'd like to have with her in a fight.

"How did you—how did you first happen to do it?" she asked, rather shyly, "to come here, I mean. Of course mother told me the story about the Pullman car."

"Oh, that——" He looked rather annoyed.

"Tell me that. I'd like to hear you tell it."

"Oh, it's nothing except what you probably know. It was evening and I'd been riding all day and thinking about—about a hundred things, Lois, and then suddenly I had a sense that some one was sitting across from me, felt that he'd been there for some time, and had a vague idea that he was another traveller. All at once he leaned over toward me and I heard a voice say: 'I want you to be a priest, that's what I want.' Well I jumped up and cried out, 'Oh, my God, not that!'—made an idiot of myself before about twenty people; you see there wasn't any one sitting there at all. A week after that I went to the Jesuit College in Philadelphia and crawled up the last flight of stairs to the rector's office on my hands and knees."

There was another silence and Lois saw that her brother's eyes wore a far-away look, that he was staring unseeingly out over the sunny fields. She was stirred by the modulations of his voice and the sudden silence that seemed to flow about him when he finished speaking.

She noticed now that his eyes were of the same fibre as hers, with the green left out, and that his mouth was much gentler, really, than in the picture—or was it that the face had grown up to it lately? He was getting a little bald just on top of his head. She wondered if that was from wearing a hat so much. It seemed awful for a man to grow bald and no one to care about it.

"Were you—pious when you were young, Kieth?" she asked. "You know what I mean. Were you religious? If you don't mind these personal questions."

"Yes," he said with his eyes still far away—and she felt that his intense abstraction was as much a part of his personality as his attention. "Yes, I suppose I was, when I was—sober."

Lois thrilled slightly.

"Did you drink?"

He nodded.

"I was on the way to making a bad hash of things." He smiled and, turning his gray eyes on her, changed the subject.

"Child, tell me about mother. I know it's been awfully hard for you there, lately. I know you've had to sacrifice a lot and put up with a great deal and I want you to know how fine of you I think it is. I feel, Lois, that you're sort of taking the place of both of us there."

Lois thought quickly how little she had sacrificed; how lately she had constantly avoided her nervous, half-invalid mother.

"Youth shouldn't be sacrificed to age, Kieth," she said steadily.

"I know," he sighed, "and you oughtn't to have the weight on your shoulders, child. I wish I were there to help you."

She saw how quickly he had turned her remark and instantly she knew what this quality was that he gave off. He was sweet. Her thoughts went of on a side-track and then she broke the silence with an odd remark.

"Sweetness is hard," she said suddenly.

"What?"

"Nothing," she denied in confusion. "I didn't mean to speak aloud. I was thinking of something—of a conversation with a man named Freddy Kebble."

"Maury Kebble's brother?"

"Yes," she said rather surprised to think of him having known Maury Kebble. Still there was nothing strange about it. "Well, he and I were talking about sweetness a few weeks ago. Oh, I don't know—I said that a man named Howard—that a man I knew was sweet, and he didn't agree with me, and we began talking about what sweetness in a man was: He kept telling me I meant a sort of soppy softness, but I knew I didn't—yet

I didn't know exactly how to put it. I see now. I meant just the opposite. I suppose real sweetness is a sort of hardness—and strength."

Kieth nodded.

"I see what you mean. I've known old priests who had it."

"I'm talking about young men," she said rather defiantly.

They had reached the now deserted baseball diamond and, pointing her to a wooden bench, he sprawled full length on the grass.

"Are these young men happy here, Kieth?"

"Don't they look happy, Lois?"

"I suppose so, but those young ones, those two we just passed—have they—are they——?

"Are they signed up?" he laughed. "No, but they will be next month."

"Permanently?"

"Yes—unless they break down mentally or physically. Of course in a discipline like ours a lot drop out."

"But those boys. Are they giving up fine chances outside—like you did?"

He nodded.

"Some of them."

"But Kieth, they don't know what they're doing. They haven't had any experience of what they're missing."

"No, I suppose not."

"It doesn't seem fair. Life has just sort of scared them at first. Do they all come in so young?"

"No, some of them have knocked around, led pretty wild lives—Regan, for instance."

"I should think that sort would be better," she said meditatively, "men that had seen life."

"No," said Kieth earnestly, "I'm not sure that knocking about gives a man the sort of experience he can communicate to others. Some of the broadest men I've known have been absolutely rigid about themselves. And reformed libertines are a notoriously intolerant class. Don't you thank so, Lois?"

She nodded, still meditative, and he continued:

"It seems to me that when one weak reason goes to another, it isn't help they want; it's a sort of companionship in guilt, Lois. After you were born, when mother began to get nervous she used to go and weep with a certain

Mrs. Comstock. Lord, it used to make me shiver. She said it comforted her, poor old mother. No, I don't think that to help others you've got to show yourself at all. Real help comes from a stronger person whom you respect. And their sympathy is all the bigger because it's impersonal."

"But people want human sympathy," objected Lois. "They want to feel the other person's been tempted."

"Lois, in their hearts they want to feel that the other person's been weak. That's what they mean by human.

"Here in this old monkery, Lois," he continued with a smile, "they try to get all that self-pity and pride in our own wills out of us right at the first. They put us to scrubbing floors—and other things. It's like that idea of saving your life by losing it. You see we sort of feel that the less human a man is, in your sense of human, the better servant he can be to humanity. We carry it out to the end, too. When one of us dies his family can't even have him then. He's buried here under plain wooden cross with a thousand others."

His tone changed suddenly and he looked at her with a great brightness in his gray eyes.

"But way back in a man's heart there are some things he can't get rid of—an one of them is that I'm awfully in love with my little sister."

With a sudden impulse she knelt beside him in the grass and, Leaning over, kissed his forehead.

"You're hard, Kieth," she said, "and I love you for it—and you're sweet."

III

Back in the reception-room Lois met a half-dozen more of Kieth's particular friends; there was a young man named Jarvis, rather pale and delicate-looking, who, she knew, must be a grandson of old Mrs. Jarvis at home, and she mentally compared this ascetic with a brace of his riotous uncles.

And there was Regan with a scarred face and piercing intent eyes that followed her about the room and often rested on Kieth with something very like worship. She knew then what Kieth had meant about "a good man to have with you in a fight."

He's the missionary type—she thought vaguely—China or something.

"I want Kieth's sister to show us what the shimmy is," demanded one young man with a broad grin.

Lois laughed.

"I'm afraid the Father Rector would send me shimmying out the gate. Besides, I'm not an expert."

"I'm sure it wouldn't be best for Jimmy's soul anyway," said Kieth solemnly. "He's inclined to brood about things like shimmys. They were just starting to do the—maxixe, wasn't it, Jimmy?—when he became a monk, and it haunted him his whole first year. You'd see him when he was peeling potatoes, putting his arm around the bucket and making irreligious motions with his feet."

There was a general laugh in which Lois joined.

"An old lady who comes here to Mass sent Kieth this ice-cream," whispered Jarvis under cover of the laugh, "because she'd heard you were coming. It's pretty good, isn't it?"

There were tears trembling in Lois' eyes.

IV

Then half an hour later over in the chapel things suddenly went all wrong. It was several years since Lois had been at Benediction and at first she was thrilled by the gleaming monstrance with its central spot of white, the air rich and heavy with incense, and the sun shining through the stained-glass window of St. Francis Xavier overhead and falling in warm red tracery on the cassock of the man in front of her, but at the first notes of the "O salutaris hostia" a heavy weight seemed to descend upon her soul. Kieth was on her right and young Jarvis on her left, and she stole uneasy glance at both of them.

What's the matter with me? she thought impatiently.

She looked again. Was there a certain coldness in both their profiles, that she had not noticed before—a pallor about the mouth and a curious set expression in their eyes? She shivered slightly: they were like dead men.

She felt her soul recede suddenly from Kieth's. This was her brother—this, this unnatural person. She caught herself in the act of a little laugh.

"What is the matter with me?"

She passed her hand over her eyes and the weight increased. The incense sickened her and a stray, ragged note from one of the tenors in the choir grated on her ear like the shriek of a slate-pencil. She fidgeted, and raising her hand to her hair touched her forehead, found moisture on it.

"It's hot in here, hot as the deuce."

Again she repressed a faint laugh and, then in an instant the weight on her heart suddenly diffused into cold fear. . . . It was that candle on the altar. It was all wrong—wrong. Why didn't somebody see it? There was something in it. There was something coming out of it, taking form and shape above it.

She tried to fight down her rising panic, told herself it was the wick. If the wick wasn't straight, candles did something—but they didn't do this! With incalculable rapidity a force was gathering within her, a tremendous, assimilative force, drawing from every sense, every corner of her brain, and as it surged up inside her she felt an enormous terrified repulsion. She drew her arms in close to her side away from Kieth and Jarvis.

Something in that candle . . . she was leaning forward—in another moment she felt she would go forward toward it—didn't any one see it? . . . anyone?

"Ugh!"

She felt a space beside her and something told her that Jarvis had gasped and sat down very suddenly . . . then she was kneeling and as the flaming monstrance slowly left the altar in the hands of the priest, she heard a great rushing noise in her ears—the crash of the bells was like hammer-blows . . . and then in a moment that seemed eternal a great torrent rolled over her heart—there was a shouting there and a lashing as of waves . . .

. . . She was calling, felt herself calling for Kieth, her lips mouthing the words that would not come:

"Kieth! Oh, my God! Kieth!"

Suddenly she became aware of a new presence, something external, in front of her, consummated and expressed in warm red tracery. Then she knew. It was the window of St. Francis Xavier. Her mind gripped at it, clung to it finally, and she felt herself calling again endlessly, impotently—Kieth—Kieth!

Then out of a great stillness came a voice:

"Blessed be God."

With a gradual rumble sounded the response rolling heavily through the chapel:

"Blessed be God."

The words sang instantly in her heart; the incense lay mystically and sweetly peaceful upon the air, and the candle on the altar went out.

"Blessed be His Holy Name."

"Blessed be His Holy Name."

Everything blurred into a swinging mist. With a sound half-gasp, half-cry she rocked on her feet and reeled backward into Kieth's suddenly outstretched arms.

V

"Lie still, child."

She closed her eyes again. She was on the grass outside, pillowed on Kieth's arm, and Regan was dabbing her head with a cold towel.

"I'm all right," she said quietly.

"I know, but just lie still a minute longer. It was too hot in there. Jarvis felt it, too."

She laughed as Regan again touched her gingerly with the towel.

"I'm all right," she repeated.

But though a warm peace was falling her mind and heart she felt oddly broken and chastened, as if some one had held her stripped soul up and laughed.

VI

HALF AN HOUR LATER SHE WALKED LEANING ON KIETH'S ARM DOWN THE LONG central path toward the gate.

"It's been such a short afternoon," he sighed, "and I'm so sorry you were sick, Lois."

"Kieth, I'm feeling fine now, really; I wish you wouldn't worry."

"Poor old child. I didn't realize that Benediction'd be a long service for you after your hot trip out here and all."

She laughed cheerfully.

"I guess the truth is I'm not much used to Benediction. Mass is the limit of my religious exertions."

She paused and then continued quickly:

"I don't want to shock you, Kieth, but I can't tell you how—how inconvenient being a Catholic is. It really doesn't seem to apply any more. As far as morals go, some of the wildest boys I know are Catholics. And the brightest boys—I mean the ones who think and read a lot, don't seem to believe in much of anything any more."

"Tell me about it. The bus won't be here for another half-hour."

They sat down on a bench by the path.

"For instance, Gerald Carter, he's published a novel. He absolutely roars when people mention immortality. And then Howa—well, another man I've known well, lately, who was Phi Beta Kappa at Harvard says that no intelligent person can believe in Supernatural Christianity. He says Christ was a great socialist, though. Am I shocking you?"

She broke off suddenly.

Kieth smiled.

"You can't shock a monk. He's a professional shock-absorber."

"Well," she continued, "that's about all. It seems so—so narrow. Church schools, for instance. There's more freedom about things that Catholic people can't see—like birth control."

Kieth winced, almost imperceptibly, but Lois saw it.

"Oh," she said quickly, "everybody talks about everything now."

"It's probably better that way."

"Oh, yes, much better. Well, that's all, Kieth. I just wanted to tell you why I'm a little—luke-warm, at present."

"I'm not shocked, Lois. I understand better than you think. We all go through those times. But I know it'll come out all right, child. There's that gift of faith that we have, you and I, that'll carry us past the bad spots."

He rose as he spoke and they started again down the path.

"I want you to pray for me sometimes, Lois. I think your prayers would be about what I need. Because we've come very close in these few hours, I think."

Her eyes were suddenly shining.

"Oh we have, we have!" she cried. "I feel closer to you now than to any one in the world."

He stopped suddenly and indicated the side of the path.

"We might—just a minute——"

It was a pietà, a life-size statue of the Blessed Virgin set within a semicircle of rocks.

Feeling a little self-conscious she dropped on her knees beside him and made an unsuccessful attempt at prayer.

She was only half through when he rose. He took her arm again.

"I wanted to thank Her for letting as have this day together," he said simply.

Lois felt a sudden lump in her throat and she wanted to say something that would tell him how much it had meant to her, too. But she found no words.

"I'll always remember this," he continued, his voice trembling a little——"this summer day with you. It's been just what I expected. You're just what I expected, Lois."

"I'm awfully glad, Keith."

"You see, when you were little they kept sending me snap-shots of you, first as a baby and then as a child in socks playing on the beach with a pail and shovel, and then suddenly as a wistful little girl with wondering, pure eyes—and I used to build dreams about you. A man has to have something living to cling to. I think, Lois, it was your little white soul I tried to keep near me—even when life was at its loudest and every intellectual idea of God seemed the sheerest mockery, and desire and love and a million things came up to me and said: 'Look here at me! See, I'm Life. You're turning your back on it!' All the way through that shadow, Lois, I could always see your baby soul flitting on ahead of me, very frail and clear and wonderful."

Lois was crying softly. They had reached the gate and she rested her elbow on it and dabbed furiously at her eyes.

"And then later, child, when you were sick I knelt all one night and asked God to spare you for me—for I knew then that I wanted more; He had taught me to want more. I wanted to know you moved and breathed in the same world with me. I saw you growing up, that white innocence of yours changing to a flame and burning to give light to other weaker souls. And then I wanted some day to take your children on my knee and hear them call the crabbed old monk Uncle Kieth."

He seemed to be laughing now as he talked.

"Oh, Lois, Lois, I was asking God for more then. I wanted the letters you'd write me and the place I'd have at your table. I wanted an awful lot, Lois, dear."

"You've got me, Kieth," she sobbed "you know it, say you know it. Oh, I'm acting like a baby but I didn't think you'd be this way, and I—oh, Kieth—Kieth——"

He took her hand and patted it softly.

"Here's the bus. You'll come again won't you?"

She put her hands on his cheeks, add drawing his head down, pressed her tear-wet face against his.

"Oh, Kieth, brother, some day I'll tell you something."

He helped her in, saw her take down her handkerchief and smile bravely at him, as the driver kicked his whip and the bus rolled off. Then a thick cloud of dust rose around it and she was gone.

For a few minutes he stood there on the road his hand on the gate-post, his lips half parted in a smile.

"Lois," he said aloud in a sort of wonder, "Lois, Lois."

Later, some probationers passing noticed him kneeling before the pietà, and coming back after a time found him still there. And he was there until twilight came down and the courteous trees grew garrulous overhead and the crickets took up their burden of song in the dusky grass.

VII

THE FIRST CLERK IN THE TELEGRAPH BOOTH IN THE BALTIMORE STATION
whistled through his buck teeth at the second clerk:

"S'matter?"

"See that girl—no, the pretty one with the big black dots on her veil.
Too late—she's gone. You missed somep'n."

"What about her?"

"Nothing. 'Cept she's damn good-looking. Came in here yesterday and
sent a wire to some guy to meet her somewhere. Then a minute ago she
came in with a telegram all written out and was standin' there goin' to give
it to me when she changed her mind or somep'n and all of a sudden tore
it up."

"Hm."

The first clerk came around tile counter and picking up the two pieces
of paper from the floor put them together idly. The second clerk read them
over his shoulder and subconsciously counted the words as he read. There
were just thirteen.

"This is in the way of a permanent goodbye. I should suggest Italy.

"Lois."

"Tore it up, eh?" said the second clerk.

DALYRIMPLE GOES WRONG

I

In the millennium an educational genius will write a book to be given to every young man on the date of his disillusion. This work will have the flavor of Montaigne's essays and Samuel Butler's note-books—and a little of Tolstoi and Marcus Aurelius. It will be neither cheerful nor pleasant but will contain numerous passages of striking humor. Since first-class minds never believe anything very strongly until they've experienced it, its value will be purely relative . . . all people over thirty will refer to it as "depressing."

This prelude belongs to the story of a young man who lived, as you and I do, before the book.

II

THE GENERATION WHICH NUMBERED BRYAN DALYRIMPLE DRIFTED OUT OF ADolescence to a mighty fan-fare of trumpets. Bryan played the star in an affair which included a Lewis gun and a nine-day romp behind the re-treating German lines, so luck triumphant or sentiment rampant awarded him a row of medals and on his arrival in the States he was told that he was second in importance only to General Pershing and Sergeant York. This was a lot of fun. The governor of his State, a stray congressman, and a citizens' committee gave him enormous smiles and "By God, Sirs" on the dock at Hoboken; there were newspaper reporters and photographers who said "would you mind" and "if you could just"; and back in his home town there were old ladies, the rims of whose eyes grew red as they talked to him, and girls who hadn't remembered him so well since his father's business went blah! in nineteen-twelve.

But when the shouting died he realized that for a month he had been the house guest of the mayor, that he had only fourteen dollars in the world and that "the name that will live forever in the annals and legends of this State" was already living there very quietly and obscurely.

One morning he lay late in bed and just outside his door he heard the up-stairs maid talking to the cook. The up-stairs maid said that Mrs. Hawkins, the mayor's wife, had been trying for a week to hint Dalyrimple out of the house. He left at eleven o'clock in intolerable confusion, asking that his trunk be sent to Mrs. Beebe's boarding-house.

Dalyrimple was twenty-three and he had never worked. His father had given him two years at the State University and passed away about the time of his son's nine-day romp, leaving behind him some mid-Victorian furniture and a thin packet of folded paper that turned out to be grocery bills. Young Dalyrimple had very keen gray eyes, a mind that delighted the army psychological examiners, a trick of having read it—whatever it was—some time before, and a cool hand in a hot situation. But these things did not save him a final, unresigned sigh when he realized that he had to go to work—right away.

It was early afternoon when he walked into the office of Theron G. Macy, who owned the largest wholesale grocery house in town. Plump, prosperous, wearing a pleasant but quite unhumorous smile, Theron G. Macy greeted him warmly.

"Well—how do, Bryan? What's on your mind?"

To Dalyrimple, straining with his admission, his own words, when they came, sounded like an Arab beggar's whine for alms.

"Why—this question of a job." ("This question of a job" seemed somehow more clothed than just "a job.")

"A job?" An almost imperceptible breeze blew across Mr. Macy's expression.

"You see, Mr. Macy," continued Dalyrimple, "I feel I'm wasting time. I want to get started at something. I had several chances about a month ago but they all seem to have—gone——"

"Let's see," interrupted Mr. Macy. "What were they?"

"Well, just at the first the governor said something about a vacancy on his staff. I was sort of counting on that for a while, but I hear he's given it to Allen Gregg, you know, son of G. P. Gregg. He sort of forgot what he said to me—just talking, I guess."

"You ought to push those things."

"Then there was that engineering expedition, but they decided they'd have to have a man who knew hydraulics, so they couldn't use me unless I paid my own way."

"You had just a year at the university?"

"Two. But I didn't take any science or mathematics. Well, the day the battalion paraded, Mr. Peter Jordan said something about a vacancy in his store. I went around there to-day and I found he meant a sort of floor-walker—and then you said something one day"—he paused and waited for the older man to take him up, but noting only a minute wince continued—"about a position, so I thought I'd come and see you."

"There was a position," confessed Mr. Macy reluctantly, "but since then we've filled it." He cleared his throat again. "You've waited quite a while."

"Yes, I suppose I did. Everybody told me there was no hurry—and I'd had these various offers."

Mr. Macy delivered a paragraph on present-day opportunities which Dalyrimple's mind completely skipped.

"Have you had any business experience?"

"I worked on a ranch two summers as a rider."

"Oh, well," Mr. Macy disparaged this neatly, and then continued: "What do you think you're worth?"

"I don't know."

"Well, Bryan, I tell you, I'm willing to strain a point and give you a chance."

Dalyrimple nodded.

"Your salary won't be much. You'll start by learning the stock. Then you'll come in the office for a while. Then you'll go on the road. When could you begin?"

"How about to-morrow?"

"All right. Report to Mr. Hanson in the stock-room. He'll start you off."

He continued to regard Dalyrimple steadily until the latter, realizing that the interview was over, rose awkwardly.

"Well, Mr. Macy, I'm certainly much obliged."

"That's all right. Glad to help you, Bryan."

After an irresolute moment, Dalyrimple found himself in the hall. His forehead was covered with perspiration, and the room had not been hot.

"Why the devil did I thank the son of a gun?" he muttered.

III

Next morning Mr. Hanson informed him coldly of the necessity of punching the time-clock at seven every morning, and delivered him for instruction into the hands of a fellow worker, one Charley Moore.

Charley was twenty-six, with that faint musk of weakness hanging about him that is often mistaken for the scent of evil. It took no psychological examiner to decide that he had drifted into indulgence and laziness as casually as he had drifted into life, and was to drift out. He was pale and his clothes stank of smoke; he enjoyed burlesque shows, billiards, and Robert Service, and was always looking back upon his last intrigue or forward to his next one. In his youth his taste had run to loud ties, but now it seemed to have faded, like his vitality, and was expressed in pale-lilac four-in-hands and indeterminate gray collars. Charley was listlessly struggling that losing struggle against mental, moral, and physical anæmia that takes place ceaselessly on the lower fringe of the middle classes.

The first morning he stretched himself on a row of cereal cartons and carefully went over the limitations of the Theron G. Macy Company.

"It's a piker organization. My Gosh! Lookit what they give me. I'm quittin' in a coupla months. Hell! Me stay with this bunch!"

The Charley Moores are always going to change jobs next month. They do, once or twice in their careers, after which they sit around comparing their last job with the present one, to the infinite disparagement of the latter.

"What do you get?" asked Dalyrimple curiously.

"Me? I get sixty." This rather defiantly.

"Did you start at sixty?"

"Me? No, I started at thirty-five. He told me he'd put me on the road after I learned the stock. That's what he tells 'em all."

"How long've you been here?" asked Dalyrimple with a sinking sensation.

"Me? Four years. My last year, too, you bet your boots."

Dalyrimple rather resented the presence of the store detective as he resented the time-clock, and he came into contact with him almost immediately through the rule against smoking. This rule was a thorn in his side. He was accustomed to his three or four cigarettes in a morning, and after three days without it he followed Charley Moore by a circuitous route up a flight of back stairs to a little balcony where they indulged in peace. But this was not for long. One day in his second week the detective met him in a nook of the stairs, on his descent, and told him sternly that next time he'd be reported to Mr. Macy. Dalyrimple felt like an errant schoolboy.

Unpleasant facts came to his knowledge. There were "cave-dwellers" in the basement who had worked there for ten or fifteen years at sixty dollars a month, rolling barrels and carrying boxes through damp, cement-walled corridors, lost in that echoing half-darkness between seven and five-thirty and, like himself, compelled several times a month to work until nine at night.

At the end of a month he stood in line and received forty dollars. He pawned a cigarette-case and a pair of field-glasses and managed to live— to eat, sleep, and smoke. It was, however, a narrow scrape; as the ways and means of economy were a closed book to him and the second month brought no increase, he voiced his alarm.

"If you've got a drag with old Macy, maybe he'll raise you," was Charley's disheartening reply. "But he didn't raise me till I'd been here nearly two years."

"I've got to live," said Dalyrimple simply. "I could get more pay as a laborer on the railroad but, Golly, I want to feel I'm where there's a chance to get ahead."

Charles shook his head sceptically and Mr. Macy's answer next day was equally unsatisfactory.

Dalyrimple had gone to the office just before closing time.

"Mr. Macy, I'd like to speak to you."

"Why—yes." The unhumorous smile appeared. The voice was faintly resentful.

"I want to speak to you in regard to more salary."

Mr. Macy nodded.

"Well," he said doubtfully, "I don't know exactly what you're doing. I'll speak to Mr. Hanson."

He knew exactly what Dalyrimple was doing, and Dalyrimple knew he knew.

"I'm in the stock-room—and, sir, while I'm here I'd like to ask you how much longer I'll have to stay there."

"Why—I'm not sure exactly. Of course it takes some time to learn the stock."

"You told me two months when I started."

"Yes. Well, I'll speak to Mr. Hanson."

Dalyrimple paused irresolute.

"Thank you, sir."

Two days later he again appeared in the office with the result of a count that had been asked for by Mr. Hesse, the bookkeeper. Mr. Hesse was engaged and Dalyrimple, waiting, began idly fingering in a ledger on the stenographer's desk.

Half unconsciously he turned a page—he caught sight of his name —it was a salary list:

Dalyrimple

Demming

Donahoe

Everett

His eyes stopped—

Everett.........................$60

So Tom Everett, Macy's weak-chinned nephew, had started at sixty —and in three weeks he had been out of the packing-room and into the office.

So that was it! He was to sit and see man after man pushed over him: sons, cousins, sons of friends, irrespective of their capabilities, while he was cast for a pawn, with "going on the road" dangled before his eyes—put off with the stock remark: "I'll see; I'll look into it." At forty, perhaps, he would be a bookkeeper like old Hesse, tired, listless Hesse with a dull routine for his stint and a dull background of boarding-house conversation.

This was a moment when a genii should have pressed into his hand the book for disillusioned young men. But the book has not been written.

A great protest swelling into revolt surged up in him. Ideas half forgotten, chaoticly perceived and assimilated, filled his mind. Get on— that was the rule of life—and that was all. How he did it, didn't matter— but to be Hesse or Charley Moore.

"I won't!" he cried aloud.

The bookkeeper and the stenographers looked up in surprise.

"What?"

For a second Dalyrimple stared—then walked up to the desk.

"Here's that data," he said brusquely. "I can't wait any longer."

Mr. Hesse's face expressed surprise.

It didn't matter what he did—just so he got out of this rut. In a dream he stepped from the elevator into the stock-room, and walking to an unused aisle, sat down on a box, covering his face with his hands.

His brain was whirring with the frightful jar of discovering a platitude for himself.

"I've got to get out of this," he said aloud and then repeated, "I've got to get out"—and he didn't mean only out of Macy's wholesale house.

When he left at five-thirty it was pouring rain, but he struck off in the opposite direction from his boarding-house, feeling, in the first cool moisture that oozed soggily through his old suit, an odd exultation and freshness. He wanted a world that was like walking through rain, even though he could not see far ahead of him, but fate had put him in the world of Mr. Macy's fetid storerooms and corridors. At first merely the overwhelming need of change took him, then half-plans began to formulate in his imagination.

"I'll go East—to a big city—meet people—bigger people—people who'll help me. Interesting work somewhere. My God, there must be."

With sickening truth it occurred to him that his facility for meeting people was limited. Of all places it was here in his own town that he should be known, was known—famous—before the water of oblivion had rolled over him.

You had to cut corners, that was all. Pull—relationship—wealthy marriages——

For several miles the continued reiteration of this preoccupied him and then he perceived that the rain had become thicker and more opaque in the heavy gray of twilight and that the houses were falling away. The district of full blocks, then of big houses, then of scattering little ones, passed and great sweeps of misty country opened out on both sides. It was hard walking here. The sidewalk had given place to a dirt road, streaked with furious brown rivulets that splashed and squashed around his shoes.

Cutting corners—the words began to fall apart, forming curious phrasings—little illuminated pieces of themselves. They resolved into sentences, each of which had a strangely familiar ring.

Cutting corners meant rejecting the old childhood principles that success came from faithfulness to duty, that evil was necessarily punished or virtue necessarily rewarded—that honest poverty was happier than corrupt riches.

It meant being hard.

This phrase appealed to him and he repeated it over and over. It had to do somehow with Mr. Macy and Charley Moore—the attitudes, the methods of each of them.

He stopped and felt his clothes. He was drenched to the skin. He looked about him and, selecting a place in the fence where a tree sheltered it, perched himself there.

In my credulous years—he thought—they told me that evil was a sort of dirty hue, just as definite as a soiled collar, but it seems to me that evil is only a manner of hard luck, or heredity-and-environment, or "being found out." It hides in the vacillations of dubs like Charley Moore as certainly as it does in the intolerance of Macy, and if it ever gets much more tangible it becomes merely an arbitrary label to paste on the unpleasant things in other people's lives.

In fact—he concluded—it isn't worth worrying over what's evil and what isn't. Good and evil aren't any standard to me—and they can be a devil of a bad hindrance when I want something. When I want something bad enough, common sense tells me to go and take it—and not get caught.

And then suddenly Dalyrimple knew what he wanted first. He wanted fifteen dollars to pay his overdue board bill.

With a furious energy he jumped from the fence, whipped off his coat, and from its black lining cut with his knife a piece about five inches square. He made two holes near its edge and then fixed it on his face, pulling his hat down to hold it in place. It flapped grotesquely and then dampened and clung clung to his forehead and cheeks.

Now . . . The twilight had merged to dripping dusk . . . black as pitch. He began to walk quickly back toward town, not waiting to remove the mask but watching the road with difficulty through the jagged eye-holes. He was not conscious of any nervousness . . . the only tension was caused by a desire to do the thing as soon as possible.

He reached the first sidewalk, continued on until he saw a hedge far from any lamp-post, and turned in behind it. Within a minute he heard several series of footsteps—he waited—it was a woman and he held his breath until she passed . . . and then a man, a laborer. The next passer, he felt, would be what he wanted . . . the laborer's footfalls died far up the drenched street . . . other steps grew nears grew suddenly louder.

Dalyrimple braced himself.

"Put up your hands!"

The man stopped, uttered an absurd little grunt, and thrust pudgy arms skyward.

Dalyrimple went through the waistcoat.

"Now, you shrimp," he said, setting his hand suggestively to his own hip pocket, "you run, and stamp—loud! If I hear your feet stop I'll put a shot after you!"

Then he stood there in sudden uncontrollable laughter as audibly frightened footsteps scurried away into the night.

After a moment he thrust the roll of bills into his pocket, snatched off his mask, and running quickly across the street, darted down an alley.

IV

YET, HOWEVER DALYRIMPLE JUSTIFIED HIMSELF INTELLECTUALLY, HE HAD many bad moments in the weeks immediately following his decision. The tremendous pressure of sentiment and inherited ambition kept raising riot with his attitude. He felt morally lonely.

The noon after his first venture he ate in a little lunch-room with Charley Moore and, watching him unspread the paper, waited for a remark about the hold-up of the day before. But either the hold-up was not mentioned or Charley wasn't interested. He turned listlessly to the sporting sheet, read Doctor Crane's crop of seasoned bromides, took in an editorial on ambition with his mouth slightly ajar, and then skipped to Mutt and Jeff.

Poor Charley—with his faint aura of evil and his mind that refused to focus, playing a lifeless solitaire with cast-off mischief.

Yet Charley belonged on the other side of the fence. In him could be stirred up all the flamings and denunciations of righteousness; he would weep at a stage heroine's lost virtue, he could become lofty and contemptuous at the idea of dishonor.

On my side, thought Dalyrimple, there aren't any resting-places; a man who's a strong criminal is after the weak criminals as well, so it's all guerilla warfare over here.

What will it all do to me? he thought with a persistent weariness. Will it take the color out of life with the honor? Will it scatter my courage and dull my mind?—despiritualize me completely—does it mean eventual barrenness, eventual remorse, failure?

With a great surge of anger, he would fling his mind upon the barrier—and stand there with the flashing bayonet of his pride. Other men who broke the laws of justice and charity lied to all the world. He at any rate would not lie to himself. He was more than Byronic now: not the spiritual rebel, Don Juan; not the philosophical rebel, Faust; but a new psychological rebel of his own century—defying the sentimental a priori forms of his own mind——

Happiness was what he wanted—a slowly rising scale of gratifications of the normal appetites—and he had a strong conviction that the materials, if not the inspiration of happiness, could be bought with money.

V

THE NIGHT CAME THAT DREW HIM OUT UPON HIS SECOND VENTURE, AND AS HE walked the dark street he felt in himself a great resemblance to a cat—a certain supple, swinging litheness. His muscles were rippling smoothly and sleekly under his spare, healthy flesh—he had an absurd desire to bound along the street, to run dodging among trees, to turn "cart-wheels" over soft grass.

It was not crisp, but in the air lay a faint suggestion of acerbity, inspirational rather than chilling.

"The moon is down—I have not heard the clock!"

He laughed in delight at the line which an early memory had endowed with a hushed awesome beauty.

He passed a man and then another a quarter of mile afterward.

He was on Philmore Street now and it was very dark. He blessed the city council for not having put in new lamp-posts as a recent budget had recommended. Here was the red-brick Sterner residence which marked the beginning of the avenue; here was the Jordon house, the Eisenhaurs', the Dents', the Markhams', the Frasers'; the Hawkins', where he had been a guest; the Willoughbys', the Everett's, colonial and ornate; the little cottage where lived the Watts old maids between the imposing fronts of the Macys' and the Krupstadts'; the Craigs—

Ah . . . there! He paused, wavered violently—far up the street was a blot, a man walking, possibly a policeman. After an eternal second be found himself following the vague, ragged shadow of a lamp-post across a lawn, running bent very low. Then he was standing tense, without breath or need of it, in the shadow of his limestone prey.

Interminably he listened—a mile off a cat howled, a hundred yards away another took up the hymn in a demoniacal snarl, and he felt his heart dip and swoop, acting as shock-absorber for his mind. There were other sounds; the faintest fragment of song far away; strident, gossiping laughter from a back porch diagonally across the alley; and crickets, crickets singing in the patched, patterned, moonlit grass of the yard. Within the house there seemed to lie an ominous silence. He was glad he did not know who lived here.

His slight shiver hardened to steel; the steel softened and his nerves became pliable as leather; gripping his hands he gratefully found them supple, and taking out knife and pliers he went to work on the screen.

So sure was he that he was unobserved that, from the dining-room where in a minute he found himself, he leaned out and carefully pulled the screen up into position, balancing it so it would neither fall by chance nor be a serious obstacle to a sudden exit.

Then he put the open knife in his coat pocket, took out his pocket-flash, and tiptoed around the room.

There was nothing here he could use—the dining-room had never been included in his plans for the town was too small to permit disposing of silver.

As a matter of fact his plans were of the vaguest. He had found that with a mind like his, lucrative in intelligence, intuition, and lightning decision, it was best to have but the skeleton of a campaign. The machine-gun episode had taught him that. And he was afraid that a method preconceived would give him two points of view in a crisis—and two points of view meant wavering.

He stumbled slightly on a chair, held his breath, listened, went on, found the hall, found the stairs, started up; the seventh stair creaked at his step, the ninth, the fourteenth. He was counting them automatically. At the third creak he paused again for over a minute—and in that minute he felt more alone than he had ever felt before. Between the lines on patrol, even when alone, he had had behind him the moral support of half a billion people; now he was alone, pitted against that same moral pressure—a bandit. He had never felt this fear, yet he had never felt this exultation.

The stairs came to an end, a doorway approached; he went in and listened to regular breathing. His feet were economical of steps and his body swayed sometimes at stretching as he felt over the bureau, pocketing all articles which held promise—he could not have enumerated them ten seconds afterward. He felt on a chair for possible trousers, found soft garments, women's lingerie. The corners of his mouth smiled mechanically.

Another room . . . the same breathing, enlivened by one ghastly snort that sent his heart again on its tour of his breast. Round object—watch; chain; roll of bills; stick-pins; two rings—he remembered that he had got rings from the other bureau. He started out winced as a faint glow flashed in front of him, facing him. God!—it was the glow of his own wrist-watch on his outstretched arm.

Down the stairs. He skipped two crumbling steps but found another. He was all right now, practically safe; as he neared the bottom he felt a slight boredom. He reached the dining-room —considered the silver— again decided against it.

Back in his room at the boarding-house he examined the additions to his personal property:

Sixty-five dollars in bills.

A platinum ring with three medium diamonds, worth, probably, about seven hundred dollars. Diamonds were going up.

A cheap gold-plated ring with the initials O. S. and the date inside—'03—probably a class-ring from school. Worth a few dollars. Unsalable.

A red-cloth case containing a set of false teeth.

A silver watch.

A gold chain worth more than the watch.

An empty ring-box.

A little ivory Chinese god—probably a desk ornament.

A dollar and sixty-two cents in small change.

He put the money under his pillow and the other things in the toe of an infantry boot, stuffing a stocking in on top of them. Then for two hours his mind raced like a high-power engine here and there through his life, past and future, through fear and laughter. With a vague, inopportune wish that he were married, he fell into a deep sleep about half past five.

VI

THOUGH THE NEWSPAPER ACCOUNT OF THE BURGLARY FAILED TO MENTION THE false teeth, they worried him considerably. The picture of a human waking in the cool dawn and groping for them in vain, of a soft, toothless breakfast, of a strange, hollow, lisping voice calling the police station, of weary, dispirited visits to the dentist, roused a great fatherly pity in him.

Trying to ascertain whether they belonged to a man or a woman, he took them carefully out of the case and held them up near his mouth. He moved his own jaws experimentally; he measured with his fingers; but he failed to decide: they might belong either to a large-mouthed woman or a small-mouthed man.

On a warm impulse he wrapped them in brown paper from the bottom of his army trunk, and printed false teeth on the package in clumsy pencil letters. Then, the next night, he walked down Philmore Street, and shied the package onto the lawn so that it would be near the door. Next day the paper announced that the police had a clew—they knew that the burglar was in town. However, they didn't mention what the clew was.

VII

AT THE END OF A MONTH "BURGLAR BILL OF THE SILVER DISTRICT WAS THE nurse-girl's standby for frightening children. Five burglaries were attributed to him, but though Dalyrimple had only committed three, he considered that majority had it and appropriated the title to himself. He had once been seen—"a large bloated creature with the meanest face you ever laid eyes on." Mrs. Henry Coleman, awaking at two o'clock at the beam of an electric torch flashed in her eye, could not have been expected to recognize Bryan Dalyrimple at whom she had waved flags last Fourth of July, and whom she had described as "not at all the daredevil type, do you think?"

When Dalyrimple kept his imagination at white heat he managed to glorify his own attitude, his emancipation from petty scruples and remorses—but let him once allow his thought to rove unarmored, great unexpected horrors and depressions would overtake him. Then for reassurance he had to go back to think out the whole thing over again. He found that it was on the whole better to give up considering himself as a rebel. It was more consoling to think of every one else as a fool.

His attitude toward Mr. Macy underwent a change. He no longer felt a dim animosity and inferiority in his presence. As his fourth month in the store ended he found himself regarding his employer in a manner that was almost fraternal. He had a vague but very assured conviction that Mr. Macy's innermost soul would have abetted and approved. He no longer worried about his future. He had the intention of accumulating several thousand dollars and then clearing out—going east, back to France, down to South America. Half a dozen times in the last two months he had been about to stop work, but a fear of attracting attention to his being in funds prevented him. So he worked on, no longer in listlessness, but with contemptuous amusement.

VIII

THEN WITH ASTOUNDING SUDDENNESS SOMETHING HAPPENED THAT CHANGED his plans and put an end to his burglaries.

Mr. Macy sent for him one afternoon and with a great show of jovial mystery asked him if he had an engagement that night. If he hadn't, would he please call on Mr. Alfred J. Fraser at eight o'clock. Dalyrimple's wonder was mingled with uncertainty. He debated with himself whether it were not his cue to take the first train out of town. But an hour's consideration decided him that his fears were unfounded and at eight o'clock he arrived at the big Fraser house in Philmore Avenue.

Mr. Fraser was commonly supposed to be the biggest political influence in the city. His brother was Senator Fraser, his son-in-law was Congressman Demming, and his influence, though not wielded in such a way as to make him an objectionable boss, was strong nevertheless.

He had a great, huge face, deep-set eyes, and a barn-door of an upper lip, the melange approaching a worthy climax in a long professional jaw.

During his conversation with Dalyrimple his expression kept starting toward a smile, reached a cheerful optimism, and then receded back to imperturbability.

"How do you do, sir?" he laid, holding out his hand. "Sit down. I suppose you're wondering why I wanted you. Sit down."

Dalyrimple sat down.

"Mr. Dalyrimple, how old are you?"

"I'm twenty-three."

"You're young. But that doesn't mean you're foolish. Mr. Dalyrimple, what I've got to say won't take long. I'm going to make you a proposition. To begin at the beginning, I've been watching you ever since last Fourth of July when you made that speech in response to the loving-cup."

Dalyrimple murmured disparagingly, but Fraser waved him to silence.

"It was a speech I've remembered. It was a brainy speech, straight from the shoulder, and it got to everybody in that crowd. I know. I've watched crowds for years." He cleared his throat as if tempted to digress on his knowledge of crowds—then continued. "But, Mr. Dalyrimple, I've seen too many young men who promised brilliantly go to pieces, fail through want of steadiness, too many high-power ideas, and not enough willingness to work. So I waited. I wanted to see what you'd do. I wanted to see if you'd go to work, and if you'd stick to what you started."

Dalyrimple felt a glow settle over him.

"So," continued Fraser, "when Theron Macy told me you'd started down at his place, I kept watching you, and I followed your record through him. The first month I was afraid for awhile. He told me you were getting restless, too good for your job, hinting around for a raise———"

Dalyrimple started.

"———But he said after that you evidently made up your mind to shut up and stick to it. That's the stuff I like in a young man! That's the stuff that wins out. And don't think I don't understand. I know how much harder it was for you after all that silly flattery a lot of old women had been giving you. I know what a fight it must have been———"

Dalyrimple's face was burning brightly. It felt young and strangely ingenuous

"Dalyrimple, you've got brains and you've got the stuff in you— and that's what I want. I'm going to put you into the State Senate."

"The what?"

"The State Senate. We want a young man who has got brains, but is solid and not a loafer. And when I say State Senate I don't stop there. We're up against it here, Dalyrimple. We've got to get some young men into politics—you know the old blood that's been running on the party ticket year in and year out."

Dalyrimple licked his lips.

"You'll run me for the State Senate?"

"I'll put you in the State Senate."

Mr. Fraser's expression had now reached the point nearest a smile and Dalyrimple in a happy frivolity felt himself urging it mentally on—but it stopped, locked, and slid from him. The barn-door and the jaw were separated by a line strait as a nail. Dalyrimple remembered with an effort that it was a mouth, and talked to it.

"But I'm through," he said. "My notoriety's dead. People are fed up with me."

"Those things," answered Mr. Fraser, "are mechanical. Linotype is a resuscitator of reputations. Wait till you see the herald, beginning next week—that is if you're with us—that is," and his voice hardened slightly, "if you haven't got too many ideas yourself about how things ought to be run."

"No," said Dalyrimple, looking him frankly in the eye. "You'll have to give me a lot of advice at first."

"Very well. I'll take care of your reputation then. Just keep yourself on the right side of the fence."

Dalyrimple started at this repetition of a phrase he had thought of so much lately. There was a sudden ring at the door-bell.

"That's Macy now," observed Fraser, rising. "I'll go let him in. The servants have gone to bed."

He left Dalyrimple there in a dream. The world was opening up suddenly— The State Senate, the United States Senate—so life was this after all—cutting corners—common sense, that was the rule. No more foolish risks now unless necessity called—but it was being hard that counted— Never to let remorse or self-reproach lose him a night's sleep—

let his life be a sword of courage—there was no payment—all that was drivel—drivel.

He sprang to his feet with clinched hands in a sort of triumph.

"Well, Bryan," said Mr. Macy stepping through the portières.

The two older men smiled their half-smiles at him.

"Well Bryan," said Mr. Macy again.

Dalyrimple smiled also.

"How do, Mr. Macy?"

He wondered if some telepathy between them had made this new appreciation possible—some invisible realization. . . .

Mr. Macy held out his hand.

"I'm glad we're to be associated in this scheme—I've been for you all along—especially lately. I'm glad we're to be on the same side of the fence."

"I want to thank you, sir," said Dalyrimple simply. He felt a whimsical moisture gathering back of his eyes.

THE FOUR FISTS

I

At the present time no one I know has the slightest desire to hit Samuel Meredith; possibly this is because a man over fifty is liable to be rather severely cracked at the impact of a hostile fist, but, for my part, I am inclined to think that all his hitable qualities have quite vanished. But it is certain that at various times in his life hitable qualities were in his face, as surely as kissable qualities have ever lurked in a girl's lips.

I'm sure every one has met a man like that, been casually introduced, even made a friend of him, yet felt he was the sort who aroused passionate dislike—expressed by some in the involuntary clinching of fists, and in others by mutterings about "takin' a poke" and "landin' a swift smash in ee eye." In the juxtaposition of Samuel Meredith's features this quality was so strong that it influenced his entire life.

What was it? Not the shape, certainly, for he was a pleasant-looking man from earliest youth: broad-bowed with gray eyes that were frank and friendly. Yet I've heard him tell a room full of reporters angling for a "success" story that he'd be ashamed to tell them the truth that they wouldn't believe it, that it wasn't one story but four, that the public would not want to read about a man who had been walloped into prominence.

It all started at Phillips Andover Academy when he was fourteen. He had been brought up on a diet of caviar and bell-boys' legs in half the capitals of Europe, and it was pure luck that his mother had nervous prostration and had to delegate his education to less tender, less biassed hands.

At Andover he was given a roommate named Gilly Hood. Gilly was thirteen, undersized, and rather the school pet. From the September day when Mr. Meredith's valet stowed Samuel's clothing in the best bureau and asked, on departing, "hif there was hanything helse, Master Samuel?" Gilly cried out that the faculty had played him false. He felt like an irate frog in whose bowl has been put goldfish.

"Good gosh!" he complained to his sympathetic contemporaries, "he's a damn stuck-up Willie. He said, 'Are the crowd here gentlemen?' and I said, 'No, they're boys,' and he said age didn't matter, and I said, 'Who said it did?' Let him get fresh with me, the ole pieface!"

For three weeks Gilly endured in silence young Samuel's comments on the clothes and habits of Gilly's personal friends, endured French phrases in conversation, endured a hundred half-feminine meannesses that show what a nervous mother can do to a boy, if she keeps close enough to him— then a storm broke in the aquarium.

Samuel was out. A crowd had gathered to hear Gilly be wrathful about his roommate's latest sins.

"He said, 'Oh, I don't like the windows open at night,' he said, 'except only a little bit,'" complained Gilly.

"Don't let him boss you."

"Boss me? You bet he won't. I open those windows, I guess, but the darn fool won't take turns shuttin' 'em in the morning."

"Make him, Gilly, why don't you?"

"I'm going to." Gilly nodded his head in fierce agreement. "Don't you worry. He needn't think I'm any ole butler."

"Le's see you make him."

At this point the darn fool entered in person and included the crowd in one of his irritating smiles. Two boys said, "'Lo, Mer'dith"; the others gave him a chilly glance and went on talking to Gilly. But Samuel seemed unsatisfied.

"Would you mind not sitting on my bed?" he suggested politely to two of Gilly's particulars who were perched very much at ease.

"Huh?"

"My bed. Can't you understand English?"

This was adding insult to injury. There were several comments on the bed's sanitary condition and the evidence within it of animal life.

"S'matter with your old bed?" demanded Gilly truculently.

"The bed's all right, but——"

Gilly interrupted this sentence by rising and walking up to Samuel. He paused several inches away and eyed him fiercely.

"You an' your crazy ole bed," he began. "You an' your crazy——"

"Go to it, Gilly," murmured some one.

"Show the darn fool——"

Samuel returned the gaze coolly.

"Well," he said finally, "it's my bed——"

He got no further, for Gilly hauled off and hit him succinctly in the nose.

"Yea! Gilly!"

"Show the big bully!"

"Just let him touch you—he'll see!"

The group closed in on them and for the first time in his life Samuel realized the insuperable inconvenience of being passionately detested. He gazed around helplessly at the glowering, violently hostile faces. He towered a head taller than his roommate, so if he hit back he'd be called a bully and have half a dozen more fights on his hands within five minutes; yet if he didn't he was a coward. For a moment he stood there facing Gilly's blazing eyes, and then, with a sudden choking sound, he forced his way through the ring and rushed from the room.

The month following bracketed the thirty most miserable days of his life. Every waking moment he was under the lashing tongues of his contemporaries; his habits and mannerisms became butts for intolerable witticisms and, of course, the sensitiveness of adolescence was a further thorn. He considered that he was a natural pariah; that the unpopularity at school would follow him through life. When he went home for the Christmas holidays he was so despondent that his father sent him to a nerve specialist. When he returned to Andover he arranged to arrive late so that he could be alone in the bus during the drive from station to school.

Of course when he had learned to keep his mouth shut every one promptly forgot all about him. The next autumn, with his realization that consideration for others was the discreet attitude, he made good use of the clean start given him by the shortness of boyhood memory. By the beginning of his senior year Samuel Meredith was one of the best-liked boys of his class—and no one was any stronger for him than his first friend and constant companion, Gilly Hood.

II

SAMUEL BECAME THE SORT OF COLLEGE STUDENT WHO IN THE EARLY NINETIES drove tandems and coaches and tallyhos between Princeton and Yale and New York City to show that they appreciated the social importance of football games. He believed passionately in good form—his choosing of gloves, his tying of ties, his holding of reins were imitated by impressionable freshmen. Outside of his own set he was considered rather a snob, but as his set was the set, it never worried him. He played football in the autumn, drank high-balls in the winter, and rowed in the spring. Samuel despised all those who were merely sportsmen without being gentlemen or merely gentlemen without being sportsmen.

He lived in New York and often brought home several of his friends for the week-end. Those were the days of the horse-car and in case of a crush it was, of course, the proper thing for any one of Samuel's set to rise and deliver his seat to a standing lady with a formal bow. One night in Samuel's junior year he boarded a car with two of his intimates. There were three vacant seats. When Samuel sat down he noticed a heavy-eyed laboring man sitting next to him who smelt objectionably of garlic, sagged slightly against Samuel and, spreading a little as a tired man will, took up quite too much room.

The car had gone several blocks when it stopped for a quartet of young girls, and, of course, the three men of the world sprang to their feet and proffered their seats with due observance of form. Unfortunately, the laborer, being unacquainted with the code of neckties and tallyhos, failed to follow their example, and one young lady was left at an embarrassed stance. Fourteen eyes glared reproachfully at the barbarian; seven lips curled slightly; but the object of scorn stared stolidly into the foreground in sturdy unconsciousness of his despicable conduct. Samuel was the most violently affected. He was humiliated that any male should so conduct himself. He spoke aloud.

"There's a lady standing," he said sternly.

That should have been quite enough, but the object of scorn only looked up blankly. The standing girl tittered and exchanged nervous glances with her companions. But Samuel was aroused.

"There's a lady standing," he repeated, rather raspingly. The man seemed to comprehend.

"I pay my fare," he said quietly.

Samuel turned red and his hands clinched, but the conductor was looking their way, so at a warning nod from his friends he subsided into sullen gloom.

They reached their destination and left the car, but so did the laborer, who followed them, swinging his little pail. Seeing his chance, Samuel no longer resisted his aristocratic inclination. He turned around and, launching a full-featured, dime-novel sneer, made a loud remark about the right of the lower animals to ride with human beings.

In a half-second the workman had dropped his pail and let fly at him. Unprepared, Samuel took the blow neatly on the jaw and sprawled full length into the cobblestone gutter.

"Don't laugh at me!" cried his assailant. "I been workin' all day. I'm tired as hell!"

As he spoke the sudden anger died out of his eyes and the mask of weariness dropped again over his face. He turned and picked up his pail. Samuel's friends took a quick step in his direction.

"Wait!" Samuel had risen slowly and was motioning back. Some time, somewhere, he had been struck like that before. Then he remembered— Gilly Hood. In the silence, as he dusted himself off, the whole scene in the room at Andover was before his eyes— and he knew intuitively that he had been wrong again. This man's strength, his rest, was the protection of his family. He had more use for his seat in the street-car than any young girl.

"It's all right," said Samuel gruffly. "Don't touch 'him. I've been a damn fool."

Of course it took more than an hour, or a week, for Samuel to rearrange his ideas on the essential importance of good form. At first he simply admitted that his wrongness had made him powerless—as it had made him powerless against Gilly—but eventually his mistake about the workman influenced his entire attitude. Snobbishness is, after all, merely good breeding grown dictatorial; so Samuel's code remained but the necessity of imposing it upon others had faded out in a certain gutter. Within that year his class had somehow stopped referring to him as a snob.

III

AFTER A FEW YEARS SAMUEL'S UNIVERSITY DECIDED THAT IT HAD SHONE LONG enough in the reflected glory of his neckties, so they declaimed to him in Latin, charged him ten dollars for the paper which proved him irretrievably educated, and sent him into the turmoil with much self-confidence, a few friends, and the proper assortment of harmless bad habits.

His family had by that time started back to shirt-sleeves, through a sudden decline in the sugar-market, and it had already unbuttoned its vest, so to speak, when Samuel went to work. His mind was that exquisite tabula rasa that a university education sometimes leaves, but he had both energy and influence, so he used his former ability as a dodging half-back in twisting through Wall Street crowds as runner for a bank.

His diversion was—women. There were half a dozen: two or three débutantes, an actress (in a minor way), a grass-widow, and one sentimental little brunette who was married and lived in a little house in Jersey City.

They had met on a ferry-boat. Samuel was crossing from New York on business (he had been working several years by this time) and he helped her look for a package that she had dropped in the crush.

"Do you come over often?" he inquired casually.

"Just to shop," she said shyly. She had great brown eyes and the pathetic kind of little mouth. "I've only been married three months, and we find it cheaper to live over here."

"Does he—does your husband like your being alone like this?"

She laughed, a cheery young laugh.

"Oh, dear me, no. We were to meet for dinner but I must have misunderstood the place. He'll be awfully worried."

"Well," said Samuel disapprovingly, "he ought to be. If you'll allow me I'll see you home."

She accepted his offer thankfully, so they took the cable-car together. When they walked up the path to her little house they saw a light there; her husband had arrived before her.

"He's frightfully jealous," she announced, laughingly apologetic.

"Very well," answered Samuel, rather stiffly. "I'd better leave you here."

She thanked him and, waving a good night, he left her.

That would have been quite all if they hadn't met on Fifth Avenue one morning a week later. She started and blushed and seemed so glad to see him that they chatted like old friends. She was going to her dressmaker's, eat lunch alone at Taine's, shop all afternoon, and meet her husband on the ferry at five. Samuel told her that her husband was a very lucky man. She blushed again and scurried off.

Samuel whistled all the way back to his office, but about twelve o'clock he began to see that pathetic, appealing little mouth everywhere—and those brown eyes. He fidgeted when he looked at the clock; he thought of the grill down-stairs where he lunched and the heavy male conversation thereof, and opposed to that picture appeared another; a little table at Taine's with the brown eyes and the mouth a few feet away. A few minutes before twelve-thirty he dashed on his hat and rushed for the cable-car.

She was quite surprised to see him.

"Why—hello," she said. Samuel could tell that she was just pleasantly frightened.

"I thought we might lunch together. It's so dull eating with a lot of men."

She hesitated.

"Why, I suppose there's no harm in it. How could there be!"

It occurred to her that her husband should have taken lunch with her—but he was generally so hurried at noon. She told Samuel all about him: he was a little smaller than Samuel, but, oh, much better-looking. He was a book-keeper and not making a lot of money, but they were very happy and expected to be rich within three or four years.

Samuel's grass-widow had been in a quarrelsome mood for three or four weeks, and through contrast, he took an accentuated pleasure in this meeting; so fresh was she, and earnest, and faintly adventurous. Her name was Marjorie.

They made another engagement; in fact, for a month they lunched together two or three times a week. When she was sure that her husband would work late Samuel took her over to New Jersey on the ferry, leaving her always on the tiny front porch, after she had gone in and lit the gas to use the security of his masculine presence outside. This grew to be a ceremony—and it annoyed him. Whenever the comfortable glow fell out through the front windows, that was his congé; yet he never suggested coming in and Marjorie didn't invite him.

Then, when Samuel and Marjorie had reached a stage in which they sometimes touched each other's arms gently, just to show that they were very good friends, Marjorie and her husband had one of those ultrasensitive, supercritical quarrels that couples never indulge in unless they care a great deal about each other. It started with a cold mutton-chop or a leak in the gas-jet—and one day Samuel found her in Taine's, with dark shadows under her brown eyes and a terrifying pout.

By this time Samuel thought he was in love with Marjorie—so he played up the quarrel for all it was worth. He was her best friend and patted her hand—and leaned down close to her brown curls while she whispered in little sobs what her husband had said that morning; and he was a little more than her best friend when he took her over to the ferry in a hansom.

"Marjorie," he said gently, when he left her, as usual, on the porch, "if at any time you want to call on me, remember that I am always waiting, always waiting."

She nodded gravely and put both her hands in his. "I know," she said. "I know you're my friend, my best friend."

Then she ran into the house and he watched there until the gas went on.

For the next week Samuel was in a nervous turmoil. Some persistently rational strain warned him that at bottom he and Marjorie had little in common, but in such cases there is usually so much mud in the water that one can seldom see to the bottom. Every dream and desire told him that he loved Marjorie, wanted her, had to have her.

The quarrel developed. Marjorie's husband took to staying in New York until late at night, came home several times disagreeably overstimulated, and made her generally miserable. They must have had too much pride to talk it out—for Marjorie's husband was, after all, pretty decent—so it drifted on from one misunderstanding to another. Marjorie kept coming more and more to Samuel; when a woman can accept masculine sympathy at is much more satisfactory to her than crying to another girl. But Marjorie didn't realize how much she had begun to rely on him, how much he was part of her little cosmos.

One night, instead of turning away when Marjorie went in and lit the gas, Samuel went in, too, and they sat together on the sofa in the little parlor. He was very happy. He envied their home, and he felt that the man who neglected such a possession out of stubborn pride was a fool and unworthy of his wife. But when he kissed Marjorie for the first time she cried softly and told him to go. He sailed home on the wings of desperate excitement, quite resolved to fan this spark of romance, no matter how big the blaze or who was burned. At the time he considered that his thoughts were unselfishly of her; in a later perspective he knew that she had meant no more than the white screen in a motion picture: it was just Samuel— blind, desirous.

Next day at Taine's, when they met for lunch, Samuel dropped all pretense and made frank love to her. He had no plans, no definite intentions, except to kiss her lips again, to hold her in his arms and feel that she was very little and pathetic and lovable. . . . He took her home, and this time they kissed until both their hearts beat high—words and phrases formed on his lips.

And then suddenly there were steps on the porch—a hand tried the outside door. Marjorie turned dead-white.

"Wait!" she whispered to Samuel, in a frightened voice, but in angry impatience at the interruption he walked to the front door and threw it open.

Every one has seen such scenes on the stage—seen them so often that when they actually happen people behave very much like actors. Samuel felt that he was playing a part and the lines came quite naturally: he announced that all had a right to lead their own lives and looked at Marjorie's husband menacingly, as if daring him to doubt it. Marjorie's husband spoke of the sanctity of the home, forgetting that it hadn't seemed very holy to him lately; Samuel continued along the line of "the right to happiness"; Marjorie's husband mentioned firearms and the divorce court. Then suddenly he stopped and scrutinized both of them— Marjorie in pitiful collapse on the sofa, Samuel haranguing the furniture in a consciously heroic pose.

"Go up-stairs, Marjorie," he said, in a different tone.

"Stay where you are!" Samuel countered quickly.

Marjorie rose, wavered, and sat down, rose again and moved hesitatingly toward the stairs.

"Come outside," said her husband to Samuel. "I want to talk to you."

Samuel glanced at Marjorie, tried to get some message from her eyes; then he shut his lips and went out.

There was a bright moon and when Marjorie's husband came down the steps Samuel could see plainly that he was suffering—but he felt no pity for him.

They stood and looked at each other, a few feet apart, and the husband cleared his throat as though it were a bit husky.

"That's my wife," he said quietly, and then a wild anger surged up inside him. "Damn you!" he cried—and hit Samuel in the face with all his strength.

In that second, as Samuel slumped to the ground, it flashed to him that he had been hit like that twice before, and simultaneously the incident altered like a dream—he felt suddenly awake. Mechanically he sprang to his feet and squared off. The other man was waiting, fists up, a yard away, but Samuel knew that though physically he had him by several inches and many pounds, he wouldn't hit him. The situation had miraculously and entirely changed—a moment before Samuel had seemed to himself heroic; now he seemed the cad, the outsider, and Marjorie's husband, silhouetted against the lights of the little house, the eternal heroic figure, the defender of his home.

There was a pause and then Samuel turned quickly away and went down the path for the last time.

IV

Of course, after the third blow Samuel put in several weeks at conscientious introspection. The blow years before at Andover had landed on his personal unpleasantness; the workman of his college days had jarred the snobbishness out of his system, and Marjorie's husband had given a severe jolt to his greedy selfishness. It threw women out of his ken until a year later, when he met his future wife; for the only sort of woman worth while seemed to be the one who could be protected as Marjorie's husband had protected her. Samuel could not imagine his grass-widow, Mrs. De Ferriac, causing any very righteous blows on her own account.

His early thirties found him well on his feet. He was associated with old Peter Carhart, who was in those days a national figure. Carhart's physique was like a rough model for a statue of Hercules, and his record was just as solid—a pile made for the pure joy of it, without cheap extortion or shady scandal. He had been a great friend of Samuel's father, but he watched the son for six years before taking him into his own office. Heaven knows how many things he controlled at that time—mines, railroads, banks, whole cities. Samuel was very close to him, knew his likes and dislikes, his prejudices, weaknesses and many strengths.

One day Carhart sent for Samuel and, closing the door of his inner office, offered him a chair and a cigar.

"Everything O. K., Samuel?" he asked.

"Why, yes."

"I've been afraid you're getting a bit stale."

"Stale?" Samuel was puzzled.

"You've done no work outside the office for nearly ten years?"

"But I've had vacations, in the Adiron——"

Carhart waved this aside.

"I mean outside work. Seeing the things move that we've always pulled the strings of here."

"No," admitted Samuel; "I haven't."

"So," he said abruptly "I'm going to give you an outside job that'll take about a month."

Samuel didn't argue. He rather liked the idea and he made up his mind that, whatever it was, he would put it through just as Carhart wanted it. That was his employer's greatest hobby, and the men around him were as dumb under direct orders as infantry subalterns.

"You'll go to San Antonio and see Hamil," continued Carhart. "He's got a job on hand and he wants a man to take charge."

Hamil was in charge of the Carhart interests in the Southwest, a man who had grown up in the shadow of his employer, and with whom, though they had never met, Samuel had had much official correspondence.

"When do I leave?"

"You'd better go to-morrow," answered Carhart, glancing at the calendar. "That's the 1st of May. I'll expect your report here on the 1st of June."

Next morning Samuel left for Chicago, and two days later he was facing Hamil across a table in the office of the Merchants' Trust in San Antonio. It didn't take long to get the gist of the thing. It was a big deal in oil which concerned the buying up of seventeen huge adjoining ranches. This buying up had to be done in one week, and it was a pure squeeze. Forces had been set in motion that put the seventeen owners between the devil and the deep sea, and Samuel's part was simply to "handle" the matter from a little village near Pueblo. With tact and efficiency the right man could bring it off without any friction, for it was merely a question of sitting at the wheel and keeping a firm hold. Hamil, with an astuteness many times valuable to his chief, had arranged a situation that would give a much greater clear gain than any dealing in the open market. Samuel shook hands with Hamil, arranged to return in two weeks, and left for San Felipe, New Mexico.

It occurred to him, of course, that Carhart was trying him out. Hamil's report on his handling of this might be a factor in something big for him, but even without that he would have done his best to put the thing through. Ten years in New York hadn't made him sentimental and he was quite accustomed to finish everything he began—and a little bit more.

All went well at first. There was no enthusiasm, but each one of the seventeen ranchers concerned knew Samuel's business, knew what he had behind him, and that they had as little chance of holding out as flies on a window-pane. Some of them were resigned—some of them cared like the devil, but they'd talked it over, argued it with lawyers and couldn't see any possible loophole. Five of the ranches had oil, the other twelve were part of the chance, but quite as necessary to Hamil's purpose, in any event.

Samuel soon saw that the real leader was an early settler named McIntyre, a man of perhaps fifty, gray-haired, clean-shaven, bronzed by forty New Mexico summers, and with those clear steady eye that Texas and New Mexico weather are apt to give. His ranch had not as yet shown oil, but it was in the pool, and if any man hated to lose his land McIntyre did. Every one had rather looked to him at first to avert the big calamity, and he had hunted all over the territory for the legal means with which to do it, but he had failed, and he knew it. He avoided Samuel assiduously, but Samuel was sure that when the day came for the signatures he would appear.

It came—a baking May day, with hot wave rising off the parched land as far as eyes could see, and as Samuel sat stewing in his little improvised office—a few chairs, a bench, and a wooden table—he was glad the thing was almost over. He wanted to get back East the worst way, and join his wife and children for a week at the seashore.

The meeting was set for four o'clock, and he was rather surprised at three-thirty when the door opened and McIntyre came in. Samuel could not help respecting the man's attitude, and feeling a bit sorry for him. McIntyre seemed closely related to the prairies, and Samuel had the little flicker of envy that city people feel toward men who live in the open.

"Afternoon," said McIntyre, standing in the open doorway, with his feet apart and his hands on his hips.

"Hello, Mr. McIntyre." Samuel rose, but omitted the formality of offering his hand. He imagined the rancher cordially loathed him, and he hardly blamed him. McIntyre came in and sat down leisurely.

"You got us," he said suddenly.

This didn't seem to require any answer.

"When I heard Carhart was back of this," he continued, "I gave up."

"Mr. Carhart is——" began Samuel, but McIntyre waved him silent.

"Don't talk about the dirty sneak-thief!"

"Mr. McIntyre," said Samuel briskly, "if this half-hour is to be devoted to that sort of talk——"

"Oh, dry up, young man," McIntyre interrupted, "you can't abuse a man who'd do a thing like this."

Samuel made no answer.

"It's simply a dirty filch. There just are skunks like him too big to handle."

"You're being paid liberally," offered Samuel.

"Shut up!" roared McIntyre suddenly. "I want the privilege of talking." He walked to the door and looked out across the land, the sunny, steaming pasturage that began almost at his feet and ended with the gray-green of the distant mountains. When he turned around his mouth was trembling.

"Do you fellows love Wall Street?" he said hoarsely, "or wherever you do your dirty scheming——" He paused. "I suppose you do. No critter gets so low that he doesn't sort of love the place he's worked, where he's sweated out the best he's had in him."

Samuel watched him awkwardly. McIntyre wiped his forehead with a huge blue handkerchief, and continued:

"I reckon this rotten old devil had to have another million. I reckon we're just a few of the poor he's blotted out to buy a couple more carriages or something." He waved his hand toward the door. "I built a house out there when I was seventeen, with these two hands. I took a wife there at twenty-one, added two wings, and with four mangy steers I started out. Forty summers I've saw the sun come up over those mountains and drop down red as blood in the evening, before the heat drifted off and the stars came out. I been happy in that house. My boy was born there and he died there, late one spring, in the hottest part of an afternoon like this. Then the wife and I lived there alone like we'd lived before, and sort of tried to have a home, after all, not a real home but nigh it—cause the boy always seemed around close, somehow, and we expected a lot of nights to see him runnin' up the path to supper." His voice was shaking so he could hardly speak and he turned again to the door, his gray eyes contracted.

"That's my land out there," he said, stretching out his arm, "my land, by God— It's all I got in the world—and ever wanted." He dashed his sleeve across his face, and his tone changed as he turned slowly and faced Samuel. "But I suppose it's got to go when they want it—it's got to go."

Samuel had to talk. He felt that in a minute more he would lose his head. So he began, as level-voiced as he could—in the sort of tone he saved for disagreeable duties.

"It's business, Mr. McIntyre," he said. "It's inside the law. Perhaps we couldn't have bought out two or three of you at any price, but most of you did have a price. Progress demands some things——"

Never had he felt so inadequate, and it was with the greatest relief that he heard hoof-beats a few hundred yards away.

But at his words the grief in McIntyre's eyes had changed to fury.

"You and your dirty gang of crooks!" he cried. "Not one of you has got an honest love for anything on God's earth! You're a herd of money-swine!"

Samuel rose and McIntyre took a step toward him.

"You long-winded dude. You got our land—take that for Peter Carhart!"

He swung from the shoulder quick as lightning and down went Samuel in a heap. Dimly he heard steps in the doorway and knew that some one was holding McIntyre, but there was no need. The rancher had sunk down in his chair, and dropped his head in his hands.

Samuel's brain was whirring. He realized that the fourth fist had hit him, and a great flood of emotion cried out that the law that had inexorably ruled his life was in motion again. In a half-daze he got up and strode from the room.

The next ten minutes were perhaps the hardest of his life. People talk of the courage of convictions, but in actual life a man's duty to his family may make a rigid corpse seem a selfish indulgence of his own righteousness. Samuel thought mostly of his family, yet he never really wavered. That jolt had brought him to.

When he came back in the room there were a log of worried faces waiting for him, but he didn't waste any time explaining.

"Gentlemen," he said, "Mr. McIntyre has been kind enough to convince me that in this matter you are absolutely right and the Peter Carhart interests absolutely wrong. As far as I am concerned you can keep your ranches to the rest of your days."

He pushed his way through an astounded gathering, and within a half-hour he had sent two telegrams that staggered the operator into complete unfitness for business; one was to Hamil in San Antonio; one was to Peter Carhart in New York.

Samuel didn't sleep much that night. He knew that for the first time in his business career he had made a dismal, miserable failure. But some instinct in him, stronger than will, deeper than training, had forced him to do what would probably end his ambitions and his happiness. But it was done and it never occurred to him that he could have acted otherwise.

Next morning two telegrams were waiting for him. The first was from Hamil. It contained three words:

"You blamed idiot!"

The second was from New York:

"Deal off come to New York immediately Carhart."

Within a week things had happened. Hamil quarrelled furiously and violently defended his scheme. He was summoned to New York and spent a bad half-hour on the carpet in Peter Carhart's office. He broke with the Carhart interests in July, and in August Samuel Meredith, at thirty-five years old, was, to all intents, made Carhart's partner. The fourth fist had done its work.

I suppose that there's a caddish streak in every man that runs crosswise across his character and disposition and general outlook. With some men it's secret and we never know it's there until they strike us in the dark one night. But Samuel's showed when it was in action, and the sight of it made people see red. He was rather lucky in that, because every time his little devil came up it met a reception that sent it scurrying down below in a sickly, feeble condition. It was the same devil, the same streak that made him order Gilly's friends off the bed, that made him go inside Marjorie's house.

If you could run your hand along Samuel Meredith's jaw you'd feel a lump. He admits he's never been sure which fist left it there, but he wouldn't lose it for anything. He says there's no cad like an old cad, and that sometimes just before making a decision, it's a great help to stroke his chin. The reporters call it a nervous characteristic, but it's not that. It's so he can feel again the gorgeous clarity, the lightning sanity of those four fists.

Actress Mildred Davis

READING BREAK!!!

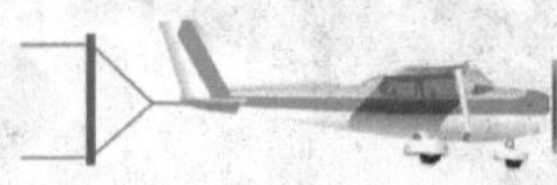

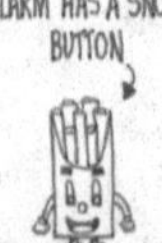

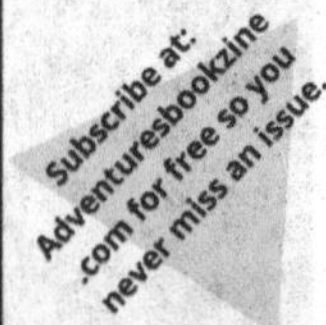

SUDOKU

(MEDIUM DIFFICULTY; ANSWERS IN BACK OF BOOK)

							5	8
7							4	
1				8			7	
					3	9		
	3			5				2
4				7	6			
	8	6				4		
	9							
		4	1			3		

> Freedom is not a reward for compliance.
> -Unknown

Explore the Books at

flick-it-books.com

Small Independant Publishing House

R.RIVETER

AMERICAN ★ HANDMADE

Want your short story published in *Adventures*?

Email your entire story, with "Submission" in Subject to: OffBeatReads@pm.me

Lucifer & the Child by Ethel Mannin

FROM ITS FIRST SENTENCE ("ON THE 18th March, 1618, Margaret and Philippa Flower were burnt at the stake…for witchcraft.") *Lucifer and the Child* (1945) sets up what ostensibly will be a novel of witchcraft, black magic and the evolution of a child cursed by her afflicted past. The title is deceptive. True there is a man with horns, there is a child, there is even a bona fide witch, but it is so much more than bubbling cauldrons, sinister incantations, a mysterious and seductive man and the child entranced with his charismatic personality and all things forbidden to her by conservative often indifferent foster parents.

Ethel Mannin explores ethics, morality, faith, love, the inherent magic of the natural world and the ultimate mystery of devotion -- both earthly and spiritual -- and does so with stark frankness, uncensored sexuality and near mockery of convention. Jenny Flower meets the man she will come to nickname Lucifer – for he is so much like the Angel of Light fallen from grace – when she is seven years old in 1930. We follow her first meeting of the mysterious man and subsequent meetings, each taking place on one of the four witch's sabbaths over the next seven years. Her introduction takes place in a forest and like Adam and Eve after eating the forbidden fruit Jenny has hers eyes opened to a natural world of splendor and mystery. Her first act of daring, her first lesson of this new world, involves intently staring at a toad in attempt to strike it dead. Much to her surprise she is entranced by the toad, an animal she never actually looked at before. While staring supposedly with true hate she cannot bring herself to kill it and she spares its life. But the more time she spends with Lucifer the less kind she will be with her experiments.

Later she is drawn to the hovel of Mrs. Beadle, the town crone often shunned for being a witch herself. Mrs. Beadle sees in Jenny her younger self and nonchalantly begins to impart some of her arcane knowledge to the girl. They start with astrology, the names of the fallen angels, Lucifer and his followers whose names have become synonymous with demonology, and the Chart of the Characters of Evil Spirits. It is an education in complete reversal of her school and church learning. Soon Jenny and Mrs. Beadle are practicing spells together. The crone is always standing over her bubbling pot stirring up ingredients for unctions, philters and potions, while simultaneously feeding Jenny's insatiable curiosity for forgotten magic and unnameable rites.

Illustrated front board of Swan River Press reissue

Marian Drew, a schoolteacher, begins to notice a change in Jenny. She is concerned about her desire to run off to Mrs. Beadle's, her derision of other schoolchildren. Jenny's constant talk of the man with the horns is alarming and her eager anticipation of his return on Candlemas or Lammas or Halloween, which fatefully happens to be Jenny's birthday, inspire Miss Drew on a mission to save Jenny from both Mrs. Beadle's baleful influence and the friendship of the mysterious man -- if indeed he even exists.

Along the way we also meet Jenny's only real friend who she thinks is her aunt. Actually Nell Flower is Jenny's real mother who gave her up to her sister to raise. Nell is a free spirit, glamorous, unconventional who can't be bothered with the responsibility of being a mother. She doesn't even know the identity of Jenny's father nor does she care. She lives for her freedom, her life as a barmaid, her elaborate head-turning wardrobe, her cosmetics. Jenny loves her. Despite Nell's surface friendship and her referring to Jenny as a brat she is devoted and protective of her daughter. However, she never wants Jenny to know that she is her real mother. In an interesting twist of the plot Nell will also try to save Jenny from Mrs. Beadle and sever what the crone and the mysterious man assure is Jenny's cursed past.

Finally there are Jenny's foster parents -- aunt Ivy and her husband Joe. Jenny has two brothers, too, in this sadly loveless household. Ivy loses her patience with her willful but friendless child and never seems able to keep her disciplined. She resorts to screaming, yelling threats, and on occasion beating. Joe, the indifferent father, is also violent. Jenny, however, is immune to punishment of any sort. She seems to be a child of the devil himself. Yet Ivy doesn't seem too worried for Jenny or her slow transformation from a misbehaving yet innocent girl to a worldly, cynical and vengeful teen.

Mannin's novel is a wondrous book that raises intriguing questions about faith and love. Miss Drew acts the voice of reason and common sense who argues with Lucifer, a literal Devil's advocate. She and Jenny are forced to reckon with the inextricably connected dichotomies of good and evil. One cannot believe in God without also believing in the devil, Lucifer constantly reminds the woman and the girl. Are not miracles the scared version of black magic? If you believe in Jesus raising the dead, changing water into wine and walking on water how can you easily dismiss the ability to communicate with dead spirits, making love potions, and flying through the air at midnight? Angels cannot exist without devils. Light is the forever companion of dark. What you truly believe in, your faith, shapes who you are for life. And that faith ultimately makes what you believe in exist.

The writing often transcends a deceptively straightforward didactic style to achieve true poetry, especially in the sequences when Mannin celebrates the creatures of the forest, the flowers of a spring afternoon, the wild fury of the ocean where Lucifer who says he is a merchant seaman spends much of his life. The words carry a rhythm like beautifully constructed verses, and her frequent repetition of phrases like "the ice-green, ice-cold waters of the Gulf of Finland' are like the chanting of Mrs. Beadle over her pot of mystery potions. Mannin calls on myth and legend when describing "the bells of lost Atlantis ringing under the sea." She resorts to ancient archaic spelling like magicke and is compelled to quote Marlowe's Faustus. Miss Drew cannot help but recall the line "Tis magic, a magic that hath ravished me" when she discovers that she has been willfully seduced by Lucifer despite all her attempts to resist him and draw him away from Jenny. In uttering that line Marian comes to realize that she welcomed the seduction and longs to see him again with a fervor almost as powerful as Jenny's rabid devotion.

The conflict comes in the fight for Lucifer's attention. Jenny grows ever jealous of his closeness to Marian Drew. Marian slowly realizes she cannot save Jenny and must resort to bargaining. When she asks Lucifer to promise to leave Jenny alone for seven years she cannot foresee that promise will set in motion a fateful plot that will be the undoing for the trio.

Lucifer and the Child uses a supernatural motif that makes one recognize that magic is ever present in the world. That the wonders of the natural world are as hypnotic as any spell or incantation chanted in a candlelit kitchen. And yet there is danger in that attractiveness and seduction of the unknown. In the hands of Mannin's contemporary writers of supernatural and horror this novel might have become a lurid piece filled with gruesome scenes and nightmarish apparitions. But as Mannin would have it the horror is more subtle, heartwrenching rather than blood spilling. We watch the irrevocable destruction of a soul, the dissolution of friendships, and a fulfillment of what amounts to a fatalistic worldview.

After being out of print for decades Lucifer and the Child has been reissued. The adventurous Swan River Press based in Dublin, mostly devoted to reprinting forgotten works by Irish writers of supernatural and fantasy fiction, has published a gorgeous new volume of Ethel Mannin's cult masterpiece. Only available for purchase directly from the publisher ordering info can be found on their website here. The book includes a well researched foreword by scholar Rosanne Rabinowitz which sheds light on the novel's re-discovery and Ethel Mannin's fascinating life as an iconoclast and counterculture figure.

JF Norris is a part time writer and bookseller. In 1999 he started an internet bookselling business from which his blog gets its name. The blog is solely devoted to of out-of-print & vintage crime, supernatural, adventure and other genre fiction. JF has also written critical essays and reviews on detective & supernatural fiction for fanzines, internet sites, and small press publishers. The Blog: prettysinister.blogspot.com

FORWARD

In it's time, The Picture of Dorian Gray by Oscar Wilde was considered controversial. Many were shocked at what was perceived as a celebration of immorality. There were others, such as author Arthur Conan Doyle, who believed Gray's tale was a moral one—and in that moral tale is the decline of a man who eventually suffers the punishments of his sins.

Within Oscar Wilde's story, Dorian Gray receives a gift from Lord Henry Wotton. The gift is a French book, yellow in color, so that it could be easily recognized by others who knew of the book. It is widely believed the book to which Wilde was referring to was *A Rebours*.

In Richard Ellmann's biography of Oscar Wilde, we find out that *A Rebours* had become the author, "Bible and bedside book". So it does stand to reason that Oscar Wilde would find a way to also include this book in Dorian Gray's narrative—especially considering that he needed something to spur Dorian Gray forward toward his downfall.

For you bibliophiles, what follows is for your enjoyment as well as the pure nostalgia of it: the yellow book that greatly influenced Dorian Gray: *A Rebourse.*

A REBOURS

(AGAINST THE GRAIN)

BY JORIS-KARL HUYSMANS
(TRANSLATED BY GROVES & MICHAUX)

PREFACE

(WRITTEN BY THE AUTHOR TWENTY YEARS AFTER THE BOOK.)

I SUPPOSE ALL MEN OF LETTERS ARE LIKE MYSELF IN THIS, THAT THEY NEVER reread their works once they have appeared. Nothing in fact is more disenchanting, more painful than examine one's phrases again after an interval of years. They have been in bottle, so to speak, and form a deposit at the bottom of the book; and, most times, volumes are not like wines which improve with age; once clarified in the fullness of time, the chapters grow flat and their bouquet evaporates.

Such is the impression certain bottles stacked in the Against the Grain bin made upon me when I had to uncork them.

Now, sadly enough, I endeavour to recall, as I turn over the pages, what precise state of mind I could have been in at the time I wrote them.

Naturalism was then at full tide; but that school, which was destined to perform the never-to-be-forgotten good service of showing real personages in accurate surroundings, was condemned to go on repeating itself, marking time forever on the same spot.

It would allow, in theory at any rate, almost no exception; it was therefore bound to limit its range to the delineation of everyday existence, forced, under pretext of making its characters alive, to create beings as like as they could possibly be made to the general average of people. This ideal was, in its class, realized in a masterpiece which has been, far more than L'Assommoir, the type and paragon of Naturalism, viz. the Education Sentimentale of Gustave Flaubert. This book was for all of us, men of the Soirées de Médan, a veritable Bible; but it brought little grist to our mill. It was done and ended, a thing not to be begun again even by Flaubert himself. Consequently we found ourselves reduced in those days to tack about, to prowl round all the countryside by roads more or less thoroughly explored before.

Virtue, being, we are compelled to admit, an exception here below, was for that very reason barred from the Naturalistic author's scheme. Not possessing the orthodox Christian conception of the Temptation and Fall, we had no knowledge from what struggles and what tribulations it has arisen; the soul's heroism, triumphant over snares and pitfalls, was inappreciable by us. It would never have occurred to us to describe this combat, with its ups and downs, its feints and flank attacks, not to speak of its skilled auxiliaries arming themselves very often far from the individual against whom the Evil One's assault is directed, in the quiet of some remote Cloister; to us Virtue seemed the attribute of creatures devoid of intelligent curiosity or wanting in common sense—hardly a stimulating subject, in any case, to treat from the point of view of art. Remained the Vices; but here the area capable of cultivation was restricted. It was confined to the territories of the Seven Deadly Sins, and even of these seven, one only, that against the Sixth Commandment, was fairly accessible.

The rest had been cropped cruelly bare, and hardly a grape was left to pluck in those vineyards. Avarice, for instance, had been squeezed to the last drop of liquor by Balzac and Hello. Pride, Anger, Envy had played their parts in every publication of the Romantics, and as dramatic motifs had been so violently distorted by the abuse of stage exigencies that it would have called for a veritable genius to rejuvenate them in a book. As for Gluttony and Idleness, these seemed to lend themselves to realization rather in subsidiary characters, to be more suitable to supers than to leading actors or prima donnas in the novel of manners.

The truth is that Pride would have been the most magnificent of all sins to study, in its infernal ramifications of cruelty towards others and false humility, that Gluttony, towing in its wake Lust and Idleness, and Theft would have supplied subjects for surprising investigations, if only writers had examined these offences with the lamp and blowpipe of the Church and possessing Faith. But as a fact not one of us was qualified for the task. We were therefore driven to handle and re-handle the sin of all others most easily laid bare, Lust, in all its various manifestations; God knows we did our best, but this amusement was in the nature of things short-lived. Invent what one chose, the story could be summed up in half-a-dozen words, to wit, why did Monsieur So-and-So commit or not commit adultery with Madame This or That? If you wished to be distinguished and stand out as a writer of the most polite taste, you made the work of the flesh take place between a Marquise and a Count; if on the other hand, you wanted to pose as a popular author, a writer knowing what's what, you chose a lover from the slums and the first street girl to hand. Only the frame was different. High life, it appears to me, has carried the day at present in the reader's good graces, for I notice that for the moment he hardly cares to regale himself on plebeian or middle-class amours, but still continues to savour the scruples and hesitations of the Marquise on her way to meet her seducer at a dainty little flat, whose aspect changes according to the varying fashion in furniture. Will she fall? Will she not fall? This is called a study in Psychology. Well, I have no objection.

Nevertheless I must own that, if I happen to open a book and come upon this everlasting seduction and not less everlasting adultery, I make haste to shut it again, being in no sort of way anxious to know how the promised idyll will finish. Any volume that does not contain authenticated documents, any book that does not teach me something, loses all interest in my eyes.

At the date when Against the Grain was published, in 1884 that is to say, the state of things therefore was this: Naturalism was getting more and more out of breath by dint of turning the mill forever in the same round. The stock of observations that each writer had stored up by self scrutiny or study of his neighbours was getting exhausted. Zola, who was a first-rate scene-painter, got out of the difficulty by designing big, bold canvases more or less true to life; he suggested fairly well the illusion of movement and action; his heroes were devoid of soul, governed simply and solely by impulses and instincts, which greatly simplified the work of analysis. They moved about, carried out sundry summary activities, peopled the scene with tolerably convincing sketches of lay-figures that became the principal characters of his dramas. In this fashion he celebrated the Central Markets, and the big stores of Paris, the railways and mines of the country at large; and the human beings wandering lost amid these surroundings played no more than the part of utility men and supers therein. But Zola was Zola artist a trifle ponderous, but endowed with powerful lungs and massive fists.

The rest of us, less robust and concerned about a more subtle method and a truer art, were constrained to ask ourselves the question whether Naturalism was not marching up a blind alley and if we were not bound soon to knock up against an impassable wall.

To tell the truth, these reflections did not actually occur to me till much later. I was striving in vain to escape from a cul-de-sac in which I was suffocating, but I had no settled plan, and Against the Grain, which, by letting in fresh air, let me get away from a literature that had no door of escape, is a purely unpremeditated work, imagined without any preconceived ideas, without definite intentions for the future, without any predetermined plan whatever.

It had appeared to me at first in the light of a brief fantasy, under the form of an extravagant tale; I saw in it something like a pendant to À vau-l'eau transferred into another milieu; I pictured to myself a Monsieur Folantin, more cultured, more refined, more wealthy and who has discovered in artificiality a relief from the disgust inspired by the worries of life and the American habits of his time; I outlined him winging a swift flight to the land of dreams, seeking refuge in the illusion of extravagant fancies, living alone and aloof, remote from his own country, amid the association called up by memory of more cordial epochs, and less villainous surroundings.

The more I pondered over it, the more the subject grew and the more it seemed to demand long and patient researches. Each chapter became the extract of a speciality, the sublimate of a different art; I found it condensing into a "meat essence" of precious stones, of perfumes, of flowers, of literature religious and lay, of profane music and plainsong.

The strange thing was that, without having had an inkling of this at the beginning, I was led by the very nature of my task to study the Church under many aspects. It was in fact impossible to go back to the only really characteristic eras humanity has ever known, the Middle Ages that is, without realizing that She embraced everything, that art existed only in Her and by Her. Being outside the Faith, I looked upon Her with some suspicion, surprised at Her greatness and glory, asking myself how a Religion which seemed to me only made for children had been able to suggest such marvellous works.

I prowled a little round Her in a groping way, guessing more than I saw, reconstructing a whole for myself with the fragments I recovered in Museums and old books. And today as I skim, after more lengthy and more trustworthy investigations, the pages of Against the Grain, that deal with Catholicism and religious art, I note that that miniature panorama I then sketched on leaves of block-books, is accurate. What I depicted then was succinct, wanting elaboration, but it was veracious. I have confined myself subsequently to enlarging and developing my outline drawings. I might quite well sign my name at the present moment to the pages of Against the Grain relating to the Church, for they appear in very deed to have been written by a Catholic.

Yet I supposed myself far from Religion all the time! I did not dream that from Schopenhauer, whom I admired beyond all reason, to Ecclesiastes and the Book of Job was only a step. The premises as to Pessimism are identical, only when it comes to action, the Philosopher shirks away. I like his ideas on the horror of existence, on the stupidity of the world, on the harshness of fate; I like them just as well in the Holy Books. But Schopenhauer's observations end in nothing; he leaves you, so to say, in the lurch; his aphorisms, in fact, are but a hortus siccus of lifeless specimens. The Church for her part explains origins and causes, certifies results, offers remedies; she is not satisfied with giving you a spiritual consultation, she treats you and cures you, while the German quack, after clearly showing you that the complaint you suffer from is incurable, turns his back on you with a sardonic grin.

His Pessimism is no different from that of the Scriptures from which he borrowed it. He has said no more than Solomon or than Job, no more even than the Imitation, which long before his day summed up his whole philosophy in a sentence: "Verily it is a wretched thing to be alive on the earth!"

Looked at from a distance, these similarities and dissimilarities stand out clearly, but at that period, if I saw them at all, I paid no heed; the necessity of coming to a conclusion did not appeal to me; the road laid down by Schopenhauer was practicable and offered diversified views, I travelled contentedly along it, without a thought of where it led. In those days I had no real illumination as to debts to be paid, no apprehension of penalties to be exacted; the mysteries of the Catechism struck me as childish; like the mass of Catholics, indeed, I was entirely ignorant of my religion; I failed to realize that everything is mysterious, that we live only in mystery, that if chance existed, chance would be yet more mysterious than Providence. I could not admit the fact of pain inflicted by a God, I persuaded myself that Pessimism could act as the consoler of lofty souls.

What foolishness! Of all notions this had the smallest basis of experience, was the least of a "human document," use a phase dear to Naturalism. Never yet has Pessimism consoled either the sick of body or the afflicted of soul!

I smile when after so many years I reread the pages where these theories, determinedly false, are affirmed.

But what strikes me most forcibly in this perusal is another fact: all the romances I have written since Against the Grain are contained in embryo in that book. The successive chapters are nothing more nor less than the priming of the volumes that followed.

The chapter on the Latin Literature of the Decadence I have, if not developed, at any rate probed deeper into, when treating of the Liturgy in En Route and L'Oblat.

I shall now reprint it without any alteration save in connection with St. Ambrose, whose watery prose and turgid rhetoric I continue to dislike. I still think him what I called him then, a "tiresome Christian Cicero," but, in compensation, as a poet he is charming; his hymns and those of his school are among the finest the Church has preserved. I will add that the literature, of a rather special sort it is true, of the Hymnary might well have found a place in the reserved compartment of that chapter.

No more than in 1884 am I at the present moment enamoured of the Classical Latin of Maro and the "Chickpea," (Cicero); as in the days of Against the Grain, I prefer the language of the Vulgate to that of the Augustan Age, nay, even to that of the Decadent Period, more curious though it be with its gamey flavour and its discolourations as of over-high venison. The Church, which after disinfecting and rejuvenating it, created, to deal with an order of ideas hitherto unexpressed, a vocabulary of grandiloquent words and diminutives of exquisite tenderness, appears to me to have fashioned Herself a diction far superior to the dialect of Paganism, and Durtal still holds the same views on this point as did Des Esseintes.

The chapter on precious stones I have recapitulated in La Cathédrale, in the second case treating the matter from the point of view of the symbolism of gems. I have there given life to the dead stones of Against the Grain. Of course I do not deny that a fine emerald may be admired for the flashes that sparkle in the fire of its green depths, but, if we are ignorant of the idiom of symbols, is it not an unknown being, a stranger, a foreigner with whom no talk can be had and who has no word to say himself, because we do not understand his language? But he is surely something more and better than that.

Without admitting with an old writer of the sixteenth century, Estienne de Clave, that precious stones propagate their species, like human beings, with a seed disseminated in the womb of mother earth, we may truly say that they are minerals with a meaning, substances that talk—that in one word they are symbols. They have been regarded under this aspect from the remotest times and the tropology of gems is one branch of that Christian symbolism so absolutely forgotten by priests and laymen alike in our own day, and which I have endeavoured to reconstruct in its main features in my volume on the basilica of Chartres.

The chapter in Against the Grain is therefore only superficial, a flush-bezel setting, so to speak. It is not what it should be, a display ranging beyond the mere material stones, it is made up of caskets of jewels more or less well described, more or less artistically arranged in a showcase—but that is all, and that is not enough.

The painting of Gustave Moreau, the engravings of Luyken, the lithographs of Bresdin and Redon make the same impression on me now as then. I have no modification to make in the arrangement of the little collection.

As for the terrible Chapter VI, the number of which corresponds, without any preconceived purpose on my part, to the Commandment it offends against, as also for some portions of Chapter IX that may be classed with it, I should obviously not write them in the same vein again. They should at least have been accounted for, in a more studious spirit, by that diabolic perversity of the will which affects, especially in matters of sensual aberration, the exhausted brains of sick folk. It would seem, in fact, that nervous invalids expose fissures in the soul's envelope whereby the Spirit of Evil effects an entrance. But this is a riddle that remains unsolved; the word hysteria explains nothing; it may suffice to define a material condition, to mark invincible disturbances of the senses, it does not account for the spiritual consequences attached to the phenomena and, more particularly, the sins of dissimulation and falsehood that are almost always engrafted on them. What are the details and attendant circumstances of this malady of sinfulness, in what degree is the responsibility diminished of the individual whose soul is attacked by a sort of demoniac possession that takes root in the disorganization of his unhappy body? None can tell: on this point Medicine talks mere folly, Theology holds her peace.

In default of a solution which manifestly he could not supply, Des Esseintes should have viewed the question from the point of view of sinfulness and expressed at any rate some regret. He refrained from abusing himself, and he did wrong; but then, though educated by the Jesuits, whose panegyrist he is, and a more ardent one than Durtal—he had grown subsequently so recalcitrant to the Divine constraints, so obstinately resolved to wallow in the mire of his carnal appetites!

In any case, these chapters seem to be markstakes unconsciously planted to indicate the road Là-Bas was to follow. It is noteworthy moreover that Des Esseintes' library contained a certain number of old books of magic and that the ideas expressed in Chapter VII of Against the Grain on sacrilege are the hooks on which to hang a subsequent volume treating the subject more thoroughly.

As for this book Là-Bas, which frightened so many people, neither should I write it, if I had to do the thing again, in the same manner, now I am become a Catholic once more. There is no doubt indeed that the wicked and sensual side therein developed is reprehensible; but at the same time I declare I have glazed over things, I have said nothing of the worst; the documents it embodies are in comparison with those I have omitted, but which I have among my papers, very insipid sweetmeats, very tasteless titbits.

I believe, nevertheless, that in spite of its cerebral aberrations and its abdominal follies, the work, by mere virtue of the subject it laid bare, has done good service. It has recalled attention to the wiles of the Evil One, who had succeeded in getting men to deny his existence; it has been the starting-point of all the studies, revived of late years, on the never-changing procedure of Satanism; it has helped, by exposing them, to put an end to the odious practices of sorcery; it had taken sides, in fact, and fought a very strenuous fight for the Church against the Devil,

To come back to Against the Grain, of which this book is only a succedaneum, I may repeat in connection with the flower chapter what I have already stated with regard to precious stones.

Against the Grain considers them only from the point of view of shapes or colours, in no wise from that of the significations they disclose; Des Esseintes chose only rare orchids, strange blossoms, but without a tongue. It is fair to add that he would have found it hard to give speech in the book to a flora attacked by aphasia, a dumb flora, for the symbolic language of plants died with the Middle Ages, and the vegetable creoles cherished by Des Esseintes were unknown to the allegorists of those days.

The counterpart of this flower study I have written since in La Cathédrale, when dealing with that liturgical horticulture which has suggested such quaint pages in the works of St. Hildegard, St. Meliton and St. Eucher.

It is different with the question of odours, the mystic emblems of which I have expounded in the same book.

Des Esseintes had concerned himself only with lay perfumes, simple scents or extracts, and profane perfumes, compound essences or bouquets.

He might have extended his experiments to the aromas of the Church, incense, myrrh and that strange Thymiama mentioned in the Bible and which is still noted in the ritual books as proper to be burned, together with incense, under the mouths of Church bells when they are baptised, after the Bishop has washed them with holy water and made the sign of the cross on them with the Holy Chrism and the oil of the sick. But this fragrant essence seems forgotten even by the Church, and I imagine a curé would be not a little startled if asked for Thymiama.

Yet the recipe is given in Exodus. The Thymiama was compounded of styrax, galbanum, incense and onycha, and this last ingredient would seem to be nothing else but the operculum of a certain shell of the tribe of the "purples" which is dredged up in the Indian seas.

Now it is difficult, not to say impossible, given the insufficient description of this shell and the locality it comes from, to prepare an authentic Thymiama. This is a pity, for had it been otherwise, this lost perfume would have surely called up before Des Esseintes' imagination sumptuous pictures of the religious festivals and liturgical rites of Eastern lands.

As for the chapters on contemporary literature, lay and clerical, they still, in my opinion, remain, as does that on Latin literature, well founded. That dealing with profane writing has helped to set in due relief several poets very little known to the public of that day, Corbière, Mallarmé, Verlaine. I have nothing to retract in what I wrote nineteen years ago; I still keep my admiration for these authors; the admiration I professed for Verlaine has even increased. Arthur Rimbaud and Jules Laforgue would have well deserved to figure in Des Esseintes' florilegium, but at that date they had not yet printed anything and it was only long after that their works saw the light.

I do not anticipate, on the other hand, that I shall ever come to appreciate the modern religious authors scourged in Against the Grain. Nothing will ever change my view that the criticism of the late lamented Nettement is idiotic and that Mme. Augustin Craven and Mlle. Eugénie de Guérin are bluestockings of a very lymphatic sort and pious pedants of a very barren kind. Their juleps strike me as insipid; Des Esseintes has passed his taste for spices on to Durtal, and I think they would come to a good understanding together, both of them, at the present moment, to prepare, in lieu of these emulsions, an essence savoury with the stimulating condiment of art.

Nor have I changed my mind about the literature of the confraternity of the Poujoulats and Genoudes, but I should be less severe nowadays on the Père Chocarne, named among a miscellaneous lot of pious scribblers, for he has at any rate composed some pithy pages on Mysticism in his introduction to the works of Saint Jean de la Croix; in the same way I should deal more gently with De Montalembert who, despite his lack of talent, has bestowed on the world a work, incoherent indeed and ill-arranged, but still moving, on the monastic orders. Above all I should not now describe the visions of Angèle de Foligno as silly, insipid stuff; the exact contrary is the truth, but I must plead in my excuse that I had then read them only in Hello's translation. Now the latter was possessed with a mania for pruning, sugaring, softening down the mystics for fear of offending the mock modesty of Catholic readers. He has set under the press a work, strong and full of sap, to extract therefrom only a vapid and colourless juice, feebly warmed up again in a pipkin over the poor night-light of his style.

So much being allowed, that as a translator Hello showed himself a mollycoddle and a pious fraud, it is only fair to add that when he was working on original matter he was an originator of fresh ideas, a sagacious commentator, an analyst of true power. He was indeed, among the writers of his type, the only thinker; I came to the support of Aurévilly in commending the work of this writer, so incomplete, but so interesting, and Against the Grain has, I think, had some share in securing what little success his best book, L'Homme, won after his death.

The conclusion arrived at in this chapter on modern ecclesiastical literature was that among the geldings of religious art, there was only one stallion, to wit Barbey d'Aurévilly; and this opinion remains absolutely and entirely accurate. He was the one and only artist, in the proper sense of the word, that Catholicism produced at that period; he was a great prose stylist, an admirable novelist whose boldness set all beadledom screaming, enraged by the explosive vehemence of his phraseology.

To conclude the list, if ever chapter can be considered the starting point of other books, it is surely the one on plainchant which I afterwards amplified in all my publications, in En Route and above in L'Oblat.

As result of this brief review of each of the special articles exhibited in the showcases of Against the Grain the conclusion is forced upon us—the book was priming for my Catholic propaganda, which is implicit in it in its entirety, though in embryo.

Indeed the misunderstanding and stupidity of sundry pedants and agitated members of the priesthood strike me, yet once again, as unfathomable. Year after year they clamoured for the destruction of the book, the copyright of which, by the by, I do not own, without ever realizing that the mystic volumes that came after it are incomprehensible without being as it is, I reiterate the statement, the root from which they all sprang. Besides this, how is it possible to appreciate the work of an author in its entirety, if it is not taken from its first beginnings and followed up step by step; above all, how is it possible to realize the progress of God's Grace in a soul, if the traces of its passage are neglected, if the first tokens left by its presence are effaced? One thing at any rate is certain, that Against the Grain marked a definite rupture with its predecessors, with Les Sœurs Vatard, En Ménage, À vau-l'eau, that with it I entered on a path the goal of which I did not so much as suspect.

More sagacious than the Catholics, Zola saw this clearly. I remember how, after the first appearance of À Rebours, I went to spend a few days at Médan. One afternoon when we were out walking, the two of us, in the country, he stopped suddenly, and his face grown dark, reproached me for having written the book, declaring I was dealing a terrible blow'at Naturalism, that I was leading the school astray, that, into the bargain, I was burning my ships with such a book, inasmuch as no class of literature was possible of this sort, where a single volume exhausted the subject; finally, as a friend—he was the best of good fellows—he urged me to return to the beaten track, to put myself in harness and write a study of manners.

I listened to what he said, thinking that he was at one and the same time right and wrong—right, when he accused me of undermining Naturalism and entirely blocking my own road; wrong, in this sense that the novel as he conceived it seemed to me moribund, worn to a shadow by the wearisome repetitions that, whether he liked it or no, possessed no interest for me.

There were many things Zola could not understand; in the first place, the craving I felt to open the windows, to escape from surroundings that were stifling me; secondly, the desire that filled me to shake off preconceived ideas, to break the limitations of the novel, to introduce into it art, science, history; in a word not to use this form of literature except as a frame in which to put more serious kinds of work. For my part, the thing that seemed to me most indispensable at that period was to do away with the traditional plot of intrigue, even to eliminate love and woman altogether, to concentrate the ray of light on a single character, to strike out a new line at any price.

Zola vouchsafed no answer to the arguments by which I endeavoured to convince him, but went on repeating over and over again the one phrase:—"I cannot allow that a man may change his ways of working and his view of art; I cannot allow that he may burn what he once adored."

Well, well! has he not too played the part of the good Sicambrian? He has, as a matter of fact, if not modified his methods of composition and writing, at least varied his manner of conceiving humanity and explaining life. After the black pessimism of his first books, have we not had, under colour of socialism, the self-satisfied optimism of his latest productions?

It must be freely confessed that nobody ever showed less comprehension of the soul than the "Naturalists" who undertook the task of investigating it. They saw existence all of a piece; they would have nothing to do with it except as manifested under probable conditions. But I have learned since by experience to know that the improbable is not always, in this world, exceptional, that the adventures of Rocambole sometimes as true to nature as those of Gervaise and Coupeau.

But the mere thought that Des Esseintes might be as truly drawn as the dramatis personae of his own novels disconcerted and came near to angering Zola.

So far, in these few pages of introduction, I have spoken of Against the Grain mainly from the point of view of literature and art. Now I must discuss it from that of God's Grace, show how large a share the unconscious, the workings of a soul ignorant of its own tendencies, may often have in the production of a book.

The definite set of Against the Grain towards Catholicism, manifest and clearly-marked as it is, remains, I confess, an insoluble problem to me.

I was not brought up in the schools of any religious order, but just in a Lycée. I was never a pious boy, and the influences of childish associations, of first Communion, of religious teaching, which often loom so large in conversion, never had any effect on me. What still further complicates the difficulty and defies analysis is this: in the days when I wrote Against the Grain, I never set foot in a church, I did not know a single Catholic who regularly performed his religious duties, I had not a single priest among my acquaintance; I felt no Divine impulse drawing me towards the Church, I lived calmly and comfortably in my own style; it seemed to me perfectly natural to satisfy the calls of my sensual appetites, and the thought never so much as entered my head that that sort of amusement was forbidden.

Against the Grain appeared in 1884, and I set off to be converted at a Trappist House in 1892; nearly eight years had elapsed before the seeds of the book had germinated. Give two years, or even three, of the working of

Grace—a working slow and secret, only occasionally visible; there would still remain five years at least during which I can remember having felt no Christian stirrings at all, no remorse for the life I was leading, no wish to alter it. Why, by what impulse, have I been incited to take a road at that time shrouded in darkness from my view? I am utterly unable to say; nothing, save perhaps an ancestry not unconnected with Béguinages and Religious Houses and the prayers of a very devout Dutch family, which however I knew hardly anything of, will account for the purely unconscious unction of the concluding cry, the pious appeal of the last page of Against the Grain.

Yes, I am quite aware, there are people of very sturdy fibre who trace out plans, organize beforehand itineraries of existence and follow them; it is even to be understood, if I am not mistaken, that by force of will any end may be reached. I can quite believe it, but for me, I confess, I have never been either tenacious of purpose as a man or worldly wise as an author. My life and my writings have something of passive receptivity about them, some unknown element, some trace of direction from outside myself which cannot be questioned.

Providence was merciful to me and the Virgin kind. I confined myself simply to not resisting them when they gave token of their purposes; I merely obeyed; I was led by what they call extraordinary ways. If any man can have the certainty of the worthless thing he would be without God's help, it is I.

Persons who do not belong to the Faith will object that, with such ideas, one is like to end in fatalism and the negation of all scientific psychology.

Not so, for Faith in Our Lord is not fatalism. Free will remains free. I could, if I chose, continue to yield to the temptations, of the senses and stay on at Paris, instead of going to suffer tribulations at a Trappist Monastery. God doubtless would not have insisted; but, while certifying that the will is intact, we must nevertheless allow that the Saviour has much to do in the matter, that he harasses the sinner, tracks him down, shadows him, to use a forcible phrase of the police; but I say again, one can, at one's own risk and peril, reject his offices.

As to Psychology, the thing is otherwise. If we regard it, as I am doing, from the point of view of a conversion, it is, in its preliminaries, impossible to unravel; certain points tangible, but the rest, no; the subterranean workings of the soul are beyond our ken. There was no doubt at the date when I was writing Against the Grain, a shifting of the soil, a delving of the earth, to lay the foundations, of which I was all unconscious. God was digging to lay His wire, and he was at work only in the darkness of the soul, in the night. Nothing was visible on the surface; it was only years after that the spark began to run along the wires. Then I could feel my soul stirred by the shock; as yet it was neither very painful nor very distinct. The Church offices, mysticism, art were the vehicles and the means; it occurred mostly in churches, at Saint Séverin in particular, where I used to go out of curiosity, for lack of other things to do. I experienced as I watched the services only an inward tremor, the little shiver one feels on seeing, hearing or reading a fine work of art; but there was no definite movement, no positive impulse to come to a decision.

Only, little by little, I was shaking myself loose from my shell of impurity; I was beginning to have a disgust of myself, but at the same time I kicked against the articles of the Faith. The objections I raised in my own mind seemed irresistible; and lo one fine morning when I woke they were solved, I never knew how. I prayed for the first time, and the catastrophe was over.

For such as do not believe in the Grace of God, all this seems folly. For those who have experienced its effects, no surprise is possible; or, if surprise there were, it could continue only over the period of incubation, the period when one sees nothing and notices nothing, the period of the clearing of the ground and laying of the foundations of which one never had even a suspicion.

I can understand, in fact, up to a certain point what befell between the year 1891 and the year 1895, between Là-Bas and En Route, nothing at all between the year 1884 and the year 1891, between Against the Grain and Là-Bas.

If I failed to understand them myself, a fortiori others could not understand the impulses that moved Des Esseintes. Against the Grain fell like an aerolite into the literary fairground, to be received with mingled amazement and indignation; the Press completely lost their heads; such an outburst of incoherent ravings had never been known before. After first calling me a misanthropic impressionist and describing Des Esseintes as a maniac and lunatic of a complex sort, the Schoolmasters, with M.

Lemaître at their head, were furious that I had not eulogized Virgil, and declared in authoritative tones that the decadent exponents of the Latin tongue in the Middle Ages were simply "drivellers and idiots." Other would-be critics were kind enough to advise me that it would do me a world of good to be confined in a hydropathic establishment and suffer the discipline of cold douches. Then, the public lecturers took their turn to join in the abuse. At the Salle des Capucines, the high archon Sarcey was crying in bewilderment: "I am quite ready to be hanged if I understand one blessed word of the book." Finally, to make all complete, the serious reviews, such as the Revue des Deux Mondes, deputed their fugleman, M. Brunetière, to liken the novel to the vaudevilles of Waflard and Fulgence.

In all this hurly-burly, a single writer alone saw clear, Barbey d'Aurévilly, who, be it said, had no personal acquaintance with me. In an article in the Constitutionnel, bearing date July 28th, 1884, and which has been reprinted in his Le Roman Contemporain published in 1902, he wrote:

"After such a book, it only remains for the author to choose between the muzzle of a pistol or the foot of the cross."

The choice has been made.

J.-K. Huysmans.

(1903)

NOTICE

To judge by such family portraits as were preserved in the Château de Lourps, the race of the Floressas des Esseintes had been composed in olden days of stalwart veterans of the wars, grim knights with scowling visages. Imprisoned in the old-fashioned picture frames that seemed all too narrow to contain their broad shoulders, they glared out alarmingly at the spectator, who was equally impressed by the fixed stare in the eyes, the martial curl of the moustaches and the noble development of the chests encased in enormous steel cuirasses.

These were ancestral portraits; those representing subsequent generations were conspicuous by their absence. There was a gap in the series, a gap which one face alone served to fill and so connect the past and present—a mysterious, world-weary countenance. The features were heavy and drawn, the prominent cheekbones touched with a spot of rouge, the hair plastered to the head and entwined with a string of pearls, the slender neck rising from amid the pleatings of a stiff ruff.

Already in this picture of one of the most intimate friends of the Duc d'Epernon and the Marquis d'O, the vitiation of an exhausted race, the excess of lymph in the blood, were plainly to be traced.

No doubt the gradual degeneration of this ancient house had followed a regular and unbroken course; the progressive effemination of the men had gone on continuously from bad to worse. Moreover, to complete the deteriorating effect of time, the Des Esseintes had for centuries been in the habit of intermarrying among themselves, thus wasting the small remains of their original vigour and energy.

Sole surviving descendant of this family, once so numerous that it covered nearly all the domains of the Ile-de-France and of La Brie, was the Duc Jean des Esseintes, a frail young man of thirty, anaemic and nervous, with hollow cheeks, eyes of a cold, steely blue, a small but still straight nose, and long, slender hands.

By a curious accident of heredity, this last scion of a race bore a strong resemblance to the far-off ancestor, the mignon of Princes, from whom he had got the pointed beard of the very palest possible blonde and the ambiguous look of the eyes, at once languid and energetic in expression, which marked the portrait.

His childhood had been beset with perils. Threatened with scrofulous affections, worn out with persistent attacks of fever, he had nevertheless successfully weathered the breakers of puberty, after which critical period his nerves had recovered the mastery, vanquished the languors and depressions of chlorosis and permitted the constitution to reach its full and complete development.

The mother, a tall, silent, white-faced woman, died of general debility; then the father succumbed to a vague and mysterious malady. At the time Des Esseintes was approaching his seventeenth birthday.

The only recollection he retained of his parents was one of fear rather than of anything resembling gratitude or affection. His father, who generally resided in Paris, was almost a total stranger; his mother he only remembered as a chronic invalid, who never left the precincts of a shuttered bedroom in the Château de Lourps. It was only on rare occasions that husband and wife met, and of these meetings all he recalled was the drab, colourless dullness—his father and mother seated on either side of a table lighted only by a deeply shaded lamp, for the Duchess could not endure light and noise without suffering from nervous attacks. In the semidarkness, they would exchange two or three sentences at most; then the Duke would slip away with a yawn and take his departure by the first available train.

At the Jesuits' College to which Jean was sent to be educated, his life proved pleasanter and less trying. The Fathers made much of the lad, whose intelligence amazed them; yet, in spite of all their efforts, they entirely failed to induce him to pursue any definite and disciplined course of study. He devoted himself eagerly to certain tasks, acquired a precocious mastery of the Latin tongue; but on the other hand, he was absolutely incapable of construing three words of Greek, displayed no aptitude whatever for living languages and showed himself a perfect fool directly any attempt was made to teach him the merest rudiments of the physical sciences.

His family pretty much washed their hands of him; occasionally his father would pay him a visit at the College, but, "Good day, good evening, be a good boy and work hard," was about all he ever said to him. His summer holidays he used to spend at the Château de Lourps, where his presence quite failed to rouse his mother from her reveries; she hardly seemed to see him or, if she did, would gaze at him for a few moments with a painful smile, then sink back again into the artificial night in which the heavy curtains drawn across the windows wrapped the apartment.

The domestics were old and tiresome. The boy, left to himself, would turn over the books in the library on wet days, or on fine afternoons take long walks in the country.

It was his great delight to make his way down into the valley to Jutigny, a village standing at the foot of the hills—a little cluster of cottages with thatched roofs tufted with moss. He would lie out in the meadows under the lee of the tall hayricks, listening to the dull rumble of the water-mills, filling his lungs with the fresh air of the Voulzie. Sometimes he would wander as far as the peat-workings, to the hamlet of Longueville with its hovels painted green and black; at another time climb the windswept hills and gaze out over the vast prospect. There he had below him on one side the valley of the Seine, losing itself in immensity and melting into the blue haze of the far distance; on the other, high on the horizon line, the churches and Castle keep of Provins that seemed to shake and shiver in a sunlit dust-cloud.

He spent the hours in reading or dreaming, drinking his fill of solitude till nightfall. By dint of constantly brooding over the same thoughts, his mind gained concentration and his still undeveloped ideas ripened towards maturity. After each vacation, he went back more thoughtful and more stubborn to his masters. These changes did not escape their notice, clearsighted and shrewd, taught by their profession to sound the deepest depths of the human soul, they were well aware of the qualities and limitations of this alert but indocile intelligence; they realized that this pupil of theirs would never enhance the fame of the House, and as his family was wealthy and appeared to take little interest in his future, they soon abandoned all idea of directing his energies towards any of the lucrative careers open to the successful student. Though he was ready enough to enter with them into those theological disputations that attracted him by their subtleties and casuistical distinctions, they never even thought of preparing him for Holy Orders, for despite their efforts, his faith remained feeble. In the last resort, out of prudence and a fear of the unknown, they left him to himself to work at such studies as he chose and neglect the rest, unwilling to alienate this independent spirit by petty restrictions such as lay ushers are so fond of imposing.

So he lived a perfectly contented life, scarcely conscious of the priests' fatherly yoke. He pursued his Latin and French studies after his own fashion, and, albeit Theology found no place in the curriculum of his classes, he completed the apprenticeship to that science which he had begun at the Château de Lourps in the library of books left by his great great-uncle Dom Prosper, erstwhile Prior of the Canons Regular of Saint-Ruf.

The time, however, arrived when he must quit the Jesuit College; he was coming of age and would be master of his fortune; his cousin and guardian, the Comte de Montchevrel, gave him an account of his stewardship. The intimacy thus established was of short duration, for what point of contact could there be between the two, one of whom was an old man, the other a young one? Out of curiosity, lack of occupation, courtesy, Des Esseintes kept up relations with this family, and on several occasions, at his hotel in the Rue da la Chaise, endured evenings of a deadly dullness at which good ladies of his kin, as ancient as the hills, conversed about quarterings of nobility, heraldic scutcheons and ceremonial observances of years gone-by.

Even more than these worthy dowagers, the men, gathered round a whist-table, betrayed their hopeless nullity; these descendants of the old preux chevaliers, last scions of the feudal houses, appeared to Des Esseintes under the guise of a parcel of snuffling, grotesque greybeards, repeating ad nauseam a wearisome string of insipid outworn platitudes. Just as when you cut the stalk of a fern, you can see the mark of a lily, really a fleur-de-lis seemed to be the one and only impress left on the softened pulp that took the place of brains in these poor old heads.

The young man was filled with an ineffable pity for these mummies buried in their rococo catafalques; for these crusty dandies who lived with eyes forever fixed on a vaguely defined Land of Promise, an imaginary Canaan of good hope.

After a few experiences of the kind, he firmly resolved, in spite of all invitations and reproaches, never again to set foot in this society.

Thereupon he began to spend his days among young men of his own age and rank. Some of these, who had been brought up like himself at religious seminaries, had retained from this training a special character of their own. They attended church, communicated at Easter, frequented Catholic clubs and dropping their eyes in mock modesty, hid from each other, as if they had been crimes, their enterprises with women. For the most part they were witless fellows, with a sufficiency of good looks, but without a spark of mind or spirit; prime dunces who had exhausted their masters' patience, but had nevertheless fulfilled the latters' ambition to send out into the world obedient and pious sons of the Church.

Others, reared in the Colleges of the State or at Lycées, were more outspoken and less of hypocrites, but they were neither more interesting nor less narrow-minded. These were men of pleasure, devotees of operettas and races, playing lansquenet and baccarat, stalking fortunes on horses and cards—all the diversions in fact that empty-headed folks love. After a year's trial of this life an enormous weariness resulted; he was sick and tired of these people whose indulgences struck him as paltry and commonplace, carried out without discrimination, without excitement, without any real stirring of blood or stimulation of nerves.

Little by little, he left off frequenting their society, and approached the men of letters, with whom his mind must surely find more points of sympathy and feel itself more at ease in their company. It was a fresh disappointment; he was revolted by their spiteful and petty judgments, their conversation that was as hackneyed as a church-door, their nauseous discussions invariably appraising the merit of a work solely according to the number of editions and the amount of profit on the sales. At the same time, he discovered the apostles of freedom, the wiseacres of the bourgeoisie, the thinkers who clamoured for entire liberty—liberty to strangle the opinions of other people—to be a set of greedy, shameless hypocrites, whom as men of education he rated below the level of the village cobbler.

His scorn of humanity grew by what it fed on; he realized in fact that the world is mostly made up of solemn humbugs and silly idiots. There was no room for doubt; he could entertain no hope of discovering in another the same aspirations and the same antipathies, no hope of joining forces with a mind that, like his own, should find its satisfaction in a life of studious idleness; no hope of uniting a keen and doctrinaire spirit such as his, with that of a writer and a man of learning.

His nerves were on edge, he was ill at ease; disgusted at the triviality of the ideas exchanged and received, he was growing to be like the men Nicole speaks of, who are unhappy everywhere; he was continually being chafed almost beyond endurance by the patriotic and social exaggerations he read every morning in the papers, overrating the importance of the triumphs which an all-powerful public reserves always and under all circumstances for works equally devoid of ideas and of style.

Already he was dreaming of a refined Thebaïd, a desert hermitage combined with modern comfort, an ark on dry land and nicely warmed, whither he could fly for refuge from the incessant deluge of human folly.

One passion and one only, woman, might have arrested him in this universal disdain that was rising within him; but this too was exhausted. He had tasted the sweets of the flesh with the appetite of a sick man, an invalid debilitated and full of whimsies, whose palate quickly loses savour. In the days when he had consorted with the coarse and carnal-minded men of pleasure, he had participated like the rest in some of those unconventional supper parties where tipsy women bare their bosoms at dessert and beat the table with dishevelled heads; he had been a visitor likewise behind the scenes, had had relations with actresses and popular singers, had endured, added to the natural and innate folly of the sex, the frantic vanity of women of the stage; then he had kept mistresses already famous for their gallantry and contributed to swell the exchequer of those agencies that supply, for a price, highly dubious gratifications; last of all, sick and satiated with this pretence of pleasure, of these stale caresses that are all alike, he had plunged into the nether depths, hoping to revive his flagging passions by sheer force of contrast, thinking to stimulate his exhausted senses by the very foulness of the filth and beastliness of lowbred vice.

Try what he would, an overpowering sense of ennui weighed him down. But still he persisted, and presently had recourse to the perilous caresses of the experts in amorousness. But his health was unable to bear the strain and his nerves gave way; the back of the neck began to prick and the hands were tremulous—steady enough still when a heavy object had to be lifted, but uncertain if they held anything quite light such as a wineglass.

The physicians he consulted terrified him. It was indeed high time to change his way of life, to abandon these practices that were draining away his vitality. For a while, he led a quiet existence; but before long his passions awoke again and once more piped to arms. Like young girls who, under the stress of poverty, crave after highly spiced or even repulsive foods, he began to ponder and presently to practise abnormal indulgences, unnatural pleasures. This was the end; as if all possible delights of the flesh were exhausted, he felt sated, worn out with weariness; his senses fell into a lethargy, impotence was not far off.

So he found himself stranded, a lonely, disillusioned, sobered man, utterly and abominably tired, beseeching an end of it—an end the cowardice of his flesh forbade his winning.

His projects of finding some retreat far from his fellows, of burying himself in a hermit's cell, deadening, as they do the noise of the traffic for sick people by laying down straw in the streets, the inexorable turmoil of life, these projects more and more attracted him.

Besides, it was quite time to come to some definite decision for other reasons; he reckoned up the state of his finances and was appalled at the result. In reckless follies and riotous living generally, he had squandered the major part of his patrimony, while the balance, invested in land, brought him in only an insignificant revenue.

He determined to sell the Château de Lourps, which he never visited and where he would leave behind him no tender memories, no fond regrets; by this means he paid off all claims on the rest of his property, bought Government annuities and so secured himself an annual income of fifty thousand francs, while reserving, over and above, a round sum to buy and furnish the little house where he proposed to steep himself in a peace and quiet that should last his lifetime.

He searched the outer suburbs of the capital and presently discovered a cottage for sale, above Fontenay-aux-Roses, in a remote spot, far from all neighbours, near the Fort. His dream was fulfilled; in this district, still unspoilt by intruders from Paris, he was secure against all harassment; the very difficulties of communication—the place was wretchedly served by a grotesquely inefficient railway at the far end of the little town and a rustic tramway that went and came according to a self-appointed timetable— were a comfort to him.

As he thought over the new existence he meant to make for himself, he experienced a lively sense of relief, seeing himself just far enough withdrawn for the flood of Paris activity not to touch his retreat, yet near enough for the proximity of the metropolis to add a spice to his solitariness. Indeed, in view of the well-known fact that for a man to find himself in a situation where it is impossible for him to visit a particular spot is of itself quite enough to fill him with an instant wish to go there, he was really guarding himself, by thus not entirely barring the road, from any craving to renew intercourse with the world or any regret for having abandoned it.

He set the masons to work on the house he had bought; then suddenly one day, without telling a soul of his plans, he got rid of his furniture, dismissed his servants and disappeared without leaving any address with the concierge.

A REBOURS

CHAPTER I

MORE THAN TWO MONTHS SLIPPED BY BEFORE THE TIME CAME WHEN DES ESseintes found it feasible to immerse himself definitely in the peace and silence of his house at Fontenay; purchases of all kinds still kept him perambulating the Paris streets, tramping the town from end to end.

And yet, what endless inquiries had he not instituted, what lengthy lucubrations had he not indulged in, before finally entrusting his new home to the hands of the upholsterers! He had long been an expert in the right and wrong combinations and contrasts of tints. In other days, when he was still in the habit of inviting women to his house, he had fitted up a boudoir where, amid dainty carved furniture of the light-yellow camphorwood of Japan, under a sort of tent of pink Indian satin, the flesh tints borrowed a soft, warm glow from the artfully disposed lights sifting down through the rich material.

This room, where mirrors hung on every wall, reflecting backwards and forwards from one to another an infinite succession of pink boudoirs, had enjoyed a great renown among his various mistresses, who loved to bathe their nakedness in this flood of warm crimson amid the aromatic odours given off by the Oriental wood of the furniture.

But, quite apart from the miracles wrought by this artificial atmosphere in the way of transfusing, or so it seemed, a new blood into tired veins and freshening up complexions tarnished and worn by the habitual use of cosmetics and too frequent nights of love, he also tasted in his own person, in this luxurious retreat, special and peculiar satisfactions, pleasures exaggerated and rendered in a way more entrancing by the recollections of evil days overpast and vexations now outlived.

So, in a spirit of hate and scorn of his unhappy boyhood, he had suspended from the ceiling of the room we speak of, a little cage of silver wire in which a cricket was kept prisoner to chirp as they had been used to do in old days among the cinders in the great fireplaces at the Château de Lourps. Whenever he heard this sound, which he had so often listened to on many an evening of constraint and silence in his mother's chamber, all the miseries of a wretched and neglected childhood would come crowding before the eye of memory. At such times, roused from his reveries by the movements of the woman he was fondling mechanically at the moment and whose words and laughter interrupted his thoughts of the past and recalled him to reality, there as he lay in the pink boudoir, a sudden commotion would shake his soul, a longing for revenge on dreary hours endured in former times, a mad craving to befoul with base and carnal acts his recollections of bygone family life, an overmastering temptation to assuage his lustful propensities on the soft cushion of a woman's body, to drain the cup of sensuality to its last and bitterest dregs.

Other times again, when despondency weighed heavy on his spirit, when on rainy Autumn days he felt a sick aversion for everything—for the streets, for his own house, for the dingy mud-coloured sky, for the stony-looking clouds, he would fly to this refuge, set the cricket's cage swinging gently to and fro and watch its movement repeated ad infinitum in the surrounding mirrors, till at last his eyes would grow dazed and he seemed to see the cage itself at rest, but all the room tossing and turning, filling the whole apartment with a dizzy whirl of pink walls.

Then, in the days when Des Esseintes still deemed it incumbent on him to play the eccentric, he had also installed strange and elaborate dispositions of furniture and fittings, partitioning off his salon into a series of niches, each differently hung and carpeted, and each harmonizing in a subtle likeness by a more or less vague similarity of tints, gay or sombre, refined or barbaric, with the special character of the Latin and French books he loved. He would then settle himself down to read in whichever of these recesses displayed in its scheme of decoration the closest correspondence with the intimate essence of the particular book his caprice of the moment led him to peruse.

Last fancy of all, he had prepared a lofty hall in which to receive his tradesmen. These would march in, take seats side by side in a row of church stalls; then he would mount an imposing pulpit and preach them a sermon on dandyism, adjuring his bookmakers and tailors to conform with the most scrupulous fidelity to his commandments in the matter of cut and fashion, threatening them with the penalty of pecuniary excommunication if they failed to follow out to the letter the instructions embodied in his monitories and bulls.

He won a great reputation as an eccentric—a reputation he crowned by adopting a costume of black velvet worn with a gold-fringed waistcoat and sticking by way of cravat a bunch of Parma violets in the opening of a very low-necked shirt. Then he would invite parties of literary friends to dinners that set all the world talking. In one instance in particular, modelling the entertainment on a banquet of the eighteenth century, he had organized a funeral feast in celebration of the most unmentionable of minor personal calamities. The dining room was hung with black and looked out on a strangely metamorphosed garden, the walks being strewn with charcoal, the little basin in the middle of the lawn bordered with a rim of black basalt and filled with ink; and the ordinary shrubs superseded by cypresses and pines. The dinner itself was served on a black cloth, decorated with baskets of violets and scabiosae and illuminated by candelabra in which tall tapers flared.

While a concealed orchestra played funeral marches, the guests were waited on by naked negresses wearing shoes and stockings of cloth of silver besprinkled with tears.

The viands were served on black-bordered plates—turtle soup, Russian black bread, ripe olives from Turkey, caviar, mule steaks, Frankfurt smoked sausages, game dished up in sauces coloured to resemble liquorice water and boot-blacking, truffles in jelly, chocolate-tinted creams, puddings, nectarines, fruit preserves, mulberries and cherries. The wines were drunk from dark-tinted glasses—wines of the Limagne and Roussillon vintages, wines of Tenedos, the Val de Penas and Oporto. After the coffee and walnuts came other unusual beverages, kvass, porter and stout.

The invitations, which purported to be for a dinner in pious memory of the host's (temporarily) lost virility, were couched in the regulation phraseology of letters summoning relatives to attend the obsequies of a defunct kinsman.

But these extravagances, that had once been his boast, had died a natural death; nowadays his only feeling was one of self-contempt to remember these puerile and out-of-date displays of eccentricity—the extraordinary clothes he had donned and the grotesque decorations he had lavished on his house. His only thought henceforth was to arrange, for his personal gratification only and no longer in order to startle other people, a home that should be comfortable, yet at the same time rich and rare in its appointments, to contrive himself a peaceful and exquisitely organized abode, specially adapted to meet the exigencies of the solitary life he proposed to lead.

When at length the new house at Fontenay was ready and fitted up in accordance with his wishes and intentions by the architect he had engaged; when nothing else was left save to settle the scheme of furniture and decoration, once again he passed in review, carefully and methodically, the whole series of available tints.

What he wanted was colours the effect of which was confirmed and strengthened under artificial light; little he cared even if by daylight they should appear insipid or crude, for he lived practically his whole life at night, holding that then a man was more truly at home, more himself and his own master, and that the mind found its only real excitant and effective stimulation in contact with the shades of evening; moreover, he reaped a special and peculiar satisfaction from finding himself in a room brilliantly lighted up, the only place alive and awake among surrounding houses all buried in sleep and darkness—a sort of enjoyment that is not free from a touch of vanity, a selfish mode of gratification familiar enough to belated workers when, drawing aside the window curtains, they note how all about them the world lies inert, dumb and dead.

Slowly, one by one, he sifted out the different tones.

Blue, by candlelight, assumes an artificial green tinge; if deep blue, like cobalt or indigo, it becomes black; if light, it changes to grey; it may be as true and soft of hue as a turquoise, yet it looks dull and cold.

Yes, it could only be employed as a supplement to help out some other colour; there could be no question of making blue the dominating note of a whole room.

On the other hand, the iron greys are even more sullen and heavy; the pearl greys lose their azure tinge and are metamorphosed into a dirty white; as for the deep greens, such as emperor green and myrtle green, these suffer the same fate as the blues and become indistinguishable from black. Only the pale greens therefore remained, peacock green for instance, or the cinnabars and lacquer greens, but then in their case lamplight extracts the blue in them, leaving only the yellow, which for its part shows only a poor false tone and dull, broken sheen.

Nor was it any use thinking of such tints as salmon-pink, maize, rose; their effeminate note would go dead against all his ideas of self-isolation; nor again were the violets worth considering, for they shed all their brightness by candlelight; only red survives undimmed at night—but then what a red! a sticky red, like wine lees, a base, ignoble tint! Moreover, it struck him as quite superfluous to resort to this colour, inasmuch as after imbibing a certain small dose of santonin, a man sees violet, and it becomes the easiest thing in the world to change about at will and without ever altering the actual tint of his wall hangings.

All these colours being rejected, three only were left, viz. red, orange, yellow.

Of these three, he preferred orange, so confirming by his own example the truth of a theory he used to declare was almost mathematically exact in its correspondence with the reality, to wit: that a harmony is always to be found existing between the sensual constitution of any individual of a genuinely artistic temperament and whatever colour his eyes see in the most pronounced and vivid way.

In fact, if we leave out of account the common run of men whose coarse retinas perceive neither the proper cadence peculiar to each of the colours nor the subtle charm of their various modifications and shades; similarly leaving on one side those bourgeois eyes that are insensible to the pomp and splendour of the strong, vibrating colours; regarding therefore only persons of delicate, refined visual organs, well trained in appreciation by the lessons of literature and art, it appeared to him to be an undoubted fact that the eye of that man amongst them who has visions of the ideal, who demands illusions to satisfy his aspirations, who craves veils to hide the nakedness of reality, is generally soothed and satisfied by blue and its cognate tints, such as mauve, lilac, pearl-grey, provided always they remain tender and do not overpass the border where they lose their individuality and change into pure violets and unmixed greys.

The blustering, swaggering type of men, on the contrary, the plethoric, the sanguine, the stalwart go-ahead fellows who scorn compromises and byroads to their goal, and rush straight at their object whatever it is, losing their heads at the first go-off, these for the most part delight in the startling tones of the reds and yellows, in the clash and clang of vermilions and chromes that blind their eyes and surfeit their senses.

Last comes the class of persons, of nervous organization and enfeebled vigour, whose sensual appetite craves highly seasoned dishes, men of a hectic, over-stimulated constitution. Their eyes almost invariably hanker after that most irritating and morbid of colours, with its artificial splendours and feverish acrid gleams—orange.

What Des Esseintes' final choice then would be hardly admitted of a doubt; but indubitable difficulties still remained unsolved. If red and yellow are accentuated under artificial light, this is not always the case with their composite, orange, which is a hotheaded fellow and often blazes out into a crimson or a fire red.

He studied carefully by candlelight all its different shades, and finally discovered one he thought should not lose equilibrium or refuse to fulfil the offices he claimed of it.

These preliminaries disposed of, he made a point of eschewing, so far as possible, at any rate in his study, the use of Oriental stuffs and rugs, which in these days, when rich tradesmen can buy them in the fancy shops at a discount, have become so common and so much a mark of vulgar ostentation.

Eventually he made up his mind to have his walls bound like his books in large-grained crushed morocco, of the best Cape skins, surfaced by means of heavy steel plates under a powerful press.

The panelling once completed, he had the mouldings and tall plinths painted a deep indigo, a blue lacquer like what the coach-builders use for carriage bodies, while the ceiling, which was slightly coved, was also covered in morocco, displaying, like a magnified œil-de-bœuf, framed in the orange leather, a circle of sky, as it were, of a rich blue, wherein soared silver angels, figures of seraphim embroidered long ago by the Weavers' Guild of Cologne for an ancient cope.

After the whole was arranged and finished, all these several tints fell into accord at night and did not clash at all; the blue of the woodwork struck a stable note that was pleasing and satisfying to the eye, supported and warmed, so to say, by the surrounding shades of orange, which for their part shone out with a pure, unsullied gorgeousness, itself backed up and in a way heightened by the near presence of the blue.

As to furniture, Des Esseintes had no long or laborious searches to undertake, inasmuch as the one and only luxury of the apartment was to be books and rare flowers; while reserving himself the right later on to adorn the naked walls with drawings and pictures, he confined himself for the present to fitting up almost all round the room a series of bookshelves and bookcases of ebony, scattering tiger skins and blue-foxes' pelts about the floor: and installing beside a massive money-changer's table of the fifteenth century, several deep-seated, high-backed armchairs, together with an old church lectern of wrought iron, one of those antique service-desks whereon the deacon of the day used once to lay the Antiphonary, and which now supported one of the ponderous volumes of du Cange's Glossarium medaie et infimae Latinitatis.

The windows, the glass of which was coarse and semiopaque, bluish in tinge and with many of the panes filled with the bottoms of bottles, the protuberances picked out with gilt, allowed no view of the outside world and admitted only a faint dim "religious" light. They were further darkened by curtains made out of old priestly stoles, the dull dead gold of whose embroideries faded off into a background of a subdued, almost toneless red.

To complete the general effect, above the fireplace, the screen of which was likewise cut from the sumptuous silk of a Florentine dalmatic, midway between two monstrances of gilded copper in the Byzantine style which had come originally from the Abbaye-aux-Bois at Bièvre, stood a marvellously wrought triptych, each of the three separate panels carved with a lacelike delicacy of workmanship; this now contained, guarded under glass let into the triple frame, copied on real vellum in beautiful missal lettering and adorned with exquisite illuminations, three pieces of Baudelaire's: right and left, the sonnets called "The Lovers' Death" and "The Enemy," in the middle, the prose poem that goes by the English title of "Anywhere Out of the World."

CHAPTER II

After the sale of his household goods, Des Esseintes kept on the two old servants who had looked after his invalid mother and between them had filled the double office of general factotum and hall-porter at the Château de Lourps. The latter had, up to the date of its being put up for sale, remained empty and untenanted.

He took with him to Fontenay this pair of domestics broken in to play the part of sick-nurses, trained to the methodical habits of wardsmen at a hospital, accustomed to administer at stated hours spoonfuls of physic and doses of medicinal draughts, subdued to the rigid quietude of cloistered monks, shut off from all communication with the outer world, content to spend their lives in close rooms with doors and windows always shut.

The husband's duty was to keep the rooms clean and fetch the provisions, the wife's to attend to the cooking. Their master gave up the first floor of the house for their accommodation, made them wear thick felt shoes, had double doors installed with well-oiled hinges and covered the floors with heavy carpeting so as to prevent his hearing the faintest sound of their footsteps overhead.

Then he arranged with them a code of signals, fixing the precise significance of different rings on his bell, few or many, long or short, and appointed a particular spot on his writing desk where each month the account books were to be left; in fact, made every possible disposition so as to avoid the obligation of seeing them or speaking to them more often than was absolutely indispensable.

More than this, as the woman must needs pass along the front of the house occasionally on her way to an outhouse where the wood was stored and he was resolved not to suffer the annoyance of seeing her commonplace exterior, he had a costume made for her of Flemish grogram, with a white mutch and a great black hood to muffle face and head, such as the Béguines still wear to this day at Ghent. The shadow of this medieval coif gliding by in the dusk gave him a conventual feeling, reminding him of those peaceful, pious settlements, those abodes of silence and solitude buried out of sight in a corner of the bustling, busy city.

He fixed the hours of meals, too, in accordance with a never varying schedule; indeed his table was of the plainest and simplest, the feebleness of his digestion no longer permitting him to indulge in heavy or elaborate repasts.

At five o'clock in winter, after dusk had closed in, he ate an abstemious breakfast of two boiled eggs, toast and tea; then came dinner at eleven; he used to drink coffee, sometimes tea or wine, during the night, and finally played with a bit of supper about five in the morning, before turning in.

These meals, the details and menu of which were settled once for all at the beginning of each season of the year, he took on a table placed in the middle of a small room communicating with his study by a padded corridor, hermetically closed and allowing neither smell nor sound to penetrate from one to the other of the two apartments it served to connect.

The dining room in question resembled a ship's cabin with its wooden ceiling of arched beams, its bulkheads and flooring of pitch-pine, its tiny window-opening cut through the woodwork as a porthole is in a vessel's side.

Like those Japanese boxes that fit one inside the other, this room was inserted within a larger one—the real dining room as designed by the architect.

This latter apartment was provided with two windows; one of these was now invisible, being hidden by the bulkhead or partition wall, which could however be dropped by touching a spring, so that fresh air might be admitted to circulate freely around and within the pitch-pine enclosure;

the other was visible, being situated right opposite the porthole contrived in the woodwork, but was masked in a peculiar way, a large aquarium filling in the whole space intervening between the porthole and the real window in the real house-wall. Thus the daylight that penetrated into the cabin had first to pass through the outer window, the panes of which had been replaced by a single sheet of plain mirror glass, then through the water and last of all through the glazing of the porthole, which was permanently fixed in its place.

At the hour when the steaming samovar stood on the table, the moment when in Autumn the sun would be setting in the west, the water in the aquarium, dull and opaque by daylight, would redden and throw out fiery flashes as if from a glowing furnace over the light-coloured walls.

Sometimes, of an afternoon, if Des Esseintes happened to be up and about at that time of day, he would turn the taps connected with a system of pipes and conduits that enabled the tank to be emptied and refilled with fresh water, and then by pouring in a few drops of coloured essences, he could enjoy at his pleasure all the tints, green or grey, opaline or silvery, that real rivers assume according to the hue of the heavens, the greater or less ardour of the sun's rays, the more or less threatening aspect of the rain-clouds, in a word according to the varying conditions of season and weather.

This done, he could picture himself in the 'tween-decks of a brig as he gazed curiously at a shoal of ingenious mechanical fishes that were wound up and swam by clockwork past the porthole window and got entangled in artificial water-weeds; at other times, as he inhaled the strong smell of tar with which the room had been impregnated before he entered it, he would examine a series of coloured lithographs on the walls, of the sort one sees in packet-boat offices and shipping agencies, representing steamers at sea bound for Valparaiso or the River Plate, alongside framed placards giving the itineraries of the Royal Mail Steam Packet services and of the various Ocean liners, freighting charges and ports of call of the Transatlantic mail boats, etc.

Then presently, when he was tired of consulting these timetables, he would rest his eyes by looking over the collection of chronometers and mariner's compasses, sextants and dividers, binoculars and charts scattered about the table, whereon figured only a single book, bound in sea-green morocco, The Adventures of Arthur Gordon Pym, specially printed for his behoof on pure linen-laid paper, hand picked, bearing a seagull for watermark.

In the last resort, he could turn his gaze upon a litter of fishing-rods, brown tanned nets, rolls of russet-coloured sails, a miniature anchor made of cork painted black, all heaped together near the door that communicated with the kitchen by a passage padded, like the corridor joining the dining room and study, in such a way as to absorb every unpleasant smell and disturbing noise.

By these means he could procure himself, without ever stirring from home, in a moment, almost instantaneously, all the sensations of a long voyage; the pleasure of moving from place to place, a pleasure which indeed hardly exists save as a matter of after recollection, almost never as a present enjoyment at the moment of the actual journey, this he could savour to the full at his ease, without fatigue or worry, in this improvised cabin, whose ordered disorder, whose transitional look and temporary arrangement, corresponded closely enough with the nature of the flying visits he paid it and the limited time he devoted to his meals, while it offered an absolute contrast to his working-room—a fixed and final spot, a place of system and settled habit, a room manifestly contrived for the definite enjoyment of a life of cloistered and learned leisure. In fact it appeared to him a futile waste of energy to travel when, so he believed, imagination was perfectly competent to fill the place of the vulgar reality of actual prosaic facts. To his mind it was quite possible to satisfy all the cravings commonly supposed to be the hardest to content under the normal conditions of life, and this merely by a trifling subterfuge, by a more or less close simulation of the object aimed at by these desires. Thus it is a sufficiently well-known fact that in these days the epicure who frequents those restaurants that have a reputation for the excellence of their cellars is really and truly gratifying his palate by drinking rare vintages artificially manufactured out of common, cheap wines treated after M. Pasteur's methods. Now, whether genuine or faked, these wines have the same aroma, the same colour, the same bouquet, whence it follows that the pleasure experienced in imbibing these fictitious, doctored beverages is absolutely identical with the satisfaction that would be enjoyed from tasting the pure, unsophisticated liquor now unprocurable even at its weight in gold.

Transferring this artful sophistication, this clever system of adulteration, into the world of the intellect, there is no doubt we can, and just as easily as in the material world, enjoy false, fictitious pleasures every whit as good as the true; no doubt, for instance, a man can undertake long voyages of exploration sitting in his armchair by the fireside, helping out, if needful, his recalcitrant or sluggish imagination by the perusal of some work descriptive of travels in distant lands; no doubt again that it is quite possible—without ever stirring from Paris—to obtain the health-giving impression of sea-bathing. In two words, all that is required in this last case is simply to take a walk to the Bain Vigier, on a pontoon moored right out in the middle of the Seine.

There, by just salting your bath and mixing with the water, according to the formula given in the Pharmacopoeia, a compound of sulphate of soda, hydrochlorate of magnesia and lime; by drawing from a box carefully secured by a screw-top a ball of twine or a scrap of rope's end bought for the purpose at one of those great marine store dealers' emporiums whose huge warehouses and cellars reek with the salty smell of the sea and seaports; by inhaling these odours which the twine or ropes end are bound to retain; by examining a lifelike photograph of the casino and industriously reading the Guide Joanne describing the beauties of the seaside resort where you would like to be; by letting yourself be lulled by the waves raised in the bath by the passing river steamers as they steer close past the bathing pontoon, by listening to the sobbing of the wind as it blusters through the arches of the bridges and the dull rumble of the omnibuses rolling six feet above your head across the Pont Royal; just by doing and suffering these simple things, the illusion is undeniable, overmastering, perfect; you are as good as at the seaside.

The whole secret is to know how to set about it, to be able to concentrate the mind on a single point, to attain to a sufficient degree of self-abstraction to produce the necessary hallucination and so substitute the vision of the reality for the reality itself.

To tell the truth, artifice was in Des Esseintes' philosophy the distinctive mark of human genius.

As he used to say, Nature has had her day; she has definitely and finally tired out by the sickening monotony of her landscapes and skyscapes the patience of refined temperaments. When all is said and done, what a narrow, vulgar affair it all is, like a petty shopkeeper selling one article of goods to the exclusion of all others; what a tiresome store of green fields and leafy trees, what a wearisome commonplace collection of mountains and seas!

In fact, not one of her inventions, deemed so subtle and so wonderful, which the ingenuity of mankind cannot create; no Forest of Fontainebleau, no fairest moonlight landscape but can be reproduced by stage scenery illuminated by the electric light; no waterfall but can be imitated by the proper application of hydraulics, till there is no distinguishing the copy from the original; no mountain crag but painted pasteboard can adequately represent; no flower but well chosen silks and dainty shreds of paper can manufacture the like of!

Yes, there is no denying it, she is in her dotage and has long ago exhausted the simple-minded admiration of the true artist; the time is undoubtedly come when her productions must be superseded by art.

Why, to take the one of all her works which is held to be the most exquisite, the one of all her creations whose beauty is by general consent deemed the most original and most perfect—woman to wit, have not men, by their own unaided effort, manufactured a living, yet artificial organism that is every whit her match from the point of view of plastic beauty? Does there exist in this world of ours a being, conceived in the joys of fornication and brought to birth amid the pangs of motherhood, the model, the type of which is more dazzlingly, more superbly beautiful than that of the two locomotives lately adopted for service on the Northern Railroad of France?

One, the Crampton, an adorable blonde, shrill-voiced, slender-waisted, with her glittering corset of polished brass, her supple, catlike grace, a fair and fascinating blonde, the perfection of whose charms is almost terrifying when, stiffening her muscles of steel, pouring the sweat of steam down her hot flanks, she sets revolving the puissant circle of her elegant wheels and darts forth a living thing at the head of the fast express or racing seaside special!

The other, the Engerth, a massively built, dark-browed brunette, of harsh, hoarse-toned utterance, with thickset loins, panoplied in armour-plating of sheet iron, a giantess with dishevelled mane of black eddying smoke, with her six pairs of low, coupled wheels, what overwhelming power when, shaking the very earth, she takes in tow, slowly, deliberately, the ponderous train of goods wagons.

Of a certainty, among women, frail, fair-skinned beauties or majestic, brown-locked charmers, no such consummate types of dainty slimness and of terrifying force are to be found. Without fear of contradiction may we say: man has done, in his province, as well as the God in whom he believes.

Thoughts like these would come to Des Esseintes at times when the breeze carried to his ears the far-off whistle of the baby railroad that plies shuttlewise backwards and forwards between Paris and Sceaux. His house was within a twenty minutes' walk or so of the station of Fontenay, but the height at which it stood and its isolated situation left it entirely unaffected by the noise and turmoil of the vile hordes that are inevitably attracted on Sundays by the neighbourhood of a railway station.

As for the village itself, he had hardly seen it. Only at night, from his window, he had looked out over the silent landscape that stretches down to the foot of a hill on the summit of which rise the batteries of the Bois de Verrieres.

In the shadow, to right and left, loomed other dimly seen masses, terracing the hillside and dominated by other far-off batteries and fortifications, the high revetments of which seemed in the moonlight as if washed in with silver pigment upon a dark background of sky.

The plain lay partly in the shadows cast by the hills, while the centre, where the moonlight fell, looked as if it were powdered with starch and smeared with cold-cream; in the warm air that fanned the pale grass and brought with it a spicy perfume, the trees stood out clearly silhouetted with their shaggy leaves and thin stems, which threw black bars of shadow across the chalky earth strewed with pebbles that sparkled like shards of broken crockery.

The artificial, rather theatrical air of this landscape was to Des Esseintes' taste; but after that one afternoon devoted to the search for a house at the hamlet of Fontenay, he had never again trodden its streets by daylight. In fact, the green-cry of this district inspired him with no sort of interest, not offering even the dainty, melancholy charm to be found in the pitiful, sickly vegetation that has so sore a struggle to live on the rubbish-heaps of suburban spots near the ramparts.

Besides, on that memorable day, he had caught sight of paunchy citizens with flowing whiskers and smartly dressed individuals with moustaches, carrying their heads high, as if they were something sacrosanct, evidently magistrates or military officers; and after such a sight, his usual horror of the human face had been still further accentuated.

During the last months of his residence in Paris, at the period when, utterly disillusioned, depressed by hypochondria, eaten up by spleen, he had reached such a pitch of nervous irritability that the mere sight of an unpleasant object or disagreeable person was deeply graven on his brain and several days were needed to efface the impress, even to a slight degree, of the human form that had formed one of his most agonizing torments when passed casually in the street.

In positive fact, he suffered pain at the sight of certain types of face, resented almost as insults the condescending or crabbed expressions of particular visages, and felt himself sorely tempted to box the ears of such and such a worthy citizen who strolled by with half closed lids and a magisterial air, another who stood swinging his cane and admiring himself in the shop windows, or yet another who seemed to be pondering the fate of the universe, as he absorbed with frowning brows the titbits and gossipy paragraphs of his morning paper.

He scented such a depth of stupidity, such a lively hatred of all his own ideals, such a contempt for literature and art and everything he himself adored, implanted and profoundly fixed in the meagre brains of these tradesmen preoccupied to the exclusion of all else by schemes of swindling and money-grubbing and only accessible to the ignoble distraction that alone appeals to mean minds, politics, that he would rush back home in a fury and lock himself up with his books.

Worst of all, he loathed with all his powers of hate the new types of self-made men, the hideous boors who feel themselves bound to talk loud and laugh uproariously in restaurants and cafés, who elbow you, without apology, on the pavements, who, without a word of polite excuse or so much as a bow, drive the wheels of a child's go-cart between your legs.

CHAPTER III

One division of the shelves fixed against the walls of his blue and orange working-room was occupied exclusively by Latin works—those works which minds broken in to conventionality by listening year after year to the miserable teaching of School and College lecturers designate under the generic name of "The Decadence."

The truth is, the Latin language, as it was written at the period which learned professors still persist in calling the "Golden Age," roused his interest scarcely at all. That idiom, confined within such narrow limits, with its carefully counted, almost invariable turns of phrase, without suppleness of syntax, without colour or light and shade; that idiom, ironed smooth on every seam, pruned of the rugged but often picturesque expressions of earlier epochs, could at a pinch enunciate the pompous nullities, the vague commonplaces repeated ad nauseam by the rhetoricians and poets of that day, but so lacking was it in originality, so instinct with tediousness, that we must, in our studies of language and literature, come down to the French style of the age of Louis XIV, to find one so wilfully emasculated, so solemnly tiresome and sapless.

Among other authors, the gentle Virgil, he whom school ushers name the Swan of Mantua, presumably because he was not born in that city, appeared to him as one of the most terrible of pedants, one of the most dismal twaddlers Antiquity ever produced; his shepherd swains, all washed and beribboned, taking turn and turn about to empty over the unfortunate reader's head their slops of sententious, chilly verses, his Orpheus whom he compares with a weeping nightingale, his Aristaeus blubbering over bees, his Aeneas, that weak-kneed, fluent personage who stalks, like a shadow figure at a show, with wooden gestures behind the ill-fitted and badly oiled screen of the poem, set him beside himself with exasperation. He might indeed have put up with the tedious fiddle-faddle these marionettes exchange by way of dialogue as a stage device; he might even have excused the impudent plagiarisms perpetrated on Homer, Theocritus, Ennius, Lucretius, the flagrant theft Macrobius has revealed to us of the whole Second Book of the Aeneid, copied almost word for word from a poem of Pisander's, he might have forgiven, in fact, all the indescribable dullness of this farrago of borrowed verses; but what revolted him more than all was the false ring of those hexameters, with their tinny tinkle like the rattle of a cracked pot, with their longs and shorts weighed out by the pound according to the unalterable laws of a pedantic, barren prosody; it was the framework of these stiff and formal lines that was beyond all bearing, with their official stamp and cringing subservience to grammatical propriety, these verses each mechanically bisected by an unmodifiable caesura, then stopped off at the tail, always in precisely the same way, by a dactyle knocking up against a final spondee.

Borrowed from the cast-iron system perfected by Catullus, that unvarying metrical scheme, unimaginative, inexorable, stuffed full of useless verbiage and endless amplifications, an array of ingeniously contrived pegs each fitting into its corresponding and expected hole, that poor trick of the Homeric "standing epithet," dragged in again and again without rhyme or reason, all that scanty vocabulary with its dull, flat tones, were a torment to his sensibility.

It is only fair to add that, if his admiration for Virgil was decidedly lukewarm and his appreciation of the light lucubrations of Ovid anything but marked, the disgust he felt for the elephantine graces of Horace, the twaddle of this unmitigated lout who smirks at his audience with the painted face and villainous jests of a superannuated clown, was limitless.

In prose, his enthusiasm was not a whit greater for the redundant figures and nonsensical digressions of "Chickpea" (Cicero); the braggadocio of his apostrophes, the claptrap of his never-ending appeals to patriotism, the exaggerated emphasis of his harangues, the ponderousness of his style, well-fed and full-fleshed, but run to fat and devoid of bones and marrow, the intolerable litter of his sonorous adverbs opening every sentence, the monotonous structure of his portly periods tied awkwardly to each other by a thread of conjunctions, worst of all his wearisome habits of tautology, were anything but attractive to him. Caesar again was little more to his taste, for all his reputation for conciseness; his was the opposite excess—a dry-as-dust aridity, a deadly dullness, an unseasonable constipation of phrase that passes belief.

The end of it all was that he could find mental pabulum neither among these writers nor among that other class which still forms the delight of dilettante scholars—Sallust, who indeed is less insipid than most of the rest; Livy, sentimental and pompous; Seneca, turgid and jejune; Suetonius, lymphatic and horrifying; Tacitus, the most nervous in his studied concision, the most biting, the most sinewy of them all. In poetry, Juvenal, despite some vigorously conceived lines, Persius, despite his mysterious insinuations, both left him cold. Neglecting Tibullus and Propertius, Quintilian and the two Plinies, Statius, Martial of Bilbilis, Terence even and Plautus, whose jargon, full as it is of neologisms, made-up words and diminutives, might have pleased him, had not his low wit and coarse jocosity repelled him, Des Esseintes only began to be interested in the language of Rome on the appearance of Lucan, with whom it took on a wider range, becoming henceforth more expressive and less harsh; that author's laboured workmanship, his verse, veneered with enamels, studded with jewels, caught his fancy, albeit his exclusive preoccupation with form, his tinkling sonorities, his metallic brilliancies, did not entirely hide from his eyes this author's vacuity of thought and the emptiness of the windbag phrases that plump out the carcase of the "Pharsalia."

The writer he really loved and who made him reject for good and all from among the books he read, Lucan and his sounding periods, was Petronius.

Petronius was an acute observer, a delicate analyst, a marvellous delineator; calmly, without prejudice, without animosity, he described the daily life of Rome, setting down in the lively little chapters of the Satyricon the manners, customs and morals of his day.

Noting facts as they occurred, putting them down in positive black and white, he disclosed the trivial, everyday existence of the commonalty, its incidents, its bestialities, its sensualities.

Here, we have the Inspector of Lodgings coming to inquire the names of the travellers lately arrived; there, it is a brothel where men are prowling round naked women standing beside placards giving name and price, while through the half-open doors of the rooms the couples can be seen at work; elsewhere again, now in country houses full of insolent luxury, amid a mad display of wealth and ostentation, now in poverty-stricken taverns with their brokendown pallet-beds swarming with fleas, the society of the period runs its race—debauched cutpurses like Ascyltos and Eumolpus on the lookout for a piece of luck; old wantons of the male sex with their tucked-up gowns and cheeks plastered with ceruse and acacia red; minions of sixteen, plump and curly-headed; women frantic with hysteria; legacy hunters offering their boys and girls to gratify the lustful caprices of rich men; all these and more gallop across the pages, quarrel in the streets, finger each other at the baths, belabour each other with fisticuffs like the characters in a pantomime.

All this told with an extraordinary vigour and precision of colouring, in a style that borrows from every dialect, that cribs words from every language imported into Rome, that rejects all the limitations, breaks all the fetters of the so-called "Golden Age," that makes each man speak in his own peculiar idiom—freemen, without education, the vernacular Latin, the argot of the streets; foreigners, their barbarian lingo, saturated with African, Syrian, Greek expressions; idiotic pedants, like the Agamemnon of the Satyricon, a rhetoric of invented words. All these people are drawn with a free pencil, squatted round a dining-table, exchanging the imbecile conversation of tipsy revellers, mouthing dotards' wise saws and pointless proverbs, all eyes turned upon Trimalchio, the giver of the feast, who sits picking his teeth, offers the company chamberpots, discourses of his insides, begging his guests to make themselves at home.

This realistic romance, this slice cut from the raw of Roman life, without one thought, whatever people may say, whether of reforming or satirizing society, without any moral purpose whatever or idea of moralizing, this tale—there is neither intrigue nor action in it—bringing before the reader the love adventures of male prostitutes, analyzing with calm address the joys and griefs of these amours and these amorous couples, depicting in language wrought to the perfection of a piece of goldsmith's work, without the writer once showing himself, without a word of comment, without one phrase of approbation or disapproval of his characters' deeds and thoughts, the vices of a decrepit civilization, an Empire falling to ruin, rivetted Des Esseintes' attention; he saw in the refinements of its style, the keenness of its observation, its closely knit, methodical construction, a strange likeness, a curious analogy with the three or four modern French novels that he could stomach.

We may be sure he bitterly regretted the loss of the Eustion and the Albutia, two works by Petronius mentioned by Planciades Fulgentius, but now vanished beyond possibility of recovery; however, the bibliophile side of him came in to console the scholarly, as he fondled in reverent hands the example he owned of the superb edition of the Satyricon, the octavo edition bearing date 1585 printed by J. Dousa at Leyden.

After Petronius, his collection of Latin authors came to the Second Century of the Christian era, skipping over the declaimer Fronto, with his old-fashioned turns of speech and his ill-adjusted, ill-polished style, leaving on one side the Noctes Atticae of Aulus Gellius, his disciple and friend, a sagacious and inquisitive mind, but as a writer embarrassed by a sticky, glutinous style—only stopping when he reached Apuleius, the editio princeps of which author he possessed the folio printed at Rome in 1469.

This African rhetorician was his delight; the Latin language was surely at its best and richest in him, rolling along in a full, copious flood, fed by many tributary streams from all the Provinces of the Empire, and combining all these different elements to form one strange, exotic dialect, hardly dreamed of before; in it new mannerisms, new details of Latin society found expression in new turns of phrase, invented in the stress of conversation in a little Roman town in a corner of Africa. Moreover, the man's bonhomie—he was a fat, jovial boon companion, there could be no doubt of that—and the warm-blooded exuberance of his southern nature tickled our hero's fancy. He had the air of a gay and genial comrade, not mealymouthed by any means, alongside of the Christian apologists, his contemporaries—the soporific Minutius Felix, a pseudoclassic, ladling out in his Octavius Cicero's heavy periods, grown heavier than ever, or even Tertullian himself, whom he kept on his shelves more perhaps for the sake of the Aldine edition of his works than for any love of the matter.

Well equipped as he was for Theological disquisitions, the argumentations of the Montanists against the Catholic Church, the polemics of the latter against gnosticism, left him cold; so, despite the preciosity of Tertullian's style, a style rigorously compressed, full of quibbles and amphibologies, based on a liberal use of participles, emphasized by continual antitheses, crammed with puns and plays upon words, variegated with words borrowed from the language of jurisprudence and the diction of the Greek Fathers, he hardly ever now opened the Apologetica or the Tractate on Patience; the most he ever did was to skim through a page or two of the De Cultu Feminarum, in which Tertullian charges the sex not to bedeck their persons with jewels and precious stuffs and forbids them to make use of cosmetics because they are thereby trying to correct and improve on Nature.

These ideas, the precise opposite of his own, made him smile; though the part played by Tertullian as Bishop of Carthage seemed to him suggestive in the way of pleasant daydreams. In a word, it was really the man more than his works that attracted him.

He had, in truth, lived in stormy times, at a period of fearful stress and strain, under Caracalla, under Macrinus, under that amazing personage, the High-Priest of Emessa, Elagabalus; and he had gone on calmly and quietly writing his sermons, composing his dogmatic treatises, preparing his apologies and homilies, while the Roman Empire was tottering to its foundations, while the frantic follies of Asia and the foul vices of Paganism were at their worst; he was preaching with an air of perfect self-possession carnal abstinence, frugality of diet, sobriety of dress at the very moment when, treading on powder of silver and sand of gold, his head crowned with a tiara, his robes studded with precious stones, Elagabalus was at work, among his eunuchs, at women's tasks, calling himself by the title of Empress and every night lying with a new Emperor, selecting him for choice from the ranks of the Court barbers and scullions, or the charioteers from the Circus.

This contrast delighted him; then the Latin language, after attaining to supreme maturity in Petronius, was beginning to break up; the literature of

Christianity was claiming its place, bringing in along with new ideas new words, unfamiliar constructions, strange verbs, adjectives of farfetched meanings, abstract nouns, hitherto scarce in the Roman tongue, and of which Tertullian had been one of the first to introduce the usage.

Only this degeneration, which was carried further after Tertullian's death by his pupil St. Cyprian, by Arnobius, by the muddy Lactantius, was eminently unattractive. It was a gradual decay, slow and incomplete, marked by awkward attempts to return to the emphasis of the Ciceronian periods, not yet possessing that special raciness which in the Fourth and still more in the succeeding Centuries the odour of Christianity will give to the Pagan tongue, as it decomposes little by little, acquires a stronger and stronger aroma of decay, dropping bit by bit to pieces pari passu with the crumbling of the civilization of the Ancient World, with the collapse, before the advance of the Barbarian hordes, of the Empires rotted by the putrescence of the ages.

Only one Christian poet, Commodian of Gaza, was to be found in his library as representative of the art of the Third Century. The Carmen Apologeticum, written about 259 AD, is a compendium of rules of conduct, tortured into acrostics, composed in rude hexameters, divided by a caesura after the fashion of heroic verse, but without any attention to quantity or the rules of hiatus and often eked out with rhymes of the kind ecclesiastical Latin later on afforded numerous examples of.

These strained, sombre verses, with their touch of savagery, full of common, vernacular expressions, of words deflected from their original meanings, appealed to him, interested him even more than the style, overripe and already decadent, the historians Ammianus Marcellinus and Aurelius Victor, of the letter-writer Symmachus and the compiler and grammarian Macrobius; he even preferred them to the lines, correctly scanned, and the variegated and superbly picturesque diction of Claudian, Rutilius and Ausonius.

These were in their day the masters of the art; they filled the dying Empire with their swan songs—the Christian Ausonius with his Cento Nuptialis and his copious and elaborate poem on the Moselle; Rutilius, with his hymns to the glory of Rome, his anathemas against the Jews and against the Monks, his itinerary of Cisalpine Gaul, where he manages sometimes to render certain aspects of the beauties of Nature, the vague charm of landscapes reflected in water, the mirage of mists, the flying vapours about the mountain tops.

Then there is Claudian, a kind of avatar of Lucan, who dominates all the Fourth Century with the terrific clarion of his verse—a poet who wrought a striking and sonorous hexameter, beating out, amid showers of sparks, the right epithet at a blow, attaining a certain grandeur, filling his work with a puissant breath of life. In the Western Empire falling more and more into ruin, amid the confusion of the repeated disasters that fall upon it, unchecked by the constant threat of invasion by the Barbarians now pressing in hordes at the very gates of the Empire whose bolts and bars are cracking under the strain, he revivifies Antiquity, sings of the Rape of Proserpine, lays on his brilliant colours, goes by with all his fires ablaze in the gathering gloom that is overspreading the world.

Paganism lives again in him, sounding its last fanfare, raising its last great poet high above the Christianity that is from his day onwards utterly to submerge the language and forever after remain absolute arbiter and master of poetry—with Paulinus, pupil of Ausonius, with the Spanish priest Juvenous, who paraphrases the Gospels in verse, with Victorinus, author of the Macchabaei, with Sanctus Burdigalensis, who in an Eclogue copied from Virgil makes the herdsmen Egon and Buculus deplore the maladies of their flocks. Then these are succeeded by all the series of the Saints— Hilary of Poitiers, the champion of the faith of Nicaea, the Athanasius of the West, as he was called; Ambrosius, the author of indigestible homilies, the wearisome Christian Cicero; Damasus, the fabricator of epigrams cut and polished like precious stones; Jerome, the translator of the Vulgate, and his adversary Vigilantius of Comminges who attacks the worship of the saints, the abuse of miracles and the practice of fasts, and already preaches, using arguments the ages will go on repeating one to the other, against monastic vows and the celibacy of the clergy.

At last, in the Fifth Century, comes Augustine, Bishop of Hippo. Him Des Esseintes knew only too well, for he was the writer of all others most highly reputed by the Church, the founder of Christian orthodoxy, the theologian whom good Catholics regard as an oracle, a sovereign authority. Result: he never opened his books any more, albeit he had celebrated, in his Confessions, his disillusionment with this world and with groans of pious contrition; in his Civitas Dei, had endeavoured to assuage the woeful distress of the age by seductive promises of better things to come in a future life. In the years when he was an active theologian, he was already a tired man, sated with his own preachings and jeremiads, weary of his theories on predestination and grace, exhausted by his fights against the schisms.

Des Esseintes liked better to dip into the Psychomachia of Prudentius, the inventor of the allegorical poem, destined later on to flourish uninterruptedly in the Middle Ages, or the Works of Sidonius Apollinaris, whose correspondence, stuffed with sallies, points of wit, archaisms, enigmas, attracted him. He was always ready to read the panegyrics, wherein, in support of his pompous praises, he invokes the deities of Paganism, and in spite of his better judgment, could not but acknowledge a weakness for the affectations and hidden meanings of these poems put together by an ingenious mechanic who loves his machine, scrupulously oils its working parts, and is prepared at a pinch to invent new ones just as complicated and as useless as the old.

After Sidonius, again, he kept on familiar terms with the panegyrist Merobaudes; Sedulius, author of rhymed poems and alphabetical hymns of which the Church has appropriated portions to incorporate in her offices; Marius Victor, whose dark and dismal tractate on the "Perversity of Morals" is lit up here and there by lines that glitter like phosphorus; Paulinus of Pella, the poet of that icy production the "Eucharisticon"; Orientius, Bishop of Auch, who in the distichs of his "Monitoria" rails at the licence of women, whose faces, he declares, destroy the nations.

The interest that Des Esseintes felt in the Latin language remained as strong as ever even now when, rotten through and through, it hung a decaying carcase, losing its limbs, distilling its pus, barely keeping, in the utter corruption of its body, a few sound parts which the Christians abstracted to preserve them in the salt pickle of their new dialect.

The second half of the Fifth Century was come, the appalling period when unspeakable troubles afflicted the world. The Barbarians were ravaging Gaul; Rome, paralyzed, sacked by the Visigoths, felt her life frozen within her veins as she saw her outlying limbs, the East and the West, struggling in a sea of blood, growing more and more exhausted from day to day.

Amid the general dissolution, amid the assassinations of Caesars that follow close on each other's heels, amid the uproar of slaughter that rolls from end to end of Europe, a wild hurrah broke forth, terrifying men's hearts, and drowning all other sounds. On the banks of the Danube, thousands of men, perched on little horses, wrapt in rat-skin coats, hideous Tartars with immense heads, flat noses, chins furrowed with wounds and scars, jaundiced, hairless faces, are rushing down helter-skelter on the provinces of the Lower Empire, overwhelming everything in the whirlwind of their advance.

Civilization disappeared in the dust of their gallop, in the smoke of their fires. Darkness fell upon the world and the peoples trembled in consternation as they heard the dread host rush by with a sound of thunder. The horde of Huns swept over Europe, precipitated itself on Gaul, to be overwhelmed on the plains of Châlons where Aëtius heaped up its dead in a fearful carnage. The land was gorged with blood—a very sea of rolling purple; two hundred thousand corpses barred the road and broke the onrush of this avalanche that, turned aside, fell like a thunderclap on Italy, whose ruined cities flamed up to heaven like so many fired hayricks.

The Eastern Empire crumbled under the shock; the expiring life it still dragged out in decrepitude and corruption was extinguished. The last end of the universe indeed seemed near at hand; the cities Attila had passed over were decimated by plague and famine. The Latin tongue, too, seemed to be perishing amid the ruins of a world.

Years rolled by; presently the Barbarian idioms grew more regular, began to emerge from their uncouth envelopes, to develop into true languages; Latin, rescued in the general cataclysm by the Monasteries, was limited to the Religious Houses and the secular cures. Only here and there a few poets appeared, cold, difficult versifiers—the African Dracontius with his "Hexameron"; Claudius Mamert, with his liturgical poems; Avitus of Vienna; then presently biographers, such as Ennodius, who relates the miracles of St. Epiphanes, the acute and venerated diplomatist, the upright and vigilant pastor, such as Eugippus, who has recorded for us the incomparable life of St. Séverin, the mysterious anchorite, the humble ascetic, who appeared like an angel of mercy to the mourning nations, mad with pain and fear; then again writers like Veranius of the Gevaudan, who composed a little treatise on Continence, like Aurelian and Ferreolus who compiled Church canons; historians like Rotherius of Agde, famed for a History of the Huns, now lost.

Works of the next succeeding centuries were few and far between on Des Esseintes' shelves. Still the Sixth Century was represented by Fortunatus, Bishop of Poitiers, whose hymns and the "Vexilla Regis", hacked out of the ancient carcase of the Latin language, and flavoured with the aromatic spices of the Church, haunted his thoughts on certain days; by Boetius Gregory of Tours, and Jornandes. Then, in the Seventh and Eighth Centuries, inasmuch as, (over and above the Low Latin of the Chroniclers, such as Fredegarius and Paul the Deacon, and verses comprised in the "Bangor Antiphonary", one hymn in which, the one that forms an acrostic and has one and the same rhyme ending every line, composed in honour of St. Comgill, he sometimes looked at), contemporary literature was almost exclusively confined to Lives of the Saints—the legend of St. Columba by the cenobite Jonas and that of the Blessed Cuthbert compiled by the Venerable Bede from the notes of an anonymous monk of Lindisfarne, he confined himself to turning over at odd moments the pages of these Hagiographers and rereading extracts from the Lives of St. Rusticula and St. Radegonde, related, the former by Defensorius, Synodite of Liguge, the latter by the modest and simple-hearted Baudonivia, a Nun of Poitiers.

However, certain singular productions of Latin literature in Anglo-Saxon lands were more to his liking; there was for instance the whole series of the enigmas of Aldhelm, of Tatwine, of Eusebius, those inheritors of Symphosius' mantle, and in especial the riddles composed by St. Boniface in the form of acrostics, where the answer is given by the initial letters of the lines of each stanza.

His predilection grew less and less towards the end of these two Centuries; finding small pleasure indeed in the ponderous prose of the Carlovingian Latinists, the Alcuins and Eginhards, he contented himself, by way of specimens of the language of the Ninth Century, with the anonymous chronicler of St. Gall, with Freculf and Reginon, with the poem on the Siege of Paris indited by Abbo Le Courbé, with the "Hortulus", the didactic poem of the Benedictine Walafrid Strabo, whose canto devoted to the glorification of the pumpkin, symbol of fecundity, charmed his sense of humour. Another favourite was the poem of Ermold the Black, celebrating the exploits of Louis le Débonnaire, a poem written in regular hexameters, in a severe, black style, in a diction of iron tempered in monastic waters, with here and there threads of sentiment imbedded in the hard metal; yet another, the "De Viribus Herbarum", a poem of Macer Floridus on simples, which particularly delighted him by its poetical recipes and the extraordinary virtues he attributes to certain herbs and flowers—to the aristolochia or birthwort, for example, which mixed with beef and laid as a plaster on a woman's abdomen is an infallible specific to make her bear a male child, or the borage, which sprinkled in an infusion about a dining hall, ensures the guests being all merry, or the peony, the pounded root of which cures headache for good and all, or the fennel, which, applied to a woman's bosom, clarifies her discharges and stimulates the sluggishness of her periods.

Except for a few special volumes, unclassed, certain works, modern or undated, cabalistic, medical and botanical, sundry odd tomes of Migne's Patrology, preserving Christian poems not to be found elsewhere, and Wernsdorff's Anthology of the Minor Latin Poets, except for Meursius, Forberg's Manual of Classical Erotology, the Moechialogy and the Diaconals for the use of Father Confessors, which he would take down from the shelves to dust at long intervals, with these exceptions, his Latin collections stopped with the beginning of the Tenth Century.

For truly the quaint originality, the complex simplicity of Christian Latinity had likewise come to an end. Henceforth the fiddle-faddle of philosophers and scholiasts, the vain logomachies of the Schoolmen, were to reign in undisputed mastery. The sooty masses of chronicles and books of history, the leaden lumps of the Cartularies, were to rise in more and more mountainous heaps, while the stammering grace, the clumsy but often exquisite simplicity of the Monks setting in a pious hotchpotch the poetical relics of Antiquity were no more, the fabrication of verses of refined sweetness, of substantives smelling of incense, of quaint adjectives, roughly shaped out of gold, in the barbarous, fascinating taste of Gothic jewelry, ceased. The old editions, fondly cherished by Des Esseintes, came to an end—and making a prodigious jump over the centuries, he loaded the rest of his shelves with modern, vernacular works that, heedless of the slow progression of the ages, came down at once to the French of the present day.

CHAPTER IV

A CARRIAGE STOPPED LATE ONE AFTERNOON BEFORE THE HOUSE AT FONTENAY. As Des Esseintes never received a visitor; as even the postman did not venture within these deserted precincts, never having either newspaper, review or letter to leave there, the servants hesitated, asking themselves if they ought to open. But presently, at the repeated summons of the bell outside the wall pulled with a vigorous hand, they went so far as to draw aside the judas let into the door; this done, they beheld a Gentleman whose whole breast was covered, from neck to waist, with a vast buckler of gold.

They informed their master, who was at breakfast.

"By all means," said he, "bring the gentleman in,"—for he remembered having on one occasion given his address to a lapidary to enable the man to deliver an article he had ordered.

The gentleman came in, made his bow and deposited in the dining room, on the pitch-pine flooring, his gold shield, which swayed backwards and forwards, rising a little bit from the ground and extending at the extremity of a snakelike neck a turtle's head which next instant it drew back in a scare under its shell.

This turtle was the result of a whim that had suddenly occurred to Des Esseintes a short while before his leaving Paris. Looking one day at an Oriental carpet with iridescent gleams of colour and following with his eyes the silvery glints that ran across the web of the wool, the colours of which were an opaque yellow and a plum violet, he had told himself: it would be a fine experiment to set on this carpet something that would move about and the deep tint of which would bring out and accentuate these tones.

Possessed by this idea, he had strolled at random through the streets; had arrived at the Palais-Royal, and in front of Chevet's window had suddenly struck his forehead—a huge turtle met his eyes there, in a tank. He had bought the creature; then, once it was left to itself on the carpet, he had sat down before it and gazed long at it, screwing up his eyes.

Alas! there was no doubt, the negro-head hue, the raw sienna tone of the shell dimmed the sheen of the carpet instead of bringing out the tints; the dominant gleams of silver now barely showed, clashing with the cold tones of scraped zinc alongside this hard, dull carapace.

He gnawed his nails, searching in vain for a way to reconcile these discordances, to prevent this absolute incompatibility of tones. At last he discovered that his original notion of lighting up the fires of the stuff by the to-and-fro movements of a dark object set on it was mistaken; the fact of the matter was, the carpet was still too bright, too crude, too new-looking. Its colours were not sufficiently softened and toned down; the thing was to reverse the proposed expedient, to deaden the tints, to stifle them by the contrast of a brilliant object that should kill everything round it, casting the flash of gold over the pale sheen of silver. Thus looked at, the problem was easier to solve. Accordingly he resolved to have his turtle's back glazed over with gold.

Once back from the jeweller's who had taken it in to board at his workshop, the beast blazed like a sun in splendour, throwing its flashing rays over the carpet, whose tones were weak and cold in comparison, looking for all the world like a Visigothic targe inlaid with shining scales, the handiwork of some Barbaric craftsman.

At first, Des Esseintes was enchanted with the effect; but he soon came to the conclusion that this gigantic jewel was only half finished, that it would not be really complete and perfect till it was incrusted with precious stones.

He selected from a collection of Japanese curios a design representing a great bunch of flowers springing from a thin stalk, took it to a jeweller's, sketched out a border to enclose this bouquet in an oval frame, and informed the dumbfounded lapidary that every leaf and every petal of the flowers was to be executed in precious stones and mounted in the actual scales of the turtle.

The choice of the stones gave him pause; the diamond had grown singularly hackneyed now that every businessman wears one on his little finger; Oriental emeralds and rubies are less degraded and dart fine, flashing lights, but they are too reminiscent of those green and red eyes that shine as headlights on certain lines of Paris omnibuses; as for topazes, burnt or raw, they are cheap stones, dear to the humble housewife who loves to lock up a jewel-case or two in a glass cupboard; of another sort, the amethyst, albeit the Church has given it something of a sacerdotal character, is yet a stone spoilt by its frequent use to ornament the red ears and bulbous hands of butchers' wives who are fain at a modest cost to bedeck their persons with genuine and heavy jewels. Alone among all these, the sapphire keeps its fires inviolate, unharmed by the folly of tradesmen and moneygrubbers. The brilliance of its fire that sparkles from a cold, limpid background has to some degree guaranteed against defilement its discreet and haughty nobility. But unfortunately by artificial light its bright flames flash no longer; the colour sinks back into itself and seems to go to sleep, only to wake and sparkle again at daybreak.

No, not one of these stones satisfied Des Esseintes; besides, they were all too civilized, too familiar. He preferred other, more startling and uncommon, sorts. After fingering a number of these and letting them trickle through his hands, he finally picked out a series of stones, some real, some artificial, the combination of which should produce a harmony, at once fascinating and disconcerting.

He combined together the several parts of his bouquet in this way: the leaves were set with stones of a strong and definite green colour—chrysoberyls, asparagus green; peridots, leek green; olives, olive green, springing from twigs of almandine and ouvarovite of a purple red, gems throwing out sparkles of a clear, dry brilliance like the incrustations of tartar that glitter on the insides of wine-casks.

For the blossoms that stood isolated, far removed from the stalk, he used an ashen blue, rejecting, however, definitely the Oriental turquoise that is used for brooches and rings, and which, along with the commonplace pearl and the odious coral form the delight of vulgar souls; he selected exclusively those European turquoises that, strictly speaking, are only a fossil ivory impregnated with coppery infiltrations and whose sea-green blue is heavy, opaque, sulphurous, as if jaundiced with bile.

This done, he could now proceed to incrust the petals of such blossoms as grew in the middle of the bunch, those in closest neighbourhood of the stem, with certain translucent stones, possessing a glassy, sickly sheen with feverish, vivid bursts of fire.

Three gems, and only three, he employed for this purpose—Ceylon cat's-eyes, cymophanes and sapphirines.

All three were stones that flashed with mysterious, incalculable sparkles, painfully drawn from the chill interior of their turbid substance— the cat's eye of a greenish grey, striped with concentric veins that seem to be endowed with motion, to stir and shift every instant according to the way the light falls; the cymophane with bluish waterings running across the milky hue that appears afloat within; the sapphirine that lights up blue, phosphorescent fires on a dull, chocolate-brown background.

The lapidary took careful notes and measures as to the exact places where the stones were to be let in. "And the edges of the shell?" he presently asked Des Esseintes.

The latter had thought at first of a border of opals and hydrophanes. But these stones, interesting as they are by their curious variations of colour and changes of sparkle, are too difficult and untrustworthy to deal with; the opal has a quite rheumatic sensitiveness, the play of its rays is entirely modified according to the degree of moisture, and of heat and cold, while the hydrophane has no fire, refuses to light up the grey glow of its furnace except in water, after it has been wetted.

Finally he settled on stones whose hues would supplement each other— the hyacinth of Compostella, mahogany red; the aquamarine, sea green; the balass ruby, vinegar rose; the Sudermania ruby, pale slate-colour. Their comparatively feeble play of colours would suffice to light up the deadness of the dull, grey shell, while leaving its full value to the brilliant bouquet of jewelled blossoms which they framed in a slender garland of uncertain splendours.

Des Esseintes stood gazing at the turtle where it lay huddled together in one corner of the dining room, flashing fire in the dim half light.

He felt perfectly happy; his eyes were intoxicated with the splendours of these flowers flashing in jewelled flames against a golden background. Then, contrary to his use, he had an appetite and was dipping his slices of toast spread with super-excellent butter in a cup of tea, an impeccable blend of Si-a-Fayoun, Mo-you-tann and Khansky—yellow teas, imported from China into Russia by special caravans.

This liquid perfume he drank from those cups of Oriental porcelain known as eggshell china, so delicate and transparent are they; in the same way, just as he would have nothing to say to any other save this adorably dainty ware, he refused to use as dishes and plates anything else but articles of genuine antique silver-gilt, a trifle worn so that the underlying silver shows a little here and there under the film of gold, giving a tender, old-world look as of something fading away in a quiet death of exhaustion.

After swallowing his last mouthful, he went back to his study, whither he directed a servant to bring the turtle, which obstinately declined to make the smallest effort towards locomotion.

Outside the snow was falling. In the lamplight, ice arabesques glittered on the dark windows and the hoarfrost sparkled like crystals of sugar on the bottle-glass panes speckled with gold.

A deep silence wrapped the little house that lay asleep in the darkness.

Des Esseintes stood lost in dreams; the logs burning on the hearth filled the room with hot, stifling vapours, and presently he threw the window partly open.

Like an overhanging canopy of reversed ermine, the sky rose before him, a black curtain dappled with white.

An icy wind was blowing, that sent the snow spinning before it and soon reversed this first arrangement of black and white. The sky returned to the correct heraldic blazon, became a true ermine, white dappled with sable, where the black of night showed here and there through the general whiteness of the snowy mantle of descending snowflakes.

He closed the window again. But this quick change, without any intermediate transition, from the torrid heat of the room to the cold of midwinter had given him a shock; he crouched back beside the fire and thought he would swallow a dose of spirits to restore his bodily temperature.

He made his way to the dining room, where in a recess in one of the walls, a cupboard was contrived, containing a row of little barrels, ranged side by side, resting on miniature stocks of sandal wood and each pierced with a silver spigot in the lower part.

This collection of liquor casks he called his mouth organ.

A small rod was so arranged as to connect all the spigots together and enable them all to be turned by one and the same movement, the result being that, once the apparatus was installed, it was only needful to touch a knob concealed in the panelling to open all the little conduits simultaneously and so fill with liquor the tiny cups hanging below each tap.

The organ was then open. The stops, labelled "flute," "horn," "vox humana," were pulled out, ready for use. Des Esseintes would imbibe a drop here, another there, another elsewhere, thus playing symphonies on his internal economy, producing on his palate a series of sensations analogous to those wherewith music gratifies the ear.

Indeed, each several liquor corresponded, so he held, in taste with the sound of a particular instrument. Dry curaçao, for instance, was like the clarinet with its shrill, velvety note; kummel like the oboe, whose timbre is sonorous and nasal; crème de menthe and anisette like the flute, at one and the same time sweet and poignant, whining and soft. Then, to complete the orchestra, comes kirsch, blowing a wild trumpet blast; gin and whisky, deafening the palate with their harsh outbursts of comets and trombones; liqueur brandy, blaring with the overwhelming crash of the tubas, while the thunder peals of the cymbals and the big drum, beaten might and main, are reproduced in the mouth by the rakis of Chios and the mastics.

He was convinced too that the same analogy might be pushed yet further, that quartettes of stringed instruments might be contrived to play upon the palatal arch, with the violin represented by old brandy, delicate and heady, biting and clean-toned; with the alto, simulated by rum, more robust, more rumbling, more heavy in tone; with vespetro, long-drawn, pathetic, as sad and tender as a violoncello; with the double-bass, full-bodied, solid and black as a fine, old bitter beer. One might even, if anxious to make a quintette, add yet another instrument—the harp, mimicked with a sufficiently close approximation by the keen savour, the silvery note, clear and self-sufficing, of dry cumin.

Nay, the similarity went to still greater length, analogies not only of qualities of instruments, but of keys were to be found in the music of liquors; thus, to quote only one example, Bénédictine figures, so to speak, the minor key corresponding to the major key of the alcohols which the scores of wine-merchants' price-lists indicate under the name of green Chartreuse.

These assumptions once granted, he had reached a stage, thanks to a long course of erudite experiments, when he could execute on his tongue a succession of voiceless melodies; noiseless funeral marches, solemn and stately; could hear in his mouth solos of crème de menthe, duets of vespetro and rum.

He even succeeded in transferring to his palate selections of real music, following the composer's motif step by step, rendering his thought, his effects, his shades of expression, by combinations and contrasts of allied liquors, by approximations and cunning mixtures of beverages.

Sometimes again, he would compose pieces of his own, would perform pastoral symphonies with the gentle blackcurrent ratafia that set his throat resounding with the mellow notes of warbling nightingales; with the dainty cacao-chouva, that sung sugar-sweet madrigals, sentimental ditties like the "Romances d'Estelle"; or the "Ah! vous di-rai-je maman," of former days.

But tonight, Des Esseintes had no wish to "taste" the delights of music; he confined himself to sounding one single note on the keyboard of his instrument, filling a tiny cup with genuine Irish whisky and taking it away with him to enjoy at his leisure.

He sank down in his armchair and slowly savoured this fermented spirit of oats and barley—a strongly marked, almost poisonous flavour of creosote diffused itself through his mouth.

Little by little, as he drank, his thoughts followed the impression thus reawakened on his palate, and stimulated by the suggestive savour of the liquor, were roused by a fatal similarity of taste and smell to recollections half obliterated years ago.

The acrid, carbolic flavour forcibly recalled the very same sensation that had filled his mouth and burned his tongue while the dentists were at work on his gums.

Once started on this track, his recollections, at first wandering vaguely over all the different practitioners he had had to do with, drew to a point, converging on one of the whole number, the eccentric memory of whose proceedings was graven with particular emphasis on his memory.

The thing had happened three years before: seized in the middle of the night with an abominable toothache, he had done everything a man does in such a case—plugging his jaws with cotton-wool, stumbling against the furniture, pacing up and down his room like a madman.

It was a molar that had been stopped again and again, and was past cure; only the dentist's forceps could end his misery. In a fever of agony, he waited for daylight, firmly resolved to bear the most atrocious operation if only it would put an end to his sufferings.

Still holding his jaws between his hands, he asked himself what to do. The dentists he usually consulted were well-to-do practitioners who could not be seen at a moment's notice; a visit must be arranged beforehand, a regular appointment made. "That is out of the question, I cannot wait," he told himself; so he made up his mind to go to the first dentist he could find, to resort to any common, low-class tooth-drawer, one of those fellows with fists of iron, who, ignorant as they may be of the art (a mighty useless art, be it said by the way) of attending to decayed teeth and stopping hollow ones, know how to extirpate with unparalleled rapidity the most obstinate of aching stumps. Places of the sort open at daybreak, and there is no waiting. Seven o'clock struck at last. He dashed out of doors, and remembering a name he knew of such a mechanic calling himself a dentist and living at the corner of a neighbouring street, he hurried thither, biting his handkerchief and keeping back his tears as best he might.

Arrived in front of the house, which was advertised by a huge wooden placard, whereon the name "Gatonax" sprawled in enormous yellow letters on a black background and two little glazed cases in which artificial teeth were ranged in symmetrical lines in gums of pink composition joined together by mechanical springs of brass wire, he stood panting for breath, the sweat rolling from his temples; a horrid spasm shook him, a shudder ran over his skin—and lo! relief came, the pain stopped, the tooth ceased to ache.

He halted irresolute on the pavement. But eventually he mastered his terror, climbed a dark staircase, mounting four steps at a time to the third floor. There he found on a door an enamelled plaque repeating in sky-blue lettering the same legend as on the board below. He pulled the bell; then, appalled at the great red blotches of expectoration he caught sight of on the steps, he suddenly turned tail, resolved to endure toothache all his life long, when a fearful screech reached his ears through the partition and reechoed in the well of the staircase, nailing him to the spot in a trance of horror, while at the same instant a door opened and an old woman begged him to come in.

Shame had won the day over fear; he was shown into a dining room; then another door opened noisily, admitting a formidable grenadier of a man, dressed in a frock coat and black trousers that seemed carved in wood. Des Esseintes followed him into an inner sanctum.

From that moment his sensations had been vague. Confusedly he remembered dropping into an armchair before a window, and stammering out, as he put a finger to his tooth: "It has been stopped already; I am afraid there's nothing can be done."

The man had cut short this explanation peremptorily, inserting an enormous forefinger into his mouth; then, muttering something from under his lacquered, pointed moustaches, he had picked up an instrument from a table.

Thereupon the drama had begun. Clinging to the arms of the operating chair, Des Esseintes had felt a sensation of cold in his cheek, then his eyes had seen three dozen candles all at once, and so unspeakable were the tortures he was enduring, he had started beating the floor with his feet and bellowing like an animal under the slaughterer's knife.

There was a loud crack, the molar had broken in coming away; he thought they were pulling off his head, smashing in his skull; he lost all control of himself, howled at the top of his voice; fought furiously against the man who now came at him again as if he would plunge his arm to the bottom of his belly; had then suddenly stepped back a pace and lifting the patient bodily by the tooth still sticking in his jaw, had let him fall back again violently in a sitting posture into the chair; next moment he was standing up blocking the window, and puffing and panting as he brandished at the end of his pincers a blue tooth with a red thread hanging from it.

Half fainting, Des Esseintes had spit out a basin full of blood, waved away the old woman who now came in offering him the stump of his tooth, which she was preparing to wrap up in a piece of newspaper, and had fled, after paying two francs, taking his turn to leave his signature in bloody spittle on the steps; then he was once more in the street, a happy man, feeling ten years younger, ready to be interested in the veriest trifles.

"B'rrr...." he shivered, horrified at these dismal reminiscences. He sprang up to break the horrid nightmare of his thoughts, and coming back to everyday matters, began to feel anxious about the turtle.

It still lay quite still; he touched it, it was dead. Accustomed no doubt to a sedentary life, an uneventful existence spent under its humble carapace, it had not been able to support the dazzling splendour imposed on it, the glittering garment in which it had been clad, the pavement of precious stones wherewith they had inlaid its poor back like a jewelled pyx.

CHAPTER V

Simultaneously with his craving to escape a hateful world of degrading restrictions and pruderies, the longing never again to see pictures representing the human form toiling in Paris between four walls or roaming the streets in search of money, had obtained a more and more complete mastery over his mind.

Having once divorced himself from contemporary existence, he was resolved to suffer in his hermit's cell no spectres of old repugnances and bygone dislikes; accordingly he had chosen only to possess pictures of a subtle, exquisite refinement, instinct with dreams of Antiquity, reminiscent it may be of antique corruption, but at any rate remote from our modern times and modern manners.

He had selected for the diversion of his mind and the delight of his eyes works of a suggestive charm, introducing him to an unfamiliar world, revealing to him traces of new possibilities, stirring the nervous system by erudite fantasies, complicated dreams of horror, visions of careless wickedness and cruelty.

Of all others there was one artist who most ravished him with unceasing transports of pleasure—Gustave Moreau.

He had purchased his two masterpieces, and night after night he would stand dreaming in front of one of these, a picture of Salomé.

The conception of the work was as follows: A throne, like the high altar of a Cathedral, stood beneath an endless vista of vaulted arches springing from thickset columns resembling the pillars of a Romanesque building, encased in many coloured brickwork, incrusted with mosaics, set with lapis lazuli and sardonyx, in a Palace that recalled a basilica of an architecture at once Saracenic and Byzantine.

In the centre of the tabernacle surmounting the altar, which was approached by steps in the shape of a recessed half circle, the Tetrarch Herod was seated, crowned with a tiara, his legs drawn together, with hands on knees.

The face was yellow, like parchment, furrowed with wrinkles, worn with years; his long beard floated like a white cloud over the starry gems that studded the gold-fringed robe that moulded his breast.

Round about this figure, that sat motionless as a statue, fixed in a hieratic pose like some Hindu god, burned cressets from which rose clouds of scented vapour. Through this gleamed, like the phosphoric glint of wild beasts' eyes, the flash of the jewels set in the walls of the throne; then the smoke rolled higher, under the arcades of the roof, mingling its misty blue with the gold dust of the great beams of sunlight pouring in from the domes.

Amid the heady odour of the perfumes, in the hot, stifling atmosphere of the great basilica, Salomé, the left arm extended in a gesture of command, the right bent, holding up beside the face a great lotus-blossom, glides slowly forward on the points of her toes, to the accompaniment of a guitar whose strings a woman strikes, sitting crouched on the floor.

Her face wore a thoughtful, solemn, almost reverent expression as she began the wanton dance that was to rouse the dormant passions of the old Herod; her bosoms quiver and, touched lightly by her swaying necklets, their rosy points stand pouting; on the moist skin of her body glitter clustered diamonds; from bracelets, belts, rings, dart sparks of fire; over her robe of triumph, bestrewn with pearls, broidered with silver, studded with gold, a corselet of chased goldsmith's work, each mesh of which is a precious stone, seems ablaze with coiling fiery serpents, crawling and creeping over the pink flesh like gleaming insects with dazzling wings of brilliant colours, scarlet with bands of yellow like the dawn, with patterned diapering like the blue of steel, with stripes of peacock green.

With concentrated gaze and the fixed eyes of a sleep walker, she sees neither the Tetrarch, who sits there quivering, nor her mother, the ruthless Herodias, who watches her, nor the hermaphrodite or eunuch who stands sabre in hand on the lowest step of the throne, a terrible figure, veiled to below the eyes, the sexless dugs of the creature hanging like twin gourds under his tunic barred with orange stripes.

The thought of this Salomé, so full of haunting suggestion to the artist and the poet, had fascinated Des Esseintes for years. How often had he read in the old Bible of Pierre Variquet, translated by the Doctors in Theology of the University of Louvain, the Gospel of St. Matthew where it recounts in brief, naive phrases the beheading of the Precursor; how often had he dreamed dreams between the simple lines:

"But when Herod's birthday was kept, the daughter of Herodias danced before them, and pleased Herod.

"Whereupon, he promised with an oath to give her whatsoever she would ask.

"And she, being before instructed of her mother, said 'Give me here John Baptist's head in a charger.'

"And the king was sorry: nevertheless, for the oath's sake, and them which sat with him at meat, he commanded it to be given her.

"And he sent, and beheaded John in the prison.

"And his head was brought in a charger, and given to the damsel: and she brought it to her mother."

But neither St. Matthew, nor St. Mark, nor St. Luke, nor any other of the Sacred Writers had enlarged on the maddening charms and the active allurements of the dancer. She had always remained a dim, obliterated figure, lost with her mysterious fascination in the far-off mist of the centuries, not to be realized by exact and pedestrian minds, only appealing to brains shaken and sharpened, made visionary as it were by hysteria; she had always eluded the grasp of fleshy painters, such as Rubens who travestied her as a Flemish butcher's wife; always baffled the comprehension of writers who have never yet succeeded in rendering the delirious frenzy of the wanton, the subtle grandeur of the murderess.

In the work of Gustave Moreau, going for its conception altogether beyond the meagre facts supplied by the New Testament, Des Esseintes saw realized at last the Salomé, weird and superhuman, he had dreamed of. No longer was she merely the dancing-girl who extorts a cry of lust and concupiscence from an old man by the lascivious contortions of her body; who breaks the will, masters the mind of a King by the spectacle of her quivering bosoms, heaving belly and tossing thighs; she was now revealed in a sense as the symbolic incarnation of world-old Vice, the goddess of immortal Hysteria, the Curse of Beauty supreme above all other beauties by the cataleptic spasm that stirs her flesh and steels her muscles—a monstrous Beast of the Apocalypse, indifferent, irresponsible, insensible, poisoning, like Helen of Troy of the old Classic fables, all who come near her, all who see her, all who touch her.

So understood, she belonged to the ancient Theogonies of the Far East; no longer she drew her origin from Biblical tradition; could not even be likened to the living image of Babylonish Whoredom, or the Scarlet Woman, the Royal Harlot of Revelations, bedecked like her with precious stones and purple, tired and painted like her; for she was not driven by a fateful power, by a supreme, irresistible force, into the alluring perversities of debauch.

Moreover, the painter seemed to have wished to mark his deliberate purpose to keep outside centuries of history; to give no definite indication of race or country or period, setting as he does his Salomé in the midst of this strange Palace, with its confused architecture of a grandiose complexity; clothing her in sumptuous, fantastic robes, crowning her with a diadem of no land or time shaped like a Phoenician tower such as Salammbô wears, putting in her hand the sceptre of Isis, the sacred flower of Egypt and of India, the great lotus-blossom.

Des Esseintes strove to fathom the meaning of this emblem. Did it bear the phallic signification the primordial religions of India give it; did it proclaim to the old Tetrarch a sacrifice of a woman's virginity, an exchange of blood, an incestuous embrace asked for and offered on the express condition of a murder? Or was it intended to suggest the allegory of Fertility, the Hindu myth of Life, an existence held betwixt the fingers of woman, snatched away and defiled by the lustful hands of man, who is seized by a sudden madness, bewildered by the cry of the flesh?

Perhaps, too, in arming his enigmatic goddess with the revered lotus-flower, the painter had thought of the dancing harlot of all times, the mortal woman the temple of whose body is defiled—cause of all the sins and all the crimes; perhaps he had remembered the sepulchral rites of ancient Egypt, the ritual ceremonies of the embalmment, when surgeons and priests stretch the dead woman's body on a slab of jasper, then with curved needles extract her brains through the nostrils, her entrails through an incision opened in the left side; finally, before gilding the nails and teeth, before coating the corpse with bitumen and precious essences, insert into her sexual parts, to purify them, the chaste petals of the divine flower.

Be this as it may, an irresistible fascination breathed from the canvas; but the watercolour entitled The Apparition was perhaps even yet more troubling to the senses.

In it, Herod's Palace towered aloft like an Alhambra on light columns iridescent with Moorish chequer-work, joined as with silver mortar, consolidated with cement of gold; arabesques surrounded lozenges of lapis lazuli and wound all along the cupolas, where on marquetries of mother-of-pearl, wandered glittering rainbows, flashes of prismatic colour.

The murder had been done; now the headsman stood there impassive, his hands resting on the pommel of his long sword, stained with blood.

The decapitated head of the Saint had risen up from the charger where it lay on the flags, and the eyes were gazing out from the livid face with its discoloured lips and open mouth; the neck all crimson, dripping tears of gore.

A mosaic encircled the face whence shone an aureola darting gleams of fire under the porticoes, illuminating the ghastly lifting of the head, revealing the glassy eyeballs, that seemed fixed, glued to the figure of the dancing wanton.

With a gesture of horror, Salomé repulses the appalling vision that holds her nailed to the floor, balanced on her toe tips; her eyes are dilated, her hand grips her throat convulsively.

She is almost naked; in the ardour of the dance the veils have unwound themselves, the brocaded draperies of her robes have slipped away; she is clad now only in goldsmith's artistries and translucent gems; a gorget clips her waist like a corselet; and for clasp a superb, a wondrous jewel flashes lightnings in the furrow between her bosoms; lower, on the hips, a girdle swathes her, hiding the upper thighs, against which swings a gigantic pendant, a falling river of carbuncles and emeralds; to complete the picture: where the body shows bare betwixt gorget and girdle, the belly bulges, dimpled by the hollow of the navel that recalls a graven seal of onyx with its milky sheen and tint as of a rosy fingernail.

Beneath the ardent rays flashing from the Precursor's head, every facet of her jewelled bravery catches fire; the stones burn, outlining the woman's shape in flaming figures; neck, legs, arms, glitter with points of light, now red as burning brands, now violet as jets of gas, now blue as flames of alcohol, now white as moonbeams.

The dreadful head flashes and flames, bleeding always, dripping gouts of dark purple that point the beard and hair. Visible to Salomé, alone, it embraces in the stare of its dead eyes neither Herodias, who sits dreaming of her hate satiated at last, nor the Tetrarch, who, leaning rather forward with hands on knees, still pants, maddened by the sight of the woman's nakedness, reeking with heady fumes, dripping with balms and essences, alluring with scents of incense and myrrh.

Like the old King, Des Esseintes was overwhelmed, overmastered, dizzied before this figure of the dancing-girl, less majestic, less imposing, but more ensnaring to the senses than the Salomé of the oil painting.

In the callous and pitiless statue, in the innocent and deadly idol, the emotion, the terror of the human being had dawned; the great lotus-flower had disappeared, the goddess vanished; an atrocious nightmare now gripped the throat of the mime, intoxicated by the whirl of the dance, of the courtesan, petrified, hypnotized by terror.

In this, she was altogether feminine, obedient to her temperament of a passionate, cruel woman; she was active and alive, more refined and yet more savage, more hateful and yet more exquisite; she was shown awakening more powerfully the sleeping passions of man; bewitching, subjugating more surely his will, with her unholy charm as of a great flower of concupiscence, born of a sacrilegious birth, reared in a hothouse of impiety.

As Des Esseintes used to maintain: never before at any epoch had the art of watercolour succeeded in reaching such a brilliancy of tint; never had the poverty of chemical pigments been able thus to set down on paper such coruscating splendours of precious stones, such glowing hues as of painted windows illumined by the noonday sun, glories so amazing, so dazzling of rich garments and glowing flesh tints.

And, falling into a reverie, he would ask himself what were the origin and antecedents of the great painter, the mystic, the Pagan, the man of genius who could live so remote from the outside world as to behold, here and now in Paris, the splendid, cruel visions, the magic apotheoses of other ages.

Who had been his predecessors? This Des Esseintes found it hard to say; here and there, he seemed influenced by vague recollections of Mantegna and Jacopo de Barbari; here and there, by confused memories of Da Vinci and the feverish colouring of Delacroix. But in the main, the effect produced by these masters' work on his own was imperceptible; the real truth was that Gustave Moreau was a pupil of no man. Without provable ancestors, without possible descendants, he remained, in contemporary art, a unique figure. Going back to the ethnographic sources of the nations, to the first origins of the mythologies whose bloodstained enigmas he compared and unriddled, reuniting, combining in one the legends derived from the Far East and metamorphosed by the beliefs of other peoples, he thus justified his architectonic combinations, his sumptuous and unexpected amalgamations of costumes, his hieratic and sinister allegories, made yet more poignant by the restless apperceptions of a nervous system altogether modern in its morbid sensitiveness; but his work was always painful, haunted by the symbols of superhuman loves and superhuman vices, divine abominations committed without enthusiasm and without hope.

There breathed from his pictures, so despairing and so erudite, a strange magic, a sorcery that moved you to the bottom of the soul, like that of certain of Baudelaire's poems, and you were left amazed, pensive, disconcerted by this art that crossed the last frontier-lines of painting, borrowing from literature its most subtle suggestions, from the art of the enameller its most marvellous effects of brilliancy, from the art of the lapidary and the engraver its most exquisite delicacies of touch. These two images of Salomé, for which Des Esseintes' admiration was boundless, were living things before his eyes where they hung on the walls of his working study on special panels reserved for them among the shelves of books.

But this was by no means the end of the purchases of pictures he had made with a view to beautifying his solitude.

True he had sacrificed all the first storey of his house, the only one above the ground floor, and occupied none of its rooms for his personal use, but the latter even by itself demanded a large number of pictures to cover the nakedness of its walls.

This ground floor was distributed as follows: A dressing-room, communicating with the bedroom, occupied one angle of the building; from the bedroom you passed into the library, from the library into the dining room, which formed the other angle.

These rooms, making up one front of the house, extended in a straight line, pierced with windows giving on the valley of Aunay.

The opposite side of the edifice consisted of four rooms exactly corresponding, so far as size and disposition went, with the former. Thus a kitchen stood at the corner, answering to the dining room; a large vestibule, serving as entrance hall to the dwelling, matched the library; a kind of boudoir, the bedroom; the closets and bathrooms, the dressing-room.

All these latter rooms looked out on the side opposite to the valley of Aunay, towards the Tour du Croy and Châtillon.

As to the staircase, it was built against one side of the house, on the outside, so that the servants' footsteps, trampling up the steps, reached Des Esseintes deadened and less noisy.

He had had the boudoir hung with tapestry of a vivid red, and on each of the four walls were displayed in ebony frames prints by Jan Luyken, an old Dutch engraver, almost unknown in France.

The works he possessed of this artist, at once fantastic and depressing, vigorous and brutal, included the series of his Religious Persecutions, a collection of appalling plates representing all the tortures which the savagery of religious intolerance has invented, plates exhibiting all the horrors of human agony—men roasted over braziers, skulls laid open by sword cuts, pierced with nails, riven asunder with saws, bowels drawn out of the belly, and twisted round rollers, fingernails torn out one by one with pincers, eyes put out, eyelids turned back and transfixed with pins, limbs dislocated or carefully broken bones laid bare and scraped for hours with knives.

These productions, replete with abominable imaginations, stinking of the stake, reeking with blood, echoing with curses and screams of agony, made Des Esseintes' flesh creep as he stood stifled with horror in the red boudoir.

But, over and above the qualms of disgust they provoked, over and above the dreadful genius of the man and the extraordinary vividness he gave his figures, there were likewise to be found among the thronging multitudes that people his marvellous drawings, among the hosts of spectators sketched with a dexterity of hand reminding us of Callot, but with a power that amusing but trivial draughtsman never possessed, curious reconstructions of the life of other places and periods; architecture, costumes, manners and customs in the days of the Maccabees, at Rome during the persecutions of the Christians, in Spain under the Inquisition, in France in the Middle Ages and at the date of the St. Bartholomew and the Dragonnades, were all noted with a scrupulous exactitude, and put on paper with a supreme skill.

These prints were mines of curious information; a man could look at them for hours and never weary; profoundly suggestive of ideas, they often helped Des Esseintes to kill the time on days when books refused to interest him.

Moreover, Luyken's own life was yet another attraction to him, explaining indeed the wildness of his work. A fervent Calvinist, a hidebound sectary, a fanatic of hymns and prayers, he composed religious poems, which he illustrated with his burin, paraphrased the Psalms in verse, lost himself in deep studies of the Bible, from which he would emerge, haggard and enraptured, his brain haunted by bloody pictures, his mouth full of the maledictions of the Reformation, and roused to an ecstasy by its songs of terror and fury.

Added to this, he was one who scorned this world, gave up his goods to the poor, lived on a crust of bread himself; in the end, he had taken boat along with an old servant-maid, carried away by a fanatic admiration of the man, put to sea at a venture, landing wherever his vessel came ashore and preaching the Gospel to all peoples, trying to live without eating, a madman and a savage almost at the last.

In the adjoining room, the vestibule, a larger apartment panelled with cedar wood the colour of a cigar-box, were ranged in rows other engravings and drawings equally extraordinary.

Bresdin's Comedy of Death was one, where in an impossible landscape, bristling with trees, coppices and thickets taking the shape of demons and phantoms, swarming with birds having rats' heads and tails of vegetables, from a soil littered with human bones, vertebrae, ribs and skulls, spring willows, knotted and gnarled, surmounted by skeletons tossing their arms in unison and chanting a hymn of victory, while a Christ flies away to a sky dappled with little clouds; a hermit sits pondering, his head between his hands, in the recesses of a grotto; a beggar dies worn out with privations, exhausted with hunger, stretched on his back, his feet extended towards a stagnant pool.

Another was the Good Samaritan by the same artist, an immense pen-and-ink drawing, lithographed—a wild entanglement of palms, service-trees, oaks, growing all together in defiance of seasons and climates, an outburst of virgin forest, crammed with apes, owls and screech-owls, cumbered with old stumps shapeless as roots of coral—a magic wood, pierced by a clearing dimly revealing far away, beyond a camel and the group of the Samaritan and the man who fell by the wayside, a river and behind it again a fairylike city climbing to the horizon line, rising to meet a strange-looking sky, dotted with birds, woolly with rolling clouds, swelling, as it were, with bales of vapour.

You would have thought it the work of an Early Italian master or a half-developed Albert Durer, composed under the influence of opium.

But, much as he admired the delicacy of detail and the imposing conception of this plate, Des Esseintes was more particularly attracted by the other pictures that decorated the room. These were signed Odilon Redon.

In their light frames of unpainted pear-wood, with a gold beading, they contained productions of an inconceivable eccentricity—a head in a Merovingian style, placed upon a cup; a bearded man, having something about him recalling at one and the same time a Buddhist priest and an orator at a public meeting, touching with the tip of his finger a colossal cannonball; a horrible spider, with a human face lodged in the middle of its body. Then there were crayons that went further yet in the horrors of a nightmare dream. Here it was an enormous die that winked a mournful eye; there, a series of landscapes—barren, parched, burnt-up plains, riven by earthquakes, rising in volcanic heights wreathed with wild clouds under a livid, stagnant sky. Sometimes even the subjects seemed to be borrowed from the dreams of science, to go back to prehistoric times; a monstrous flora spread over the rocks; everywhere were erratic blocks, glacial mud streams, and amongst them human beings whose apelike type—the heavy jaws, the projecting arches of the brows, the receding forehead, the flattened top of the skull, recalled the ancestral head, the head of the earliest quaternary period, when man was still a fruit-eater and speechless, a contemporary of the mammoth, the woolly-haired rhinoceros and the giant bear. These drawings passed all bounds, transgressing in a thousand ways the established laws of pictorial art, utterly fantastic and revolutionary, the work of a mad and morbid genius.

In fact, there were some of these faces, staring out with great, wild, insane eyes, some of these shapes exaggerated out of all measure or distorted as if seen refracted through water, that evoked in Des Esseintes' memory recollections of typhoid fever, remembrances that had stuck persistently in his head of hot nights of misery and horrid childish nightmares.

Overcome by an indefinable sense of distress before these designs—the same distress he had formerly experienced at the sight of certain Proverbs of Goya's which they resembled, as also after reading some of Edgar Allan Poe's stories, whose mirages of hallucination and effects of terror Odilon Redon seemed to have transferred into a sister art, he would rub his eyes and gaze at a radiant figure that, amid these frenzied designs, rose calm and serene, a figure of Melancholia, seated before a round sun's disk, on rocks, in an attitude of depression and despondency.

Then the gloom would be dissipated as if by magic; a pleasing sadness, a languor of gentle mournfulness, would fill his thoughts, and he would meditate for hours before this work, which, with its splashes of colour-wash gleaming amid the heavy chalks, struck a brilliant note of liquid green and pale gold to relieve the unbroken black of all these crayons and engravings.

Besides this series of Redon's works, covering nearly all the panels of the vestibule, he had hung in his bedroom an extravagant design, a sketch by Théocopuli, a Christ with livid flesh tints, the drawing of which was exaggerated, the colouring crude, the vigour excessive and undisciplined, an example of that painter's second manner, when he was tormented with the one haunting idea of avoiding any resemblance to Titian at all costs.

This gloomy work of art, with its tints of dead black and unhealthy green, corresponded in Des Esseintes' ideas with certain conclusions he came to with regard to the furnishing of the same apartment.

There existed, according to him, two ways and only two of arranging a bedroom; either to make it a place for pleasure, contrived to excite the passions for nightly adventure; or else to regard it as a retreat dedicated to sleep and solitude, a home of quiet thoughts, a kind of oratory.

In the first case, the Louis XV style, was preeminently the one for refined minds, for people exhausted above all by stress and strain of mental sensibility; indeed, only the Eighteenth Century has known how to envelope woman in a vicious atmosphere, shaping its furniture on the model of her charms, copying the contortions of her ardour, imitating the spasms of her amorousness in the waving lines and intricate convolutions of wood and copper, adding a spice to the sugar-sweet languor of the blonde by the vivid, bright tone of its ornamentation, mitigating the salty savour of the brunette by tapestries of subdued, liquid, almost insipid hues.

A chamber of the sort he had already included in his Paris abode, with the broad, white bed that gives an added titillation, an enhanced satisfaction to the depraved senses of an old voluptuary, that is like a cynic's grin in face of pretended chastity, before Greuze's innocent sprigs of girlhood, before the artificial purity of naughty sheets that seem spread for children and young virgins.

In the other case—and now that he was determined to break with the agitating memories of his past life, this was the only one possible—he must contrive a bedchamber to resemble a monk's cell in a Religious House; but here came difficulty upon difficulty, for he refused absolutely to endure for his personal occupation the austere ugliness that marks such refuges for penitence and prayer.

By dint of turning the question over this way and that and looking at it from every side, he arrived at the conclusion that the result to be aimed at amounted to this—to arrange by means of objects cheerful in themselves a melancholy whole, or rather, while preserving its character of plain ugliness, to impress on the general effect of the room thus treated a kind of elegance and distinction; to reverse, in fact, the optical delusion of the stage, where cheap tinsel plays the part of expensive and sumptuous robes, to gain indeed precisely the opposite effect, using costly and magnificent materials so as to give the impression of common rags; in a word, to fit up a Trappist's cell that should have the look of the genuine article, and yet of course be nothing of the sort.

He set about the task as follows: to imitate the ochre wash that is the invariable mark of administrative and clerical direction, he had the walls hung with saffron silk; to represent the chocolate brown of the wainscot, the regulation colour for suchlike places, he panelled the lower part of these same walls with wood painted a rich, deep purple. The effect was charming, recalling—though how different really!—the bald stiffness of the pattern he was copying—with modifications. The ceiling, in the same way, was covered with unbleached white cloth, giving the appearance of plaster, but without its crude shiny look; then for the cold tiles of the floor; he mimicked these very successfully, thanks to a carpet with a pattern of red squares, interspersed with spots of a whitish hue where the occupants' sandals might have been supposed to leave their mark.

This room he furnished with a little iron bedstead, a sham hermit's couch, constructed out of old pieces of wrought and polished iron, its plainness relieved at head and foot by a leaf and flower ornamentation— tulips and vine-tendrils intertwined, once part of the balustrade of the great staircase of an old château.

By way of night-table, he installed an antique prie-Dieu, the inside of which would hold a utensil, while the top supported a book of offices of the Church; he erected against the opposite wall a state pew, surmounted by an openwork canopy decorated with ornaments carved in the solid wood; he used candelabra that had come from a desecrated church, in which he burned real wax tapers purchased at a special house patronized by the clergy, for he felt a genuine repugnance for all the modern methods of illumination, whether petroleum, rock-oil, gas or composite candles, all alike in their crude, dazzling effects.

In bed in the morning, as he lay with his head on the pillow before falling asleep, he would gaze at his Théocopuli, the painful colouring of which modified to some degree the soft cheerfulness of the yellow silk on the walls and gave it a graver tone; at these times, he could easily picture himself living a hundred leagues from Paris, far from the world of men, in the depths of a Monastery.

And, after all, the illusion was not difficult to sustain for truly he was living a life largely analogous to that of a Monk. In this way, he enjoyed the advantages of confinement in a cloister, while he escaped its inconveniences—the quasi-military discipline, the lack of comfort, the dirt and herding together and the monotonous idleness. Just as he had made his cell into a warm, luxurious bedchamber, so he had procured himself an existence carried on under normal conditions, without hardship or incommodity, sufficiently occupied, yet free from irksome restraints.

Like an eremite, he was ripe for solitude, harassed by life's stress, expecting nothing more of existence; like a monk again, he was overwhelmed with an immense fatigue, a craving for peace and quiet, a longing to have nothing more to do henceforth with the vulgar, who were in his eyes all utilitarians and fools.

In short, though he was conscious of no vocation for the state of grace, he felt in himself a genuine sympathy for the folks shut up in Monasteries, persecuted by a society that hates them and can never forgive the well-grounded contempt they entertain for it nor the wish they manifest to redeem, to expiate by long years of silence the ever-increasing licentiousness of its grotesque or silly conversations.

CHAPTER VI

Buried in a vast hooded armchair, his feet resting on the silver-gilt balls of the firedogs, his slippers roasting before the burning logs that shot out bright, crackling flames as if lashed by the furious blast of a blowpipe, Des Esseintes laid down on a table the old quarto he was reading, stretched himself, lit a cigarette and presently lapsed into a delicious reverie, his mind hurrying full chase in pursuit of old-time reminiscences. For months he had not given these a thought, but now they were suddenly revived by the associations of a name that recurred without apparent reason to his memory.

Once more he could see with surprising clearness his friend D'Aigurande's embarrassment when once, at a gathering of confirmed old bachelors, he had been forced to confess to the final completion of the arrangements for his marriage. Everybody protested and drew a harrowing picture for his benefit of the abominations of sleeping two in a bed. Nothing availed; he had lost his head, he believed implicitly in the good sense of his future wife and would have it he had discovered in her quite exceptional gifts of tenderness and devotion.

Among them all, Des Esseintes had been the only one to encourage him in his design—this after learning the fact that his comrade's fiancée wished to live at the corner of a newly constructed boulevard, in one of those modern flats that are built on a circular ground-plan.

Convinced of the merciless influence exerted by petty vexations, more disastrous as these are for highly strung temperaments than the great sorrows of life, and basing his calculations on the fact that D'Aigurande possessed no fortune of his own, while his wife's dowry was all but nonexistent, he foresaw in this harmless wish an indefinite vista of ludicrous miseries to come.

D'Aigurande proceeded in due course to buy furniture all made on the round—console-tables hollowed out at the back so as to form a semicircle, curtain-poles curved like a bow, carpets cut crescent-shaped—a whole suite of furniture made specially to order. He spent twice as much as other people; then presently, when his wife, finding herself short of money for her dress, got tired of living in this roundhouse and removed to an ordinary square habitation at a lower rent, no single piece of furniture would fit in or look right. Little by little, these unconscionable chairs and tables and chests of drawers gave rise to endless squabbles; conjugal happiness, already worn thin by the friction of a life in common, grew week by week more and more ambiguous; mutual recriminations followed, as they found it impossible to live in their drawing-room where sofas and console-tables refused to touch the wall and, in spite of wedges and props, shook and shivered whenever you came near them. Funds were lacking for repairs and improvements, which, to tell the truth, were quite impracticable. Everything became a subject of bitterness and quarrelling, from the drawers that had warped in the wobbling furniture to the petty thefts of the maidservant who took advantage of her master and mistress's squabbles to rob the cashbox. In one word, their life grew unbearable; he sought amusement out of doors, she tried to find in the arms of lovers an anodyne for the wretchedness of her overcast and monotonous life. By common consent, they cancelled the settlements and petitioned for a separation.

"Yes, my plan of campaign was quite correct," Des Esseintes had told himself on hearing the news; he enjoyed the same satisfaction a strategist feels when his manoeuvres, planned long beforehand, end in victory.

Now, sitting there before his fire and thinking over the breakup of this household which he had helped by his advice to bring together, he threw a fresh armful of wood onto the hearth, and so off again full cry in his dreams.

Belonging to the same order of ideas, other memories now began to crowd upon him.

It was some years ago now since one evening in the Rue de Rivoli, he had come across a young scamp of sixteen or so, a pale-faced, quick-eyed child, as seductive as a girl. He was sucking laboriously at a cigarette, the paper of which was bursting where the sharp ends of the coarse caporal had come through. Cursing the stuff, the lad was rubbing kitchen matches down his thigh; they would not light, and soon he came to the end of the box. Catching sight of Des Esseintes who was watching him, he came up, touching his peaked cap, and asked politely for a light. Des Esseintes offered some of his own scented Dubeques, after which he entered into conversation with the lad and urged him to tell the story of his life.

Nothing could well be more ordinary; his name was Auguste Langlois, and he worked at making pasteboard boxes; he had lost his mother and had a father who beat him unmercifully.

Des Esseintes' thoughts were busy as he listened. "Come and have a drink," he said—and took him to a café where he regaled him with goes of heady punch. The child drank his liquor without a word. "Look here," broke in Des Esseintes suddenly, "would you like some fun this evening? I'll pay the piper." And he had thereupon carried off the youngster to Madame Laure's, a lady who kept an assortment of pretty girls on the third floor of a house in the Rue Mosnier; there was a series of rooms with red walls diversified by circular mirrors, the rest of the furniture consisting mainly of couches and washbasins.

There, petrified with surprise, Auguste as he fingered his cloth cap, had stared with round eyes at a battalion of women whose painted lips exclaimed all together:

"Oh! the little lad! Why, he is sweet!"

"But, tell us, my angel, you're not old enough yet, surely?" a brunette had interjected, a girl with prominent eyes and a hook nose who filled at Mme. Laure's establishment the indispensable role of the handsome Jewess.

Quite at his ease, and very much at home, Des Esseintes was talking familiarly in a low voice with the mistress of the house.

"Don't be afraid, stupid," he turned to the child to say; "come now, make your choice, it's my treat,"—and he pushed the lad gently towards a divan, onto which he fell between two women. They drew a little closer together, on a sign from Madame Laure, enveloping Auguste's knees in their peignoirs and bringing under his nose their powdered shoulders that emitted a warm, heady perfume. The child never stirred, but sat there with burning cheeks, a dry mouth and downcast eyes, darting from under their lids downward glances of curiosity, that refused obstinately to leave the upper part of the girls' thighs.

Vanda, the handsome Jewess, kissed him, giving him good advice, telling him to do what father and mother told him, while her hands were straying all the time over the lad's person; a change came over his face and he threw himself back in a kind of transport on her bosom.

"So it's not on your own account you've come tonight," observed Madame Laure to Des Esseintes. "But where the devil did you get hold of that baby?" she added, when Auguste had disappeared with the handsome Jewess.

"In the street, my dear lady."

"Yet you're not drunk," muttered the old woman. Then, after thinking a bit, she proceeded, with a motherly smile: "Ah, I understand; you rascal, you like 'em young, do you?"

Des Esseintes shrugged his shoulders. — "You're wide of the mark! oh! miles away from it," he laughed; "the plain truth is I am simply trying to train a murderer. Now just follow my argument. This boy is virgin and has reached the age when the blood begins to boil; he might, of course, run after the little girls of his neighbourhood, and still remain an honest lad while enjoying his bit of amusement; in fact, have his little share of the monotonous happiness open to the poor. On the contrary, by bringing him here and plunging him in a luxury he had never even suspected the existence of and which will make a lasting impression on his memory; by offering him every fortnight a treat like this, I shall make him acquire the habit of these pleasures which his means forbid his enjoying; let us grant it will take three months for them to become absolutely indispensable to him—and by spacing them out as I do, I avoid all risk of satiating him— well, at the end of the three months, I stop the little allowance I am going to pay you in advance for the benevolence you show him. Then he will take to thieving to pay for his visits here; he will stop at nothing that he may take his usual diversions on this divan in this fine gas-lit apartment.

"If the worst comes to the worst, he will, I hope, one fine day kill the gentleman who turns up just at the wrong moment as he is breaking open his desk; then my object will be attained, I shall have contributed, so far as in me lay, to create a scoundrel, an enemy the more for the odious society that wrings so heavy a ransom from us all."

The woman gazed at the speaker with eyes of amazement.

"Ah! so there you are!" he exclaimed, as he saw Auguste creeping back into the room, red and shy, skulking behind the fair Vanda. "Come, youngster, it is getting late, make your bow to the ladies." Then he explained to him on their way downstairs that, once every fortnight, he might pay a visit to Madame Laure's without putting hand in pocket. Finally, on reaching the street, as they stood together on the pavement, he looked the abashed child in the face and said:

"We shall not meet again after this; do you go back hot foot to your father, whose hand is itching for work to do, and never forget this half divine command: 'Do unto others as you would not have them do unto you.' With that to guide you will go far."

"Good night, sir."

"But whatever you do, do not be ungrateful, let me hear tidings of you soon as may be—in the columns of the Police News."

"The little Judas!" Des Esseintes muttered to himself on this occasion, as he stirred the glowing embers; "to think that I have never once seen his name in the newspapers! True, it has been out of my power to play a sure game; that I have foreseen, yet been unable to prevent certain contingencies—old mother Laure's little tricks, for instance, pocketing the money and not delivering the goods; the chance of one of the women getting infatuated with Auguste, and, when the three months was up, letting him have his whack on tick; or even the possibility of the handsome Jewess's highly-spiced vices having scared the lad, too young and impatient to brook the slow and elaborate preliminaries, or stand the exhausting consummations of her caprices. Unless, therefore, he has been in trouble with the criminal courts since I have been at Fontenay where I never read the papers, I am dished."

He got up from his chair and took two or three turns up and down the room.

"It would be a thousand pities all the same," he mused, "for, by acting in this way, I had really been putting in practice the parable of lay instruction, the allegory of popular education, which, while tending to nothing else than to turn everybody into Langlois, instead of definitely and mercifully putting out the wretched creatures' eyes, tries its hardest to force them wide open that they may see all about them other lots unearned by any merit yet more benignant, pleasures keener and more brightly gilded, and therefore more desirable and harder to come at."

"And the fact is," went on Des Esseintes, pursuing his argument, "the fact is that, pain being the effect of education, seeing that it grows greater and more poignant the more ideas germinate, the more we endeavour to polish the intelligence and refine the nervous system of the poor and unfortunate, the more we shall be developing the germs, always so fiercely ready to sprout, of moral suffering and social hatred."

The lamps were smoking. He turned them up and looked at his watch. Three o'clock in the morning. He kindled a cigarette and plunged himself again in the perusal, interrupted by his dreaming, of the old Latin poem "De Laude Castitatis", written, in the reign of Gondebald, by Avitus, Bishop Metropolitan of Vienne.

CHAPTER VII

After this evening when, without any apparent cause, he had dwelt upon the melancholy memory of Auguste Langlois, Des Esseintes lived his whole life over again.

He was now incapable of understanding one word of the volumes he perused; his eyes themselves refused to read; it seemed to him that his mind, satiated with literature and art, declined absolutely to absorb any more.

He lived on himself, fed on his own substance, like those hibernating animals that lie torpid in a hole all the winter; solitude had acted on his brain as a narcotic. At first, it had nerved and stimulated him, but its later effect was a somnolence haunted by vague reveries; it checked all his plans, broke down his will, led him through a long procession of dreams which he accepted with passive endurance without even an attempt to escape them.

The confused mass of reading and meditation on artistic themes which he had accumulated since he had lived alone as a barrier to arrest the current of old recollections, had been suddenly carried away, and the flood was let loose, sweeping away present and future, submerging them under the waves of the past, drowning his spirit in a vast lake of melancholy, on the surface of which floated, like grotesque derelicts, trivial episodes of his existence, ridiculously unimportant incidents.

The book he was holding tumbled on to his knees; he did not try to resume it, but sat reviewing, full of fear and disgust, the years of his dead past; his thoughts pivoted, like swirling waters round a stake that stands firm and immovable in their midst, about the memories connected with Madame Laure and Auguste. What a time that was!—the period of evening parties, of race-meetings, of card-playing, of love scenes, ordered in advance and served to the minute, at the stroke of midnight, in his pink boudoir! His mind was obsessed by glimpses of faces, looks, unmeaning words that stuck in his memory in the way popular tunes have of doing, which for a while you cannot help humming over and over, but are as suddenly forgotten without your being aware of it.

This epoch was of short duration; then followed a siesta of memory, during which he buried himself once more in his Latin studies, anxious to efface every last trace of these recollections of bygone years.

But the game was fairly started; a second phase followed almost immediately on the first, when his thoughts clung persistently about his boyhood, and especially the part of it spent with the Jesuit fathers.

These memories were more distant, yet clearer than the others, engraved on his heart more deeply and more ineffaceably; the leafy park, the long garden walks, the flower beds, the benches, all the material details rose before him.

Then the gardens filled with a throng of boys and masters; he could hear the former's shouts at play, the latter's laughter as they mingled in the lads' sports, playing tennis with tucked-up cassocks, the skirts passed between their legs, or else talking under the trees to their pupils without the least affectation of superiority, as if conversing with comrades of their own age.

He recalled that paternal yoke which discountenanced any form of punishment, declined to inflict impositions of five hundred or one thousand lines, was content to have the unsatisfactory task done over again while the rest of the class were at recreation, more often than not preferred a mere reprimand, watched over the growing child with an active but loving care, striving to please his tastes, agreeing to walks in whatever direction he liked on Wednesday half-holidays, seizing the opportunity offered by all the little semiofficial feast-days of the Church to add to the ordinary fare at meals a treat of cakes and wine or organize a country expedition—a yoke under which the pupil was never brutalized, but was admitted to open discussion, was treated in fact like a grown man, while still being pampered like a spoilt child.

In this way the Fathers succeeded in gaining a real ascendancy over the young, moulded to some extent the minds they cultivated, guided them in the desired direction, engrafted particular modes of thought on their intelligence, secured the development of their character after the required pattern by an insinuating, wheedling method of treatment which they continued to pursue afterwards, making a point of following their subsequent course of life, backing them in their career, keeping up an affectionate correspondence with them—letters of the sort the Dominican Lacordaire knew well how to write to his former pupils at Sorrèze.

One by one, Des Esseintes went over the points of the training he had undergone, as he himself supposed without result; he quite appreciated its merits, albeit his temperament, recalcitrant and stubborn, carping and critical, eager to argue out every proposition, had prevented his being modelled by their discipline or ruled by what they taught him. Once outside the College walls, his scepticism had grown more acute; his intercourse with legitimist society, intolerant and narrow to the last degree, his talks with puzzle-headed church officials and half educated priests whose blunders tore away the veil so cleverly contrived by the Jesuits, had still further fortified his spirit of independence and increased his distrust in any and every form of belief.

He deemed himself, in a word, released from every tie, free from every obligation; all he had hitherto preserved, differing herein from all his friends who had been educated at Lycées or lay boarding-schools, was a highly favourable memory of his school and schoolmasters; yet now, he was actually examining his conscience, beginning to ask himself if the seed heretofore fallen on barren ground was not showing signs of fructifying.

The fact is for some days he had been in an indescribably strange state of mind. For a brief moment he was a believer, an instinctive convert to religion; then, after the shortest interval of reflection, all his attraction towards the Faith would evaporate. But all the time and in spite of everything, he was anxious and disturbed in spirit.

Yet he was perfectly well aware, if he looked into his own heart, that he could never have the humility and contrition of a truly Christian soul; he knew beyond all possibility of doubt that the moment of which Lacordaire speaks, the moment of grace, "when the final ray of right penetrates the soul and draws together to a common centre the truths that lie dispersed therein," would never come for him; he experienced none of that craving for prayer and mortification without which, if we are to listen to the majority of priests, no conversion is possible; he felt no wish to supplicate a God, whose loving-kindness seemed to him highly problematical. At the same time the sympathy he still had for his former instructors was sufficient to interest him in their works and teachings; the inimitable accents of conviction he remembered, the ardent voices of men of superior intelligence he recalled, haunted his mind and made him doubt his own ability and strength of intellect. Living the lonely life he now did, with no fresh food for thought, no novel impressions to stimulate imagination, no exchange of sensations coming from outside, from meeting friends or society, from living the same life as other men, confined within an unnatural prison-house which he refused to escape from, all sorts of problems, never thought of during his residence in Paris, demanded a solution with irritating persistency.

His study of the Latin works he delighted in, works almost without exception written by bishops and monks, had no doubt played their part in determining this crisis. Surrounded by a cloistered atmosphere, wrapt in a fragrance of incense that intoxicated his brain, he had got into an overwrought condition of nerves, and then, by a natural association of ideas, these books had ended by dimming his recollections of his life as a young man, while throwing into high relief those connected with his boyhood among the Fathers.

"There is no difficulty," Des Esseintes told himself with an effort after self-examination, "in accounting for this irruption of the Jesuit element at Fontenay; ever since I was a child, and without my knowing it myself, I have had this leaven, which had not previously fermented; is not this inclination I have always felt towards religious thoughts and things perhaps a proof of this?"

But his efforts were all directed to persuading himself of the contrary, annoyed as he was to find himself no longer absolute master of his own soul. He sought for motives to account for the change in himself; yes, he must have been forcibly drawn in the direction of the priesthood because the Church, and the Church only, has preserved the art, the lost beauty of the centuries; she has stereotyped, even in the cheap modern reproductions, the patterns of metal work, preserved the charm of chalices slim and tall as petunias, of sacred vessels of exquisite curves and contours, safeguarded, even in aluminium, in sham enamel, in coloured glass, the grace of the models of olden days. As a matter of fact, the main part of the precious objects exhibited in the Musée de Cluny, having escaped by a miracle the foul savagery of the sans-culottes, come from the old Abbeys of France. Just as in the Middle Ages the Church saved from barbarism, philosophy, history and letters, so she has saved plastic art, brought down to our own days those wondrous patterns in ecclesiastical robes and jewelry which the manufacturers of Church furniture and ornaments do their best to spoil, though they can never quite ruin the original beauty of form and colour. There was therefore no cause for surprise in the fact that he had sought eagerly for these antique curios, that like many another collector, he had acquired suchlike relics from the shops of the Parisian antiquaries and the stores of country dealers.

But, despite all the good reasons he could call up to his aid, he could not quite manage to convince himself. No doubt, after due consideration, he still continued to look upon religion merely as a superb myth, as a magnificent imposture; and yet, heedless of all his excuses and explanations, his scepticism was beginning to wear thin.

There was the fact, odd as it might seem: he was less confident at the present moment than he had been in his boyhood, in the days when the Jesuits exercised direct supervision over his training, when their teaching had to be received, when he was entirely in their hands, was theirs, body and soul, without family ties, without any outside influences of any kind to react against their ascendancy. Moreover, they had instilled in him a certain taste for the marvellous that had slowly and stealthily taken root in his soul, and was now coming to a head in this solitary life that could not but exert its influence on his silent, self-centred nature, forever moving within the narrow limits of certain fixed ideas.

By dint of examining the processes of his thought, of striving to connect its threads together and discover its causes and conditioning circumstances, he eventually persuaded himself that its activities during his life in the world of men had their origin in the education he had received. Thus, his tendencies to artificiality, his longings for eccentricity, were these not, after all, results of plausible studies, supra-terrestrial refinements, semi-theological speculations; in ultimate analysis they amounted to the same thing as religious enthusiasms, aspirations towards an unknown universe, towards a far-off beatitude, just as ardently to be desired as that promised to believers by the Scriptures.

He pulled himself up short, broke off the thread of his reflections. "Come, come," he chid himself angrily, "I am more seriously hit than I thought: here I am argufying with myself, like a casuist."

He remained pensive, troubled by a secret fear. No doubt, if Lacordaire's theory was correct, he had nothing to dread, seeing that the magic touch of conversion does not come about in an instant; to produce the explosion, the ground must have been long and systematically mined. But if the novelists talk about the thunderclap of love at first sight, there is also a certain number of theologians who speak of the thunderclap of religion. Admitting the truth of this doctrine, no man then was safe against succumbing. There was no room left for self-analysis, no use in weighing presentiments, no object gained by taking preventive measures; the psychology of mysticism was futile. It was so because it was so, and there was no more to be said.

"Why, I am growing crazy," Des Esseintes told himself; "the dread of the disease will end by bringing on the disease itself, if this goes on."

He managed to shake off the influence of these preoccupations to some extent, but other morbid symptoms supervened. Now it was the subject matter of various discussions that haunted him to the exclusion of everything else. The College garden, the school lessons, the Jesuit Fathers sank into the remote background, his whole mind was dominated by abstractions, his thoughts were busy, in spite of himself, with contradictory interpretations of dogmas, with long forgotten apostasies, denounced in his work on the Councils of the Church by Père Labbe. Fragments of these schisms, scraps of these heresies, which for centuries divided the Western and the Eastern Churches, haunted his memory. Here it was Nestorius, protesting against the Virgin's bearing the title of Mother of God, because in the mystery of the Incarnation, it was not God, but rather the human creature, she had carried in her womb; there it was Eutyches, maintaining that the image of Christ could not be like that of the rest of mankind, inasmuch as the Divinity had been domiciled in his body and had thereby changed its nature utterly and entirely; elsewhere again other quibblers would have it that the Redeemer had had no human body at all, that the language of the Holy Books on this point must be understood figuratively, while yet again Tertullian was found positing his famous quasi-materialistic axiom: "Nothing is incorporal save what is not; whatever is, has a body that is proper to itself," till finally we come to the old, old question debated for years: was the Christ bound alone to the cross, or did the Trinity, one in three persons, suffer, in its threefold hypostasis, on the gibbet of Calvary? All these difficulties tormented him, pressing for an answer—and mechanically, like a lesson already learnt by rote, he kept asking himself the questions and repeating the replies.

For several succeeding days, his brain was seething with paradoxies and subtleties, puzzling over a host of hairsplitting distinctions, wrestling with a tangle of rule as complicated as so many points of law, open to any and every interpretation, admitting of every sort of quirk and quibble, leading up to a system of celestial jurisprudence of the most tenuous and burlesque subtlety. Then the abstract side fell in its turn into abeyance, and a whole world of plastic impressions took its place, under the influence of the Gustave Moreaus hanging on the walls.

He beheld a long procession pass before his eyes of prelates, archimandrites, patriarchs, blessing the kneeling multitudes with uplifted arms of gold, wagging their white beards in reading of the Scriptures and in prayer; he saw dim crypts receive the silent ranks of innumerable penitents; he looked on while men raised vast cathedrals where white-robed monks thundered from the pulpit. In the same fashion as de Quincey, after a dose of opium, would at the mere sound of the words "Consul Romanus" recall whole pages of Livy, would see the consuls coming on in solemn procession and the pompous array of the Roman legionaries marching stately by, so Des Esseintes, struck by some theological phrase, would halt in breathless awe as he pondered the flux and reflux of Nations, and beheld the forms of bishops of other days standing forth in the lamplit gloom of basilicas; visions like these kept him entranced, travelling in fancy from age to age, coming down at last to the religious ceremonies of the present day, enfolded in an endless flood of music, mournful and tender. Now he was beyond all self-justification, the thing was decided beyond appeal; it was just an indefinable impression of veneration and fear; the artistic sense was dominated by the well-calculated scenes of Catholic ceremonial. At these memories his nerves quivered; then, in a sudden mood of revolt, of swift revolution, ideas of monstrous depravity would attack him—thoughts of the profanities foreseen in the Confessors' Manual, degraded and filthy abuses of the holy water and the consecrated oil. Face to face with an omnipotent God now stood up a rival full of energy, the Demon; and he thought a hideous glory must needs result from a crime committed in open church by a believer fiercely resolved, in a mood of horrid merriment, of a sadic satisfaction, to blaspheme, to overwhelm with insult and recrimination the things most deserving veneration; mad doings of magic, the black mass, the witches' sabbath, horrors of demoniac possession and exorcism rose before his imagination; he began to ask himself if he were not guilty of sacrilege in possessing articles once consecrated to holy uses—church service-books, chasubles, pyx-covers. And, strange to say, this notion of living in a state of sin afforded him a sense of proud satisfaction and pleasure; he found a delight in these acts of sacrilege—after all a possibly innocent sacrilege; in any case not a very serious offence, seeing he really loved these articles and put them to no base usage. Thus he comforted himself with prudent, coward considerations, his halfhearted condition of soul forbidding open crimes, robbing him of the needful courage to accomplish real sins, deliberate, damning iniquities.

Eventually, little by little, these casuistries disappeared. He looked out, as it were, from the summit of his mind, over the panorama of the Church and her hereditary influence over humanity, as old as the centuries; he pictured her to himself, solitary and impressive, proclaiming to mankind the horror of life, the inclemency of fate; preaching patience, contrition, the spirit of sacrifice; essaying to heal men's sores by exhibiting the bleeding wounds of the Christ; guaranteeing divine privileges, promising the best part of paradise to the afflicted; exhorting the human creature to suffer, to offer to God as a holocaust his tribulations and his offences, his vicissitudes and his sorrows. He saw her truly eloquent, a mother to the unfortunate, a pitiful father to the oppressed, a stern judge to oppressors and tyrants.

At this point, Des Esseintes recovered footing. Doubtless he was content to accept this admission of social rottenness, but his mind revolted against the vague remedy offered, the hope of another life. Schopenhauer was more exact; his doctrine and the Church's started from a common point of view; he, too, took his stand on the wickedness and baseness of the world; he, too, cried out, with the Imitation of Our Lord, in bitterness of spirit: "Verily it is a pitiful thing to be alive on the earth!" He, too, preached the nullity of existence, the advantages of solitude; warned humanity that, whatever it did, whichever way it turned, it must still be unhappy—the poor man, because of the sufferings that spring from privations; the rich, by reason of the invincible ennui engendered by abundance. But he proclaimed no panacea, consoled you, as a cure for inevitable evils, with no alluring bait.

Nor did he maintain the revolting dogma of original sin; did not try to convince you of the existence of a God supremely good and kind who protects the scoundrel, succours the fool, crushes infancy, brutalizes old age, chastises the innocent; he did not extol the benefits of a Providence which has invented that abomination, useless, incomprehensible, unjust and inept, physical pain; far from endeavouring, like the Church, to justify the necessity of torments and trials, he exclaimed in his indignant pity: "If a God had made this world, I should not like to be that God; the misery of the world would break my heart."

Schopenhauer had seen the truth! What were all the evangelical pharmacopoeias beside his treatises of spiritual hygiene? He made no professions of healing, offered the sick no compensation, no hope; but his theory of Pessimism was, after all, the great consoler of chosen intellects, of lofty souls; it revealed society as it was, insisted on the innate foolishness of women, pointed you out the beaten tracks, saved you from disillusions by teaching you to restrict, so far as possible, your expectations; never, if you felt yourself strong enough to check the impulse, to let yourself come to the state of mind of believing yourself happy at last if only, when you least expected it, heaven did not send crashing on your head some murderous tile from the housetops.

Setting out from the same starting-point as the Imitation, this theory found the very same goal, but without losing itself on the road among mysterious mazes and impossible bypaths, in resignation and passivity.

Only, if this resignation, frankly based on the observation of a deplorable condition of things and the impossibility of effecting any alteration in them, was accessible to the rich in spirit, it was only the more hardly to be received by the poor, whose grievances and indignation the kindly hand of Religion was better adapted to appease.

These reflections relieved Des Esseintes of a heavy burden; the aphorisms of the great German thinker calmed the tumult of his thoughts, while at the same time the points of similarity between the two doctrines mutually helped each other to find a firm place in his memory, and he could never forget Catholicism, so poetical, so touching, in which he had been bathed as a boy and whose essence he had absorbed through every pore.

These returns towards religious convictions, these fears and doubts of uncertain faith had tormented him, especially since new complications had begun to show themselves in his health; they coincided with certain nervous disturbances that had lately arisen.

Since his earliest childhood he had been tormented by inexplicable repulsions, shuddering spasms that froze his backbone and clenched his teeth, whenever, for instance, he saw a servant-maid in the act of wringing out wet linen. These instinctive dislikes had never changed, and to that day it caused him genuine suffering to hear a piece of stuff torn in two, to rub his finger over a lump of chalk, to stroke the surface of watered silk.

The excesses of his bachelorhood, the abnormal strains put upon his brain had extraordinarily aggravated his original nervous weakness, still further impoverished the exhausted blood of his race; in Paris he had been obliged to resort to hydropathic treatment for trembling of the hands, for atrocious pains, for neuralgic agonies that seemed to cut his face in two, that beat with a never-ceasing hammering at his temples, sent stabbing throbs through his eyelids, provoked fits of nausea he could only subdue by stretching himself flat on his back in the dark.

These inconveniences had gradually disappeared, thanks to a better regulated and quieter life; now they were making themselves felt again, though in a different shape, diffused through the body generally; the pain left the head and attacked the stomach, which was swollen and hard; scorched the inwards as with a red-hot iron, brought on a condition of the bowels at once uneasy and constipated. Presently a nervous cough, dry and hacking, beginning always exactly at a set hour and lasting for precisely the same number of minutes, woke him half choking in his bed. Finally he lost all appetite; hot, gassy eructations rose like fire in his throat; the stomach was distended; he felt stifled, after each attempt to eat; he could not endure the least constriction about the body, a buttoned trouser-belt or a buckled waistcoat.

He gave up spirituous liquors, coffee and tea, confined himself to a milk diet, resorted to bathing the body with cold water, stuffed himself with assafoetida, valerian and quinine; he even consented to leave the house and take strolls in the country when the days of rain came that make the roads silent and deserted; he forced himself to walk, to take exercise; as a last resource, he renounced reading altogether for the time being and, consumed with ennui, determined by way of filling up this time of enforced leisure to carry out a project the execution of which he had again and again postponed out of laziness and dislike of change since the first day of his settling at Fontenay.

No longer able to intoxicate himself afresh with the magical enchantments of style, to fall into an ecstasy over the delicious witchery of the rare and well-chosen epithet that, while still definite and precise, yet opens infinite perspectives, to the imagination of the initiate he resolved to complete the decoration of his dwelling, to fill it with costly hothouse flowers and so procure himself a material occupation that should distract his thoughts, calm his nerves and rest his brain. Moreover, he had hopes that the sight of their strange and magnificent colours might console him somewhat for the loss of the fancied or real shades of literary style which his abstention from all reading was to make him forget for the moment or lose altogether.

CHAPTER VIII

He had always been madly fond of flowers, but this passion which, during his residence at Jutigny, had at the first embraced all flowers without distinction of species or genus, had in the end grown more discriminating and precise, limiting itself to a single type.

For a long time now he had scorned the everyday plants that blossom on the counters of Parisian florists, in dripping flowerpots, under green awnings or red umbrellas.

At the same time that his literary tastes, his preferences in art, had become more refined, no longer caring for any works but such as had been tried and sifted, the distillation of overwrought and subtle brains; at the same time that his disgust with generally accepted notions had reached its height, simultaneously his love of flowers had rid itself of all base residuum, all dregs of commonness, had been clarified, as it were, and purified.

He pleased his fancy by likening a horticulturist's shop to a microcosm wherein were represented all the different categories of society—poor, vulgar flowers, hovel flowers, so to speak, that are really in their proper place only on the windowsill of a garret, roots that are crammed in milk-tins and old earthen pots, the gilliflower for instance; pretentious, conventional, silly flowers, whose only place is in porcelain vases painted by young ladies, such as the rose; lastly, flowers of high lineage, such as the orchids, dainty and charming, trembling and delicate, such as the exotic flowers, exiles in Paris, kept in hothouses, in palaces of glass, Princesses of the vegetable world, living apart, having nothing whatever in common with the flowers of the street, the blossoms that are the delight of grocers' wives.

In a word, he could do no more than feel a trivial interest, a slight pity, for the people's flowers, fading under the poisonous breath of sewers and sinks in squalid districts; to make up, he loathed those that go with the cream and gold reception-rooms in new houses; he reserved, in fact, for the full and perfect delectation of his eyes, rare plants of high-bred type, coming from distant lands, kept alive by skill and pains in an artificial equatorial temperature maintained by carefully regulated furnaces.

But this choice of his, that had deliberately fallen on greenhouse flowers, had itself been further modified under the influence of his general ideas, his opinions that had now come to definite conclusions on all matters. In former days, in Paris, his innate preference for the artificial had led him to neglect the real flower for its copy, faithfully executed thanks to india-rubber and twine, glazed cotton and lustring, paper and velvet.

He possessed in accordance with this taste a marvellous collection of tropical plants, produced by the cunning fingers of supreme masters of the craft, following Nature step by step, recreating her, taking the flower from its birth, carrying it to maturity, imitating it to its final decease, observing every shade of its infinite variety, the most fleeting changes of its awakening and its sleep, noting the pose of its petals blown back by the wind or beaten down by the rain, sprinkling on its morning leaves little drops of gum to represent dew, fashioning it according to every season—in full bloom, when the twigs bend under the weight of sap; or when it lifts its parched stem and ragged corolla as the petals drop away and the leaves fall.

This admirable art had long fascinated him; but now he was dreaming of the construction of another sort of flora.

He had done with artificial flowers aping the true; he wanted natural flowers imitating the false.

He set himself to work out this problem, nor had he to search long or go far, for was not his house situated in the very middle of the district specially favoured by the great flower-growers? He went straight off to pay a visit to the hothouses of the Avenue de Châtillon and the valley of

Aunay, to return tired out and his purse empty, thinking of nothing but the strange species he had bought, ceaselessly haunted by his memories of superb and extraordinary blooms.

Two days later the carts arrived.

List in hand, Des Esseintes called the roster, verified his purchases one by one.

The gardeners unloaded from their vans a collection of Caladiums whose swollen, hairy stalks carried enormous leaves, shaped like a heart; while keeping a general look of kinship, they were every one different.

They included some extraordinary specimens—some rosy-red, like the Virginale which seemed cut out in glazed cloth, in shiny court-plaster; some all white, like the Albane, that looked as if made of the semitransparent membrane that lines an ox's ribs, or the diaphanous film of a pig's bladder. Others again, especially the one called Madame Maine, mimicked zinc, parodied pieces of stencilled metal coloured emperor-green, blotched with drops of oil paint, streaks of red-lead and ceruse: these—the Bosphorus was an example—gave the illusion of starched calico, spotted with crimson and myrtle-green; those, the Aurora Borealis for instance, had broad leaves the colour of raw meat, intersected by striations of a darker red and purplish threads, leaves that seemed swollen and sweating with dark liquor and blood.

This plant, the Aurora Borealis, and the Albane between them displayed the two opposite poles of constitution, the former bursting with apoplexy, the latter pallid with bloodlessness.

The men brought other and fresh varieties, in this case presenting the appearance of a fictitious skin marked by an imitation network of veins. Most of them, as if disfigured by syphilis or leprosy, displayed livid patches of flesh, reddened by measles, roughened by eruptions; others showed the bright pink of a half-closed wound or the red brown of the crusts that form over a scar; others were as if scorched with cauteries blistered with burns; others again offered hairy surfaces eaten into holes by ulcers and excavated by chancres. To finish the list, there were some that had just come from the doctor's hands, it seemed, plastered with black mercury dressing, smeared with green belladonna ointment, dusted over with the yellow grains of iodoform powder.

Thus assembled all together, these strange blossoms struck Des Esseintes as more monstrous yet than when he had first seen them ranged side by side with others, like patients in a hospital ward, down the long conservatories.

"Sapristi!" he exclaimed, stirred to the depths.

A new plant, of a type similar to the Caladiums, the Alocasia Metallica, moved his enthusiasm to a still higher pitch. Its leaves were overlaid with a layer of green bronze, shot with gleams of silver; it was the masterpiece, the fine flower of counterfeit; you might have thought it a bit of stovepipe, cut out of sheet iron in the shape of a spearhead, by a jobbing blacksmith.

Next the men unloaded a tangled mass of leaves, lozenge-shaped, bottle-green in hue; from their midst rose a switch on top of which trembled a great ace of hearts, as smooth and shiny as a capsicum; then, as if to defy all the familiar aspects of plants, from the middle of this ace of hearts, of an intense vermillion, sprang a fleshy tail, downy, white and yellow, upright in some cases, corkscrewed above the heart, like a pig's tail, in others.

It was the Anthurium, one of the arum family, recently imported from Colombia; it formed part of a section of the same family to which also belonged an Amorphophallus, a plant from Cochin China, with long black stalks seamed with scars, like a negro's limbs after a thrashing.

Des Esseintes' cup of joy was brimming over.

Then they got out of the carts a fresh batch of monstrosities, the Echinopsis, showing a pink blossom like the stump of an amputated limb rising out of a compress of cotton-wool; the Nidularium, displaying in its sword-like leaves gaping, ragged hollows; the Tillandsia Lindeni, like a broken-toothed cury-comb, of the colour of wine-must: the Cypripedium, with its involved, incoherent, incongruous contours that seem the invention of a madman. It was shaped like a wooden shoe, or a little ragbag, above which was a human tongue retracted, with the tendon drawn tight, as you may see it represented in the plates of medical works treating of diseases of the throat and mouth; two miniature wings, of a jujube red, that seemed borrowed from a child's toy windmill, completed this grotesque conjunction of the underside of a tongue, colour of wine lees and slate, and a little glossy pocket, the lining of which distilled a viscous glue.

He could not take his eyes off this impossible-looking orchid, indigenous to India, till the gardeners, exasperated by these delays, began to read out aloud for themselves the labels fixed in the pots as they carried them in.

Des Esseintes looked on in wonder, listened open-mouthed to the barbarous names of the herbaceous plants—the Encephalartos horridus, a gigantic artichoke, an iron spike painted rust colour, like the ones they stick on the top of park gates to prevent intruders climbing over; the Cocos Micania, a sort of palm, with a notched and slender stem, everywhere surrounded with tall leaves like paddles and oars; the Zamia Lehmanni, a huge pineapple, like an immense Cheshire cheese, growing in peaty soil and bristling at the apex with barbed spears and cruel looking arrows; the Cibotium Spectabile, going one better ever than its congeners in the wild caprice of its structure, defying the maddest nightmare, throwing out from amid a clustered foliage of palm leaves a prodigious orangutan's tail, a brown, hairy tail curling over at the tip like a bishop's crozier.

These, however, he barely glanced at, waiting impatiently for the series of plants that particularly fascinated him, those vegetable ghouls, the carnivorous plants—the Flycatcher of the Antilles, with its shaggy edge, secreting a digestive liquid, provided with curved thorns folding into each other to form a barred grating over the insect it imprisons; the Drosera of the peat mosses, furnished with rows of stiff, glandulous hairs; the Sarracena; the Cephalothus, with deep, voracious cups capable of absorbing and digesting actual lumps of meat; last, but not least amazing, the Nepenthes whose eccentricity of shape overpasses all known limits.

It seemed as though he could never weary of turning about in his hands the pot in which trembled this extravagant vagary of the flower tribe. It resembled the gum-tree in its long leaves of a sombre, metallic green, but from the end of these leaves depended a green string, a sort of umbilical cord, carrying a greenish coloured urn, veined with purple, a sort of German pipe in porcelain, a strange kind of bird's nest, that swung quietly to and fro, exhibiting an interior carpeted with a hairy growth.

"That one is a veritable miracle," Des Esseintes murmured to himself.

But he was forced to cut short his manifestations of delight, for now the gardeners, in a hurry to be gone, were unloading the last of their wares and setting down side by side tuberous Begonias and black Crotons, flecked with red-lead spots, like rusty iron.

Then he noticed that one name was still left on the list, the Cattleya of New Granada. They pointed out to him a little winged bellflower of a pale lilac, an almost invisible mauve; he drew near, put his nose to it and started back; it exhaled an odour of varnished deal, just the smell of a new box of toys, recalling irresistibly all the horrors of the New Year and New Year's presents.

It struck him it would be well for him to beware of it, almost regretted having admitted among the scentless plants he had become possessor of the orchid that brought up the most unpleasant associations.

He cast only one glance over this flood-tide of vegetation that swelled in his vestibule; there they were, all confounded together, intercrossing their sword-blades, their kreeses, their lance-heads, forming a tangled mass of green weapons of war, over which floated like barbarian pennons of battle, blossoms dazzling and cruel in their brilliance.

The atmosphere of the room was clearer by now, and soon, in a dark corner, just above the floor, a light crept out, soft and white.

He went up to it, to discover it was a cluster of Rhizomorphs, each of which, as it breathed, was shedding this gleam like that cast by nightlights.

"All the same, these plants are amazing things," he muttered to himself; then he stepped back and embraced in one view the whole collection. Yes, his object was attained; not one of them looked real; cloth, paper, porcelain, metal seemed to have been lent by man to Nature to enable her to create these monstrosities. When she had found herself incapable of copying human workmanship, she had been reduced to mimick the membranes of animals' insides, to borrow the vivid tints of their rotting flesh, the superb horrors of their gangrened skin.

"It is all a matter of syphilis," reflected Des Esseintes, his eyes attracted, riveted on the hideous marking of the Caladiums, lit up at that moment by a shaft of daylight. And he had a sudden vision of the human race tortured by the virus of long past centuries. Ever since the beginning of the world, from sire to son, all living creatures were handing on the inexhaustible heritage, the everlasting malady that has devastated the ancestors of the men of today, has eaten to the very bone old fossil forms which we dig up at the present moment.

Never wearying, it had travelled down the ages, to this day it was raging everywhere, disguised under ordinary symptoms of headache or bronchitis, hysteria or gout; from time to time, it would climb to the surface, attacking for choice badly cared-for, badly-fed people breaking out in gold pieces, setting, in horrid irony, a Nautch-girl's parure of sequins on its wretched victim's brows, inscribing their skin, for a crown to their misery, with the very symbol of wealth and well-being.

And lo! here it was reappearing, in its pristine splendour, on the bright-coloured petals of flowers!

"It is true," pursued Des Esseintes, going back to the starting point of his argument, "it is true that, for most of the time, Nature is by herself incapable of producing species so morbid and perverse; she supplies the raw material, the germ and the soil, the procreative womb and the elements of the plant, which mankind rears, models, paints, carves afterwards to suit his caprice."

Obstinate, confused, limited though she be, she has at last submitted, and her master has succeeded in changing by chemical reactions the substances of the earth, to utilize combinations long ripened for use, crossings slowly prepared for, to employ artful buddings, systematic graftings, so that nowadays he can make her produce blooms of different colours on the same bough; invents new hues for her; modifies, at his good pleasure, the age-old shapes of her plants. He clears off the rough from her half-hewn blocks, puts the finishing touches to her rude sketches, marks them with his signet, impresses on them his sign-manual of art.

"There is no more to be said," he cried, resuming his train of thought; "mankind is able in the course of a few years to bring about a selection which sluggish Nature can never effect but after centuries of time; no doubt of it, in these present times, the gardeners are the only and the true artists."

He was a little weary and felt stifled in this atmosphere of hothouse plants; the walks he had taken during the last few days had exhausted him; the change from the open air to the warmth of the house, from the sedentary life of a recluse to the free activity of an outdoor existence, had been too sudden. He left the hall and went to lie down on his bed; but, bent on one single absorbing subject, as if wound up with a spring, the mind, though asleep all the while, went on paying out its chain, and he was soon wallowing in the gloomy fancies of a nightmare.

He was standing in the middle of a ride in a great forest at dusk; he was walking side by side with a woman he did not know, had never seen before; she was tall and thin, had pale flaxen hair, a bulldog face, freckled cheeks, irregular teeth projecting below a flat nose. She wore a servant's white apron, a long kerchief crossed like a soldier's buff-belt over her chest, a Prussian grenadier's half-boots, a black bonnet trimmed with ruchings and a big bow.

She had the look of a show-woman at a fair, a travelling mountebank or the like.

He asked himself who the woman was whom he somehow knew to have been a long while in the room, to have long been an intimate part of his life; in vain he strove to remember her origin, her name, her business, the explanation of her presence; no recollection would come to him of this inexplicable liaison, of which however there could be no doubt.

He was still searching his memory when suddenly a strange figure appeared in front of them; it was on horseback and trotted on for a minute, then turned round in the saddle.

His blood gave one bound within him and he remained nailed to the spot in utter horror. The ambiguous, sexless creature was green, and from under purple lids shone a pair of pale blue eyes, cold and terrible; two arms of an inordinate leanness, like a skeleton's bare to the elbows, shaking with fever, projected from ragged sleeves, and the fleshless thighs shuddered in churn-boots, a world too wide.

The awful eyes were fixed on Des Esseintes, piercing him, freezing him to the marrow of his bones; more terrified still, the bulldog woman pressed against him and yelled death and destruction, her head thrown back, her neck stiffened with a spasm of wild terror.

And lo! in an instant he knew the meaning of the appalling vision. He had before his eyes the image of the Pox.

Mad with fear, beside himself with consternation, he dashed into a side path, ran at headlong speed to a summerhouse standing among laburnums to the left of the road, where he dropped into a chair in a passage.

In a few minutes when he was beginning to get his breath, the sound of sobs made him look up. The bulldog woman was before him; a piteous, grotesque spectacle. She stood weeping hot tears, declaring she had lost her teeth in her panic, and, drawing from the pocket of her servant's apron a number of clay pipes, she proceeded to break them and stuff bits of the stems into the holes in her gums.

"Come now, she's quite ridiculous," Des Esseintes kept telling himself; "the pipes will never stick in,"—and as a matter of fact, they all came tumbling out of her jaws one after the other.

At that moment, a galloping horse was heard approaching. A paralysing fear seized Des Esseintes; his limbs failed him. But the sound of hoofs grew momentarily louder; despair stung him to action like the lash of a whip; he threw himself upon the woman, who was now trampling the pipe bowls underfoot, beseeching her to be quiet and not betray him by the noise of her boots. She struggled; but he dragged her to the end of the passage, throttling her to stop her crying out. Suddenly, he saw an alehouse door, with green painted shutters, pushed it open, darted in and stopped dead.

In front of him, in the middle of a vast clearing in the woods, enormous white pierrots were jumping like rabbits in the moonlight.

Tears of disappointment rose to his eyes; he could never, no, never cross the threshold of the door. — "I should be dashed to pieces," he thought— and as if to justify his fears, the troop of giant pierrots was reinforced; their bounds now filled the whole horizon, the whole sky, which they knocked alternately with their heels and their heads.

The horse came to a standstill, it was there, close by, behind a round window in the passage; more dead than alive, Des Esseintes turned round and saw through the circular opening two pricked ears, two rows of yellow teeth, nostrils breathing clouds of vapour that stank of phenol.

He sank to the earth, abandoning all idea of resistance or even of flight; he shut his eyes so as not to see the dreadful eyes of the Syphilis glaring at him through the wall, which nevertheless forced their way under his lids, glided down his spine, enveloped his body, the hairs of which stood up on end in pools of cold sweat. He expected any and every torment, only hoped to have done with it with one final annihilating blow; an age, that beyond a doubt lasted a whole minute, went by; then he opened his eyes again with a shudder.

All had vanished; without transition, as if by a change of scene, by a stage delusion, a hideous metallic landscape was disappearing in the distance, a landscape wan, desert, cloven with ravines, dead and dreary; a light illumined this desolate place, a calm, white light, recalling the glint of phosphorus dissolved in oil.

On the surface, something moved which took a woman's shape, a pallid, naked woman, green silk stockings moulding the legs.

He gazed at her curiously. Like horsehair curled by over-hot irons, her locks were frizzled, with broken ends; urns of the Nepenthes hung at her ears; tints of boiled veal showed in her half-opened nostrils. With entranced eyes, she called him in a low voice.

He had no time to answer, for already the woman was changing; gleams of iridescent colours flashed in her eyes; her lips assumed the fierce red of the Anthuriums; the nipples of her bosom blazed out like two bright red pods of capsicum.

A sudden intuition came to him; it is the Flower, he told himself; and the spirit of reasoning still persisted in the nightmare, drew the same conclusions as he had already in the daytime from the plants as the malevolence of the Virus.

Then he noticed the terrifying irritation of the bosoms and of the mouth, discovered on the skin of the body stains of bistre and copper, and recoiled in horror; but the woman's eye fascinated him, and he crept slowly, reluctantly towards her, trying to drive his heels into the ground to stay his advance, dropping to the earth, only to rise again to go to her. He was all but touching her when black Amorphophalli sprang up on every side, and made darts at her belly that was rising and falling like a sea. He put them away from him, pushed them back, feeling an infinite loathing to see these hot, moist, firm stems coiling between his fingers. Then, in a moment, the odious plants disappeared, and two arms were seeking to wind themselves about him. An agony of terror set his heart beating wildly, for the eyes, the dreadful eyes of the woman, had become pale, cold blue, terrible to look at. He made a superhuman effort to free himself from her embraces, but with an irresistible gesture she seized and held him, and haggard with horror, he saw the savage Nidularium blossom under her meagre thighs, with its sword blades gaping in blood-red hollows.

His body was almost in contact with the hideous open wound of the plant; he felt himself a dying man, and awoke with a start, choking, frozen, frantic with fear, sobbing out: "Thank God, thank God! it is only a dream."

CHAPTER IX

THESE NIGHTMARES RECURRED AGAIN AND AGAIN, TILL HE WAS AFRAID TO GO to sleep. He would lie stretched on his bed, sometimes the victim of obstinate fits of insomnia and feverish restlessness, at others of abominable dreams only interrupted by the spasmodic awakening of a man losing foothold, pitching from top to bottom of a staircase, plunging into the depths of an abyss, without power to stop himself.

For several days, the exhausting nervous disturbance gained the upper hand again, showing itself more violent and more obstinate than ever, though under new forms.

Now the bedclothes were a weight not to be borne; he felt stifled under the sheets, while his whole body was tormented with tinglings; his thighs burned, his legs itched. To these symptoms were soon added a dull aching of the jaws and a sensation as if his temples were confined within a vice.

His distress of mind grew more and more acute, but unfortunately the proper means of mastering the merciless complaint were lacking. He had tried without success to fit up an installation of hydropathic appliances in his dressing room; but the impossibility of bringing water to the top of the hill on which his house was perched, the preliminary difficulty indeed of getting water at all in sufficient quantity in a village supplied by public fountains which only trickled sparingly at fixed hours, made his attempt abortive. Finding it impracticable to get himself douched with jets of water, which, shot freely and forcible against the bony rings of the vertebral columns, formed the only method powerful enough to subdue the insomnia and bring back peace of mind, he was reduced to the employment of short aspersions in his bathroom or his tub; mere cold aspersions followed by an energetic rubbing down with a horsehair glove at the hands of his valet.

But these half measures were very far from scotching the disease; the most he felt was a temporary relief of a few hours, dearly bought, moreover, by a fresh access of the paroxysms returning to the charge with increased violence.

He was consumed with infinite ennui. The pleasure he had felt in the possession of his amazing flowers was exhausted; he was tired already of looking at the texture of their leaves and the shades of their blossoms. Besides, for all the care he lavished upon them, most of his plants had died; these he had removed from the rooms, and then, to such a pitch of nervous irritability had he come, that the sight of the places left vacant for want of them wounded his eye and reduced him to a condition of further exasperation.

To distract his attention and kill the interminable hours, he had recourse to his portfolios of prints and sorted his Goyas. The early states of certain plates of the Caprices, proofs distinguishable by their reddish tone, which he had bought in former days at sales, at extravagant prices, struck his fancy, and he lost himself in their contemplation, as he followed the weird fancies of the artist with an unfailing delight in his bewildering imaginations—witches riding black cats, women extracting a dead man's teeth at the foot of the gallows, bandits, succubi, devils and dwarfs.

After this, he went through all the other series of the artist's etchings and aquatints, his Proverbs, so grotesque in their gloomy horror, his battle subjects, so ferocious in their bloodthirstiness, his plate of the Garotte, of which he possessed a superb proof before letters, printed on heavy paper, unsized, with visible watermark-lines showing in its substance.

The savage vigour, the uncompromising, reckless talent of this artist captivated him. Yet, at the same time, the universal admiration his works had won put him off somewhat, and for years he had always refused to frame them, fearing, if he exhibited them, that the first noodle who might happen to see them would feel himself bound to talk inanities and fall into an ecstasy in stereotyped phrases as he stood in front of them.

It was the same with his Rembrandts, which he would examine now and again on the sly; and indeed it is very true that, just as the finest air in the world is vulgarized beyond all bearing once the public has taken to hum it and the street organs to play it, so the work of art that has appealed to the sham connoisseurs, that is admired by the uncritical, that is not content to rouse the enthusiasm of only a chosen few, becomes for this very reason, in the eyes of the elect, a thing polluted, commonplace, almost repulsive.

This diffusion of appreciation among the common herd was in fact one of the sorest trials of his life; unaccountable triumphs had forever spoilt his enjoyment in pictures and books he had once held dear; the approbation of the general voice always ended by making him discover some hitherto imperceptible blemish, and he would repudiate them, asking himself if his taste was not getting blunted and untrustworthy.

He shut his portfolios and once more fell into a state of indifference and ill humour. To change the current of his ideas, he tried a course of emollient reading; essayed, with a view to cooling his brain, some of the solanaceae of art; read those books so charming for convalescents and invalids whom sensational stories or works richer in phosphates would only fatigue: Charles Dickens' novels.

But the volumes produced an effect just the opposite of what he looked for; his chaste lovers, his Protestant heroines, modestly draped to the chin, whose passions were so seraphic, who never went beyond a coy dropping of the eyes, a blush, a tear of happiness, a squeezing of hands, exasperated him. This exaggerated virtue drove him into the opposite extreme; in virtue of the law of contrasts, he rushed into the contrary excess; thought of passionate, full-bodied loves; pictured the doings of frail, human couples; of ardent embraces mouth to mouth; of pigeon kisses, as ecclesiastical prudery calls them when tongue meets tongue in naughty wantonness.

He threw away his book, and banishing the mock-modesty of Albion far from his thoughts, dreamed of the licentious practices, the salacious little sins the Church condemns. A commotion shook him; the insensibility of brain and body that he had supposed final and irrevocable was no more. Solitude has its influence, too, on broken nerves; he was filled with a craving, not now for religious conviction, but for the pleasant sins religion condemns. The habitual object of its threats and curses was the one thing that tempted him; the carnal side of his nature, that had lain dormant for months, roused, first of all, by the feebleness of the pious stuff he had been reading, then stirred to full wakefulness in a spasm of the nerves by the hateful English cant, now asserted itself, and the stimulated senses harking back to the past, he found himself wallowing in the memories of his old dissipations.

He got up and gloomily opened a little box of silver-gilt, its lid set here and there with aventurines.

It was full of bonbons of a violet colour; one of these he took and turned it about in his fingers, thinking over the strange properties of these sweetmeats, sprinkled over with a powdering of sugar, like hoarfrost; formerly, in the days when his impotency was an established fact and he could dream of women without bitterness, regret or longing, he would place one of these sweetmeats on his tongue and let it melt in his mouth; then, in a moment, would recur with an infinite tenderness recollections, almost effaced, altogether soft and languishing, of the lascivious doings of other days.

These bonbons, an invention of Siraudin's known under the ridiculous name of "Pearls of the Pyrenees," consisted of a drop of sarcanthus scent, a drop of essence of woman, crystallized in a piece of sugar; they entered by the papillae of the mouth, evoking reminiscences of water opalescent with rare vinegars; and deep, searching kisses, all fragrant with odours.

As usual, his face broke into a smile, as he drank in this amorous aroma; this shadowy semblance of caresses that revived in a corner of his brain a sense of female nudity and reawakened for a second the savour, once so adorable, of certain women. But today, it was no longer a muffled peal that was ringing; the drug's effect was no longer limited to reviving the memory of far away, half forgotten escapades; rather was it to tear the veils from before his eyes and show him the bodily reality, in all its brutal force and urgency.

Heading the procession of mistresses that the taste of the sweetmeat helped to define in clear outlines, one riveted his attention, a woman with long, white teeth, a satiny skin, rosy with health, a short nose, mouse-grey eyes, short-clipped, yellow hair.

It was Miss Urania, an American girl with a supple figure, sinewy legs, muscles of steel, arms of iron.

She had been one of the most famous of the acrobats at the Cirque.

Whole evenings, Des Esseintes had watched her performing. The first few times she had struck him as being just what she was, a powerfully made, handsome woman, but he had felt no desire to come into any closer contact with her; she had nothing about her to appeal to the tastes of a worn man of the world, yet for all this he returned again and again to the Circus, drawn by some mysterious attraction, urged by some sentiment difficult to define.

Little by little, as he watched her, his mind filled with strange notions. The more he admired her strength and suppleness, the more he seemed to see an artificial change of sex operating in her; her pretty allurements, her feminine affectations fell more and more into the background, while in their stead were developed the charms attaching to the agility and vigour of a male. In a word, after being a woman to begin with, then something very like an androgyne, she now seemed to become definitely and decisively and entirely a man.

"This being so, just as a robust athlete falls in love with a thin slip of a girl, this woman of the trapeze should by natural tendency love a feeble, backboneless weakling like myself," Des Esseintes told himself; by dint of considering his own qualities and giving the rein to his faculties of comparison, he presently arrived at the conclusion that, on his side, he was himself getting nearer and nearer the female type. This point reached, he was seized with a definite desire to possess this woman, craving for her as an anaemic young girl will for some great, rough Hercules whose arms can crush her to a jelly in their embrace.

This change of sex between Urania and himself had stirred him deeply; we are made for each other, he would declare, while, added to this sudden admiration of brute force, a thing he had hitherto detested, was the spice of the self-degradation involved in such a union—the same base delight a common prostitute enjoys in paying dear for the clumsy caresses of a bully.

Meantime, as his determination to seduce the acrobat, to make his dreams a reality, if the thing could be done, was maturing, he confined his cherished illusion by attributing the same series of inverted thoughts as his own to the unconscious brain of the woman, reading his own desires repeated in the fixed smile that hovered on the lips of the performer turning on her trapeze.

One fine evening, he made up his mind to open the campaign. Miss Urania deemed it necessary not to yield without some preliminary courting. Still she showed herself not very exacting, knowing from common report that Des Esseintes was wealthy and that his name was a help towards starting woman on a successful career.

But no sooner were his wishes granted than his disappointment passed all bounds. He had pictured the pretty American athlete to be as stolid and brutal as the strong man at a fair, but her stupidity, alas! was purely feminine in its nature. No doubt she lacked education and refinement, possessed neither good sense nor good wit, while at table she gave tokens of a brutish greediness but all the childish weaknesses of a woman were there in full force; she had all the love of chatter and finery that marks the sex specially given up to trivialities; any such thing as a transmutation of masculine ideas into her feminine person was a pure figment of the imagination.

Besides, she was quite a little Puritan and was altogether innocent of those rude, athletic caresses Des Esseintes at once desired and dreaded; she was not subject, as he had for a moment hoped she might be, to any morbid perversities of sex. Possibly, on searching the depths of her temperament, he might yet have discovered a penchant for a dainty, delicate, slimly-built paramour, for a nature precisely the opposite of her own; but in that case, it would have been a preference not for a young girl at all, but for some merryhearted little shrimp of a man; for some skinny, queer-faced clown.

Inevitably Des Esseintes resumed his part, momentarily forgotten, as a man; his impressions of femininity, of feebleness, of a sort of protection bought and paid for, of fear even, disappeared entirely. He could deceive himself no longer; Miss Urania was just a mistress like any other, not justifying in any way the cerebral curiosity she had excited.

Though, just at first, the freshness and splendour of her beauty had surprised Des Esseintes and kept him captivated, it was not long before he sought to sever the connection and bring about a speedy rupture, for his premature impotency grew yet more marked when confronted with the icy woman's caresses and prudish passivity.

Nevertheless, she was the first to halt before him in the unbroken procession of these wanton memories; but, at bottom, if she had made a deeper impression on his mind than a host of other women whose allurements had been less fallacious and the pleasures they gave less limited, this came of the smell she exhaled as of a sound and wholesome animal. Her redundant health was the very antipodes of the anaemic, perfumed savour, whose delicate fragrance breathed from Siraudin's dainty sweetmeats.

By sheer contrast of fragrance, Miss Urania was bound to hold a foremost place in his memory, but almost immediately, Des Esseintes, startled for a moment by the unexpectedness of a natural, unsophisticated aroma, came back to more civilized scents and began inevitably to think of his other mistresses. They trooped across the field of memory in crowds; but, above them all, stood out the woman whose monstrous gift had for months given him such contentment.

She was a brunette, a little lean woman, with black eyes and black hair worn in tight bandeaux, that looked as if they had been plastered on her head with a brush, and parted on one side near the temple like a boy's. He had made her acquaintance at a café-concert, where she was giving performances as a ventriloquist.

To the amazement of a crowded audience who were half frightened at what they heard, she would give voices, turn and turn about, to half a dozen dolls of graduated sizes seated on chairs like a row of Pandean pipes; she would hold conversations with the little figures that seemed all but alive, while, in the auditorium itself, flies could be heard buzzing about the chandeliers and the spectators whispering on the benches though they had never opened their mouths. Then a string of imaginary carriages would roll up the room from the door to the stage, seeming almost to graze the elbows of the seated audience, who started back, instinctively surprised to find themselves there at all.

Des Esseintes had been fascinated; a crowd of new thoughts coursed through his brain. To open the campaign, he made all haste to reduce the fortress by the battery of bank notes, the ventriloquist catching his fancy by the very fact of the utter contrast she presented to the fair American. This brown beauty reeked of artfully prepared perfumes, heady and unhealthy scents, and she burned like the crater of a volcano. In spite of all his subterfuges, Des Esseintes' vigour was exhausted in a few hours; none the less he persisted in allowing himself to be drained dry by her, for more than the woman as a woman, her phenomenal endowments attracted him.

In fact, the plans he had proposed to himself to carry out were ripe for execution. He resolved to accomplish a project hitherto impossible of realization.

One night, he had a miniature sphinx brought in, carved in black marble, couched in the classic pose with outstretched paws and the head held rigid and upright together with a chimaera, in coloured earthenware, flourishing a bristling mane, darting savage glances from ferocious eyes, lashing into furrows with its tail its flanks swollen like the bellows of a forge. He placed these monsters, one at each end of the room, put out the lamps, leaving only the red embers glowing on the hearth, to throw a vague and uncertain illumination about the chamber that exaggerated the apparent size of objects half lost in the semidarkness.

This done, he stretched himself on the bed beside his mistress, whose unsmiling face was visible by the faint glow from the fireplace, and awaited developments. With weird intonations which he had made her long and patiently rehearse beforehand, she gave life and voice to the two monsters, without so much as moving her lips, without even a glance in their direction.

Then, in the silence of the night, began the wondrous dialogue of the Chimaera and the Sphinx, spoken in deep, guttural tones, now hoarse, now shrill, like voices of another world.

"Here, Chimaera, stop, I say."

"No, never."

Under the spell of Flaubert's marvellous prose, he listened trembling to the dreadful pair and a shudder shook his body from head to foot, when the Chimaera uttered the solemn and magic sentence:

"I seek new perfumes, ampler blossoms, untried pleasures."

Ah! it was to himself this voice, mysterious as an incantation, spoke; it was to him she told of her feverish desire for the unknown, her unsatisfied longing for the ideal, her craving to escape the horrible reality of existence, to overpass the confines of thought, to grope, without ever reaching it, after a certainty, in the mists of the regions beyond the bounds of art! All the pitifulness of his own efforts filled his heart with sick disgust. Softly he pressed to his breast the silent woman by his side, clung to her for comfort like a frightened child, never even seeing the sulky looks of the actress forced to play a part, to exercise her craft, at home, in her hours of rest, far away from the footlights.

Their liaison went on, but before long Des Esseintes' feebleness grew more pronounced; the effervescence of his mental activities could no longer melt the icy fetters that held his bodily powers; the nerves refused to obey the mandates of the will; the lecherous caprices that appeal to old men dominated him. Feeling himself growing more and more inefficient as a lover, he had recourse to the most powerful stimulus of aged voluptuaries uncertain of their powers—fear.

While he held the woman clasped in his arms, a hoarse, furious voice would burst out from behind the door: "Let me in, I say! I know you have a lover with you. Just wait a minute, and I'll let you know, you trollop."— Instantly, like the libertines whose passions are stimulated by terror of being caught in flagrante delicto in the open air, on the river banks, in the Tuileries Gardens, in a summerhouse or on a bench, he would temporarily recover his powers, throw himself at the ventriloquist, whose voice went storming on outside the room, and he found an abnormal satisfaction in this rush and scurry, this alarm of a man running a risk, interrupted, hurried in his fornication.

Unhappily these sittings soon came to an end. In spite of the extravagant prices he paid, the ventriloquist sent him about his business, and the same night gave herself to a good fellow whose requirements were less complicated and his back stronger.

Des Esseintes had regretted the woman, and when he recollected her artifices, other women seemed devoid of flavour; the affected graces of depraved children even appeared insipid, and so profound became his contempt for their monotonous grimaces that he could not bring himself to put up with them any more.

Still chewing the bitter cud of his disillusionment, he was walking one day all alone in the Avenue de Latour-Maubourg when he was accosted near the Invalides by a young man, almost a boy, who begged him to tell him the shortest way to go to the Rue de Babylone. Des Esseintes indicated his road and, as he was crossing the Esplanade too, they set off together.

The lad's voice, insisting, it seemed to his companion quite needlessly, on fuller instructions as to the way;—"Then you think, do you? that by turning left, I should be taking the longer road; but I was told that if I cut obliquely across the Avenue, I should get there all the quicker,"—was timid and appealing at the same time, very low and very gentle.

Des Esseintes looked him up and down. He seemed to have just left school, was poorly dressed in a little cheviot jacket tight round the hips and barely coming below the break of the loins, a pair of close-fitting black breeches, a turndown collar cut low to display a puffed cravat, deep blue with white lines, La Vallière shape. In his hand he carried a class book bound in boards, and on his head was a brown, flat-brimmed bowler hat.

The face was at once pathetic and strangely attractive; pale and drawn, with regular features shaded by long black locks, it was lit up by great liquid eyes, the lids circled with blue, set near the nose, which was splashed with a few golden freckles and under which lurked a little mouth, but with fleshy lips divided by a line in the middle like a ripe cherry.

They examined each other for a moment, eye to eye; then the young man dropped his and stepped nearer; soon his arm was rubbing against Des Esseintes', who slackened his pace, gazing with a thoughtful look at the lad's swaying walk.

And lo! from this chance meeting sprang a mistrustful friendship that nevertheless was prolonged for months. To this day, Des Esseintes could not think of it without a shudder; never had he experienced a more alluring liaison or one that laid a more imperious spell on his senses; never had he run such risks, nor had he ever been so well content with such a grievous sort of satisfaction.

Among all the memories that pressed upon him in his solitude, the recollection of this attachment dominated all the rest. All the leaven of insanity that can torment a brain over-stimulated by nervous excitation was fermenting within him; moreover, to complete the satisfaction he found in these reminiscences, in this morose pleasure, as Theology names this recurrence of old doings of shame, he combined with the physical visions, spiritual ardours roused by his former readings of the casuists, writers like Busenbaum and Diana, Liguori and Sanchez, treating of sins against the Sixth and Ninth Commandments of the Decalogue.

While giving birth to an extra-human ideal in this soul which it had impregnated and which a hereditary tendency dating from the reign of Henry III, perhaps predisposed in the same direction, Religion had at the same time roused an illegitimate ideal of licentious pleasures; libertine and mystic obsessions haunted, in an inextricable union, his brain that thirsted with an obstinate craving to escape the vulgarities of life; to plunge, utterly regardless of revered usages, into new and original ecstasies; into excesses celestial or accursed, but equally ruinous in the waste of phosphorus they involve.

As a matter of fact, he issued from these reveries utterly exhausted, half dying; then he would at once kindle the candles and lamps, flooding the room with light, thinking in this way to hear less distinctly than in the darkness the dull, persistent, intolerable beating of the arteries that throbbed and throbbed unceasingly under the skin of the neck.

CHAPTER X

In the course of that singular malady which plays such havoc with races of exhausted vitality, sudden intervals of calm succeed the crises. Without being able to explain the reason, Des Esseintes awoke quite strong and well one fine morning; no more hacking cough, no more wedges driven with a hammer into the back of the neck, but an ineffable sensation of well-being and a delightful clearness of brain, while his thoughts became cheerful; and instead of being opaque and dull, grew bright and iridescent, like brilliantly coloured soap bubbles.

This lasted some days; then in a moment, one afternoon, hallucinations of the sense of smell appeared.

His room was strong of frangipane. He looked to see if perhaps there was a bottle of the perfume lying about anywhere uncorked; but there was no such thing in the place. He visited his working-room and then the dining room; the smell was there too.

He rang for his servant. "Don't you smell something?" he asked, but the man, after sniffing the air, declared he noticed nothing. Doubt was impossible; the nervous derangement was come again, taking the form of a fresh delusion of the senses.

Wearied by the persistency of this imaginary aroma, he resolved to plunge himself in a bath of real perfumes, hoping that his nasal homeopathy might cure him or, at any rate, moderate the force of the overpowering frangipane.

He betook himself to his study. There, beside an ancient font that served him as a wash-hand basin, under a long looking-glass in a frame of wrought iron that held imprisoned like a wellhead silvered by the moonlight the pale surface of the mirror, bottles of all sizes and shapes were ranged in rows on ivory shelves.

He placed them on a table and divided them into two series—first, the simple perfumes, extracts and distilled waters; secondly, composite scents, such as are described under the generic name of bouquets.

He buried himself in an armchair and began to think.

Years ago he had trained himself as an expert in the science of perfumes; he held that the sense of smell was qualified to experience pleasures equal to those pertaining to the ear and the eye, each of the five senses being capable, by dint of a natural aptitude supplemented by an erudite education, of receiving novel impressions, magnifying these tenfold, coordinating them, combining them into the whole that constitutes a work of art. It was not, in fact, he argued, more abnormal than an art should exist of disengaging odoriferous fluids than that other arts should whose function is to set up sonorous waves to strike the ear or variously coloured rays to impinge on the retina of the eyes; only, just as no one, without a special faculty of intuition developed by study, can distinguish a picture by a great master from a worthless daub, a motif of Beethoven from a tune by Clapisson, so no one, without a preliminary initiation, can avoid confounding at the first sniff a bouquet created by a great artist with a potpourri compounded by a manufacturer for sale in grocers' shops and fancy bazaars.

In this art of perfumes, one peculiarity had more than all others fascinated him, viz, the precision with which it can artificially imitate the real article.

Hardly ever, indeed, are scents actually produced from the flowers whose name they bear; the artist who should be bold enough to borrow his element from Nature alone would obtain only a half-and-half result, unconvincing, lacking in style and elegance, the fact being that the essence obtained by distillation from the flowers themselves could at the best present but a far-off, vulgarized analogy with the real aroma of the living and growing flower, shedding its fragrant effluvia in the open air.

So, with the one exception of the jasmine, which admits of no imitation, no counterfeit, no copy, which refuses even any approximation, all flowers are perfectly represented by combinations of alcoholates and essences, extracting from the model its inmost individuality while adding that something, that heightened tone, that heady savour, that rare touch which makes a work of art.

In one word, in perfumery the artist completes and consummates the original natural odour, which he cuts, so to speak, and mounts as a jeweller improves and brings out the water of a precious stone.

Little by little, the arcana of this art, the most neglected of all, had been revealed to Des Esseintes, who could now decipher its language—a diction as varied, as subtle as that of literature itself, a style of unprecedented conciseness under its apparent vagueness and uncertainty.

To reach this end, he had, first of all, been obliged to master the grammar, to understand the syntax of odours, to grasp the rules that govern them; then, once familiarized with this dialect, to study and compare the works of the diverse masters of the craft, the Atkinsons and Lubins, the Chardins and Violets, the Legrands and Piesses, to analyze the construction of their sentences, to weigh the proportion of their words and the disposition of their periods.

Next, in this idiom of essences, it was for experience to come to the assistance of theories too often incomplete and commonplace.

The classic art of perfumery was, in truth, little diversified, almost colourless, uniformly run in a mould first shaped by old-world chemists; it was in its dotage, hidebound in its ancient alembics, when the Romantic epoch dawned and took its part in modifying, in rejuvenating it, in making it more malleable and more supple.

Its history followed step by step that of the French language. The Louis XIII style, perfumed and full-flavoured, compounded of elements costly at that date, of iris powder, musk, civet, myrtle water, already known by the name of Angels' Water, barely sufficed to express the rude graces, the rather crude tints of the time which certain sonnets of Saint-Amand's have preserved for us. Later on, with the introduction of myrrh, frankincense, the mystic scents, powerful and austere, the pomp and stateliness of the Grand Siècle, the redundancy and artificiality of the orator's art, the full, sustained, wordy style of Bossuet and the great preachers became almost possible; later on again, the well-worn, sophisticated graces of French society under Louis XV found a readier interpretation of their charm in the frangipane and maréchale, which offered in their way the very synthesis of the period. Then finally, after the indifference and incuriousness of the First Empire, which used eau de cologne and preparations of rosemary to excess, perfumery ran for inspiration, in the train of Victor Hugo and Gautier, to the lands of the sun; it created Oriental essences, selams overpowering with their spicy odours; invented new savours; tried and approved old tones and shades now rediscovered, which it made more complex, more subtle, more choice; definitely repudiating once for all the voluntary decrepitude to which the art had been reduced by the Malesherbes, the Andrieux, the Baour-Lormians, the vulgar distillers of its poetry.

Nor had the language of perfumes remained stationary since the epoch of 1830. Again it had progressed and following the march of the century had advanced side by side with the other arts. It, too, had complied with the whims of amateurs and artists, flying for motives to China and Japan, inventing scented albums, imitating the flowery nosegays of Takeoka; by a mingling of lavender and clove obtaining the perfume Rondeletia; by a union of patchouli and camphor, the singular aroma of India-ink; by compounding citron, clove and neroli (essence of orange blossoms), the odour, the Hovenia of Japan.

Des Esseintes studied, analyzed the soul of these fluids, expounded these texts; he took a delight, for his own personal satisfaction, in playing the part of psychologist, in unmounting and remounting the machinery of a work, in unscrewing the separate pieces forming the structure of a complex odour, and by long practice of this sort, his sense of smell had arrived at the certainty of an almost infallible touch.

Just as a wine-merchant knows the vintage by imbibing a single drop; as a hop-dealer, the instant he sniffs at a bag, can there and then name its precise quality and price; as a Chinese trader can declare at once the place of origin of the teas he examines, say on what farms of the Bohea mountains, in what Buddhist Monasteries, each specimen was grown, and the date at which its leaves were gathered, can state precisely the degree of heat used and the effect produced by its contact with plum blossom, with the Aglaia, with the Olea fragrans, with all or any of the perfumes employed to modify its flavour, to give it an added piquancy, to brighten up its rather dry savour with a whiff of fresh and alien flowers; even so could Des Esseintes, by the merest sniff at a scent, detail instantly the doses of its composition, explain the psychology of its blending; all but quote the name of the particular artist who wrote it and impressed on it, the personal mark of his style.

Needless to say, he possessed a collection of all the products used by perfume-makers; he had even some of the true Balm of Mecca, a very great rarity, to be procured only in certain regions of Arabia Petraea and guarded as a monopoly of the Grand Turk.

Seated now in his study at his working table, he was pondering the creation of a new bouquet, and had reached that moment of hesitation so familiar to authors who, after months of idleness, are preparing to start upon a fresh piece of work.

Like Balzac, who was haunted by an imperious craving to blacken reams of paper by way of getting his hand in, Des Esseintes felt the necessity of recovering his old cunning by dint of executing some task of minor importance. He determined to make heliotrope, and measured out the proper quantities from phials of almond and vanilla; then he changed his mind and resolved to try sweet-pea.

The phrases, the processes had escaped his memory. So he made experiments. No doubt in the fragrance of that flower, orange blossom was the dominant factor, he tried a number of combinations and ended by getting the right tone by blending the orange with the tuberose and rose, binding the three together with a drop of vanilla.

All his uncertainties vanished; a fever of eagerness stirred him, he was ready to set to work in earnest. He compounded a fresh brew of tea, adding a mixture of cassia and iris; then, sure of himself, he resolved to march boldly forward, to strike a thundering note, the overmastering crash of which should bury the whisper of that insinuating frangipane which still stealthily impregnated the room.

He handled amber; Tonquin musk, with its overpowering scent; patchouli, the most pronounced of all vegetable perfumes, whose blossom, in the natural state, gives off an odour compounded of wet wood and rusty iron. Do what he would, the associations of the eighteenth century haunted him, gowns with paniers and furbelows hovered before his eyes; memories of Boucher's Venus, all flesh, without bones, stuffed with pink cotton-wool, besieged him; recollections of the novel Thémidore and the exquisite Rosette with skirts high lifted in a fire-red despair, pursued him. In a rage, he sprang up and, to shake himself free from the obsession, sniffed in with all his might that unadulterated essence of spikenard that is so dear to Easterns and so disagreeable to Europeans, by reason of its over-strong savour of valerian. He staggered under the violence of the shock; as if crushed under the blow of a mallet, the delicate fibrils of the dainty scent disappeared. He took advantage of the moment's respite to escape from the dead centuries, the old-time emanations, to enter, as he had been used to do in other days, on creations less limited in scope and more modern in fashion.

Of old, he had loved to soothe his spirit with harmonies in perfumery; he would use effects analogous to those of the poets, would adopt, in a measure, the admirable metrical scheme characterizing certain pieces of Baudelaire's, for instance "l'Irréparable" and "le Balcon," where the last of the five lines composing the strophe is the echo of the first, returning like a refrain to drown the soul in infinite depths of melancholy and languor.

He wandered, lost in the dreams these aromatic stanzas called up in his brain, till suddenly recalled to his starting point, to the original motif of his meditations, by the recurrence of the initial theme, reappearing at studied intervals in the fragrant orchestration of the poem.

For the actual moment, he was fain to roam in freedom amid a landscape full of surprises and changes, and he began by a simple phrase—ample, sonorous, at once opening a view over an immense stretch of country.

With the help of his vaporizers, he injected into the room an essence composed of ambrosia, Mitcham lavender, sweet-pea, compound bouquet—an essence which, if distilled by a true artist, well deserves the name bestowed on it of "extract of meadow flowers"; then, into this meadow, he introduced a carefully modulated infusion of tuberose, orange and almond blossom, and instantly artificial lilacs came into being, while lindens swayed in the breeze, shedding on the ground about them their pale emanations, mimicked by the London extract of tilia.

This scene, once arranged in a few imposing lines, melting to the horizon under his closed eyes, he insinuated a light rain of human, not to say half feline, essences, smacking of the petticoat, announcing woman powdered and painted—the stephanotis, the ayapana, the opoponax, the chypre, the champaka, the sarcanthus, over which he superimposed a dash of seringa, to suggest, amid the factitious life of makeup and make-belief which they evoked, a natural flower of hearty, uncontrolled laughter, of the joys of existence in the eye of the sun.

Then he let these fragrant waves escape by a ventilator, keeping only the country scent, which he renewed and reinforced, strengthening the dose so as to force it to recur like the burden of a song at the end of each strophe.

Little by little, the feminine aroma disappeared, the country was left without inhabitants. Then, on the enchanted horizon, rose a row of factories whose tall chimneys flamed at their tops like so many bowls of punch.

A breath as of manufactories, of chemical works now floated on the breeze which he raised by waving fans, though Nature still continued to sweeten with her fragrant emanations this foulness of the atmosphere.

Des Esseintes proceeded to turn about and warm between his hands a ball of styrax, and a very curious odour filled the room, a smell at once repugnant and exquisite, blending the delicious scent of the jonquil with the filthy stench of guttapercha and coal tar. He disinfected his hands, shut away his resin in a box hermetically sealed, and the stinking factories vanished in their turn. Then, he tossed amid the revivified vapours of lindens and meadow-grass some drops of "new mown hay," and on the magic spot, instantly bared of its lilacs, rose mounds of hay, bringing with them a new season, scattering their delicate odours reminiscent of high summer.

Last of all, when he had sufficiently savoured the sight, he hurriedly scattered about exotic perfumes, exhausted his vaporizers, concentrated his strongest essences, gave the rein to all his balms, and lo! the stifling closeness of the room was filled with an atmosphere, maddening and sublime, breathing powerful influences, impregnating with raging alcoholates an artificial breeze—an atmosphere unnatural, yet delightful, paradoxical in its union of the allspice of the Tropics, the pungent savours of the sandalwood of China and the hediosmia of Japan with native odours of jasmine, hawthorn and vervain, forcing, to grow together, in despite of seasons and climates, trees of diverse essences, flowers of colours and fragrances the most opposite, creating by the blending and shock of all these tones one common perfume, unknown, unforeseen, extraordinary, wherein reappeared at intervals as a persistent refrain, the decorative phrase of the opening, the odour of the broad meadows breathed over by the lilacs and the lindens.

Suddenly a sharp agony assailed him; it felt as though a centre-bit were boring into his temples. He opened his eyes, to find himself once more in the middle of his study, seated before his working table; he got up and walked painfully, half-stunned, to the window, which he threw part open. A current of fresh air sweetened the stifling atmosphere that enveloped him; he marched up and down the room to recover the proper use of his limbs, going to and fro, his eyes fixed on the ceiling on which crabs and seaweed powdered with sea salt stood out in relief from a grained background, yellow as the sand of a beach. A similar design decorated the plinths bordering the panels, which in their turn were covered with Japanese crape, a watery green in colour and slightly waved to imitate the ripple of a windblown river, while down the gentle current floated a rose leaf round which frolicked a swarm of little fishes dashed in with two strokes of the pen.

But his eyes were still heavy; he left off pacing the short length of floor between the font and the bath and leant his elbows on the windowsill. Presently his dizziness ceased, and after carefully recorking the bottles of scents and essences, he seized the opportunity to tidy his apparatus for making up the face—his paints and powders and the like. He had not touched these things since his arrival at Fontenay, and he was almost astonished now at the sight of this collection once visited by so many women. One on top of the other, phials and porcelain pots littered the table confusion. Here was a china box, of the green sort, containing schnouda, that marvellous white cream which, once spread on the cheeks, changes under the influence of the air to a tender pink, then to a scarlet so natural that it gives an absolutely convincing illusion of a complexion mantling with red blood; there, jars incrusted with mother-o'-pearl held Japanese gold and Athens green, coloured like the wing of the cantharides beetle, golds and greens that blend into a deep purple directly they are moistened; beside pots full of filbert paste, of serkis of the harem, of emulsions of Cashmere lilies, of lotions of strawberry and elderflower for the skin, beside little phials of solutions of India-ink and rose-water for the eyes, lay a host of different instruments, of mother-o'-pearl, of ivory and of silver, mixed up with dainty brushes for the teeth and gums—pincers, scissors, strigils, stumps, crimpers, powder-puffs, backscratchers, patches and files. He handled all this elaborate apparatus, bought in former days to please a mistress who found an ineffable pleasure in certain aromatics and certain balms, an ill-balanced, nerve-ridden woman, who loved to have her nipples macerated in scents, but who only really experienced a genuine and overmastering ecstasy when her head was tickled with a comb and she could, in the act of being caressed by a lover, breathe the smell of chimney soot, of wet plaster from a house building in rainy weather, or of dust churned up by the heavy thunder drops of a summer storm.

He pondered these recollections, recalling particularly an afternoon spent, partly for want of anything better to do, partly out of curiosity, in this woman's company at her sister's house at Pantin, the memory of which stirred in his breast a whole forgotten world of long-ago thoughts and old-time scents. While the two women were chattering and showing each other their frocks, he had gone to the window and, through the dusty panes, had looked out on the long, muddy street and heard its pavements echo under the incessant beat of heavy boots trampling through the puddles.

The scene, now far away in the past, suddenly stood out before him with extraordinary vividness. Pantin lay there in front of his eyes, bustling and alive, imaged in the green, dead water of the mirror into which his eyes involuntarily gazed. A hallucination carried him far away from Fontenay; the looking-glass reproduced for him the same reflections the street had once presented to his bodily eye, and buried in a dream, he said over the ingenious, melancholy yet consoling, anthem he had noted down on that former occasion on getting back to Paris:—

"Yes, the time of the great rains is come; behold, the gutter-pipes vomit their drippings on to the pavements, with a song of many waters, and the horse-dung lies fermenting in the puddles that fill the holes in the macadam with a coffee-coloured fluid; everywhere, for the humble wayfarer, are foot-baths full to overflowing.

"Under the lowering sky, in the dull air, the walls of the houses drip black sweat and the cellar-openings stink; loathing of life is strong within the soul and the spleen is a torment to the flesh; the seeds of filthiness that every man has in his heart begin to bud; cravings for foul pleasures trouble the austerest and in the brain of respectable folks criminal desires spring up.

"And yet, there I am, warming myself before a blazing fire, while a basket of blowing flowers on a table fills the room with a sweet savour of benzoin, geranium and bent-grass. In mid November, it is still springtime at Pantin, in the Rue de Paris, and I find myself laughing in my sleeve to think of the timorous family parties that, in order to avoid the approach of winter, fly to Antibes or Cannes as fast as steam will take them.

"Inclement Nature goes for nothing in this strange phenomenon; it is to industry, to commerce, and that alone, be it said, that Pantin owes this artificial spring.

"The truth is, these flowers are of lustring, mounted on brass-wire, and the springlike fragrance floating in through the cracks of the window-frame, is exhaled by the neighbouring factories where Pinaud and Saint-James make their perfumes.

"For the artisan exhausted by the hard labour of the workshops, for the small clerk, alas! only too often a father, the illusion of a breath or two of good air is a possibility—thanks to these manufacturers.

"Indeed, out of this scarce believable illusion of the country may be developed a quite rational medical treatment. Fast livers affected by chest complaints who are now carted off to the South mostly die, broken down by the rupture of all their habits of life, by the homesick craving to return to the Parisian pleasures that have brought them to this pass by their excess. Here, in an artificial climate, heated and regulated by stoves, libertine recollections will return, gently and harmlessly, along with the languishing feminine emanations given off by scent factories. In lieu of the deadly dreariness of provincial existence, the physician can by this device supply his patient platonically with the longed-for atmosphere of Parisian boudoirs, of Parisian haunts of pleasure.

"In the majority of cases, all that will be required to complete the cure is for the sick man to possess a little touch of imagination.

"Now, seeing that, in these times of ours, there is no single thing really genuine to be found; seeing that the wine we drink and the liberty we acclaim are equally adulterate and derisory; considering how remarkable a dose of credulity it takes to suppose the governing classes to deserve respect and the lower to be worthy either of relief or commiseration, it appears to me," concluded Des Esseintes, "neither more absurd nor more insane to demand of my neighbour a sum total of illusion barely equal to that he expends every day in his life for quite idiotic objects, that he may successfully persuade himself that the town of Pantin is an artificial Nice, a factitious Menton."

"All which," he exclaimed, rudely interrupted in his reflections by a sudden failure of all his bodily powers, "does not alter the fact that I must beware of these delicious and abominable experiments that are killing me." He heaved a sigh: "Well, well, more pleasures to moderate, more precautions to take,"—and he retired for refuge to his study, thinking in this way to escape more easily from the haunting influence of the perfumes.

He threw the window wide open, delighted to enjoy an air bath; but next moment, the wind seemed to bring with it a vague breath of essence of bergamot, mingled with a smell of jasmine, cassia and rose-water. He shuddered, asking himself if he was not surely under the tyranny of one of those possessions by the devil that the Priests used to exorcise in the Middle Ages. Soon the odour changed and altered, however. An uncertain savour of tincture of tolu, balm of Peru, saffron, blended together by a few drops of amber and musk, now floated in from the sleeping village at the bottom of the hill; then, suddenly, in an instant, the metamorphosis was wrought, the scent of frangipane, of which his nostrils had caught the elements and were so familiar with the analysis, filled all the air from the valley of Fontenay away to the Fort, assailing his exhausted sense of smell, shaking afresh his shattered nerves, prostrating him to such a degree that he fell swooning and half dying across the windowsill.

CHAPTER XI

The terrified domestics hurried off in search of the Fontenay doctor, who did not understand one word of Des Esseintes' condition. He muttered sundry medical terms, felt the invalid's pulse and examined his tongue, tried in vain to make him speak, ordered sedatives and rest, promised to come back next day, and on Des Esseintes shaking his head—he had regained strength enough to disapprove his servant's zeal and send the intruder about his business—took his departure and went off to describe to every inhabitant of the village the eccentricities of the house, the furniture and appointments of which had struck him with amazement and frozen him where he stood.

To the astonishment of the servants, who dared not stir from their quarters, their master recovered in a day or two, and they came upon him drumming on the windowpanes and gazing up anxiously at the sky.

One afternoon, the bells rang a peremptory summons, and Des Esseintes issued orders that his trunks were to be got ready for a long journey.

While the old man and his wife were selecting, under his superintendence, such articles as were necessary, he was pacing feverishly up and down the cabin of his dining room, consulting the timetables of steamers, going from window to window of his study, still scrutinizing the clouds with looks at once of impatience and satisfaction.

For a week past the weather had been atrocious. Sooty rivers pouring unceasingly across the grey plains of the heavens rolled along masses of clouds that looked like huge boulders torn up from the earth.

Every few minutes storms of rain would sweep down and swallow up the valley under torrents of wet.

But that day the firmament had changed its aspect. The floods of ink had dried up, the rugged clouds had melted; the sky was now one great flat plain, one vast watery film. Little by little this film seemed to fall lower, a moist haze wrapped the face of the land; no longer did the rain descend in cataracts, as it had the day before, but fell in a continuous drizzle, fine, penetrating, chilling, soaking the garden walks, churning up the roads, confounding together earth and sky. The daylight was darkened, and a livid gloom hung over the village now transformed into a lake of mud speckled by the raindrops that pitted with spots of silver the muddy surface of the puddles. In the general desolation, all colour had faded to a drab uniformity, leaving only the roofs glittering with wet above the lifeless hues of the walls.

"What weather!" sighed the old servant, depositing on a chair the clothes his master had called for, a suit ordered some time before from London.

The only answer Des Esseintes vouchsafed was to rub his hands and take his stand before a glass-fronted bookcase in which a collection of silk socks was arranged in the form of a fan. He hesitated a while over the best shade to choose, then rapidly, taking into consideration the gloom of the day and the depressing tints of his coat and trousers, and remembering the object he had in view, he selected a pair of drab silk and quickly drew them on. Next he donned lace-up, brogued, shooting boots; put on the suit, mouse-grey with a check of a lighter grey and whitey spots, clapped a little round hat on his head, threw an inverness-cape round his shoulders, and followed by his servant staggering under the weight of a trunk, a collapsible valise, a carpet bag, a hatbox and a travelling rug wrapped round umbrellas and sticks, he made for the railway station. Arrived there, he informed the domestic that he could fix no definite date for his return, that he might be back in a year's time, next month, next week, sooner perhaps, gave orders that nothing should be changed or moved in the house during his absence, handed over the approximate sum required to keep up the establishment during his absence, and got into the railway carriage, leaving the old fellow dumbfounded, arms dangling and mouth wide open, behind the barrier beyond which the train got into motion.

He was alone in his compartment; a blurred, murky landscape, looking as if seen through the dirty water of an aquarium, whirled past the flying, rain-splashed train. Buried in his thoughts, Des Esseintes closed his eyes.

Once more, this solitude he had so ardently desired and won at last had resulted in poignant distress; this silence that had once appealed to him as a consolation for all the fools' chatter he had listened to for years, now weighed upon him with an intolerable burden. One morning, he had awoke as frenzied in mind as a man who finds himself locked up in a prison cell; his trembling lips moved to cry out, but no sound came, tears rose to his eyes, he felt choked like one who has been sobbing bitterly for hours.

Devoured by a longing to move, to see a human face, to talk with a fellow human being, to mingle with the common life of mankind, he actually asked his servants to stay with him, after summoning them to his room on some pretext or other. But conversation was impossible; besides the fact that the two old people, bowed and bent under the weight of years of silence and broken in to the habits of sick-nurses, were next door to dumb, the distance which Des Esseintes had always maintained between himself and his dependents was not calculated to make them anxious to unclose their lips. Their brains, too, had grown sluggish and inert, and refused to supply more than monosyllabic answers to any questions they might be asked.

There was nothing therefore to be hoped for from them in the way of relief or solace. But now a fresh phenomenon came to pass. The reading of Dickens which he had in the first instance carried out with the object of composing his nerves, but which had produced just the opposite effect to what he had looked for in the matter of benefitting his health, now began to act little by little in an unexpected direction, inducing visions of English life over which he sat pondering for hours; gradually into these fictitious reveries came creeping notions of turning them into a positive reality, of making an actual voyage to England, of verifying his dreams, engrafted on all which was further a growing wish to experience novel impressions and so escape the divagations of a mind dizzied with grinding, grinding at nothing, which had so disastrously sapped his strength.

Then the abominable weather with its everlasting fog and rain helped on his purpose, confirming as it did what he remembered from his reading, keeping constantly before his eyes a picture of what a land of mist and mud is like, and in this way focusing his ideas and holding them to their original starting point.

He could resist no more, and one day had quite suddenly made up his mind. So great was his hurry to be off that he fled precipitately, impatient to be done with his present life, to feel himself hustled in the turmoil of a crowded street, in the crush and bustle of a railway station.

"I can breathe now," he said to himself as the train slowed down in its dance and came to a halt in the rotunda of the Paris terminus of the Sceaux Railway, its last pirouettes accompanied by the crashes and jerks of the turntables.

Once out in the street, on the Boulevard d'Enfer, glad to be encumbered as he was with his trunks and rugs, he hailed a cabman. By the promise of a generous pourboire he soon came to an understanding with the man of the drab breeches and red waistcoat. "By the hour"; he ordered, "drive to the Rue de Rivoli and stop at the office of Galignani's Messenger"; his idea was to purchase before starting a Baedeker's or Murray's Guide to London.

The conveyance blundered off, throwing up showers of mud from the wheels. The streets were like a swamp; under the grey sky that seemed to rest on the roofs of the houses, the walls were dripping from top to bottom, the rain-gutters overflowing, the pavements coated with mud of the colour of gingerbread in which the passersby slipped and slid. On the sidewalks, as the omnibuses swept by, people would stop in crowded masses, and women, kilted to the knees and bending under sodden umbrellas, would press against the shop windows to escape the flying mire.

The wet was coming in at the windows; so Des Esseintes had to put up the glass, which the rain streaked with little rivulets of water, while clots of mud flew like a firework in all directions from the moving vehicle. To the monotonous accompaniment of the storm beating down with a noise like a sack of pears being shaken out on his luggage and the carriage roof, Des Esseintes dreamed of his coming journey; it was already an instalment on account of rainy London he was now receiving at Paris in this dreadful weather; the picture of a London, fogbound, colossal, enormous, smelling of hot iron and soot, wrapt in a perpetual mantle of smoke and mist, unrolled itself before his mind's eye. Vistas of endless docks stretched farther than eye could see, crowded with cranes and capstans and bales of merchandise, swarming with men perched on masts, astraddle across ship's yards, while on the quays myriads of others were bending, head down and rump in air, over casks which they were storing away in cellars.

All this activity he could see in full swing on the riverbanks and in gigantic warehouses bathed by the foul, black water of an imaginary Thames, in a forest of masts, in vast entanglements of beams piercing the wan clouds of the lowering firmament, while trains raced by, some tearing full steam across the sky, others rolling along in the sewers, shrieking out horrid screams, vomiting floods of smoke through the gaping mouths of wells, while along every avenue and every street, buried in an eternal twilight and disfigured by the monstrous, gaudy infamies of advertising, streams of vehicles rolled by between marching columns of men, all silent, all intent on business, eyes bent straight ahead, elbows pressed to the sides.

Des Esseintes shuddered deliciously to feel himself lost in this terrible world of men of business, in this isolating fog, in this incessant activity, in this ruthless machine grinding to powder millions of the poor and powerless, whom philanthropists urged, by way of consolation, to repeat verses of the Bible and sing the Psalms of David.

Then, in a moment, the vision vanished as the vehicle gave a jolt that made him jump on the seat. He looked out of the window. Night had fallen; the gas lamps were winking through the fog, each surrounded by a dirty yellow halo; ribbons of fire swam in the puddles and seemed to circle round the wheels of the carriages that jogged on through a sea of liquid, discoloured flame. He tried to see where he was, caught sight of the Arc du Carrousel, and in an instant, without rhyme or reason, perhaps simply from the reaction of his sudden fall from the high regions where his imagination had been roaming, his thoughts fell back on a quite trivial incident he now remembered for the first time—how, when he stood looking on at his servant packing his trunks, the man had forgotten to put in a toothbrush among his other toilet necessaries. Then he mentally reviewed the list of objects included; yes, they had all been duly arranged in his portmanteau, but the annoyance of this one omission pursued him obstinately till the coachman pulled up his horse and so broke the current of his reminiscences and regrets.

He was now in the Rue de Rivoli, in front of Galignani's Messenger. On either side of a door of frosted glass, the panels covered with lettering and hung with Oxford frames containing cuttings from newspapers and telegrams in blue wrappers, were two broad windows crammed with books and albums of views. He came nearer, attracted by the look of these volumes, some of them in paper covers, butcher's-blue and cabbage-green, lavishly decorated with gold and silver patterning, others bound in cloth of various colours, carmelite blue, leek green, goose yellow, current red, cold tooled on back and sides with black lines. All this had an anti-Parisian touch, a mercantile flavour, more vulgar but yet less cheap and tawdry than the way the book-hawkers' wares are got up in France; here and there, among open albums showing comic scenes by Du Maurier and John Leech or chromos of mad gallops across country by Caldecott, appeared a few French novels, tempering this riot of discordant colours with the plain and soothing commonplace of their yellow backs.

At last, tearing himself away from this display, he pushed open the door and entered a vast library, crowded with people. Foreign females sat examining maps and jabbering remarks to one another in strange tongues. A clerk brought Des Esseintes a selection of guidebooks. He, too, sat down and fell to turning over the volumes, whose flexible covers bent between his fingers. He glanced through them, but was presently arrested by a page of Baedeker describing the London Museums. His interest was roused by the brief, precise details supplied by the Guide; but it was not long before his attention wandered from the works of the old English painters to those of the new school which appealed to him more strongly. He recalled certain examples he had seen at International Exhibitions, and he thought that very likely he would see them again in London—pictures by Millais, the Eve of St. Agnes, with its moonlight effect of silvery green; pictures by Watts, with their strange colouring, speckled with gamboge and indigo; works sketched by a Gustave Moreau fallen sick, painted in by a Michelangelo gone anaemic, and retouched by a Raphael lost in a sea of blue. Among other canvases he remembered a Cure of Cain, an Ida, and more than one Eve, wherein, under the weird and mysterious amalgamation of these three masters, lurked the personality, at once complex and essentially simple, of an erudite and dreamy Englishman, unfortunately haunted by a predilection for hideous tones.

All these pictures came crowding into his head at once. The shopman, surprised to see a customer sitting at a table lost in a brown study and quite oblivious of his surroundings, asked him which of the Guides he had chosen. Des Esseintes looked up in a dazed way, then, with a word of excuse for his absence of mind, purchased a Baedeker and left the shop. The cold wind froze him to the bone; it was blowing crosswise, lashing the arcades of the Rue de Rivoli with a pelting rain. "Drive there," he cried to the cabman, pointing to a shop at the end of a section of the arcade standing at the corner of the street he was in and the Rue de Castiglione. With its shining panes lighted from within, it looked like a gigantic lantern, a beacon fire amid the perils of the fog and the horrors of the vile weather.

It was the "Bodega." Des Esseintes stood wondering to find himself in a great hall that ran back, like a broad corridor, the roof carried by iron pillars and lined along the walls on either side with tall casks standing upended on stocks.

Hooped with iron, and having round their waist a miniature line of battlements resembling a pipe-rack in the notches of which hung tulip-shaped glasses upside down, with a hole drilled in the lower part in which was fixed an earthenware spigot, these barrels, blazoned with a Royal shield, displayed on coloured cards the name of the vintage each contained, the amount of liquor they held and the price of the same, whether by the hogshead, in bottle, or by the glass.

In the passageway left free between these rows of casks, under the gas jets that flared noisily in a hideous chandelier painted iron-grey, ran a long counter loaded with baskets of Palmer's biscuits, stale, salty cakes, plates piled with mince-pies and sandwiches, hiding under their greasy wrappers great blotches of miniature mustard-plasters. Beside this stood a double row of chairs extending to the far extremity of this cellar-like room, lined all along with more hogsheads having smaller barrels laid across their tops, these last lying on their sides and having their names and descriptions branded with a hot iron in the oak.

A reek of alcohol assailed his nostrils as he took a seat in this room where so many strong waters were stored. He looked about him. Here, the great casks stood in a row, their labels announcing a whole series of ports, strong, fruity wines, mahogany or amaranth coloured, distinguished by laudatory titles, such as "Old Port," "Light Delicate," "Cockburn's Very Fine," "Magnificent Old Regina"; there, rounding their formidable bellies, crowded side by side enormous hogsheads containing the martial wine of Spain, the sherries and their congeners, topaz coloured whether light or dark—San Lucar, Pasto, Pale Dry, Oloroso, Amontillado, sweet or dry.

The cellar was crammed. Leaning his elbow on the corner of a table, Des Esseintes sat waiting for the glass of port he had ordered of a "gentleman" busy opening explosive sodas in egg-shaped bottles that reminded one, on an exaggerated scale, of those capsules of gelatine and gluten which chemists use to mask the taste of certain nauseous drugs.

All round him were swarms of English—ungainly figures of pale-faced clergymen, dressed in black from head to foot, with soft hats and monstrously long coats decorated down the front with little buttons, shaven chins, round spectacles, greasy hair plastered to the head; laymen with broad pork-butcher faces and bulldog muzzles, apoplectic necks, ears like tomatoes, wine-sodden cheeks, bloodshot, foolish eyes, beards and whiskers joining in a collar like some of the great apes. Further off, at the far end of the wine-shop, a tall, thin man like a string of sausages, with towy locks and a chin adorned with straggling grey hairs like the root of an artichoke, was deciphering with a microscope the small print of an English newspaper; more to the front, a sort of American commodore, short and stout and roundabout, with a smoke-dried complexion and a bottle nose, sat half asleep, a cigar stuck in the hairy orifice of his mouth, staring at the placards on the walls advertising champagnes, the trademarks of Perrier and Roederer, Heidsieck and Mumm, and a hooded monk's head with the name in Gothic lettering of Dom Pérignon, Rheims.

A feeling of lassitude crept over Des Esseintes in this rude, garrison-town atmosphere; deafened by the chatter of these English folk talking to one another, he fell into a dream, calling up from the purple of the port wine that filled their glasses a succession of Dickens' characters, who were so partial to that beverage, peopling in imagination the cellar with a new set of customers, seeing in his mind's eye here Mr. Wickfield's white hair and red face, there, the phlegmatic and astute bearing and implacable eye of Mr. Tulkinghorn, the gloomy lawyer of Bleak House. Perfect in every detail, they all stood out clear in his memory, taking their places in the Bodega, with all their works and ways and gestures; his recollections, lately revived by a fresh perusal of the stories, were extraordinarily full and precise. The Novelist's town, the well lighted, well warmed house, cosy and comfortably appointed, the bottles slowly emptied by Little Dorrit, by Dora Copperfield, by Tom Pinch's sister Ruth, appeared to him sailing like a snug ark in a deluge of mire and soot. He loitered idly in this London of the imagination, happy to be under shelter, seeming to hear on the Thames the hideous whistles of the tugs at work behind the Tuileries, near the bridge. His glass was empty; despite the mist that filled the room overheated by the smoke of pipes and cigars, he experienced a little shudder of disgust as he came back to the realities of life in this moist and foul smelling weather.

He asked for a glass of Amontillado, but then, as he sat before this pale, dry wine, the nerve-soothing stories, the gentle lenitives of the English author were scattered and the harsh revulsives, the cruel irritants of Edgar Allan Poe rose in their place. The chill nightmare of the cask of Amontillado, the story of the man walled up in an underground chamber, seized upon his fancy; the kindly, commonplace faces of the American and English customers who filled the hall seemed to him to reflect uncontrollable and abominable cravings, odious and instinctive plans of wickedness. Presently he noticed he was nearly the last there, that the dinner hour was close at hand; he paid his score, tore himself from his chair and made dizzily for the door. He got a wet buffet in the face the instant he set foot outside; drowned by the rain and driving squalls, the street lamps flickered feebly and gave hardly a gleam of light; the clouds ruled lower than ever, having come down several pegs, right to the middle of the house fronts. Des Esseintes looked along the arcades of the Rue de Rivoli, bathed in shadow and dripping with moisture, and he thought he was standing in the dismal tunnel excavated beneath the Thames. But the cravings of hunger recalled him to reality; he went back to his cab, threw the driver the address of the tavern in the Rue d'Amsterdam, near the Saint-Lazare railway station, and looked at his watch—it was seven o'clock. He had just time enough to dine; the train did not start till eight-fifty, and he fell to counting up the time on his fingers, calculating the hours required for the crossing from Dieppe to Newhaven, and telling himself—"If the figures in the railway-guide are right, I shall be in London tomorrow on the stroke of halfpast twelve noon."

The vehicle stopped in front of the tavern, once more Des Esseintes left it and made his way into a long hall, with drab walls innocent of any gilding, and divided by means of breast-high partitions into a series of compartments like the loose-boxes in a stable. In this room, which opened out into a wider space by the door, rows of beer engines rose along a counter, side by side with hams as brown as old violins, lobsters of a bright metallic red, salted mackerel, along with slices of onion, raw carrots, pieces of lemon peel, bunches of bay leaves and thyme, juniper berries and coarse pepper swimming in a thick sauce.

One of the boxes was unoccupied. He took possession of it and hailed a young man in a black coat, who nodded, muttering some incomprehensible words. While the table was being laid, Des Esseintes examined his neighbours. It was the same as at the Bodega; a crowd of islanders with china blue eyes, crimson faces and pompous, supercilious looks, were skimming through foreign newspapers. There were some women amongst the rest, unaccompanied by male escort, dining by themselves—sturdy English dames with boys' faces, teeth as big as tombstones, fresh, apple-red cheeks, long hands and feet. They were attacking with unfeigned enthusiasm a rumpsteak pie—meat served hot in mushroom sauce and covered with a crust like a fruit tart.

After his long loss of appetite, he looked on in amazement at these sturdy trencherwomen, whose voracity whetted his own hunger. He ordered a plate of oxtail, a soup that is at once unctuous and tasty, fat and satisfying; then he scrutinized the list of fish, asked for a smoked haddock, which struck him as worthy of all praise, and seized with a rabid fit of appetite at the sight of other people stuffing themselves, he ate a great helping of roast beef and boiled potatoes and absorbed a couple of pints of ale, his palate tickled by the little musky, cow-like smack of this fine, light-coloured beer.

His hunger was nearly satisfied. He nibbled a bit of blue Stilton, a sweet cheese with an underlying touch of bitter, pecked at a rhubarb tart, and then, to vary the monotony, quenched his thirst with porter, that British black beer which tastes of liquorice juice from which the sugar had been extracted.

He drew a deep breath; for years he had not guzzled and swilled so much. The change of habits, the choice of unexpected and satisfying viands had roused the stomach from its lethargy. He sat back in his chair, lit a cigarette and prepared to enjoy his cup of coffee, which he laced with gin.

The rain was still falling steadily; he could hear it rattling on the glass skylight that roofed the far end of the room and running in torrents along the gutters. Nobody stirred a finger; all were dozing; comfortable like himself with liqueur glasses before them.

Presently tongues were lossened; as nearly everyone looked up in the air in talking, Des Esseintes concluded that these Englishmen were all discussing the weather. No one ever laughed, and all were dressed in suits of grey cheviot with nankin-yellow and blotting-paper red stripes. He cast a look of delight at his own clothes, the colour and cut of which did not sensibly differ from those of the people round him, highly pleased to find himself not out of tone with his surroundings, glad to be, in a kind of superficial way, a naturalized citizen of London. Then he gave a start—"but what of the train time?" he asked himself. He consulted his watch—ten minutes to eight; he had still nearly half-an-hour to stay there, he told himself, and once more he fell to thinking over the plan he had framed.

In the course of his sedentary life two countries only had tempted him to visit them, Holland and England.

He had fulfilled the first of these two wishes; attracted beyond his power to resist, he had left Paris one fine day and inspected the cities of the Low Countries one by one.

The general result of the journey was a series of bitter disappointments. He had pictured to himself a Holland after the pattern of Teniers' pictures and Jan Steen's, Rembrandt's and Ostade's, fashioning beforehand for his own particular use and pleasure Jewries as richly sun-browned as pieces of Cordova leather, imagining prodigal kermesses, everlasting junketings in the country, expecting to see all that patriarchal goodfellowship, that riotous joviality limned by the old masters.

No doubt Haarlem and Amsterdam had fascinated him; the common folk, seen in their unpolished state and in true rustic surroundings were very much as Van Ostade had painted them with their unlicked cubs of children and their old gossips as fat as butter, big-bosomed and huge-bellied. But of reckless merrymakings and general carousings not a sign. As a matter of fact, he found himself forced to admit that the Dutch School as represented in the Louvre had led him astray; it had merely supplied him with a springboard, as it were, to start him off on his fancies; from it he had leapt off on a false trail and wandered away into an impossible dreamland, never to discover anywhere in this world the land of faery he had hoped to find real; nowhere to see peasants and peasant-maidens dancing on the greensward littered with wine-casks, crying with sheer happiness, shouting with joy, relieving themselves under stress of uncontrollable laughter in their petticoats and their trunks!

No, decidedly, nothing of the sort was to be seen; Holland was a country like any other, and to boot, a country by no means simple and primitive, by no means specially genial, for the Protestant faith was rampant there with its stern hypocrisies and solemn scruples.

This past disillusionment recurred to his memory; again he consulted his watch—there was then some minutes more before his train left. "It is high time to ask for my bill and be going," he muttered to himself. He felt an extreme heaviness of stomach and an overpowering general lethargy. "Come now," he exclaimed, by way of screwing up his courage, "let's drink the stirrup cup,"—and he poured himself out a glass of brandy, while waiting for his account. An individual in a black coat, a napkin under one arm, a sort of majordomo, with a pointed head very bald, a harsh beard turning grey and a shaved upper lip, came forward, a pencil behind his ear, took up a position, one leg thrown forward like a singer on the platform, drew a paper-book from his pocket, and fixing his eyes on the ceiling without once looking at his writing, scribbled out the items and added up the total. "Here you are, sir," he said, tearing out the leaf from his book and handing it to Des Esseintes, who examined it curiously, as if it had been some strange animal. "What an extraordinary specimen, this John Bull," he thought, as he gazed at this phlegmatic personage whose clean-shaven lips gave him a vague resemblance to a helmsman of the American mercantile marine.

At that moment, the door into the street opened, and a number of people came in, bringing with them a stench of drowned dog mingled with a smell of cooking which the wind beat back into the kitchen as the unlatched door banged to and fro. Des Esseintes could not stir a limb;

a soothing, enervating lassitude, was creeping through every member, rendering him incapable of so much as lifting his hand to light a cigar. He kept telling himself: "Come, come now, get up, we must be off"; but instantly objections occurred to him in contravention of these orders. What was the good of moving, when a man can travel so gloriously sitting in a chair? Was he not in London, whose odours and atmosphere, whose denizens and viands and table furniture were all about him? What could he expect, if he really went there, save fresh disappointments, the same as in Holland?

He had only just time enough left now to hurry to the station, and a mighty aversion for the journey, an imperious desire to stay quiet, came over him with a force that grew momentarily more and more powerful and peremptory. He sat dreaming and let the minutes slip by, thus cutting off his retreat, telling himself: "Now I should have to dash up to the barriers, hustle with the luggage; how tiresome, what a nuisance that would be!"— Then, harking back, he told himself over again: "After all, I have felt and seen what I wanted to feel and see. I have been steeped in English life ever since I left home; it would be a fool's trick to go and lose these imperishable impressions by a clumsy change of locality. Why, surely I must be out of my senses to have tried thus to repudiate my old settled convictions, to have condemned the obedient figment of my imagination, to have believed like the veriest ninny in the necessity, the interest, the advantage of a trip abroad?—There," he concluded, glancing at his watch, "the time is ripe to go back home again." And this time he did get to his feet, left the tavern and ordered the cabman to take him back to the Gare de Sceaux; thence he returned with his trunks, his packages, his portmanteaux, his rugs, his umbrellas and walking-sticks to Fontenay, feeling all the physical exhaustion and moral fatigue of a man restored to the domestic hearth after long and perilous journeyings.

CHAPTER XII

DURING THE DAYS THAT FOLLOWED HIS RETURN HOME DES ESSEINTES occupied himself in reviewing the books of his library, drawing from the thought that he might have been parted from them for a long period as genuine a satisfaction as he would have enjoyed if he had really been coming back to them after a serious absence. Under the stimulus of this feeling, the volumes appeared to him in a new light altogether, for he found beauties in them he had quite forgotten ever since the day he first purchased them.

Everything: books, bric-a-brac, furniture, acquired a peculiar charm in his eyes. His bed struck him as more downy, in comparison with the pallet he would have occupied in London; the discreet, silent bearing of his domestics enchanted him, harassed as he was to think of the noisy loquacity of hotel waiters; the methodical organization of his daily life seemed more than ever desirable, since the haphazard of travelling had become a possibility.

He plunged himself again in the bath of fixed habits to which artificial regrets added a more bracing and tonic quality.

But it was his books that chiefly attracted his interest. He examined them, arranged them afresh on the shelves, looking to see whether, since his coming to Fontenay, the heat and wet had not injured their bindings or foxed their costly papers.

He began by turning over all his Latin library, after which he re-marshalled the special works of Archelaüs, Albertus Magnus, Raymond Lully and Arnaud de Villanova treating of the kabbala and the occult sciences; lastly he verified, one by one, his modern books and was delighted to find they were all intact, dry and in good condition.

This collection had cost him considerable sums of money; the fact is that he could not endure to see the authors he specially cherished printed, like those in other people's libraries, on rag paper, wearing hobnailed shoes like a clumsy peasant's.

In former days at Paris, he had certain volumes specially set up for him and printed off by specially hired workmen on hand-presses. Sometimes he would go to Perrin of Lyons, whose slim, clear types were suitable for archaic re-impressions of old tracts; sometimes he would send to England or the States, for new characters to print works of the present century; sometimes he would apply to a house at Lille which had for hundreds of years possessed a complete font of Gothic letters; sometimes again he would call in the help of the long-established Enschede press, of Haarlem, whose type-foundry preserves the stamps and matrices of the so-called "letters of civility."

He had followed the same course for his papers. Wearying one fine day of the ordinary papers de luxe—the silvery Chinese, the pearly golden Japanese, the white Whatmans, the brown Dutch, the Turkey-grains and Seychal-mills tinted to resemble chamois leather, and long ago disgusted with the machine-made articles, he had commissioned a laid paper run in special moulds from the ancient paper-mills at Vire, where they still use the old-fashioned stamps formerly employed to break the hemp. Then, to introduce a little variety in his collection, he had at various times imported from London dressed fabrics—flock-papers, repp-papers—while to further accentuate his scorn of the bibliophiles, a Lübeck tradesman was making him a glorified candle-paper, bluish in tint, crackling and rather brittle, in the substance of which the straw-lines were replaced by gold spangles like those that glitter in Dantzig liqueur-brandy.

By such means, he had secured a unique library, always choosing unusual sizes and shapes of page. These treasures he had had clothed by Lortic, by Trautz Bauzonnet, by Chainbolle, by the firm of Capé's Successors, in irreproachable bindings of antique silk, of stamped ox-leather, of Cape goatskin, full bindings, panelled and mosaiced, with wavy or watered silk linings instead of end-papers, adorned like Church service-books with clasps and metal corners, sometimes even ornamented by Gruel-Engelmann in oxydized silver and transparent enamel.

On these lines, he had had printed in the admirable episcopal character of the ancient firm of Le Clere, a copy of Baudelaire in a large format, recalling that of a Missal, on a very light Japanese felt, spongy in texture, as soft as elder-pith and just faintly tinged with pink over its milky white. This edition, limited to a single copy and printed in a velvety India-ink black, had been clothed outside and covered within with a marvellous and authentic sow-skin, one picked out of a thousand, flesh colour all dotted with the bristle marks and decorated with a lacework in black executed with the cold iron, the designs miraculously assorted by a great artist.

Today, Des Esseintes took down this incomparable volume from his shelves, and after fondling it reverently in his hands, reread certain pieces, which in this simple but inimitable frame seemed to him more striking and significant than ever.

His admiration for the writer in question was limitless. To his mind, Literature had hitherto confined itself to exploring the mere surface of the soul or, at most, penetrating into such of its underground chambers as were readily accessible and well lighted, verifying here and there the stratification of the deadly sins, studying their seams and their origin, noting for instance with Balzac the geological formation of the soul possessed by the monomania of an overmastering passion—by ambition, or avarice, or paternal infatuation, or senile love.

After all, it was entirely concerned with virtues and vices of a quite healthy and robust order, with the peaceable activity of brains of a perfectly ordinary conformation, with the practical reality of current ideas, with never a thought of morbid depravations, with no outlook beyond the pale of everyday; in a word, the speculations of these analysts of human nature stopped short at the ordinary classification of human acts by the Church into good and evil; it was all the simple investigation, the mere examination into normal conditions of a botanist who watches minutely the foreseen development of the everyday flora growing in common earth.

But Baudelaire had gone further; he had descended to the bottom of the inexhaustible mine, had pushed his way along abandoned or unexplored galleries, had penetrated those districts of the soul where the monstrous vegetations of the sick mind flourish.

There, near the confines where aberrations of the intellect and diseases of the will sojourn—the mystic tetanus, the burning fever of wantonness, the typhoids and yellow fevers of crime, he had found, hatching in the gloomy forcing-house of Ennui, the appalling reaction of age on the feelings and ideas.

He had revealed the morbid psychology of the mind that has reached the October of its sensations, detailed the symptoms of souls challenged by grief, set apart by spleen; had demonstrated the ever encroaching caries of the impressions at a time when the enthusiasms and beliefs of youth are faded; when there remains only the barren memory of miseries endured, of tyrannies suffered, of vexations undergone, in intelligences crushed by an incongruous fortune.

He had traced all the phases of this lamentable Autumn, as he watched the human creature, quick to grow embittered, ingenious at self-deception, forcing his thoughts to cheat each other, all to render his suffering more acute, spoiling in advance, thanks to his powers of analysis and observation, all possibility of happiness.

Next, following on this sensitiveness, this irritability of soul, on this ferocity of bitter reflection that repulses the importunate ardour of acts of devotion, the benevolent insults of charity, he saw arise little by little the horror of those passions of age, those loves of maturity, where one is still ready to comply while the other remains aloof and on guard, where lassitude claims of the pair filial caresses whose false juvenility seems a something new, or maternal fondlings whose gentleness is so restful and affords, as it were, the stimulating remorse of a vague sort of incest.

In magnificent pages he had exposed these hybrid loves, pages exasperated by their powerlessness to express the whole truth, these dangerous subterfuges of stupefying and poisonous drugs called upon to help soothe pain and conquer the weariness of the flesh. At a period when Literature was wont to attribute the grief of living exclusively to the mischances of disappointed love or the jealousy of adulterous deceptions, he had said not a word of these childish maladies, but had sounded those more incurable, more poignant and more profound: wounds that are inflicted by satiety, disillusion and contempt in ruined souls tortured by the present, disgusted with the past, terrified and desperate of the future.

And the more Des Esseintes reread his Baudelaire, the more fully he recognized an indescribable charm in this writer, who, in days when verse had ceased to serve any purpose save to depict the external aspect of men and things, had succeeded in expressing the inexpressible, thanks to a sinewy and firm-bodied diction which, more than any other, possessed the wondrous power of defining with a strange sanity of phrase the most fleeting, the most evanescent of the morbid conditions of broken spirits and disheartened souls.

After Baudelaire, the number of French books that found a place on his shelves was very limited. He was assuredly insensible to the merits of those works which it is a mark of taste and cleverness to wax enthusiastic over. The side-shaking mirth of Rabelais, "the full-bodied vis comica of Molière" failed to rouse his sense of humor; indeed his antipathy towards these comicalities even went so far that he did not hesitate to liken them, from the point of view of art, to those rows of flaring sconces that contribute to the jollity of country fairs.

So far as older poets were concerned, his reading hardly went beyond Villon, whose mournful "ballades" touched him, and some stray morsels of D'Aubigné that stirred his blood by the incredible virulence of their apostrophes and anathemas.

In prose, he made small account of Voltaire and Rousseau, or even of Diderot, whose extravagantly lauded "Salons" struck him as being stuffed to a singular excess with moral twaddlings and nonsensical aspirations. Detesting all this balderdash, he confined his reading almost entirely to the masterpieces of Christian eloquence, to Bourdaloue and Bossuet, whose sonorous and elaborate periods impressed him; but, for choicer preference, he savoured those pithy aphorisms condensed in stern, strong phrases of the sort Nicole wrought, in his meditations, and still more Pascal, whose austere pessimism and agonizing sense of sin stirred him to the bottom of his heart.

Apart from these few books, French literature, so far as his library was concerned, began with the present century. It was classified into two groups, one comprising the ordinary, profane writers, the other the

Catholic authors—a special literature, almost unknown to the generality, albeit disseminated by long established and enormous bookselling firms to the four corners of the world.

He had had the courage to wander in these hidden places, and, the same as in secular literature, he had discovered, underneath a gigantic mass of insipidities, some works written by true masters.

The distinctive characteristic of this literature was the persistency, the unchangeableness of its ideas and diction; just as the Church has perpetuated the primordial shape and form of sacred objects, in the same way has she kept intact the relics of her dogmas and piously preserved the reliquary that enshrined them—the oratorical phraseology of the Grand Siècle. As one of its own exponents even, Ozanam to wit, declared, the Christian style had nothing to learn from the language of Rousseau; its duty was to employ exclusively the dialect made use of by Bourdaloue and by Bossuet.

Despite this dictum, the Church, more tolerant than her disciple, winked at sundry expressions, sundry turns of phrase, borrowed from the lay speech of the same century, and the Catholic idiom had to some extent shaken itself free of its ponderous periods, weighed down, especially in Bossuet, by the length of its parentheses and the painful redundancy of its pronouns. But there the concessions had stopped; indeed, others would no doubt have been unavailing, for so lightened, this prose was adequate for the limited number of subjects which the Church condemned herself to treat.

Incapable of dealing with contemporary life, of making visible and palpable the simplest aspect of men and things, ill adapted to explain the complex ruses of a brain indifferent to the state of grace, this diction nevertheless excelled in the treatment of abstract subjects. Useful in the discussion of a controversy, in the demonstration of a theory, in the uncertainties of a commentary, it possessed more than any other the authority needful to lay down, without discussion, the value of a doctrine.

Unfortunately, there as everywhere, an innumerable army of pedants had invaded the sanctuary and degraded by their ignorance and want of talent its stern and uncompromising dignity. Then, to crown the calamity, pious ladies had taken up the pen, and ill-advised sacristies and rash drawing-rooms had extolled as veritable works of genius the wretched prattlings of these females.

Among other works of this sort that stirred his curiosity, Des Esseintes had read those of Madame Swetchine, the Russian General Officer's wife whose house at Paris was the rendezvous of the most fervent Catholics. They had filled him with an inexhaustible and overpowering sense of weariness; they were worse than bad, they were trivial; the whole thing suggested an echo hanging about a little chapel wherein a crowded congregation of bigoted, narrow-minded people knelt muttering prayers, asking after each others' news in whispers, repeating with looks of profound mystery a string of commonplaces on politics, the state of the barometer, the condition of the weather at the moment.

But there was a lower depth; there was Madame Augustus Craven, an accredited laureate of the Institut, the author of the Récit d'une Sœur, of Eliane, of Fleurange, applauded with blaring trumpets and rolling organ by the whole Catholic press. Never, no never, had Des Esseintes imagined that anyone could write such poor stuff. The books were, from the point of view of general conception, so utterly silly and were written in so nauseous a style, that they actually attained a sort of individuality of their own, became curiosities in their way.

In any case, it was not among female writers that Des Esseintes, whose mind was naturally sophisticated and unsentimental, could find a literary refuge adapted to his peculiar idiosyncrasies.

Still he persevered and with a conscientiousness no impatience could modify, did his best to appreciate the work of that child of genius, the bluestocking Virgin of this group, Eugénie de Guérin. His efforts were in vain, he could not stomach the famous Journal and Letters in which she extols, without tact or discretion, the prodigious talents of a brother who rhymed with such consummate ingenuity and grace that we must surely go back to the works of M. de Jouy and M. Ecouchard Lebrun to find any verses so boldly conceived and so fresh and new.

To no purpose had he tried to understand the charm of these productions in which we find such thrilling remarks as these:—"This morning I hung up beside papa's bed a cross a little girl gave him yesterday,"—"We are invited tomorrow, Mimi and I, to M. Roquiers', to attend the service of blessing a bell; I am very pleased to go,"—in which are recorded such momentous events as this: "I have just hung about my neck a medal of the Blessed Virgin, sent me by Louise as a safeguard against cholera,"—in which we come upon poetry of this calibre: "Oh, the lovely moonbeam that has just fallen on the Gospel I was reading!" or, to make an end, observations of the brilliant perspicacity of the following: "Whenever I see a man, on passing a crucifix, cross himself and take off his hat, I tell myself—That is a Christian going by."

This was the sort of thing that runs on page after page, without truce or respite, till the death of Maurice de Guérin, whom his sister bewails in still more rhapsodies, written in a wishy-washy prose interspersed here and there with tags of verse the poverty of which ended by moving Des Esseintes' pity.

Well, there was no denying it, the Catholic party was not hard to please in its choice of protégées, and far from critical! These pious muses it had made so much of and for whom it had exhausted the complaisance of its press, wrote one and all like Convent schoolgirls, in a colourless diction, in a flux of words no astringent can arrest!

The end was Des Esseintes turned away in horror from the stuff. But neither were the modern masters of sacred literature of a nature to offer him any sufficient compensations for his disappointment. These preachers and polemists were impeccable and correct in style, but the Christian dialect, in their sermons and books, had ended by becoming impersonal, stereotyped in a rhetoric whose movements and pauses were all fixed beforehand, arranged in a series of periods each constructed on one and the same model. In fact, the ecclesiastical authors all wrote alike, with a trifle more or a trifle less unconstraint and emphasis; the differences were all but imperceptible among these grey, colourless canvases, whether the work of Messeigneurs Dupanloup or Landriot, La Bouillerie or Gaume, of Dom Gueranger or the Père Ratisbonne, of Monseigneur Freppel or Monseigneur Perraud, of the Réverends Pères Ravignan or Gratry, the Jesuit Olivain, the Carmelite Dosithee, the Dominican Didon or of the erstwhile Prior of Saint-Maximin, the Réverend Chocarne.

Again and again, the conclusion had been forced upon Des Esseintes that it would need a very authentic talent, a very genuine originality, a firmly anchored conviction to thaw this frozen diction, to give life to this conventional style incapable of expressing a single unexpected idea, of upholding any thesis of the smallest audacity.

Nevertheless, one or two authors were to be found whose burning eloquence could melt and mould this inert phraseology—Lacordaire first and foremost, one of the only real authors the Church has produced for many years.

Imprisoned, like all his colleagues, within the narrow circle of orthodox speculation, obliged, like them, to mark time and refrain from touching any ideas but such as had been originated and consecrated by the Fathers of the Church and developed by the masters of the pulpit, he yet managed to turn the obstacle, to rejuvenate, almost to modify, these time-honoured commonplaces by throwing them into a more personal and more living form.

Scattered up and down his Conférences de Notre-Dame, happy phrases, bold expressions, accents of loving-kindness, outbursts of enthusiasm, cries of gladness, ecstatic outpourings of spirit occurred that made the age-old style smoke under his pen. Then, over and above his talent as an orator— and he was a true orator, this capable gentle-hearted monk whose intellect and industry were exhausted in the hopeless effort to conciliate the liberal doctrines of an advanced society with the authoritative dogmas of the Church, he was further endowed with a temperament of fervent charity, of diplomatic tenderness.

Then, again, the letters he used to write to young men often contained the loving words of a father exorting his sons—smiling reprimands, indulgent expressions of forgiveness. Some were charming where he would avow all his greed for affection, others almost impressively serious when he was sustaining his correspondents' courage or dissipating their doubts by the statement of the irrefragable certainties of his own Faith. In a word, this feeling of fatherhood, which under his pen assumed a dainty, feminine touch, impressed on his prose an accent unique amid all the mass of clerical literature.

After him, very few were the ecclesiastics and monks who showed any individuality. At most, some pages of his pupil the Abbé Peyreyve were readable. He had left touching biographical notices of his master, written some amiable letters, composed articles conceived in the sonorous language of the pulpit, pronounced panegyrics in which the declamatory note is too dominant. Undoubtedly, the Abbé Peyreyve had neither the tenderness nor the fire of Lacordaire. He was too much a priest and too little a man; here and there nevertheless his rhetoric as a preacher was illuminated by telling analogies, broad and weighty phrases, purple patches rising almost to sublimity.

But it was only among writers who had not submitted to Ordination, among secular authors attached to the interests of Catholicism and devoted to its propaganda, that a prose style was to be found worthy to arrest the attention.

The episcopal diction, so feebly handled by our Prelates, had acquired new strength, regained something of masculine force and vigour in the hands of the Comte de Falloux. Under an appearance of moderation, this Academician distilled gall; his discourses pronounced in 1848 in Parliament were diffuse and dull, but his articles contributed to the Correspondant, and afterwards collected in book form, were biting and bitter under the exaggerated courtesy of their outward expression. Conceived as set speeches, they displayed a certain caustic wit, while they startled by the intolerance of their convictions.

Dangerous as a controversialist by reason of the pitfalls he dug for his adversaries and the crookedness of his logic, forever turning the enemy's flank and striking an unexpected blow, the Comte de Falloux had also written some striking pages on the death of Madame Swetchine, whose remains he had edited and whom he revered as a Saint.

But where this author's temperament really showed itself was in two pamphlets which appeared one in 1846 and the other in 1880, the latter entitled l'Unité nationale ("National Unity").

Filled with a cold fury, this implacable Legitimist delivered for once, contrary to his custom, a frontal attack, and by way of peroration hurled at the sceptics' heads this thunder of savage invective:—

"And you, Utopians of a system, who make an abstraction of human nature, panegyrists of atheism, nourished on hallucinations and detestations, emancipators of woman, destroyers of the family, genealogists of the simian race, you, whose name was once insult enough, be well content; you will have been the prophets and your disciples will be the high-priests of an abominable future!"

The other pamphlet bore for title: le Parti catholique ("The Catholic Party") and was directed against the despotism of the Univers and its editor Veuillot, whose name it refused to utter. Here the flank attacks were resumed, poison lurked under every line of the little book in which the gentleman, bruised and battered, answered with scornful sarcasms the brutal blows of the professional bully.

Between them they represented the two parties in the Church whose differences degenerate into ungovernable hatred. De Falloux, at once more arrogant and more crafty than his opponents, belonged to that liberal coterie which already embraced both Montalembert and Cochin, both Lacordaire and de Broglie; he adhered heart and soul to the principles advocated by the Correspondant, a review which strove to overlay with a varnish of tolerance the peremptory theories of the Church. Veuillot, more outspoken and frank, threw off the mask, avowed unhesitatingly the tyranny of ultramontane aspirations, openly admitted and loudly acclaimed the pitiless yoke of her dogmas.

The latter champion had forged himself for the struggle a special language, borrowed part from La Bruyère and part from the bully of the Gros-Caillou. This style, half pompous, half familiar, wielded by this brutal personality, had the crushing weight of a bludgeon. Extraordinarily stubborn and extraordinarily courageous, he had felled with this terrible weapon freethinkers and bishops alike, hitting out might and main, rushing like a wild bull at his foes to whichever party they belonged. Distrusted by the Church, which approved neither his contraband diction nor his blackguard attitude, this religious mountebank had nevertheless made his mark by his undoubted talents, bringing about his heels the whole pack of the press, which he lashed till the blood came in his Odeurs de Paris, keeping at bay every assault, kicking off the whole base horde of low quill-drivers that tried to bite his calves.

Unfortunately, his incontestable talents only showed in a fight; in cold blood Veuillot was but an indifferent writer. His poetry and novels only inspired pity; his peppery invective lost its pungency when blows were no longer flying; the Catholic warrior was metamorphosed, in peaceful days, into a dyspeptic wheezing out trite litanies and stammering puerile canticles.

More narrow, more limited, more serious was the cherished apologist of the Church, the inquisitor of Christian diction, Ozanam. Difficult though he was to apprehend, Des Esseintes could not fail to be astonished by the aplomb of this author who would prate of the inscrutable purposes of God when he should have been adducing the proofs of the impossible assertions he was making; with the most perfect coolness he would travesty events, deny, more impudently still than the panegyrists of the other parties, the acknowledged facts of history, declare that the Church had never hidden the high esteem in which it held Science, describe heresies as foul miasmas, treat Buddhism and all other religions with such fine scorn that he excused himself from sullying Catholic prose by so much as an attack upon their doctrines.

There were occasions when religious passion breathed a certain ardour into his oratorical periods, beneath the ice of which boiled an undercurrent of suppressed violence; in his numerous writings on Dante, on St. Francis, on the author of the "Stabat," on the Franciscan poets, on Socialism, on Commercial Law, on everything, the man never failed to plead the defence of the Vatican which he deemed impeccable, judging all cases alike according as they approached more or less close or differed more or less widely from his own.

The same manner of looking at all questions from one point of view and one only equally belonged to that paltry scribbler whom some people held up as his rival, Nettement. The latter was less straitlaced and made less exalted and more worldly pretensions. He had repeatedly trespassed beyond the literary cloister in which Ozanam was a voluntary prisoner, and had dipped into profane writings with a view to appraising them. This region, indeed, he had penetrated groping, like a child in a cave, seeing nothing but darkness round him, perceiving in the general blackness only the flicker of the taper that lighted him onwards, throwing its glimmer a few feet ahead.

In this ignorance of the localities, in this obscurity, he had blundered at every step. Speaking of Mürger, he described him as "heedful of a polished and carefully finished style"; Victor Hugo was one who searched out the impure and filthy and he dared to compare N. de Laprade with him; Delacroix disdained all rules, while Paul Delaroche and the poet Reboul he extolled because they seemed to him to possess faith.

Des Esseintes could not help a shrug of the shoulders at these unfortunate criticisms, which were expressed in a laboured prose, the material of which, already worn threadbare, caught and tore on every corner of his sentences.

In another class, the productions of Poujoulat and Genoude, Montalembert, Nicolas and Carné failed to inspire him with any much more vivid interest; nor were his inclinations for History treated with painstaking erudition and in dignified language by the Duc de Broglie, nor his predilections for social and religious questions discussed by Henry Cochin, who had, however, revealed his true sentiments in a letter wherein he recounted a heart-stirring assumption of the veil at the Sacré-Coeur, very much more pronounced. For years, he had not looked into these books, and it was now a far-off day when he had thrown away as waste paper the puerile lucubrations of the dismal Pontmartin and pitiable Féval, and handed over to the servants for household purposes the little histories of Aubineau and Lesserre, those feeble hagiographers of the miracles wrought by M. Dupont de Tours and the Virgin.

In a word, Des Esseintes failed to extract from this literature even a passing distraction to his boredom; so he pushed away into the remote corners of his library this mass of volumes which he had studied in former days after leaving the Jesuits' seminary—"I should have done better to leave them behind in Paris," he muttered, as he drew out from their lurking-place behind the rest two sets of books he found particularly unendurable, the works of the Abbé Lamennais and those of that unmitigated fanatic, so supremely, so pompously tiresome and futile, Count Joseph de Maistre.

A single volume only was left still in place on a shelf within reach of the hand, that entitled l'Homme, by Ernest Hello.

This writer was the absolute antithesis of his brethren in religion. Almost isolated in the pious group which was shocked by his ways of thought, Ernest Hello had ended by abandoning the great main road that leads from earth to heaven.

Sickened no doubt by the triteness of this highway and the throng of pilgrims of letters that had for centuries filed obediently along the same track, walking each in the footmarks of his predecessor, stopping at the same halting-places, to exchange the same commonplaces on Religion, on the Fathers of the Church, on their identical beliefs, on their identical masters, he had diverged along bypaths, had come out into the gloomy forest clearing of Pascal, where he had tarried a long while to recover his wind; then he had pursued his journey and penetrated further into Jansenism, which all the time he abused, in the regions of human thought.

Full of subtlety and preciosity, erudite and elaborate, Hello with his hairsplitting minutiae of analysis reminded Des Esseintes of the laboured and meticulous studies of some of the psychological sceptics of the last and present centuries. There was in him a kind of Catholic Duranty, but more dogmatic and more astute, a practised master of the microscope, a trained engineer of the soul, a skilful watchmaker of the brain, delighting to examine the mechanism of a passion and explain minutely every wheel of the machinery.

In this oddly constituted mind were to be found associations of thought, analogies and contrasts scarcely to have been expected; added to which, a curious trick whereby he made the etymology of the words he used a springboard for leaping off to fresh ideas, the combination of which was often trivial enough, but almost invariably ingenious and stimulating.

In this way, and in spite of the faulty equilibrium of his constructions, he had taken to pieces, so to speak, with remarkable perspicacity The Miser, The Mediocre Man, analysed "Popular Taste," "The Passion of Calamity," besides revealing the interesting comparisons that can be established between the processes of photography and those of memory.

But this adroitness in wielding this perfected weapon of analysis which he had stolen from the Church's enemies represented only one of the sides of the man's temperament.

Yet another being existed in him; his mind had a double aspect, and after the good side appeared the bad—that of a religious fanatic and a Biblical prophet.

Like Hugo himself, whose contortions both of thought and phrase he recalled, Ernest Hello had loved to pose as a little St. John on Patmos to play the pontiff and enact the oracle from the top of a rock manufactured in the sacred image shops of the Rue Saint-Sulpice, haranguing the reader in an apocalyptic tongue salted here and there with the gall of an Isaiah.

He affected at that time exaggerated pretensions to profundity; some flatterers even hailed him as a genius, pretended to regard him as the great man of his day, the well of knowledge of his epoch—a well perhaps, but one where you could very often not see one drop of water.

In his volume Paroles de Dieu ("Words of God"), in which he paraphrased the Scriptures and did his best to complicate their meaning when fairly obvious; in another book of his entitled l'Homme; in his pamphlet le Jour du Seigneur ("The Day of the Lord"), composed in a Biblical style, broken and obscure, he showed the qualities of a vindictive, haughty apostle, full of gall and bitterness; he revealed himself in the character of a crackbrained deacon, half mystic, half epileptic, of a De Maistre for once endowed with talent, of a harsh and ferocious sectary.

At the same time, reflected Des Esseintes, this morbid excess of zeal barred the way to inventive sallies of casuistry; with more intolerance than Ozanam, he repudiated absolutely whatever did not pertain to his own narrow world, announced the most amazing axioms, maintained with a disconcerting air of authority that "Geology had gone back to Moses," that Natural History, Chemistry, all contemporary Science was by way of verifying the scientific accuracy of the Bible; every page was full of the "sole and only Verity," "the superhuman wisdom of the Church," the whole interspersed with aphorisms more than dangerous, and savage imprecations poured out in foul torrents on the art and literature of the last century.

To this strange alloy was superadded a love of pious studies— translations of the Visions of Angèle de Foligno, a book of an unparalleled fluidity and folly; and of selected portions from Ruysbroek l'Admirable, a mystic of the thirteenth century, whose prose presents an incomprehensible but fascinating combination of gloomy ecstasies, outpourings of unction, transports of bitterness.

All this attitude of the overbearing high-priest, which was characteristic of Hello, had come out in full force in an astounding Preface he wrote for this book. It is his own remark that "extraordinary things can only be told in stammers," and he stammered accordingly, declaring that "the holy obscurity wherein Ruysbroek spreads his eagle's wings is his ocean, his prey, his glory, and the four horizons would be for him a garment all too narrow."

Let him be what he would, Des Esseintes felt himself attracted by this ill-balanced, but subtle mind; to complete the fusion between the adroit psychologist on the one hand and the pious pedant on the other, had proved impossible, and these jolts, these incoherences even constituted the personality of the man.

Recruits to his standard were certain other writers forming little bands that operated as skirmishers on the outskirts of the Clerical camp. They did not belong to the main body, but were, properly speaking, rather the scouts of a Religion that distrusted men of talent like Veuillot and Hello, whom it deemed too independent and not colourless enough. What it really wanted was soldiers who never reasoned, regiments of the purblind, mediocre sort of men whom Hello stigmatized with the indignation of one who had endured their yoke. Accordingly, Catholicism had made all haste to expel from the columns of its organs one of its own partisans, Leon Bloy, a savage pamphleteer, who wrote a style at once furious and artificial, coquettish and uncultivated, and had turned out of doors at its official bookshops, as one plague-stricken and unclean, another author who had yet bawled himself hoarse in celebrating its praises: Barbey d'Aurévilly.

Truth to tell, he was too compromising an ally, and too indocile a disciple. The rest would always in the long run bow the head under rebuke and fall back into line; he was the "incorrigible urchin" the party could not recognize; he was a literary runagate after the girls, whom he brought bare-bosomed into the very sanctuary.

It was only due to that huge scorn with which Catholicism looks down on talent that an excommunication in due and proper form had not outlawed this strange servant who, under pretext of doing honour to his masters, was for breaking the church windows, mountebanking with the sacred vessels, executing fancy dances round the tabernacle.

Two works in particular of Barbey d'Aurévilly's fired Des Esseintes' imagination: the Prêtre marié ("Married Priest") and the Diaboliques.1 Others, such as l'Ensorcelé ("The Bewitched"), the Chevalier des Touches, Une vieille Maîtresse ("An Old Mistress"), were no doubt better balanced and more complete works, but they appealed less warmly to Des Esseintes, who was genuinely interested only in sickly books with health undermined and exasperated by fever.

In these comparatively sane volumes Barbey d'Aurévilly was perpetually tacking to and fro between those two channels of Catholicism which eventually run into one—mysticism and Sadism.

But in these two books which Des Esseintes was now turning over, Barbey had abandoned all prudence, had given the rein to his steed, had dashed off whip and spur along the roads he had then traversed to their extremest limits.

All the mysterious horror of the Middle Ages hovered over that improbable book the Prêtre marié; magic was mixed up with religion, gibberish with prayer, and more pitiless, more cruel than the Devil, the God of original sin tortured without respite or remorse the innocent Calixte, the victim of His abhorrence, branding her with a red cross on the brow, as of old He had had one of his angels mark the houses of unbelievers whom he was fain to slay.

Conceived by a fasting monk run delirious, these scenes succeeded one another in the broken language of a fever patient. But, unfortunately, among these creations as fantastic as the Coppélias galvanized into life by Hoffmann, there were some, the Néel de Néhou for example, that seemed to have been imagined in one of those periods of exhaustion that follow a crisis and were quite out of keeping amid these tales of gloom and madness, into which they imported the comic element that moves our involuntary mirth at sight of the little tin mannikin that plays the horn, in hunting boots, on the top of a mantelpiece clock.

Succeeding to these mystical divagations, the author had a period of comparative calm; then a terrible relapse followed.

The belief that man is a Buridan's ass, a being dragged this way and that by two forces of equal strength, which fight, turn and turn about victorious and vanquished, for his soul, the conviction that human life is no better than a doubtful struggle between hell and heaven, the faith in two opposed entities, Satan and the Christ, were bound fatally and inevitably to engender those inward discords where the soul, stimulated by an incessant combat, excited in a sort by promises and threats, ends by giving up the effort to resist and prostitutes itself to whichever of the two factions had been most obstinate in its pursuit.

In the Prêtre marié, the praises of the Christ, whose temptations had been successful, were sung by Barbey d'Aurévilly; in the Diaboliques, the author had surrendered to the Devil whom he then extolled. And then came the apparition of Sadism, that bastard birth of Catholicism, which

Faith has for centuries, under all its shapes, pursued with its exorcisms and its fires.

This condition of mind, so strange and so ill-defined, cannot in fact arise in the soul of an unbeliever. It does not consist solely in a mad riot amid the excesses of the flesh, further stimulated by bloody outrages of cruelty, for in that case it would be merely an aberration of the sexual feelings, an instance of satyriasis arrived at its point of supreme maturity; it consists primarily and particularly in a course of sacrilegious acts, in a moral revolt, in a spiritual debauch, in an aberration purely ideal, purely Christian. Another essential characteristic is a joy tempered by fear, analogous to the naughty pleasure of disobedient children who insist on playing with forbidden articles for no other reason than because their parents have expressly forbidden them to go near them.

In truth, if it did not involve a sacrilege, Sadism would have no raison d'être; on the other hand, sacrilege, which flows from the very existence of a religion, cannot be intentionally and effectively committed save by a believer, for a man would experience no satisfaction from profaning a faith that he did not believe in, or knew nothing of.

The force of Sadism then, the attraction it offers, lies wholly in the forbidden pleasure of transferring to Satan the homages and prayers we owe to God; it lies then in the nonobservance of the Catholic precepts which we are actually respecting, though in an inverse sense, when we commit, in order the more scornfully to mock the Christ, the sins he had most expressly banned—pollution of holy things and carnal orgies.

In reality, the vice to which the Marquis de Sade has given his name was as old as the Church herself; it had been rampant in the eighteenth century, reintroducing, to go back no farther, by a mere phenomenon of atavism, the impious practices of the medieval Witches' Sabbath.

By simply consulting the Malleus Maleficorum, Jacob Sprenger's terrible code of justice, which permitted the Church to exterminate by the fires of the stake thousands of necromancers and sorcerers, Des Esseintes was enabled to recognize in the ancient Sabbath all the obscene practices and all the blasphemies of Sadism. Over and above the unclean orgies dear to the Evil One, nights consecrated successively to lawful and unnatural coition, nights befouled by the bloody bestialities of ruttish animals, he found repeated the same parodies of Church processions, the same standing insults and defiances against God, the same ceremonies of devotion to his Rival, when was celebrated, with curses in lieu of blessings on the bread and wine, the Black Mass on the back of a woman crouching on all fours, whose rump, naked and polluted again and again, served for altar table, and the congregation communicated, in derision, with a black host on the face of which a figure of a he-goat was impressed.

The very same debauch of foul-mouthed raillery and degrading insults was to be seen in the Marquis de Sade, who added to his cruel and abominable sensualities the spice of sacrilegious profanities.

He defied Heaven, made invocation to Lucifer, called God a contemptible scoundrel, an idiot, an imbecile, spat on the communion, did all he could to degrade with vile obscenities a Deity he hoped would damn him, while declaring, the better to defy Him, that he had no existence.

This condition of soul Barbey d'Aurévilly came very near sharing. If he did not go as far as De Sade in uttering atrocious maledictions against the Saviour; if, more prudent or more timid, he always made a profession of honouring the Church, he none the less, as they did in the Middle Ages, addressed his pleadings to the Devil and fell, like the rest, by way of defying God, into demoniac erotomania, contriving sensual monstrosities of vice; borrowing even from the Philosophie dans le Boudoir a certain episode, which he seasoned with new condiments, when he wrote the tale: le Diner d'un athée ("An Atheist's Dinner-Party").

This extraordinary book was Des Esseintes' delight; he had printed for him in violet ink, Bishop's violet, within a border of Cardinal purple, on an authentic parchment which the Church officials had blessed, a copy of the Diaboliques set up in "letters of civility," whose outlandish serifs and flourishes, twisted into horns and hoofs, affect a Satanic contour.

After certain pieces of Baudelaire's which, in imitations of the psalms chanted on the nights of the Witches' Sabbath, took the form of infernal Litanies, this volume was among all the works of contemporary apostolic literature the only one that bore witness to that condition of soul at once pious and impious, towards which the remembered claims of Catholicism, stimulated by the attacks of nervous disorder, had often urged Des Esseintes.

With Barbey d'Aurévilly, the series of religious writers came to an end. To tell the truth, this pariah belonged more, from every point of view, to secular literature than to the other in which he was for claiming a place that was denied him. His language, characterized by a romanticism run wild, crammed with contorted expressions, unusual turns of phrase, extravagant similes, whipped up his sentences which tore along with roar and rattle and clang of noise of bells from top to bottom of the page. In a word, d'Aurévilly appeared like a full-blooded stallion among the geldings that people the Ultramontane stables.

Such were Des Esseintes' reflections as he reread passages chosen at random from the book and compared its nervous and varied style with the lymphatic, stereotyped diction of his fellows, thinking at the same time of the evolution of language so rightly insisted on by Darwin.

Associating with the profane, educated in the romantic school, familiar with the new literature, accustomed to the business of modern publications, Barbey found himself inevitably in possession of a dialect which had undergone many and profound modifications, which had been changed and renovated, since the days of the Grand Siècle.

Very different had been the case with the ecclesiastical writers; confined to their own domain, imprisoned within an ancient and identical range of reading, knowing nothing of the literary movements of the centuries and firmly determined, if need be, to tear out their eyes rather than see, they necessarily employed a language incapable of change, like that speech of the eighteenth century which the descendants of the French settlers in Canada still speak and write as their mother tongue, without any selection of phraseology or words having ever been possible in their idiom, isolated as it is from the ancient metropolis and surrounded on all sides by the English language.

Matters were at this point when the silvery sound of a bell tinkling a tiny angelus informed Des Esseintes that breakfast was ready. He left his books, wiped his forehead and made for the dining room, telling himself that among all the volumes he had been arranging on his shelves, the works of Barbey d'Aurévilly were still the only ones whose matter and style offered those gamey flavours, those stains of disease and decay, that cankered surface, that taste of rotten-ripeness which he so loved to savour among the decadent writers, Latin and Monastic, of the early ages.

CHAPTER XIII

The weather went from bad to worse. That year the seasons seemed to have changed places; after a long succession of rainstorms and fogs, blazing skies, like sheets of white-hot metal, now hung over the earth from horizon to horizon. In two days, without any transition whatever, cold, wet mists and lashing showers were followed by a torrid heat, an atmosphere as heavy as lead. As if stirred to a fiery fury with giants, the sun glared—a glowing furnace-mouth shooting forth an almost white light that scorched the eyes; a dust of flame rose from the burnt-up roads, grilling the parched trees, frying the dry grass. The reverberation from the whitewashed house-walls, the flames thrown back from the zinc of roofs and panes of windows, blinded the sight; the temperature of a smelting-house in full blast weighed on Des Esseintes' house.

Half stripped, he threw open a casement, to receive full in the face a puff of wind as hot as if coming from an oven; the dining room, whither he fled for refuge, was burning, the rarefied air seemed to boil. In utter exhaustion, he sat down, for the excitement that had kept his mind active with dreams and fancies during the time when he was arranging his books had come to an end.

As is the case with all sufferers from nervous disorders, the heat undermined his strength terribly; his anaemia, checked for the time being by the cold, recurred, exhausting a body debilitated by copious perspirations.

With shirt clinging to his moist back, perspiring perineum, dripping arms and legs, brow streaming with salt drops that poured down his cheeks, Des Esseintes lay back half fainting in his chair. The sight of the food on the table sickened him; he ordered it to be taken away and boiled eggs brought instead. He tried to swallow sippets of toast dipped in the yolk, but they stuck in his throat. He turned sick and drank a few drops of wine, but it seemed to burn his stomach like fire. He mopped his face; the sweat, hot just now, was now cold as it trickled from his temples; he tried sucking bits of ice to relieve the feeling of nausea—but all to no purpose. An infinite lassitude glued him to his chair by the table; at last he got up, longing for air, but the sippets of toast had swelled and risen in his throat till they came near choking him. Never before had he felt so oppressed, so feeble, so ill at ease; his eyes, too, were affected, he saw things double and turning round and round; soon the sense of distance grew confused, his glass seemed to be a mile away from his hand. He told himself he was the victim of an optical delusion, but he could not throw off the sensation. Finally, he went and lay down on the sofa in the drawing-room; but then the rolling of a ship at sea began, increasing his nausea still further. He sprang up again, resolved to take a digestive to settle the eggs in his stomach.

He returned to the dining room and sadly compared himself, in his cabin, to passengers on a vessel attacked by seasickness. With staggering steps he made his way to the cupboard that contained his "mouth-organ," and examined the latter, but without opening it he reached instead up to a higher shelf for a bottle of Bénédictine, which he selected to keep by him because of its shape which struck him as suggestive of ideas at once pleasantly festive and vaguely mystical.

But for the moment, he remained indifferent, looking with a dull eye at the thickset flagon of dark green glass which was wont at other times to call up before his mind's eye the Priors of the medieval Monastery as he looked at its antique monkish paunch, its head and neck wrapped in a parchment cowl, its stamp of red wax quartered with three silver mitres on a field azure, the cork tied over and sealed with lead like a Papal bull, and the label written in sonorous Latin, on paper yellowed and faded as if by age—liquor Monachorum Benedictinorum Abbatiae Fiscanensis (Liqueur of the Benedictine Monks of the Abbey of Fécamp).

Under this full monastic habit, certified by a cross and certain ecclesiastical initial letters—P.O.M., within these parchments and bands that guarded it like an authentic charter, slumbered a saffron-coloured liquor of an exquisite delicacy. It distilled an aroma of the quintessence of angelica and hyssop mingled with seashore herbs rich in iodines and bromines disguised by sugary matters; it stimulated the palate with a spirituous heat dissimulated under a toothsomeness altogether virginal and innocent; flattered the nose with a smack of rankness enwrapped in a soothing savour at once childlike and pious.

This hypocrisy resulting from the startling discrepancy between the containing vessel and its contents, between the liturgical form of the bottle and the soul inside it, so feminine, so modern, had before now set him dreaming; he had indeed fallen many a time into a brown study as he sat before this liqueur, thinking of the monks who sold it, the Benedictines of the Abbey of Fécamp who, while belonging to the Congregation of Saint-Maur, famous for its researches in History, served under the rule of St. Benedict, yet did not follow the observances of the white monks of Citeaux and the black monks of Cluny. Irresistibly they came crowding before his mind's eye, in their daily life as they lived in the Middle Ages, cultivating simples, heating retorts, distilling in alembics sovereign panaceas, infallible cure-alls.

He drank off a drop of the liqueur and felt a relief that lasted a minute or two; but very soon the same fire that a mouthful of wine had before kindled in his inwards burned there again. He tossed away his napkin and went back into his study, where he began pacing up and down; he felt as if he were under the bell of an air-pump in which a vacuum was being gradually produced, and a sensation of faintness, at once soothing and excruciating, ran from his brain down every limb. He pulled himself together and, unable to bear more, for the first time perhaps since his arrival at Fontenay, fled for refuge to his garden, where he found shelter in the ring of shadow cast by a tree. Seated on the turf, he gazed with a dazed look at the beds of vegetables the servants had planted. But it was only after an hour had elapsed that his eyes saw what he was looking at, for a greenish mist floated before his eyes and prevented his making out more than the blurred images, as if viewed through deep water, of objects, whose appearance and colour kept continually changing.

In the end, however, he recovered his balance and found himself able to distinguish clearly onions and cabbages, further off a broad patch of lettuce and in the background, all along the hedge, a row of white lilies standing motionless in the heavy air.

A smile flitted over his lips, for suddenly he remembered a quaint comparison old Nicander makes, likening, from the point of view of shape, the pistil of a lily to an ass's genitals, while a passage from Albertus Magnus also occurred to him where that miracle-worker gives a singular formula for discovering by the use of a lettuce whether a girl is still virgin.

These recollections gave him a moment's merriment. Then he fell to examining the garden, marking how the plants lay withered by the heat and the ground smoked in the glare of the dusty sunbeams. Presently, above the hedge separating the garden which lay at a lower level from the raised roadway leading up to the Fort, he caught sight of a band of young rascals tumbling over each other in the blazing sunshine.

His attention was still concentrated on them when another village lad appeared, a smaller mite than the rest. He was a squalid object; his hair looked like seaweed sodden with sand, his nose was filthy, his mouth was disgusting, the lips smeared with a white paste from what he had been nibbling at—skim-milk cheese spread on a piece of bread and sprinkled over with slices of raw green onion.

Des Esseintes sniffed the air; a sudden longing, a perverse craving seized him; the nauseous dainty brought the water to his mouth. He thought somehow that his stomach, that rebelled against all food, would digest this horrid repast and his palate enjoy it like a royal feast.

He sprang up, ran to the kitchen and gave instant orders to send to the village for a round loaf, some white cheese and a raw onion, directing that they should make him a meal exactly like what he had seen the child gnawing at. This done, he went back and resumed his seat under the tree.

The lads were fighting now, snatching scraps of bread out of each other's hands, shoving them into their mouths and then licking their fingers. Kicks and fisticuffs were freely exchanged, and the weaker vessels got tumbled over in the road, where they lay squalling as the jagged stones scraped their backsides.

The sight gave new life to Des Esseintes; the interest he took in the combat diverted his thoughts from his own miseries. Looking on at the fury of these naughty youngsters, he reflected on the cruel and abominable law of the struggle for existence, and ignoble as the children were, he could not help sympathizing with their lot and concluding it would have been better for them had their mother never borne them.

In fact, what was it all but scald-head, colics, fevers, measles, kicking and cuffings in infancy, hard knocks and degrading jobs of work at thirteen or so, women's trickeries, vile diseases and wives' unfaithfulness in manhood; then, in declining years, infirmities and a painful death in a workhouse or a hospital.

When all was said and done, the future was the same for all, and neither one nor the other class, if they had had a particle of common sense, could possibly have desired it. For the rich, it was, in different surroundings, the same passions, the same vexations, the same sorrows, the same diseases, and likewise the same poor satisfactions, whether these were alcoholic, literary or carnal. There was even a vague compensation for all the sufferings, a kind of rude justice that restored the balance of misery as between the classes, enabling the poor to endure more easily the physical sufferings that broke down more mercilessly the feebler and more emaciated bodies of the rich.

What madness to beget children! reflected Des Esseintes. And to think that ecclesiastics, who have taken a vow of sterility, have actually pushed unreason so far as to canonize St. Vincent de Paul because he saved innocent little ones for useless torments!

Thanks to his odious precautions, he had postponed for years the death of beings, devoid of intelligence and feeling, in such wise that, having in time grown almost understanding and at any rate capable of pain, they could foresee the future, could expect and dread the death they had hitherto not known so much as the name of; that they could, some of them, even call upon it to come, in very hatred of the condemnation to live he inflicted on them in virtue of an illogical code of Theology.

Yes, and since the old Saint's death, his ideas had come to govern the world; children abandoned to die were rescued, instead of being left to perish quietly without their being conscious of aught amiss; while, at the same time, the life they preserved them for was growing day by day harsher and more barren! Under pretext of liberty and progress, Society had discovered yet another means of aggravating the miseries of man's existence, by dragging him from his home, tricking him out in an absurd costume, putting specially contrived weapons in his hands, brutalizing him in a slavery identical with that from which they had, out of compassion, enfranchised the negro, and all this merely to put him in a condition to slaughter his fellows without risking the scaffold, as common murderers do who work in units, without uniform, with arms less noisy and less swift to kill.

What a strange epoch, Des Esseintes told himself, is this, which, while invoking the sacred name of humanity, and striving to perfect anaesthetics to abolish physical pain, at the very same time provides such irritants to aggravate moral agonies!

Ah! if ever, in the name of pity, useless procreation should be abolished, that time was now! But here, again, the laws promulgated by men like Portalis and Homais appeared, ferocious and self-contradictory.

Justice deemed quite natural the ways men use to trick Nature in the marriage bed; it was a recognized, admitted fact; there was never a household, no matter how well-to-do, that did not employ means to hinder procreation, use contrivances to be bought openly in the shops—all artifices it would never occur to anybody to disapprove. Yet, if these means, these subterfuges proved ineffectual, if the trickery failed, and to make good the failure, recourse was had to more certain methods, there were not prisons and gaols and penal settlements enough to hold in durance vile people condemned to this punishment by judge and jury, who the same night in the conjugal bed used every trickery they could devise not to beget youngsters of their own.

The trickery itself therefore was no crime, but to make good its failure was one!

In a word, Society regarded as a crime the act that consisted in killing a creature endowed with life; and yet, in expelling a foetus, the operator was surely destroying an animal, less fully formed, less alive and certainly less intelligent and more ugly than a dog or a cat, which may be strangled at birth without penalty.

It is right to add, thought Des Esseintes, for further proof how monstrous the injustice is, that it is not the unskilful operator, who generally makes off with all haste, but the woman, victim of his awkwardness, who pays the penalty for saving an innocent being from the burden of life.

Verily the world must be extraordinarily prejudiced to want to suppress manoeuvres so natural that primitive man, that the very savages of the South Seas have been led to practise them by the mere action of their own instinct.

At this moment, his servant interrupted these charitable reflections of his master by bringing Des Esseintes a silver-gilt salver on which lay the nauseous dainty he had asked for. A spasm of disgust shook him; he had not the courage to touch the thing, for the morbid craving had now ceased. A sensation of extreme malaise returned; he was forced to rise from where he sat; the sun, in moving westwards was little by little encroaching on the place, the air becoming more oppressive and the heat more scorching.

"Go and pitch the thing," he ordered the man, "to those children yonder fighting in the road; I hope the weakest ones will be maimed and never get a scrap and, what's more, be soundly whipped by their parents when they get back home with trousers torn and eyes blackened; that will give them a foretaste of the merry life that awaits them!" Then he returned to the house, where he sank half fainting in an armchair.

"Still I must try and eat something," he sighed—and he proceeded to soak a biscuit in a glass of old Constantia (J. P. Cloete brand), a few bottles of which were still left in his cellar.

This wine, the colour of onion skins slightly burnt, smacking of old Malaga and Port, but with a sugary bouquet of its own and an aftertaste of grapes whose juices have been condensed and sublimated by burning suns, had often comforted his stomach and given a fillip to his digestion enfeebled by the forced fasts he was compelled to undergo; but the cordial, generally so efficacious, failed of its effect. Then, hoping an emollient might cool the hot irons that were burning his intestines, he had recourse to Nalifka, a Russian liqueur, contained in a flask patterned over with dead-gold filigree; but this unctuous, fruity syrup was equally ineffective. Alas! the days were long past when Des Esseintes, still in the enjoyment of robust health, would, in the middle of the dog-days, mount a sledge he had at home, and then, closely wrapped in furs which he would pull up to his chin, force himself to shiver as he told himself through teeth that chattered of set purpose: "Ah! but the cold is Arctic; it's freezing, freezing hard!" till he actually persuaded himself it was cold weather!

Alas! suchlike remedies were of no avail now that his sufferings were real.

With all this, it was useless for him to have recourse to laudanum; instead of acting as a sedative, that drug only irritated his nerves and robbed him of sleep. In former times he had resorted to opium and hashish in order to see visions, but the only result had been to bring on vomiting and intense nervous disturbances; he had been obliged forthwith to give up their use and without the help of these coarse excitants to ask his brain of itself alone to bear him far away from everyday life into the region of dreams.

"What a day!" he moaned to himself on this occasion, as he sponged his neck, feeling as if every ounce of strength he had left was melting away in a fresh access of perspiration. A feverish restlessness still made it impossible for him to stay in one place; again he set off roaming through his rooms, trying all the seats one after the other. Wearied out at last, he presently sank down before his writing desk, and resting his elbow on the table, fell mechanically and without any ulterior motive to turning about in his hands an astrolabe, lying as a paperweight on a heap of books and memoranda.

He had purchased the instrument, which was of copper engraved and gilt, of German workmanship and dating from the seventeenth century, at a bric-a-brac shop in Paris, after a visit he had paid one day to the Musée de Cluny, where he had stood for hours enraptured before a wonderful astrolabe of carved ivory, the cabalistic look of which had fascinated him.

The paperweight in question stirred up in him a whole crowd of reminiscences. Influenced by the associations evoked by the sight of the little ornament, his thoughts flew from Fontenay to Paris, to the old curiosity shop where he had bought it, then returned to the Musée des Thermes, where he called up the mental picture of the ivory astrolabe, while his eyes still continued to dwell, but without seeing it, on the copper astrolabe on his writing table.

Then, still led by memory, he quitted the Museum and, without leaving town, strolled up and down the streets. After roaming along the

Rue Sommerard and the Boulevard Saint-Michel, he struck off into the adjoining streets and came to a halt in front of certain establishments whose frequency and peculiar character had often struck him.

Beginning with the astrolabe, this mental excursion ended by leading him to the beer-halls of the Quartier Latin.

He recalled the great number of these places all along the Rue Monsieur-le-Prince and at the end of the Rue Vaugirard adjoining the Odéon; sometimes they stood cheek by jowl like the old riddecks in the Rue du Canal-aux-Harengs at Antwerp, stretching one after the other down the sidewalk, which they overlook with a row of signboards all very much alike.

Through the half open doors and the windows only partially obscured by coloured panes or curtains he could remember having caught glimpses of women walking up and down with dragging step and out-thrust neck, the way geese waddle; others lounging on benches were rubbing elbows on marble-topped tables, dreaming away the hours or singing to themselves, their heads drooped between their fists; yet others would be preening themselves before the looking-glass, patting with the tips of their fingers their false hair just dressed by a barber; others again would be drawing out of reticules with broken fastenings piles of silver and copper which they amused themselves by ranging methodically in little heaps.

The majority had massive features, hoarse voices, flaccid bosoms and painted eyes, and all, like so many automata wound up at the same time with the same key, uttered in the same tone the same invitations, lavished the same smiles, talked in the same silly phrases, indulged in the same absurd reflections.

Thoughts began to crystallize in Des Esseintes' mind and he found himself coming to a definite inference, now that he could look back in memory and take a bird's-eye view, as it were, of these crowded taverns and streets.

He realized the meaning of these cafés, saw that they corresponded to the state of mind and imagination of a whole generation; he gathered from them material for the synthesis of the period.

Indeed, the symptoms were plain and unmistakable; the legalized brothel was disappearing, and each time one of these closed its doors, a beer-tavern opened.

This diminution of official prostitution, organized for the satisfaction of clandestine amours, was evidently to be accounted for by the incomprehensible illusions men indulge in from the carnal standpoint.

Monstrous as this might seem, the fact was, the beer-tavern satisfied an ideal.

True, the utilitarian tendencies transmitted hereditarily and further developed by the precocious discourtesies and constant brutalities of school and college had made the youth of the present day singularly coarse and also singularly opinionated and cold-hearted, but for all this, it had preserved, deep down in its heart, an old-fashioned flower of sentiment, a vague, half decayed ideal of love.

So nowadays, when the blood was hot within, it could no more consent just to march in, work its will, pay and go home again. This, in its eyes, was a bestial thing, like a dog covering a bitch without preliminary or preamble. Besides, vanity was in no sort of way gratified in these official houses of vice where there was no pretence of resistance on the woman's part, no semblance of victory on that of the man, where no special preference was to be expected, nor even any special liberality of favours from the prostitute who, as a tradeswoman should, measured her caresses in proportion to the price paid. On the other hand, to pay court to a girl at a beer-saloon was allowing for all these sentimentalities, all the delicacies of love. There were rivals in this case striving for her affection, and those to whom she agreed, for a sufficient consideration, to grant a rendezvous, imagined themselves, in all good faith, to have won a victory, to be the object of a flattering preference, the recipient of a precious favour.

Yet, all the time, the creatures were every whit as stolid, as mercenary, as base and degraded as those who ply their trade in the houses with numbers. Like these, the tavern waitresses drank without being thirsty, laughed without being amused, were mad after the caresses of a fancy man from the streets, blackguarded each other and quarrelled and fought on the slightest provocation. Yet, in spite of everything, the young Parisian rake had never learned that the servant wenches at these beer-halls were, from every point of view, whether of personal good looks or attractive poses or pretty dresses, altogether inferior to the women confined in the luxurious rooms of the other sort of establishment! Great God! Des Esseintes could not help exclaiming, what simpletons these fools must be who flutter round beer-halls, for, to say nothing of their ridiculous self-deception, they have positively brought themselves to ignore the danger they run from the low-class, highly suspicious quality of the goods supplied, to think nothing of the money spent in drinks, all priced beforehand by the landlady, to forget the time wasted in waiting for delivery of the commodity—a delivery put off and put off continually in order to raise the price, frittered away in delays and postponements endlessly repeated, all to quicken and stimulate the liberality of the client.

This imbecile sentimentalism combined with ferocity in practice seemed to represent the dominant feeling of the age; these same fellows who would have gouged out their best friend's eye to make a sixpence, lost all clearness of vision, all perspicacity, in dealing with the disreputable tavern-wenches who bullied them without compunction and exploited them without mercy. Workmen toiled, families cheated one another in the name of trade, all to let themselves be swindled out of money by their sons, who in their turn allowed themselves to be plundered by these women, who in the last resort were drained dry by their fancy lovers.

From end to end of Paris, East to West and North to South, it was one unbroken chain of petty trickeries, a series of organized thefts repeated continually from one to another—all this simply because, instead of satisfying lechers straight away, the suppliers of these goods were artful enough to keep their clients dangling about and waiting with what patience they might.

At bottom, human wisdom might be summed up in the precept—drag things out indefinitely, say no, then after a long time, yes; for indeed there was no way of managing mankind half so good as procrastination.

"Ah! if only the same held good of the stomach," sighed Des Esseintes, seized with a sudden spasm of pain which instantly brought his thoughts back to Fontenay, recalling them from the faraway regions they had been roaming.

CHAPTER XIV

Two or three days had jogged by more or less satisfactorily, thanks to various devices for cheating the stomach's reluctance, when one morning the highly spiced sauces which masked the smell of fat and savour of blood that go along with flesh-meat stirred Des Esseintes' gorge, and he asked himself anxiously whether his weakness, already alarming, was not getting worse and likely soon to force him to take to his bed. Suddenly, a gleam of light shone through his distress of mind; he remembered how one of his friends, who had been very ill at one time, had succeeded by using a "patent digester" in checking the anaemia, stopping the wasting, keeping what was left him of vigour from further dissipation.

He despatched his servant to Paris to procure the precious apparatus, and in accordance with the directions the maker sent with it, himself instructed the cook how to cut up the beef into little bits, put it dry into the tin digester, to add a slice of leek and carrot, then screw on the lid and set the whole thing to boil in a hot-water pan for four hours.

At the end of that time, the threads of meat were squeezed dry, and you drank a spoonful of the muddy, salty juice left at the bottom of the pot. Then you felt something slip down that was like absorbing warm marrow, something that soothed the stomach with a gentle, velvety caress.

This quintessence of nourishment stopped the spasms and nauseas of the empty stomach, stimulating its action till it no longer refused to keep down a few spoonsful of soup.

Thanks to his "digester," Des Esseintes' nervous malady made no further progress, and he told himself: "Well, that is something gained, at any rate; perhaps the temperature will fall soon; the clouds will modify the glare of that odious sun that wears me out, and I shall then get along, without overmuch suffering, to the first fogs and frosts of Autumn."

In his present state of apathy and the weariness of having nothing to occupy his thoughts, his library, the rearrangement of which still remained uncompleted, got on his nerves; no longer stirring from his chair, he had continually before his eyes the shelves appropriated to profane literature with the books on them lying about in disorder, propped up one against the other, piled up in heaps or tumbled like a pack of cards flat on their sides. This confusion shocked him the more when he contrasted it with the perfect order of his religious works, carefully drawn up, as if on parade, along the walls.

He tried to remedy this confusion, but after ten minutes' labour he found himself bathed in perspiration; the effort was too much for his strength; he lay down exhausted on a couch and rang for his servant.

Following his directions, the old domestic set to work, bringing him the books one by one, which he then examined and pointed out the chosen place for each.

The task was quite a short one, for Des Esseintes' library contained only a singularly limited number of non-religious books of the present day.

By dint of passing them through the test of a severe mental review, in the same way as the wire-drawer passes strips of metal through a steel draw-plate from which they issue attenuated and light, reduced to almost invisible threads, he had finally come to possess only books which had proved capable of withstanding such a treatment and were solid enough of frame to bear the second rolling-mill of perusal. By this process of elimination, he had checked and pretty well sterilized all pleasure in reading, accentuating yet further the irreconcilable conflict between his ideas and those of the society in which chance had ordained he should be born. It had come to this at last that he found it impossible any longer to discover a book to satisfy his secret aspirations; nay, he had even ceased to admire the very volumes that had without a doubt done much to embitter his mind and fill it so full of subtle suspicions.

Yet in literature and art, his opinions had started in the first instance from a simple enough point of view. For him, there were no such things as schools, only the writer's individual temperament mattered, only the working of the creator's brain interested him, whatever the subject treated of. Unfortunately, this true criterion of appreciation, worthy of La Palisse, was as good as useless, for the simple reason that, while desiring to be rid of prejudice, to refrain from all passion, every man goes for choice to those works which correspond most intimately with his own temperament and he ends by relegating all the rest to the background.

This work of selection had gone on slowly. He had at one time adored the great Balzac, but in proportion as his organism had lost balance, as his nerves had gained the upper hand, his inclinations had been modified and his preferences changed.

Soon even, and this although he was well aware of his injustice towards the marvellous author of the Comédie Humaine, he had given up so much as ever opening his books, the sturdy art of which irritated him; other aspirations stirred him now, that were in a sense incapable of precise definition.

By careful self-examination, however, he realized in the first place that a book to attract him must bear the character of singularity that Edgar Allan Poe craved; but Des Esseintes was ready and willing to adventure further along this road, demanding strange flowers of Byzantine fancy and complicated sophistries of diction; he preferred a vague, vexing indefiniteness, that left him to brood meditatively over it till he had made it, at will, yet more vague, or more firmly outlined, according to the condition of his spirit at the moment. He wanted, in one word, a work of art both for what it was in itself and for what it allowed him to lend it of himself; he wanted to go along with it, thanks to its support, helped on his way by it as if supported by a friend's arm, as if borne forward by a vehicle, into a sphere where the sublimated stress of sensation roused in him an unexpected commotion, the exact causes of which he would strive long and even vainly to unravel.

Lastly, ever since his leaving Paris, he shrunk more and more from the realities of life and above all from the society of his day which he regarded with an ever growing horror—a detestation which had reacted strongly on his literary and artistic tastes; he refused, as far as possible, to have anything to do with pictures and books whose subjects were in any way connected with modern existence.

Thus, losing the faculty of admiring beauty independently of the shape, whatever that may be, under which it presents itself, he now preferred, in Flaubert, the Tentation de Saint-Antoine to the Education sentimentale; in De Goncourt, Faustin to Germinie Lacerteux; in Zola, La Faute de l'Abbé Mouret to L'Assommoir.

This point of view seemed to him logical; these works, less direct indeed, but equally thrilling, equally human, let him penetrate further into the inmost secrets of temperament of these masters who displayed with a more unfeigned frankness the most mysterious impulses of their being, while at the same time they raised him also, higher than the rest, out of that trivial life he was weary of.

Moreover, he could enter in reading them into complete community ideas with the writers who had conceived them; because at the moment of writing, the authors had been in a state of mind closely analogous to his own.

The truth is, when the period at which a man of talent is condemned to live is dull and stupid, the artist is, unconsciously to himself, haunted by a sensation of morbid yearning for another century.

Unable to bring himself into harmony, save at rare intervals, with the surroundings amid which he develops, ceasing to find in the study of these surroundings and in the beings who are subjected to them sufficient pleasures of observation and analysis to divert him, he feels the birth and growth in himself of phenomena of a singular sort. Confused cravings for a change of time and place spring up, which find their satisfaction in reflection and reading. Instincts, sensations, preferences transmitted from his ancestors awake, grow more and more precise and govern his thoughts as masters. He recalls memories of persons and things he had never personally known, and there comes a time when he escapes impetuously from the prison-house of his century, and wanders forth, in freedom, in another epoch, with which, by a crowning piece of self-deception, he believes he would have been in better accord.

In some cases, it is a return to past ages, to vanished civilizations, to dead centuries; in others, it is an impulse towards the fantastic, the land of dreams, it is a vision more or less vivid of a time to come whose images reproduce, without his being aware, as a result of atavism, that of bygone epochs.

In Flaubert's case, it was a series of vast and solemn pictures, of grandiose and pompous spectacles, in the magnificent and barbaric frame of which moved beings sensitive and delicate, mysterious and proud, women endowed, in the perfection of their beauty, with sick and suffering souls, wherein he discerned secret horrors of infatuation and insane caprice, driven to desperation as they were even in their day by the miserable inadequacy of the pleasures they could hope to enjoy.

The temperament of the great author was revealed in all its brilliance in those incomparable pages of the Tentation de Saint-Antoine and Salammbô in which, far from all associations of our petty modern life, he called up the Asiatic splendours of far-off ages, their mystic aspirations and discouragements, the morbid fancies of their idleness, the ferocities springing from the oppressive ennui that flows, even before its pleasures have been drained to the dregs, from a life of opulence and prayer.

In De Goncourt, on the other hand, it was a longing for the preceding century, a craving to return to the elegant trivialities of the eighteenth century, never to be renewed.

The gigantic panorama of seas breaking upon piers of granite, of deserts beneath blazing skies stretching farther than eye can see, found no place in his work of imaginary reconstruction, which confined itself, within the boundaries of a great noble's park, to a boudoir warm with the alluring emanations of its fair occupant, a woman with a tired smile, a discontented mouth, restless yet pensive eyes. The soul wherewith he animated his characters was not now the soul Flaubert breathed into his creations, a soul in revolt beforehand at thought of the inexorable certainty that no new happiness was possible; rather was it a soul driven to revolt after trial, after experience, after all the fruitless efforts it had made to invent novel, less hackneyed liaisons, to give a new spice to the one, world-old pleasure that is repeated from age to age in the gratification, more or less ingeniously carried out, of a pair of lovers' lust.

Albeit Faustin lived among us moderns and was body and soul of our age; yet, by ancestral influences, she was a being of the bygone century, the captious heart and mental lassitude and sensual satiety of which she shared in full.

This book of Edmond de Goncourt's was one of the volumes Des Esseintes most delighted in. Indeed, that suggestiveness, that invitation to dreamy reverie which he loved, abounded in this work, where underneath the written line peeped another visible to the soul only, indicated rather than expressed, which revealed depths of passion piercing through a reticence that allowed spiritual infinities to be defined such as no idiom of human language could have encompassed. It was very different from the diction of Flaubert, no doubt one of inimitable magnificence; here the style was at once clear and morbid, vigorous and deformed, careful to note the impalpable impression that strikes the senses and determines sensation; a style expert to modulate complicated shades of distinction of a period which was itself extraordinarily complex. In a word, it was the phraseology inevitably called for by decrepit civilizations which for the due expression of their needs demand, to whatever age they belong, special acceptations, special turns of phrase, novel moulds of sentences and words.

At Rome, expiring Paganism had modified its prosody, transmuted its language, with Ausonious, Claudian, Rutilius, whose style, careful and scrupulous, full-bodied and sonorous, presented, particularly in passages descriptive of reflections, shadows, shades of meaning, an inevitable analogy with that of the De Goncourts.

At Paris, a unique phenomenon in literary history had come about; this perishing society of the eighteenth century, which had produced painters, sculptors, musicians, architects, all influenced by its predilections, imbued with its beliefs, had never succeeded in fashioning a veritable writer capable of rendering its dying elegancies, or expressing the essential juice of its feverish pleasures, that were to be so cruelly expiated. It had had to wait for De Goncourt, whose temperament was made up of memories, of regrets stirred to life by the grievous spectacle of the intellectual poverty and the base aspirations of his own day, to resuscitate, not alone in his books of history, but likewise in a retrospective work like Faustin, the very soul of the epoch, to incarnate its nervous daintinesses in his actress heroine, so painfully eager to torment heart and head alike that she might savour to the verge of exhaustion the cruel revulsives of love and art.

In Zola, the same feeling of neurotic longing, the craving to overpass the bounds of the present day, took a different form. In him there was no wish to travel to regions and systems of the past, to worlds vanished in the darkness of bygone ages. His temperament, strong and powerful, enamoured of the luxuriances of life, of full-blooded vigour, of moral sturdiness, deterred him from the artificial graces, the painted and powdered pallors of the last century, as likewise from the hieratic solemnity, the brutal ferocity and the effeminate, dubious imaginations of the ancient East. The day when he, too, in his turn, had been attacked by this same yearning, this desire that is in essence poetry itself, to fly far from this contemporary society he was studying, he had hastened to an ideal country where the sap boiled in full sunshine; he had dreamed of fantastic concupiscences of heaven, of long passionate swoonings of earth, of fertilizing showers of pollen falling on the panting genitals of flowers; he had arrived at a gigantic pantheism, had, all unconsciously perhaps, created, in these surroundings where, as in a Garden of Eden, he placed his Adam and Eve, a wondrous Hindu epic, celebrating in a style whose broad colours, laid on unmixed, had a sort of quaint brilliancy as of an Indian painting, the hymn of the flesh, matter, animated, living, revealing to human beings by its very frenzy of generation the forbidden fruit of love, its suffocating spasms, its instinctive caresses, its natural attitudes.

With Baudelaire, these were the three masters who in all the range of French literature, modern and profane, had most caught and moulded Des Esseintes' tastes; but by dint of rereading them, of saturating his mind in their works, of knowing them by heart from end to end, he had been constrained in order to gain the power of absorbing them again, to force himself to forget them and leave them for a while undisturbed on his bookshelves.

Accordingly, he barely opened them as the old servant handed them to him one by one. He confined himself to pointing out the place they were to occupy, taking care to see them arranged in good order and with plenty of elbow room.

The domestic next brought him another series of books, which caused him more trouble. These were works to which he had grown more and more partial, works which by the very fact of their imperfection, relieved the strain after the high perfections of writers of vaster powers. Here again, in his refining way, Des Esseintes had come to look for and find in pages otherwise ill put together occasional sentences which gave him a sort of galvanic shock and set him quivering as they discharged their electricity in a medium that had seemed at first entirely a nonconductor.

The very imperfections themselves pleased him, provided they did not come from base parasitism and servility, and it may well be there was a modicum of truth in his theory that the subordinate writer of the decadence, the writer still individual though incomplete, distils a balm more active, more aperitive, more acid than the author of the same period who is really truly great, really and truly perfect. In his view, it was in their ill-constructed attempts that the most acute exaltations of sensibility were to be seen, the most morbid aberrations of psychology, the most extravagant eccentricities of language pushed to its last refusal to contain, to enclose the effervescent salts of sensations and ideas.

So, in spite of himself, neglecting the masters, he now addressed himself to sundry minor writers, who were only the more agreeable and dear to him by reason of the contempt in which they were held by a public incapable of understanding them.

One of these, Paul Verlaine, had already made his debut with a volume of verse, the Poèmes Saturniens, a volume almost to be described as feeble, in which imitations of Leconte de Lisle jostled against experiments in romantic rhetoric, but which nevertheless revealed in certain pieces, such as the sonnet entitled "Un Rêve familier", the real personality of the poet.

Going back to his antecedents, Des Esseintes discovered underlying these attempts with their uncertain touch a talent already profoundly affected by Baudelaire, whose influence subsequently became much better marked, though without the contributions offered by the impeccable master being too flagrantly plagiarisms.

Then later, some of his books, the Bonne Chanson, the Fêtes Galantes, the Romances sans paroles and finally his last volume, Sagesse, contained poems in which the original writer was revealed, making his mark among the mass of his contemporaries.

Provided with rhymes contrived by using the tenses of verbs, sometimes even by lengthy adverbs preceded by a monosyllable, from which they fell as from a stone sill in a massive cascade of water, his verse, divided by impossible caesuras, was often singularly obscure with its daring ellipses and strange breaches of rule, that were yet not without a certain grace.

Handling metre better than most, he had endeavoured to rejuvenate the stereotyped forms of poetry, the sonnet, for instance, which he turned about, tail in air, like those Japanese fish of variegated earthenware we see which rest on their pedestal gills downwards. In other cases, he had degraded its form, employing only masculine rhymes, for which he seemed to show a predilection. Similarly and not unfrequently he had adopted a quaint form, a strophe of three lines, the middle one being left unrhymed, and a tercet, with one rhyme only, followed by a single line by way of refrain and recurring as an echo of itself, as in the popular pieces like "Dansons la Gigue." Yet other rhymes were to be found whose half-heard ring was only faintly to be caught in far-off strophes, like the distant sound of a bell.

But his individuality was mainly conspicuous in the fact that he had known how to suggest vague and delicious secrets, in whispered voices, in the dusk of twilight. He alone had had the art to half reveal certain mysterious and troublous instincts of the soul, certain whisperings of thought so soft and low, certain avowals so gently murmured, so brokenly expressed, that the ear catching them was left hesitating, passing on to the mind languors stirred by the mystery of this breath of sound divined rather than heard. Verlaine's very spirit is in those admirable lines of the "Fêtes Galantes":—

> Le soir tombait, un soir équivoque d'automne,
> Les belles se pendant rêveuses à nos bras,
> Dirent alors des mots si spécieux tout bas,
> Que notre âme depuis ce temps tremble et s'étonne.

2

It was not now the limitless horizon revealed through unforgettable portals by Baudelaire, but rather, on a moonlit night, a chink half opened upon a field of view more restricted and more intimate; in a word, a field peculiar to the author. Indeed the latter, in verses that Des Esseintes greatly savoured, had formulated his own poetic system:—

> Car nous voulons la nuance encore,
> Pas la couleur, rien que la nuance
> ⋮
> Et tout le reste est littérature.

3

Gladly Des Esseintes had followed him through the series of his works, even the most diverse. After the publication of his Romances sans paroles, issued from the printing-office of a local newspaper at Sens, Verlaine had written nothing for a considerable interval; then, in charming lines touched with the gentle, moving charm of Villon, he had reappeared, celebrating the Virgin, "far from our days of carnal spirit and dreary flesh." Often would Des Esseintes read and reread this book, Sagesse, and enjoy under its inspiration secret reveries, imaginations of an occult passion for a Byzantine Madonna, transmuting at a given moment into a Cyprian goddess who had strayed into our century. She was so mysterious and so troublous to the senses that none could say whether she was craving for depravities of vice so monstrous that, once accomplished they would become irresistible by mankind; or whether she herself was immersed in a dream, an immaculate reverie, where the adoration of the soul should float about her in a love forever unconfessed, forever pure.

There were other poets, too, who enticed him to trust their guidance. One was Tristan Corbière, who, in 1873, amid general indifference, had launched a volume of verses of the wildest eccentricity under the title of Les Amours Jaunes. Des Esseintes, who, in his hatred of the trivial and commonplace, would have welcomed the most unmitigated follies, the most grotesque extravagancies, spent some agreeable hours with this book where the burlesque was strangely combined with an inordinate vigour, where lines of a disconcerting brilliance occurred in poems that were as a whole utterly incomprehensible, such as the litanies in his "Sommeil", which he himself in one passage stigmatized as:—

> Obscène confesseur des dévotes mort-nées.

4

It was barely French; the author was talking negro, using a sort of telegram language, passing all bounds in the suppression of verbs, affecting a ribald humour, condescending to quips and quibbles only worthy of a commercial traveller of the baser sort; then, in a moment, in this tangle of ludicrous conceits, of smirking affectations, would rise a cry of acute pain, like a violoncello string breaking. But with all this, in this style, rugged, arid, fleshless, bristling with unusual vocables and unexpected neologisms, flashed many a happy expression, many a stray verse, rhymeless yet superb; finally, to say nothing of his Poèmes Parisiens, from which Des Esseintes used to quote this profound definition of womankind:—

Eternal féminin de l'éternel jocrisse.
5

Tristan Corbière had, in a style almost imposing in its conciseness, sung the seas of Brittany, the mariners' seraglios, the Pardon of St. Anne, and had even risen to the eloquence of hate in the invective he hurled, in connection with the Camp of Conlie, at the individuals whom he reviled under the title of "mountebanks of the Fourth of September."

This overripe flavour which Des Esseintes loved and which was offered him by this poet of the contorted epithets and beauties that are always of the rather suspect sort, he found likewise in another poet, Théodore Hannon, a disciple of Baudelaire and Gautier, a writer animated by a very special sense of far-sought elegancies and factitious pleasures.

Unlike Verlaine, who came direct, without cross, from the Baudelaire breed, particularly on the psychological side, the whimsical turn of his thought and the artful concentration of his sentiment, Théodore Hannon derived from the master, mainly on the plastic side, by his external envisagement of men and things.

His fascinating corruption bore a fatal correspondence with Des Esseintes' predilections, and, in days of fog and rain, the latter would shut himself up in the retreat imagined by this poet, intoxicating his eyes with the glitter of his rich stuffs, with the flash of his jewels, with his sumptuosities, exclusively material, which all helped to excite the brain to frenzy and rose like a cantharides powder in a cloud of hot incense towards a Brussels Idol with painted face and belly tanned with perfumes.

With the exception of these and of Stéphane Mallarmé, whom he directed his servant to set on one side, in order to give him a class apart, Des Esseintes was only very moderately drawn to the poets.

For all his magnificence of technique, for all the impressive roll of his verse which moved with so fine a stateliness that even Victor Hugo's hexameters seemed in comparison flat and dull, Leconte de Lisle could now no longer satisfy him. The ancient world, reanimated with so marvellous a vigour by Flaubert, remained dead and cold in his hands. There was no movement in his verse; it was all outside façade, with, most part of the time, never an idea to prop it up; there was no life in the dusty poems whose dull mythologies ended by chilling him.

On the other hand, after having long cherished him as a prime favourite, Des Esseintes was coming to lose interest in Gautier's work; his admiration for that incomparable painter of pictures had been melting from day to day, and now he was more amazed than delighted before his descriptions, in a way impersonal as they are. The impression of objects had fixed itself on his eminently perceptive eye, but there it had, so to say, localized itself, had penetrated no further into brain and into body; like a marvellously contrived reflector, it had confined itself to repeating all things about it with an indifferent precision.

No doubt Des Esseintes still loved the works of these two poets in the same way as he loved rare jewels, precious articles of dead matter, but none of the variations of these accomplished instrumentalists could any longer move him to ecstasy, for not one of them was conducive to reverie, not one of them opened, at any rate for him, one of those living outbursts that enabled him to speed the slow flight of the hours.

He left their books hungry and the same was true of Victor Hugo's. The Oriental and patriarchal side was too conventional, too empty to retain his interest, while the other side, at once good-natured and grandfatherly, got on his nerves. It was not till he came to the Chansons des rues et des bois that he felt himself bound to applaud the faultless jugglery of his metrical technique yet, when all was said and done, how gladly would he have given all these tours de force for one new poem of Baudelaire to match the old, for beyond a doubt the latter was almost the only author whose verses contained beneath their shining rind a really balsamic and nutritious kernel!

To leap from one extreme to the other, from form devoid of ideas to ideas devoid of form, left Des Esseintes no less cold and circumspect in his admiration. The psychological labyrinths of Stendhal, the analytical divagations of Duranty attracted him; but their diction, official, colourless, dry; their mercenary prose, at most good for the ignoble consumption of the stage, repelled him. Besides, the interesting intricacies of their analyses appealed, after all, only to brains still stirred by passions that no longer moved him. Little he cared for the common emotions of humanity, for the ordinary associations of ideas, now that his mental reserve was growing more and more pronounced; and he was sensitive to none but superfine sensations and the doubts raised by Catholicism and sensual phenomena.

To enjoy a literature uniting, as he desired, with an incisive style, a penetrating, feline power of analysis, he must resort to that master of Induction, that strange, profound thinker, Edgar Allan Poe, for whom, since the moment when he had begun to reread him, his predilection had suffered no possible diminution.

Better than any other writer perhaps, Poe possessed those close affinities of spirit that fulfilled the demands Des Esseintes had formulated in the course of his meditations.

While Baudelaire had deciphered in the hieroglyphics of the soul the period of recurrence of feelings and thoughts, he had, in the realm of morbid psychology, more particularly scrutinized the region of will.

In literature, he had been the first, under the emblematic title of "The Demon of Perversity," to explore those irresistible impulses which the will submits to without understanding their nature and which cerebral pathology now accounts for with a fair degree of certainty; again, he was the first, if not to note, at any rate to make generally known, the depressing influence of fear acting on the will, like those anaesthetics that paralyze sensibility and that curare that annihilates the nervous elements of motion; it was on this point, this lethargy of the will, that he had focused his studies, analysing the effects of this moral poison, pointing out the symptoms of its progress, the troubles incidental to it, beginning with anxiety, proceeding to anguish, culminating finally in terror which stupefies the powers of volition, yet without the intelligence, however severely shaken, actually giving way.

To death, which the dramatists had so lavishly abused, he had, in a manner, given a new and keener edge, made it other than it was, introducing into it an algebraic and superhuman element; yet, to say truly, it was not so much the actual death agony of the dying he depicted as the moral agony of the survivor, haunted before the bed of suffering by the monstrous hallucinations engendered by pain and fatigue. With a hideous fascination, he concentrated his gaze on the effects of terror, on the collapse of the will; applied to these horrors the cold light of reason; little by little choking the breath out of the throat of the reader who pants and struggles, suffocated before these mechanically reproduced nightmares of raging fever.

Convulsed by hereditary nervous disorders, maddened by moral choreas, his characters lived only by the nerves; his women, the Morellas, the Ligeias, possessed a vast erudition, deeply imbrued with the foggy mists of German metaphysics and the cabalistic mysteries of the ancient East; all had the inert bosoms of boys or angels, all were, so to say, unsexual.

Baudelaire and Poe, whose minds have often been compared because of their common poetical inspiration and the predilection they shared for the examination of mental maladies, yet differed radically in their conceptions of love—and these conceptions filled a large place in their works. Baudelaire's passion was a thirsty, ruthless thing, a thing of cruel disillusion that suggested only reprisals and tortures; Poe's a matter of chaste and ethereal amours, where the senses had no existence, and the brain alone was stirred to erethism with nothing to correspond in the bodily organs, which, if they existed at all, remained forever frozen and virgin.

This cerebral clinic where, vivisecting in a stifling atmosphere, this spiritual surgeon became, directly his attention flagged, the prey of his imagination, which sprayed about him, like delicious miasmas, apparitions whether of nightmare horrors or of angelic hosts, was for Des Esseintes a source of indefatigable conjectures. Now, however, when his nerves were all sick and on edge, there were days when such reading exhausted him, days when it left him with trembling hands and ears strained and watchful, feeling himself, like the lamentable Usher, seized by unreasoning pangs of dread, by a secret terror.

So he felt bound to moderate his zeal, to indulge sparingly in these formidable elixirs, just as he could now no longer visit with impunity his red vestibule and intoxicate himself with the sight of Odilon Redon's gloomy paintings or Jan Luyken's representations of tortures.

And yet, when he was in these dispositions of mind, all literature struck him as vapid after these terrible philtres imported from America.

Thereupon he turned his attention to Villiers de l'Isle-Adam, in whose works he noted, here and there, observations equally unorthodox, vibrations equally spasmodic, but which, at any rate, with the exception of his Claire Lenoir, did not distil so overwhelming a sense of horror.

First published in 1867 in the Revue des lettres et des arts, this Claire Lenoir opened a series of romances included under the generic title of Histoires moroses. On a background of obscure speculations borrowed from old Hegel, moved a phantasmagoria of impossible beings, a Doctor Tribulat Bonhomet, pompous and puerile, a Claire Lenoir, comic and uncanny, wearing blue spectacles, as round and big as five franc pieces, concealing her almost lifeless eyes.

The romance turned on an ordinary adultery, but ended on an unspeakable note of horror, when Bonhomet, uncovering Claire's eyeballs on her deathbed and searching them with hideous probes, beheld distinctly reflected on the retina the picture of the offended husband brandishing in his extended hand the severed head of the lover; and, like a Kanaka savage, howling a war-song of triumph.

Based on the physiological fact, more or less surely verified, that the eyes of some animals, oxen for instance, preserve till decomposition sets in, in the same way as photographic plates, the image of the persons and things lying at the instant of their death within the range of their last look, the tale evidently derived from those of Edgar Allan Poe, from whom he copied the meticulous and appalling discussion of the details.

The same might be said of the "Intersigne," subsequently incorporated in the Contes cruels, a collection of stories displaying indisputable talent, and in which occurred "Vera", a romance Des Esseintes regarded as a little masterpiece.

Here the hallucination was impressed with an exquisite tenderness; there was nothing here of the gloomy imaginings of the American author, it was a vision of warmth and gentleness, almost celestial in its beauty. It formed, in an identical mode, the antithesis of Poe's Beatrices and Ligeias, those sad, wan phantoms engendered by the inexorable nightmare of black opium!

This romance likewise brought into play the operations of the will, but it no longer treated of its enfeeblements and failures under the action of fear. On the contrary, it made a study of its exaltations under the impulse of a conviction become a fixed idea; it demonstrated its power, which even came to saturate the atmosphere and impose its faith on surrounding things.

Another book of Villiers', Isis, struck him as curious on other grounds. The philosophical lumber of Claire Lenoir cumbered this book no less than its predecessor, and it presented an incredible confusion of verbose, chaotic observations and reminiscences of old-fashioned melodramas, oubliettes, poniards, rope ladders, all those transpontine situations Villiers was to prove himself unable to revivify in his "Elen" and his "Morgane," pieces long since forgotten, published by an obscure local printer, Monsieur Francisque Guyon, of Saint-Brieuc.

The heroine of this book, a Marquise Tullia Fabriana, who was supposed to have assimilated the Chaldean learning of Poe's women together with the diplomatic wisdom of the Sanseverina-Taxis of Stendhal, had into the bargain put on the enigmatic air of a Bradamante added to an antique Circé. These incompatible mixtures developed a smoky vapour through which philosophical and literary influences elbowed each other, without having been able to take order in the author's brain at the time he was writing the prolegomena to this work, which was planned to embrace not less than seven volumes.

But in Villiers' temperament there existed another side, altogether more telling, more clearly defined, an element of grim pleasantry and savage raillery; it was no longer, when this came into play, a case of Poe's paradoxical mystifications, but rather a cruel jeering, a gloomy jesting, of the same sort as Swift's black rage against humanity. A whole series of pieces, "les Memoiselles de Bienfilâtre," "l'Affichage céleste," "la Machine à gloire," "le Plus beau dîner au monde," revealed a gift of satirical banter singularly inventive and effective. All the filth of utilitarian ideals, all the mercenary baseness of the century were glorified in pages the bitter irony of which moved Des Esseintes to ecstasy.

In this special class of serious and biting pleasantry no other book existed in France; at most, a romance of Charles Cros, La Science de l'amour, published originally in the Revue du Monde-Nouveau, might well amaze readers by its wild eccentricities, its satiric humour, its coldly comic observations, but the pleasure was no more than relative, for the execution was fatally defective. Villiers' style, strong, varied, often original, had disappeared to give place to a sort of forcemeat scraped from the shop-board of the first literary pork-butcher to hand.

"Great God! how few books then there are that one can reread," sighed Des Esseintes, watching the servant as he stepped off the stool he had been perched on and drew aside to let his master cast a general look along the shelves.

Des Esseintes nodded his approval. There now remained on his table only two thin volumes. He beckoned the old man to leave the room, and fell to skimming the pages of one of these, bound in wild ass's skin, first glazed under a hydraulic press, dappled in watercolour with silver clouds and provided with "end-papers" of old China silk, the pattern of which, now rather dim with age, had that grace of faded splendour that Mallarmé celebrated in a singularly delightful poem.

These pages, nine in all, contained extracts from unique copies of the two earliest Parnasses, printed on parchment, and preceded by a title page bearing the words: Quelques vers de Mallarmé, designed by a wonderful calligrapher in uncial letters, coloured and picked out, like the characters in an ancient manuscript, with points of gold.

Among the eleven pieces included in the collection some, "Les fentres," "l'Epilogue," "Azur," attracted him; but one of all the rest, a fragment of the "Hérodiade," mastered him like a veritable spell at certain times.

How many evenings, under the light of the lowered lamp flooding the silent room, had he not felt his senses stirred by this same Herodias who, in Gustave Moreau's masterpiece that, now half invisible in the dimness, gleamed merely as a vaguely seen white statue in the midst of a dull glowing brazier of jewels.

The darkness hid the blood, dimmed the flash of colours and gold, buried in gloom the far corners of the temple, obscured the minor actors in the murderous drama where they stood wrapped in sad-coloured garments, sparing only the high lights of the painting, showing the white figure of the woman emerging from her sheath of jewels and accentuating her nakedness.

Involuntarily he lifted his eyes and looked. There gleamed the never-to-be-forgotten outlines of her shape; she lived again, recalling to his lips those weird, sweet words that Mallarmé puts in her mouth:

"O miroir!

"Eau froide par l'ennui dans ton cadre gelée,

Que de fois, et pendant les heures désolée

Des songes et cherchant mes souvenirs qui sont

Comme des feuilles sous ta glace au trou profond,

Je m'apparus en toi comme une ombre lointaine!

Mais, horreur! des soirs, dans ta sévère fontaine,

J'ai de mon rêve épars connu ta nudité."

6

He loved these verses as he loved all the works of this poet who, in an age of universal suffrage and an epoch of filthy lucre, lived aloof from literary society; sheltered against the folly of the world about him by his fine scorn; finding joy, far from the crowd, in the surprises of the intellect, the visions of his brain; refining on thoughts already fine and specious, engrafting on them Byzantine conceits, perpetuating them in deductions just lightly hinted, deductions barely bound together by an imperceptible thread.

These thoughts, interwoven and precious, he knotted into one with an adhesive diction, aloof and secret, full of contorted phrases, elliptical turns of speech, audacious tropes.

Catching analogies the most remote, he would often designate by a word that suggests by an effect of likeness at once form, scent, colour, quality, brilliancy, the object or being to which he must have appended a host of different epithets to indicate all its aspects, all its lights and shades, if it had been merely referred to by its technical name. He thus contrived to do away with the formal statement of a comparison, which arose of itself in the reader's mind by analogy, once he had comprehended the symbol, and avoided dissipating the attention over each of the several qualities which might otherwise have been presented one by one by a series of adjectives strung in a row, concentrating it instead on one single word, on one whole, producing, as an artist does in a picture, one unique and complete effect, one general aspect.

The result was a sort of condensed literature, an essence of nutriment, a sublimate of art. It was a device which Mallarmé after first employing it only sparingly in his earlier works, had openly and boldly adopted in a piece he wrote on Théophile Gautier and in the l'Après-midi du faune, an eclogue in which the subtleties of sensual joys were unfolded in mysterious, softly suggestive verses, broken suddenly by this frantic, wild-beast cry of the Faun:

> "Alors m'éveillerai-je à la ferveur première,
> Droit et seul sous un flot antique de luminère,
> Lys! et l'un de vous tous pour l'ingénuité."
> 7

The last verse, which with its monosyllable "Lys" thrown back to the beginning called up the idea of something rigid, tall, white, an indication further strengthened by the noun "ingénuité" brought in as a rhyme, expressed allegorically, in a single word, the passion, the effervescence, the passing moment of excitement of the virgin Faun, maddened to lust at sight of the Nymphs.

In this extraordinary poem, surprises, novel images, unexpected conceptions awaited the reader in every line, as the poet went on to describe the emotions and regrets of the goat-foot standing by the marsh-side and gazing at the clumps of rushes still keeping a fleeting impress of the rounded forms of the Naïds that had lain there.

Then Des Esseintes also found a fanciful delight in handling the miniature volume, the covers of which, in Japanese felt, as white as curdled milk, were fastened with two silk cords, one China pink, the other black.

Concealed behind the binding, the black ribbon met the pink one, which gave a note of velvety softness, a suspicion as of modern Japanese rouge, a suggestion of love and licence, to the antique severity of the pure white, the frankly natural tint of the book, which it entwined, knotting together in a small rosette its sombre hue with the brighter tint of the other, suggesting a discreet intimation of the Faun's regrets, a vague foreshadowing of the melancholy that succeeds the transports of passion and the appeasing of the senses excited to frenzy by desire.

Des Esseintes replaced on the table the Après-midi du faune, and glanced through another thin volume which he had had printed for his private use—an anthology of prose poetry, a little shrine dedicated to Baudelaire as patron saint and opening with one of his pieces.

The collection included selected passages from the Gaspard de la nuit of that fantastic author Aloysius Bertrand who has transferred Da Vinci's methods to prose and painted with his metallic oxides a series of little pictures whose brilliant tints glitter like transparent enamels. To these Des Esseintes had added the "Vox populi" of Villiers, a piece superbly struck off in a style of gold recalling the type of Leconte de Lisle and Flaubert, and some extracts from that delicious trifle, the Livre de Jade, whose exotic perfume of ginseng and tea is mingled with the fresh fragrance of water babbling in the moonlight from cover to cover of the book.

But, in this selection, had likewise been gathered sundry pieces rescued from dead and gone reviews: "le Demon de l'analogie", "la Pipe", "le Pauvre enfant pâle", "le Spectacle interrompu", "le Phénomène futur", and in particular the "Plaintes d'automne et Frisson d'hiver." This last was one of Mallarmé's masterpieces, one of the masterpieces of prose poetry to boot, for they united a diction so magnificently ordered that it lulled the senses, like some mournful incantation, some intoxicating melody, with thoughts of an irresistible seductiveness, stirrings of soul of the sensitive reader whose quivering nerves vibrate with an acuteness that rises to ravishment, to pain itself.

Of all forms of literature that of the prose poem was Des Esseintes' chosen favourite. Handled by an alchemist of genius, it should, according to him, store up in its small compass, like an extract of meat, so to say, the essence of the novel, while suppressing its long, tedious analytical passages and superfluous descriptions. Again and again Des Esseintes had pondered the distracting problem, how to write a novel concentrated in a few sentences, but which should yet contain the cohobated juice of the hundreds of pages always taken up in describing the setting, sketching the characters, gathering together the necessary incidental observations and minor details. In that case, so inevitable and unalterable would be the words selected that they must take the place of all others; in so ingenious and masterly a fashion would each adjective be chosen that it could not with any justice be robbed of its right to be there, and would open up such wide perspectives as would set the reader dreaming for weeks together of its meaning, at once precise and manifold, and enable him to know the present, reconstruct the past, divine the future of the spiritual history of the characters, all revealed by the flashlight of this single epithet.

The novel, thus conceived, thus condensed in a page or two, would become a communion, an interchange of thought between a magic-working author and an ideal reader, a mental collaboration by consent between half a score persons of superior intellect scattered up and down the world, a delectable feast for epicures and appreciable by them only.

In a word, the prose poem represented in Des Esseintes' eyes the concrete juice, the osmazome of literature, the essential oil of art.

This succulence, developed and concentrated in a drop, already existed in Baudelaire, as also in those poems of Mallarmé's which he savoured with so deep a delight.

When he had closed his anthology, Des Esseintes told himself, here was the last book of his library, which would probably never receive another addition.

In fact, the decadence of a literature, attacked by incurable organic disease, enfeebled by the decay of ideas, exhausted by the excess of grammatical subtlety, sensitive only to the whims of curiosity that torment a fever patient, and yet eager in its expiring hours to express every thought and fancy, frantic to make good all the omissions of the past, tortured on its deathbed by the craving to leave a record of the most subtle pangs of suffering, was incarnate in Mallarmé in the most consummate and exquisite perfection.

Here was to be found, pushed to its completest expression, the quintessence of Baudelaire and Poe; here was the same powerful and refined basis yet further distilled and giving off new savours, new intoxications.

It was the dying spasm of the old tongue which, after a progressive decay from century to century, was ending in a total dissolution, in the same deliquium the Latin language had suffered, as it expired finally in the mystic conceptions and enigmatic phrases of St. Boniface and St. Adhelm.

For the rest, the decomposition of the French language had come about at a blow. In Latin, a lengthy period of transition, a pause of four hundred years, had intervened between the variegated and magnificent phraseology of Claudian and Rutilius and the dialect of the eighth century with its taint of decomposition. Not so in French; here no interval of time, no long-drawn series of ages, occurred; the variegated and magnificent style of the De Goncourts and the tainted style of Verlaine and Mallarmé rubbed elbows at Paris, dwelling together at the same time, in the same period, in the same century.

And Des Esseintes smiled to himself as he looked at one of the folios lying open on his church reading-desk, thinking how the moment might come when a learned scholar would compile for the decadence of the French language a glossary like that in which the erudite Du Cange has noted down the last stammering accents, the last spasmodic efforts, the last flashes of brilliancy, of the Latin tongue as it perished of old age, the death rattle sounding through the recesses of monkish cloisters.

CHAPTER XV

AFTER BLAZING UP LIKE A FIRE OF STRAW, HIS ENTHUSIASM FOR THE "DIGEST-er" was extinguished with a like rapidity. Soothed for the time being, his dyspepsia began again; presently, this over-stimulating essence of nourishment brought on such an irritation of the bowels that Des Esseintes was obliged to drop its use with all possible speed.

The complaint resumed its course, hitherto unknown symptoms going with it. First nightmares, hallucinations of smell, disturbances of vision, a hacking cough, coming on at a fixed hour with the regularity of clockwork, a beating of the arteries and heart accompanied by cold sweats; then, delusions of hearing, all the mischiefs, in fact, that mark the last stage of the malady.

Eaten up by a burning fever, Des Esseintes would suddenly hear the sound of running water, the buzz of wasps; then these noises would melt into a single one resembling the whirring of a lathe; then this would grow shriller and thinner, changing finally into the silvery tinkle of a bell.

Then he would feel his maddened brain wafted away on waves of music, rolling among the billows of harmony familiar to his boyhood. The chants he had learned from the Jesuit Fathers recurred to him, recalling the college, the college chapel, where they had echoed; then the hallucination would pass on to the olfactory and visual organs, wrapping them in the vapour of incense and the gloom of a sanctuary dimly lit through painted windows under lofty vaults.

Among the Fathers, the rites of religion were performed with great pomp and ceremony; an excellent organist and a noteworthy choir made these spiritual exercises an artistic delight, to the great end of edification. The organist was a lover of the old masters, and on days of festival he would select one of Palestrina's or Orlando Lasso's masses, Marcello's psalms, Handel's oratorios, Sebastian Bach's motets, would play in preference to the sensuous, facile compilations of Father Lambillotte so much favoured by the average priest, certain Laudi spirituali of the sixteenth century whose stately beauty had many a time fascinated Des Esseintes.

But above all, he had experienced ineffable pleasures in listening to the "plainsong," which the organist had kept up in spite of modern prejudices.

This form, now looked down upon as an effete and Gothic type of the Christian liturgy, as an antiquarian curiosity, as a relic of barbarous centuries, was the life-word of the ancient Church, the very spirit of the Middle Ages; it was the prayer of all time set to music in tones modulated in accord with the aspirations of the soul, the never-ceasing hymn of praise that had risen for hundreds of years to the throne of the Most High.

This traditional melody was the only one that, with its mighty unison, its solemn, massive harmonies, like blocks of ashlar, could fitly go with the old basilicas and fill their romanesque vaults, of which it seemed the emanation and the living voice.

How many times had not Des Esseintes been entranced and mastered by an irresistible awe when the "Christus factus est" of the Gregorian chant had swelled up in the nave whose pillars trembled amid the floating clouds of incense, or when the rolling bass of the "De profundis" groaned forth, mournful as a stifled sob, poignant as a despairing cry of mankind bewailing its mortal destiny, imploring the tender mercy of its Saviour.

In comparison with this magnificent plainsong, created by the genius of the Church, impersonal, anonymous as the organ itself, whose inventor is unknown, all other religious music seemed to him secular, profane. At bottom, in all the works of Jomelli and Porpora, of Carissimi and Durante, in the most admirable conceptions of Handel and Bach, there was no real renunciation of popular triumph, no sacrifice of artistic success, no abdication of human pride listening to itself at prayer; at best, in those imposing masses of Lesueur's performed at Saint-Roch was the true religious style renewed, grave and august, making some approach to the unadorned nudity, the austere majesty of the old plainsong.

Since those days, utterly revolted by pretentious works like the Stabat mater of Rossini or the similar compositions of Pergolese, disgusted with all this intrusion of worldly art into the liturgical sanctum, Des Esseintes had held aloof altogether from these equivocal productions tolerated by an indulgent Mother Church.

In fact, this fatal complacence, due partly to the greed for offertories, partly to a supposed attraction the music exercised on the faithful, had led directly to abuses—airs borrowed from Italian operas, trivial cavatinas, unseemly quadrilles, performed with full orchestral accompaniment in the churches transformed into fine ladies' boudoirs, entrusted to theatre actors who bellowed aloft under the roof while down below the women fought a pitched battle of fine clothes with one another and quivered with soft emotion to hear the heroes of the opera whose wanton tones defiled the sacred notes of the organ!

For years now he had positively refused to take part in these pious entertainments, resting satisfied with his memories of childhood, regretting even having heard sundry "Te Deums" by great masters, for did he not remember that admirable "Te Deum" of the plainsong, that hymn so simple and grandiose, composed by some Saint, a St. Ambrose or a St. Hilary, who, lacking the complicated resources of an orchestra, failing the mechanical music of modern music, displayed an ardent faith, a delirious joy, the essence of the soul of all humanity expressed in burning, trustful, almost heavenly accents?

In any case, Des Esseintes' ideas on music were in flagrant contradiction with the theories he professed as to the other arts. In religious music, he really cared only for the monastic music of the Middle Ages, that ascetic music that acted instinctively on the nerves, like certain pages of the old Christian Latinity; besides, he admitted it himself, he was incapable of understanding the artful devices contemporary masters might have been able to introduce into Catholic art. The truth is, he had not studied music with the same passionate ardour he had applied to painting and to literature. He could play the piano like any other amateur, had come, after many fumblings, to be competent to read a score; but he knew nothing of harmony or the technique needful for really appreciating lights and shades of expression, for understanding nice points, for entering, with proper comprehension, into refinements and elaborations.

Then, on another side, secular music is a promiscuous art which one cannot enjoy at home and alone, as one reads a book; to taste it, he must needs have mixed with that inevitable public that crowds to theatres and besieges the Cirque d'hiver where, under a broiling sun, in an atmosphere as muggy as a washhouse, you see a man with the look of a carpenter bawling a remoulade and massacring disconnected bits of Wagner to the huge delight of an ignorant crowd!

He had never had the courage to plunge into this bath of promiscuity in order to hear Berlioz; some fragments of whom had nevertheless won his admiration by their high-wrought passion and abounding fire, while he realized with no less perspicacity that there was not a scene, not a phrase in any opera of the mighty Wagner that could be detached from its context without ruining it.

The scraps thus cut from the whole and served up at a concert lost all meaning, all sense, for, like the chapters in a book that mutually complete each other and all concur to bring about the same conclusion, the same final effect, his melodies were used by Wagner to define the character of his personages, to incarnate their thoughts, to express their motives, visible or secret, and their ingenious and persistent repetitions were only intelligible for an audience which followed the subject from its first opening and watched the characters grow little by little more clearly defined, observed them develop in surroundings from which they could not be separated without seeing them perish like branches severed from a tree.

So Des Esseintes thought, convinced that of all the horde of melomaniacs who every Sunday fell into ecstasies on the benches, twenty at most knew the score the musicians were massacring, when the box-openers were kind enough to hold their tongues and let the orchestra be heard.

The circumstance also being remembered that the intelligent patriotism of the French nation forbade the production of an opera of Wagner's at a Paris theatre, there was nothing left for the curious amateur who is unskilled in the arcana of music and cannot or will not travel to

Bayreuth, save to stay at home, and that was the reasonable course Des Esseintes had adopted.

On another side, more popular, easier music and detached morceaux taken from the old-fashioned operas scarcely appealed to him; the trivial tunes of Auber and Boieldieu, of Adam and Flotow, and the commonplaces of musical rhetoric favoured by Ambroise Thomas, Bazin and their like repelled him just as much as the antiquated sentimentalities and cheap graces of the Italian composers. He had therefore resolutely refused to have anything to do with music, and for all the years this renunciation lasted, he found nothing to look back upon with any pleasure save a few chamber concerts at which he had heard Beethoven and above all Schumann and Schubert, who had stimulated his nerves as keenly as the most telling and tragical poems of Edgar Allan Poe.

Certain settings for the violoncello by Schumann had left him positively panting with emotion, gasping for breath under the stress of hysteria; but it was chiefly Schubert's lieder that had stirred him to the depths, lifted him out of himself, then prostrated him as after a wasteful outpouring of nervous fluid, after a mystic debauch of soul.

This music thrilled him to the very marrow, driving back an infinity of forgotten griefs, of old vexations, on a heart amazed to contain so many confused miseries and obscure sorrows. This music of desolation, crying from the deepest depths of being, terrified, while fascinating him. Never, without nervous tears rising to his eyes, had he been able to repeat the "Young Girl's Plaints," for in this lamento there was something more than heartbroken, something despairing that tore his entrails, something recalling the end of love's dream in a dismal landscape.

Every time they came back to his lips, these exquisite and funereal laments called up before his fancy a lonely place beyond the city boundaries, a beggarly, forsaken locality, where noiselessly, in the distance, lines of poor folks, harassed by life's wretchedness, filed away, bent double, into the gloom of twilight, while, meantime, he himself, full of bitterness, overflowing with disgust, felt himself standing alone, all alone in the midst of weeping Nature, overborne by an unspeakable melancholy, by an obstinate distress, the mysterious intensity of which brooked no consolation, no comparison, no respite. Like a passing bell, the despairing air haunted his brain now that he lay in bed, enfeebled by fever and tormented by an anxiety the more implacable because he could no longer discover its cause. Eventually he surrendered himself to the current, let himself be swept away by the torrent of the music, suddenly barred for a brief minute by the plainsong of the psalms that rose with its long-drawn bass notes in his head, whose temples seemed bruised and battered by the clappers of a hundred bells.

One morning, however, these noises fell quiet; he was in better possession of his faculties and asked the servant to hand him a mirror. He hardly knew himself; his face was earthen in hue, the lips dry and swollen, the tongue furrowed, the skin wrinkled; his straggling hair and beard, which his man had not trimmed since the beginning of his illness, added to the horror of the sunken cheeks and staring, watery eyes that burned with a feverish brightness in this death's-head bristling with unkempt hair.

Worse than his weakness, worse than his irrepressible fits of vomiting which rejected every attempt at taking food, worse than the wasting from which he suffered, this disfigurement of face alarmed him. He thought he was done for; then, in spite of the exhaustion that crushed him down, the fierce energy of a man at bay brought him to a sitting posture in his bed, lent him strength to write a letter to his Paris doctor and order his servant to go instantly to find him and bring him back with him, cost what it might, the same day.

In an instant, he passed from the most absolute despair to the most comforting hope. The physician in question was a noted specialist, renowned for the cure of nervous disorders; "he must before now have cured more obstinate and more dangerous cases than mine," Des Esseintes told himself; "not a doubt of it, I shall be set up again in a few days' time." But presently again this overconfidence was followed by a feeling of utter disenchantment; no matter how learned and how perspicacious they may be, doctors really know nothing about nervous disease, the very cause of which they cannot tell. Like all the rest, he would prescribe the everlasting oxide of zinc and quinine, bromide of potassium and valerian; "and who can say," he went on to himself, clinging to the last twig of hope, "if the reason why these remedies have hitherto failed me is not simply because I have not known how to employ them in proper doses."

Despite everything, this waiting for expected relief gave him new life; but presently a fresh dread assailed him—suppose the doctor should not be in town or should decline to disturb his arrangements; then came yet another panic lest his servant should have failed to find him at all. This threw him into the depths of despair. His mind began to fail again, jumping, moment by moment, from the most inordinate hopefulness to the most baseless apprehension, exaggerating both his chances of sudden recovery and his fears of immediate danger. Hour after hour slipped by, and a time arrived when, despairing and exhausted, convinced the doctor would never come, he told himself over and over again in impotent anger that, if only he had seen to it in time, he would undoubtedly have been saved; then after a while, his rage with his servant, his indignation at the doctor's delay, abated, and he began to cherish a bitter vexation against himself instead, blaming his own procrastination in having waited so long before sending for help, persuading himself that he would have been perfectly well by now, if, even the night before only, he had provided himself with good, strong medicines and proper nursing.

Gradually these alternate paroxysms of hope and fear that tormented his half-delirious brain grew milder, as these repeated panics wore down his strength. He dropped into a sleep of exhaustion broken by incoherent dreams, a kind of coma interrupted by periods of wakefulness too brief for consciousness to be regained. He had finally lost all notion of what he wished and what he feared so completely that he was merely bewildered, and felt neither surprise nor satisfaction, when suddenly the doctor made his appearance in the room.

The servant no doubt had informed him of the manner of life Des Esseintes led and of various symptoms he had himself been in a position to notice since the day when he had picked up his master by the window where he lay, felled by the violence of his perfumes, for he asked the patient very few questions, knowing indeed his antecedents for many years past. But he examined and sounded him and carefully scrutinized the urine, in which certain white streaks told him the secret of one of the chief determining causes of his nervous collapse. He wrote a prescription and took his leave without a word, saying he would come again.

His visit comforted Des Esseintes, albeit he was alarmed at the doctor's silence and besought his servant not to hide the truth from him any longer.

The man assured him the doctor had showed no signs of anxiety and, suspicious as he was, Des Esseintes could detect no tokens whatever of prevarication or falsehood in the old man's calm face.

Then his thoughts grew more cheerful; indeed the pain had stopped and the feebleness he had experienced in every limb had merged into a sort of agreeable languor, a feeling of placid content at once vague and slowly progressive. Then he was at once astonished and pleased to find his bedside table unlittered with drugs and medicine bottles, and a pale smile hovered over his lips when finally his servant brought him a nourishing enema compounded with peptone, and informed his master that he was to repeat the little operation three times every twenty-four hours.

The thing was successfully carried out, and Des Esseintes could not help secretly congratulating himself on the event which was the coping stone, the crowning triumph, in a sort, of the life he had contrived for himself; his predilection for the artificial had now, and that without any initiative on his part, attained its supreme fulfilment! A man could hardly go farther; nourishment thus absorbed was surely the last aberration from the natural that could be committed.

"What a delicious thing," he said to himself, "it would be if one could, once restored to full health, go on with the same simple regime. What a saving of time, what a radical deliverance from the repugnance meat inspires in people who have lost their appetite! what a definite and final release from the lassitude that invariably results from the necessarily limited choice of viands! what a vigorous protest against the degrading sin of gluttony! last but not least, what a direct insult cast in the face of old Mother Nature, whose never varying exigencies would be forever nullified!"

In this vein, he went on talking to himself under his breath. Why, it would be easy enough to sharpen one's appetite by swallowing a strong aperient, then when one could truly tell oneself: "Come, what hour is it now? seems to me it must be high time to sit down to dinner, I have a wolf in my stomach," the table would be laid by depositing the noble instrument on the cloth—and lo! before you had time so much as to say grace, the troublesome and vulgar task of eating would be suppressed.

Some days later, the man handed his master an enema altogether different in colour and smell from the peptone suppositories.

"Why, it's not the same!" exclaimed Des Esseintes, looking with consternation at the liquid poured into the apparatus. He demanded the menu as he might have done in a restaurant and unfolding the physician's prescription, he read out—

    Cod-liver oil 20 grams

    Beef-tea 200"

    Burgundy 200"

    Yolk of one egg

He sat pensive. He had never succeeded, on account of the ruined state of his stomach, in taking a serious interest in the art of cookery; now he was surprised to find himself all of a sudden pondering over combinations of a posteriori gourmandise! Then a grotesque notion shot across his brain. Perhaps the doctor had imagined his patient's abnormal palate was wearied by this time of the flavour of peptone; perhaps, like a skilful chef, he had wished to vary the savour of the foods administered, to prevent the monotony of the dishes leading to a complete loss of appetite. Once started on this train of thought, Des Esseintes busied himself in composing novel recipes, contriving dinners for fast days and Fridays, strengthening the dose of cod-liver oil and wine, while striking out the beef-tea as being meat and therefore expressly forbidden by the Church. But, before very long, the necessity disappeared of deliberating about these nourishing liquids, for the doctor managed little by little to overcome the nausea and gave him, to be swallowed by the ordinary channel, a syrup of punch mixed with powdered meat and having a vague aroma of cocoa about it that was grateful to his genuine mouth.

Weeks passed and the stomach at last consented to act; occasionally fits of nausea still recurred, which, however, ginger beer and Rivière's anti-emetic draught were effectual in subduing. Eventually, little by little, the organs recovered with the help of the pepsines, and ordinary foods were digested. Strength returned and Des Esseintes was able to stand on his feet and try to walk about his bedroom, leaning on a stick and holding on to the furniture. Instead of being pleased with this success, he forgot all his past sufferings, was irritated by the length of his convalescence, and upbraided the doctor for protracting it in this slow fashion. True, sundry ineffectual experiments had delayed matters; no better than quinine did the stomach tolerate iron, even when mitigated by the addition of laudanum, and these drugs had to be replaced by preparations of arsenic; this after a fortnight had been lost in useless efforts, as Des Esseintes noted with no small impatience.

At last, the moment was reached when he could remain up for whole afternoons at a time and walk about his rooms without assistance. Then his working-room began to get on his nerves; defects to which custom had blinded his eyes now struck him forcibly on his coming back to the room after his long absence. The colours chosen to be seen by lamplight seemed to him discordant under the glare of daylight; he thought how best to alter them and spent hours in contriving artificial harmonies of hues, hybrid combinations of cloths and leathers.

"Without a doubt I am on the high road to health," he told himself, as he noted the return of his former preoccupations and old predilections.

One morning, as he was gazing at his orange and blue walls, dreaming of ideal hangings made out of stoles of the Greek Church, of gold-fringed Russian dalmatics, of brocaded copes patterned with Slavonic lettering, adorned with precious stones from the Urals and rows of pearls, the doctor came in and, noting what his patient's eyes were looking at, questioned him.

Then Des Esseintes told him of his unrealizable ideals and began to plan out new experiments in colour, to speak of novel combinations and contrasts of hues that he meant to contrive, when the physician soused a sudden douche of cold water over his head, declaring in the most peremptory fashion that, come what might, it would not be in that house he could put his projects into execution.

Then, without giving him time to recover breath, he announced that so far he had only attacked the most urgent necessity, the reestablishment of the digestive functions, but that now he must deal with the nervous derangements which were by no means mitigated and would require for their cure years of regimen and careful living. He concluded with the ultimatum that, before trying any course of cure, before beginning any sort of hydropathic treatment—impracticable in any case at Fontenay—he was bound to abandon this solitary existence, to return to Paris and take part again in the common life of men; in a word, endeavour to find diversions the same as other people.

"But they don't divert me, the pleasures other people enjoy," protested Des Esseintes, indignantly.

Without discussing the question, the doctor simply assured his hearer that this radical change of life which he ordered was in his opinion a matter of life and death, of restored health or insanity followed at short notice by tuberculosis.

"Then it is a case either of death or deportation!" cried Des Esseintes, in exasperation.

The physician, who was imbued with all the prejudices of a man of the world, only smiled and made for the door without vouchsafing an answer.

CHAPTER XVI

es Esseintes shut himself up in his bedroom and turned a deaf
ear to the knocking of the men's hammers who were nailing
up the packing-cases the servants had got ready; each stroke
seemed to beat on his heart and send a pang of pain through his flesh.
The sentence pronounced by the doctor was being executed; the dread
of enduring all over again the same sufferings he had borne before, the
fear of an agonizing death, had exercised a more powerful influence over
Des Esseintes than his hatred of the detestable existence to which the
physician's orders condemned him could counteract.

"And yet," he kept telling himself, "there are people who live alone,
without a soul to speak to, self-absorbed and utterly aloof from society, like
the Reclusionists and Trappists for instance, and there is nothing to show
that these unfortunates, these wise men, run mad or develop consumption."

These examples he had quoted to the doctor—without effect; the
latter had merely repeated in a dry tone admitting of no reply, that his
verdict, confirmed moreover by all the writers on nervous diseases, was
that distraction, amusement, cheerfulness, were the only means of
benefitting this complaint which, on the mental side, remained unaffected
by any remedies in the nature of drugs. Finally, annoyed by his patient's

reproaches, he had once for all declared his refusal to go on with his case unless he consented to take change of air and live under altered conditions of hygiene.

Des Esseintes had immediately repaired to Paris, where he had consulted other specialists and frankly submitted his case to them; all had with one accord and unhesitatingly approved their colleague's prescriptions. Thereupon, he had taken a flat still vacant in a newly-built house; had returned to Fontenay and, white with rage, had given his servant orders to pack his boxes.

Buried in his armchair, he was now pondering these express directions of the faculty which upset all his plans, broke all the ties binding him to his present life, made his future projects futile. So, his time of bliss was over! This haven, that sheltered him from the storms, he must abandon and put out again into the storm-tost ocean of human folly that had battered and bruised him so sorely.

The doctors prated of amusement, of distraction; with whom, pray with what, did they expect him to be blithe and gay?

Had he not deliberately put himself under a social ban? did he know one single friend who would be willing to essay a life, like his, of contemplation, of dreamy abstraction? did he know a single individual capable of appreciating the delicate shades of a style, the subtle joints of a picture, the quintessence of a thought, one whose soul was so finely framed as to understand Mallarmé and love Verlaine?

Where, when, in what depths must he sound to discover a twin soul, a mind free of commonplace prejudices, blessing silence as a boon, ingratitude as a solace, suspicion as a port of security, a harbour of refuge?

In the society he had frequented before he took his departure for Fontenay?—Why, the majority of the clowns he associated with in those times must, since that date, have yet further stultified themselves in drawing-rooms, grown more degraded sitting at gaming tables, reached lower depths in the arms of prostitutes. Nay, the most part must by now be married; after having enjoyed all their life hitherto the leavings of the street-loafers, it was their wives who at present owned the leavings of the streetwalkers, for, master of the first-fruits, the vulgar herd was the one and only class that did not feed on refuse!

"What a pretty change of partners, what a gallant interchange, this custom adopted by a society that still calls itself prudish!" Des Esseintes growled to himself.

Yes, nobility was utterly decayed, dead; aristocracy had fallen into idiocy or filthy pleasures! It was perishing in the degeneracy of its members, whose faculties grew more debased with each succeeding generation till they ended with the instincts of gorillas quickened in the pates of grooms and jockeys, or else, like the once famous houses of Choiseul-Praslin, Polignac, Chevreuse, wallowed in the mud of legal actions that brought them down to the same level of baseness as the other classes.

The very mansions, the time-honoured scutcheons, the heraldic blazons, the stately pomp and ceremony of this ancient caste had disappeared. Its estates no longer yielded revenue, they and the great houses on them had come to the hammer, for money ran short to buy the smiles of women that bewitched and poisoned the besotted descendants of the old families.

The least scrupulous, the least dull-witted, threw all shame to the winds; they mixed in low plots, stirred up the filth of base finance, appeared like common pickpockets at the bar of justice, serving at any rate to set off the tact of human justice which, finding it impossible to be always impartial, ended the matter by making them librarians in the prisons.

This eagerness after gain, this itch for filthy lucre, had found a counterpart also in another class, the class that had always leant for support on the nobility—the clergy to wit. Now were to be seen on the outside sheets of the papers advertisements of corns cured by a priest. The monasteries were transformed into apothecaries' laboratories and distilleries. They sold recipes or manufactured the stuff themselves; the Cistercians, chocolate, Trappistine, semolina, tincture of arnica; the Marist Brotherhood, bisulphate of chalk for medical purposes and vulnerary water; the Jacobines, anti-apoplectic elixir; the disciples of St. Benedict, Bénédictine; the monks of St. Bruno, Chartreuse.

Business had invaded the cloisters, where, in lieu of antiphonaries, fat ledgers lay on the lecterns. Like a leprosy, the greed of the century devastated the Church, kept the monks bending over inventories and invoices, turned the Fathers Superior into confectioners and quacksalvers, the lay brothers and novices into common packers and vulgar bottle-washers.

And yet, spite of everything, it was still only among ecclesiastics that Des Esseintes could hope for relations congruent, up to a certain point, with his tastes. In the society of the clergy, generally learned and well educated men, he might have spent some affable and agreeable evenings; but then he must have shared their beliefs and not be a mere waverer between sceptical notions and spasms of conviction that came surging from time to time to the surface, buoyed up by the memories of childhood.

He must needs have held identical views, refused to accept, as he was ready enough to do in his moments of ardour, a Catholicism spiced with a touch of magic, as under Henri III, and a trifle of Sadism, as at the end of the eighteenth century. This special brand of clericalism, this vitiated and artistically perverse type of mysticism, towards which he was tending at certain seasons, could not even be discussed with a priest, who would either have failed to understand what he meant or would have excommunicated him there and then in sheer horror.

For the twentieth time, the same insoluble problem tormented him. He would fain this state of suspicion and suspense against which he had struggled in vain at Fontenay should have an end; now that he was to turn over an entirely new leaf, he would fain have forced himself to possess faith, to seize it and clothe himself in it, to fasten it with clamps in his soul, to put it beyond the reach of all the reasonings that shake it and uproot it. But the more he desired it and the less the emptiness of his mind was filled, the more the visitation of the Saviour delayed its coming. Just in proportion, indeed, as his religious faith increased, as he craved with all his strength, as a ransom for the future and a help in the new life he was to lead, this faith that showed itself in glimpses, though the distance still dividing him from it appalled him, did doubts rise crowding his ever excited brain, upsetting his ill-poised will, repudiating on grounds of common sense, of mathematical demonstrations, the mysteries and dogmas of the Church.

He should have been able to stop these discussions with himself, he told himself with a groan; he should have been able to shut his eyes, let himself be carried along with the stream, forget all the accursed discoveries that have shattered the religious edifice from top to bottom during the last two centuries.

"Yet, really and truly," he sighed, "it is neither the physiologists nor the sceptics who destroy Catholicism, it is the priests themselves, whose clumsy writings might well root up the most firmly grounded convictions."

In the Dominican collection, was there not to be found a certain Doctor of Theology, Révérend Père Rouard de Card, a Preaching Brother, who in a brochure entitled:—Of the Falsification of the Sacramental Substances, has demonstrated beyond a doubt that the major part of Masses were null and void, by reason of the fact that the materials used in the rite were sophisticated by dealers?

For years, the holy oils had been adulterated with goose-grease; the taper-wax with burnt bones; the incense with common resin and old benzoin. But worse than all, the substances indispensable for the holy sacrifice, the two things without which no oblation was possible, had likewise been falsified—the wine by repeated dilutings and the illicit addition of Pernambuco bark, elderberries, alcohol, alum, salicylate, litharge; the bread, that bread of the Eucharist that must be kneaded of the fine flour of wheat, by ground haricotbeans, potash and pipeclay!

Nay, now they had gone further yet; they had dared to suppress the wheat altogether and shameless dealers manufactured out of potato meal nearly all the hosts!

Now God declined to come down and be made flesh in potato flour. This was a surety, an indisputable fact; in the second volume of his Moral Theology, His Eminence Cardinal Gousset had also dealt at length with this question of adulteration from the divine standpoint, and, according to the authority of this master which there was no gainsaying, the celebrant could not consecrate bread made of oats, buckwheat or barley, and though the case of rye-bread at least admitted of doubt, no question could be raised, no argument sustained, when it came to using potato meal, which, to employ the ecclesiastical expression, was in no sense a substance competent for the Blessed Sacrament.

By reason of the easy manipulation of this meal and the good appearance presented by the unleavened cakes made of this substance, the unworthy and fraudulent substitution had become so widely prevalent that the mystery of the transubstantiation could hardly be said to exist any longer, and priests and faithful laymen communicated, all unwittingly, with neutral elements!

Ah! the days were far away when Rhadegond, Queen of France, used with her own hands to prepare the bread destined for the altars; the days when, by the custom of Cluny, three priests or three deacons, fasting, clad in alb and amice, after washing face and fingers, sorted out the wheat grain by grain, crushed it in the hand-mill, kneaded the dough with cold spring-water and baked it themselves over a clear fire, singing psalms the while!

"All this," Des Esseintes told himself, "cannot hinder the natural result, that this prospect of being constantly duped, even at the holy table itself, is not of a sort to establish beliefs already tottering; besides, how accept an omnipotence that is hindered by a pinch of potato meal or a drop of alcohol?"

These thoughts still further darkened the aspect of his future existence and rendered his horizon yet more dark and threatening.

Of a surety, no haven of refuge was open to him, no shore of safety left. What was to become of him in Paris yonder, where he had neither relatives nor friends? No tie bound him any more to the Faubourg Saint-Germain that was now quavering in its dotage, scaling away in a dust of desuetude, lying derelict—a worn-out, empty hull!—amid a new society! And what point of contact could there be between him and that bourgeois class that had little by little climbed to the top, taking advantage of every disaster to fill its coffers, stirring up every kind of catastrophe to make its crimes and thefts pass muster?

After the aristocracy of birth, it was now the turn of the aristocracy of money; it was the Caliphate of the countinghouse, the despotism of the Rue du Sentier, the tyranny of commerce with its narrow-minded, venal ideas, its ostentatious and rascally instincts.

More nefarious, more vile than the nobility it had plundered and the clergy it had overthrown, the bourgeoisie borrowed their frivolous love of show, their decrepit boastfulness, which it vulgarized by its lack of good manners, stole their defects which it aggravated into hypocritical vices. Obstinate and sly, base and cowardly, it shot down ruthlessly its eternal and inevitable dupe, the populace, which it had itself unmuzzled and set on to spring at the throat of the old castes!

Now the victory was won. Its task once completed, the plebs had been for its health's sake bled to the last drop, while the bourgeois, secure in his triumph, throned it jovially by dint of his money and the contagion of his folly. The result of his rise to power had been the destruction of all intelligence, the negation of all honesty, the death of all art; in fact, the artists and men of letters, in their degradation, had fallen to their knees and were devouring with ardent kisses the unwashed feet of the high-placed horse-jockeys and lowbred satraps on whose alms they lived!

In painting, it was a deluge of effeminate futilities; in literature, a welter of insipid style and spiritless ideas. What was a-lacking was common honesty in the business gambler, common honour in the freebooter who hunted for a dowry for his son while refusing to pay his daughter's, common chastity in the Voltairean who accused the clergy of incontinence while he was off himself to sniff, like a dull fool and a hypocrite, pretending to be the rake he was not, in disorderly dens of pleasure, at the greasy water in toilet vessels and the hot, acrid effluvium of dirty petticoats.

It was the vast, foul bagnio of America transported to our Continent; it was, in a word, the limitless, unfathomable, incommensurable firmament of blackguardism of the financier and the self-made man, beaming down, like a despicable sun, on the idolatrous city that grovelled on its belly, hymning vile songs of praise before the impious tabernacle of Commerce.

"Well, crumble then, society! perish, old world!" cried Des Esseintes, indignant at the ignominy of the spectacle he had conjured up—and the exclamation broke the nightmare that oppressed him.

"Ah!" he groaned, "to think that all this is not a dream! to think that I am about to go back into the degraded and slavish mob of the century!" He tried to call up, for the healing of his wounded spirit, the consoling maxims of Schopenhauer; he said over to himself Pascal's grievous axiom: "The soul sees nothing that does not afflict it when it thinks of it"; but the words rang in his brain like sounds without sense; his weariness of spirit disintegrated them, robbed them of all meaning, all consolatory virtue, all effective and soothing force.

He realized, at last, that the arguments of pessimism were powerless to comfort him; that the impossible belief in a future life could be the only calmant.

A fit of rage swept away like a hurricane his efforts after resignation, his attempts at indifference. He could deceive himself no more, there was nothing, nothing left for it, everything was over; the bourgeoisie were guzzling, as it might be at Clamart, on their knees, from paper parcels, under the grand old ruins of the Church, which had become a place of assignation, a mass of debris, defiled by unspeakable quibbles and indecent jests. Could it be that, to prove once for all that He existed, the terrible God of Genesis and the pale Crucified of Golgotha were not going to renew the cataclysms of an earlier day, to rekindle the rain of fire that consumed the ancient homes of sin, the cities of the Plain? Could it be that this foul flood was to go on spreading and drowning in its pestilential morass this old world where now only seeds of iniquity sprang up and harvests of shame flourished?

Suddenly the door was unclosed; in the distance, framed in the opening, appeared men carrying lights in their caps, with clean-shaven cheeks and a tuft on the chin, handling packing-cases and shifting furniture; then the door closed again after the servant, who marched off with a bundle of books under his arm.

Des Esseintes dropped into a chair, in despair. "In two days more I shall be in Paris," he exclaimed; "well, all is over; like a flowing tide, the waves of human mediocrity rise to the heavens and they will engulf my last refuge; I am opening the sluice-gates myself, in spite of myself. Ah; but my courage fails me, and my heart is sick within me!—Lord, take pity on the Christian who doubts, on the sceptic who would fain believe, on the galley-slave of life who puts out to sea alone, in the darkness of night, beneath a firmament illumined no longer by the consoling beacon-fires of the ancient hope."

The End

10¢
APRIL
SECRET AGENT X
G-MAN ACTION ADVENTURES
AN ACE MAGAZINE
THE MURDER BRAIN
Gripping "Secret Agent X" Novel
By BRANT HOUSE
REDHEADED DECOY
DON CAMERON

Southwest Scenarios

COMMENTARIES FROM RURAL ARIZONA
BY DARRYLE PURCELL

PETA claims are an udder story

Originally Published April 27, 2003

A FEW YEARS AGO WE WERE ALL WORRIED ABOUT MAD COW DISEASE AND whether our bovine brothers and sisters would all have to be restrained at a funny farm. Well, time has passed and Mad Cows have been placed on the back burner. We are now faced, according to the People for the Ethical Treatment of Animals (PETA), with the problem of falsely labeled "Happy Cows." (Wouldn't it be interesting if some of the Happy Cows were also Mad Cows? Would that make them manic-depressive cows?)

Apparently, the San Francisco-based California Milk Advisory Board launched a "Happy Cows" advertising campaign, which ticked off the PETA folk. One of the board's television commercials shows cows frolicking in a beautiful pasture with the slogan, "great cheese comes from happy cows. Happy cows come from California."

PETA sued the board demanding an end to the campaign because, according to PETA's wisdom, the cows are really miserable.

Now, I grew up on a farm, and I have seen a lot of cows, and bulls, engaged in a lot of bovine activities. And, truthfully, I have never seen a cow smile (although I have seen a horsefly). Cows have perfect poker faces — it's impossible, for me, to tell what they are thinking. Perhaps PETA has the assistance of Shirley MacLaine in communicating with the cloven-hoofed complainers, but I wouldn't think grumpy cow channeling would be admissible in court…. no matter what they would have to beef about.

To me, the burden of proof should be on PETA. And let's face it, from what I've heard is growing in many parts of California, especially near Frisco, those cows may not only be happy, they may be Robert Downey, Jr., ecstatic.

According to an Associated Press report, the California court (for once) made a decent decision to throw out the case. But, typical of California, they didn't base it on the stupidity of PETA's allegations. The court ruled that a government agency (California Milk Advisory Board) is exempt from false advertising laws that would apply to private individuals.

So basically, a La La Land government agency could have claimed the milk comes from zootsuit wearing, prurient tap-dancing weasels with skin problems and not be responsible for honesty. On the other hand, that private canned cream company that claims its cows are contented could be the next target of a PETA lawsuit.

PETA's actions, as well as most California court rulings, are, once again, enough to drive a happy cow mad.

Southwest Scenarios

The commentaries here and in future issues were originally published by *The Mohave Valley Daily News between 1993 & 2013--and* in many ways they apply to today. We are grateful to republish these commentaries written by Darryle Purcell in full and unedited. His own brand of humor and style can deliver insight, provoke thought, and even boil blood.

THE RAVEN MESSENGER
AN ORIGINAL STORY BY TEEL JAMES GLEN

CHAPTER 1

"You took your time getting here, Mister Corbie," Gunnar Norstrum said. "Or do you prefer the name the underworld calls you, 'The Raven?'"

Duncan Corbie was not a big man, certainly not compared to the red-bearded giant who stood across the ornate office from him, but his presence filled the room. He was dark haired, square jawed and just shy of forty. He wore a black leather trenchcoat like it was a royal robe, his body posture relaxed and aloof.

"I'm nae a serf to be summoned, Mister Norstrum," Corbie said. "Aye came at all because I owe Carson LeRoi a favor and he said ye called him to ask me. And yer gate guards, by the by, were no help fer speed."

The bearded man, dressed in an expensive grey business suit, turned from the window he had been gazing out to look directly into Corbie's eyes. "You know in my culture the Raven is the messenger of Odin, who sees all, and brings to the one-eyed god the news of the world."

"Muggin and Huggein,--memory and thought," Corbie said. "I know. And what news do ye want me ta bring you?" Corbie kept his own coal black eyes locked with the emerald green of Norstrum's.

"Mister Norstrum wants you to deliver a package for him," A young woman who entered the large, converted ballroom with brisk steps said. She was dressed in a conservative skirt suit and carried a folder under her arm. She was in middle years, with lackluster brown hair bound tight in a bun on her head and wore old style, red glasses.

She crossed to the elegantly appointed office at the back of the cavernous ballroom. The room was stuffed every inch with works of art, marble and bronze statues, an upright Egyptian sarcophagus, a Monet, a Matisse, at least two Rembrandt etchings and Norse artifacts including a Spanhelm and carved Viking axes.

Corbie suspected they were all originals. It's like Norstrum raided The City Art Museum.

The woman handed to the folder to Corbie. He noted that her fingernails were long and elegant, which seemed at odds with her tight all business look.

"We apologize for the security at the gate," she said, "But this will explain why."

There was a single sheet of typed paper in the folder that said, "If you want to see your wife again alive leave one million dollars in bearer bonds at The Soldier's Tomb Monument in the red trash bin by midnight or you will never see her again. Do not contact the authorities.

"When did ye get this?" Corbie asked. He was careful not to touch the paper itself, only the edge of the folder.

"Mister Norstrum found it tacked to the front door when he opened it to head out to work about an hour ago," the woman said.

"So much for your security guards."

"They were added after Mister Norstrum received this," the woman said. "He does not like ostentatious measures."

The Raven looked at the art all around him then gave a wry smile.

"I can take care of myself," Norstrum said.

"Why call me?" Corbie asked.

"They said no police," the woman said. "Mister Norstrum does not want to take the chance with his wife's life. I am Arwyn Datlow, Mister Norstrum's personal secretary"

"My Inga," Norstrum moaned with a deep sigh. He was running his hands possessively over a marble statue of Artemus while he stared up at a life size portrait over the mantel. The painting was of a younger Norstrum in formal attire standing next to a stunningly beautiful blonde woman. She was petite next to Norstrum, wearing a traditional wedding gown decked out in jewels.

The painter had done an amazing job of capturing a sense of vitality in his depiction of her. The green eyes of the golden-haired beauty were lambent and blazing with life. They seemed to stare down at the viewer, but Corbie couldn't help but feel that the smile on the angelic face didn't go all the way to her eyes.

"They took her from me," Norstrum said without taking his gaze off the painting. "My Inga." His hands squeezed the throat of the marble statue till the tendons stood out on the back of them.

When Corbie looked at Miss Datlow curiously waiting for an explanation she added, "Mister Norstrum wants you to handle delivering the bonds, Mister Corbie."

"Why me?"

"You have an exceptional reputation for honesty," she said. "And not being too scrupulous about the law."

"Only justice," he said with a wry grin.

"As you can see," she continued, "Mister Norstrum is too distraught to make the exchange himself. Your fee will be generous."

"Yes, yes," the upset husband said, his eyes looking up at the painting again. "Money is no object. She was my world since I heard her singing at Club Diamond. My world! She is mine."

"What fate imposes men must needs abide," Corbie quoted Shakespeare. "I'm complimented but I'm sorry, Mister Norstrum, the police are the ones equipped for this kind of thing, they have the resources to—"

"No!" Norstrum exploded, yanking the statue he'd been strangling from its base so that it smashed to pieces on the mahogany floor. "No police, no ham-fisted cops. I can't have people knowing she could be taken from me. I have a reputation, businesses where the stocks would tank if.."

"Mister Norstrum wishes to just pay these thugs to return his wife and be done."

"Yes, yes," Norstrum said. "They took her from me. I want her back, that is all that matters."

"I realize that sir, but with kidnap cases the police are the best chances of getting—ah—good result."

"They took my wife," he snarled, "They took what is mine. I want her back."

"Yes," Corbie repeated, "but there is no guarantee that they will return her safe. I promise the police are very good at this sort of thing. They will get her back."

"He makes sense, sir," the secretary said. "Please—"

"There must me absolute confidentiality," Norstrum said.

"They are good at that as well, sir," Corbie added. "I'll stand by here and help ye—it is about the lady now."

The redhaired man visibly wrestled with the decision then, with one more look up at the painting, gave a great sigh and nodded.

"Okay, call them."

CHAPTER 2

"This time you made the right decision, Corbie," Detective Gordon O'Brian said in a quiet voice. They were standing in the cavernous office of Gunnar Norstrum while several plainclothes police swarmed over the place. They had spirited the folder away and put a tap on the house phone. "We'll stake out the Tomb and we'll get the kidnapper."

"I know, Gordon. Ye fellas are good at that sort of thing."

"Nice of you to admit we know how to do our jobs, Raven."

"Och, ye know I respect the constabulary." When the officer looked at Corbie with a sour expression he added, "Most of the time."

Gordon and rushed to Norstrum's place with as little fanfare as possible.

Norstrum was still angry that they had been called in but was reduced to just grumbling while he sat at his desk and aimlessly shuffled papers. He was one of the most successful real estate moguls in the city and a familiar face on the society pages but despite his size and stature seemed reduced to confusion by what had occurred.

"She's gone," Norstrum mumbled from time to time insistently. "I want her back."

"That is our first and most important priority, sir," Gordon assured him. "We will have the area covered but only discretely. We will not interfere with the bonds being picked up—and will follow whoever recovers them without being seen."

"But they said not to—"

"I know," O'Brian said, "but we will not be seen. Trust me, there is no proof they will take your money and then still return your wife."

"No!" he bolted upright from his chair, and it looked for a second like he was going to jump the desk to go for Gordon. "I have to have her back."

The cop just gritted her teeth. "That is what we all want, sir. But if these people get away with this there is no guarantee they will not do this again to someone else."

"I don't care about anyone else," he snorted. "Just my Inga."

Gordon and Corbie exchanged a look, and it was clear they both had the same opinion of Norstrum but he was a victim. Despite him they would do what they could job to get the wife back safe.

"You have the ransom?" Gordon asked. "That's a lot of money to get on short notice."

"Not for me," Norstrum said, "Miss Datlow had gone to my banker and will be back shortly with the unregistered bonds, as specified."

"Making them untraceable," Gordon said.

"Who cares?" Norstrum shot back. "Inga is all that matters."

"Yes," O'Brian said, gritting his teeth not to snarl at him. "But after your wife is released, we wish to capture the criminals. So, we will chemically mark each of the bonds." When he looked to protest, he added, "It is invisible and only special equipment can detect it."

"It doesn't matter," Miss Datlow said as she burst through the door waving a copy of The Arling Daily Newspaper. "The kidnappers will never show up now."

She threw the newspaper on the desk in front of her employer. There on the headline was "Millionaire realtor's wife kidnapped!" and had an article about how she had been kidnapped though there were few details.

"I knew this would happen!" Norstrum roared. "I'll be a laughing-stock!"

Gordon snatched up the paper and cursed as he read it. as he read it. "When I find out who leaked this, I will nail their hide to a wall."

"It doesn't matter who," Norstrum roared. "Get out of my house—you may have killed my wife with your blundering!"

There was not much that Gordon could say to that—if the kidnappers could read it was fair bet they realized they would be dealing with the police now. Chances of another drop were almost nil.

The secretary accompanied Corbie to the door while Norstrum stood by his desk as if daring them to say anything. Datlow and Corbie stood there while the police filed out.

Gordon was the last to leave. "I'm sorry it worked out this way, Mister Norstrum," he said. "But We—"

"Get out," the realtor hissed. "I'll speak to the mayor about this..this.. gross incompetence."

The detective shot Corbie a look as if to accuse him of the way things went.

"Dinnae be scunnered, O'Brian," the Raven said. "Some people don't want to be helped."

"Later, Raven," the detective said. "We'll hash this all more completely after it plays out."

Miss Datlow stepped up to the Scotsman and put a hand on his arm as he paused in the doorway. "Mister Corbie," she said quietly, "I do not hold you responsible for this. Mister Norstrum will send a cancelation fee to you for your time."

"Don't bother yourself, lassie," he said taking another look across the foyer to the painting on the wall of Norstrum office, "Save yer pennies for the funeral wreaths."

Corbie left the mansion of Norstrum on Lake Champlain and went back to the Rook nightclub that he co-owned near the factory district of Arling. The front of the building was a century old warehouse that had been renovated, a carved image of a castle chess piece on a swinging sign over the door.

The staff was getting set to open for the late lunch crowd. The main room of the club was a vast space of a converted warehouse, made intimate with lush wooden décor, mirrors and excellent acoustics to support the bands that played on the stage in one corner. It had the feel of an old English pub made large.

There were tables and booths with the space arranged so each 'set up' felt as if it were in its own world, a world surrounded by rich jazz. It had a four-star menu and a world-wide reputation for first class musical talent.

A dark-skinned woman, well over six feet tall even without her high heels, was behind the bar with a clipboard writing down inventory when Corbie entered.

"What did that big Viking want, Ma chere? The woman called in a soft Caribbean accent when Corbie entered.

"I guess you've nae seen afternoon papers, eh?" He doffed his trench coat and settled on a stool while the bartender pulled out his private stock to single malt and poured him a drink.

"Thanks, Claude." He took a sip and let the whiskey warm his throat for a moment then related what had happened in the past few hours.

When he was done he concluded with, "I tell you, Lenore, I cannae get the look on that lassie's face in that painting out of my mind. Thinking of her being used as a bargaining chip—even if he is a tagger of a fella."

"Nothing you can do about it, Duncan," she said. Her voice was musical. Like a muted clarinet as she leaned forward over the bar to put her mouth close to his year. "No use making this another crusade."

He turned his head to give her a peck on the cheek. "Now, now, would ye still care for me if I was all that levelheaded?"

She made a tsking sound and shook her head. "So, what will you do? What can you do?"

He finished his drink. "I don't follow the society pages," he said. "What do you know about his misses?"

"I can tell you about her," Claude volunteered. "She used to sing at a nightspot off Little Broadway, The Club Arabia." The bartender, shaven headed and with a Maori tattoo on his face, smiled. "She was good, too. Real theatre royalty."

"That makes sense," I said. "He seems the type to want what he perceives as 'the best."

"Word of Norstrum and Inga's whirlwind courtship was the talk of the society pages." Claude continued, "After the marriage she sang only for him. A shame, I heard her a couple of times before the wedding. Maybe her last night, even." He got a wistful look on his rough face. "She was a delicate thing—and as you would guess kind of refined. Apparently, the mister was not the cream of the crop."

"I've met the charming tycoon," Corbie said, "I can testify to that." He picked up his coat and rose. "I'm going to head into the office and catch up on some paperwork, could you have Edgar send in a steak for me, the usual?"

"Sure, boss," Claude said.

"I'll be along shortly, Ma Chere," Lenore called. "I'll bring some creme brulee for desert."

CHAPTER 3

"**I** called a contact of mine on the Daily," Lenore said as she and Corbie relaxed with a drink after his meal. Out in the main room the sound of the band tuning up for the night drifted back through the open office door as they prepared for a busy Friday night.

"Why was that?" the Scotsman asked. He was seated in a comfortable leather couch, his legs draped casually across the Haitian woman's lap while she sat at one end.

"I knew you would not let the matter of the lady in distress rest," she said in a musical voice. "And thought I might find out more to help you."

He gave a soft laugh. "Ye know me too well, Ma Quinee, I can't get the poor lassie outta me mind."

"My source told me that the tip that came into the paper came from an anonymous call," she said, "It wasn't recorded, but it was a female voice."

"That's interesting but dinnae necessarily help."

"What will, ma chere?" She patted his thigh which made him laugh.

"Action," he said. "I have to do something; you know Ravens hate to be idle."

Now she laughed, pushed his legs off his lap and said, "Than get to it, my black bird, so I'll have your full attention again."

The Club Arabia was on the second floor of a warehouse like structure and the only way in was past two door trolls. Corbie knew one of them.

"You get tired of your own place, Raven?" The tall black man dressed like a genie asked while a second muscular doorman ran a metal detector wand up and down the Scotsman's body.

"I like to go slumming now and then," Corbie answered with a smile. "And you know I never carry a gun, Dave."

"Yeah," Dave said, "but the boss is a stickler, you know how it is."

"How's yer wee brother doing?"

"Much better now, thanks," Dave said. His brother had gotten into a beef with a numbers runner and Corbie had been able to settle things with a minimum of bloodshed. "I'll tell him you were asking after him."

Up the stairs the interior of Club Arabia was done up to resemble an Arabian Nights fantasy, with lots of marble and silk all in pastel colors, with pillowed alcoves scattered around and soft lighting. The female staff were all made up in harem-type outfits while the men wore turbans and brocade jackets.

A maitre-de greeted Corbie at the top of the stairs. "Are you expecting others?"

"Actually, I was hoping I could talk to the manager," Corbie said. "I've an inquiry about a former employee."

The expressionless maître de projected distain which was somewhat blunted by is absurd dress. He just waved me to a side corridor. "The Boss' office is down there." He then turned his attention from Corbie as if he didn't exist to focus on an elegantly dressed couple who came up the stairs behind him.

At the end of the corridor was a white oak door that was carved with scenes of Middle Eastern mythology, specifically a blue bird of happiness. Standing right beside the door was a hired gun in a three-piece suit. He was doing his best to not look bored and came to attention when The Raven entered the hallway.

"Wrong room, sir," the guard said. He shifted his weight as if to be ready to fight.

"Ali Baba back there sent me to see the manager, laddie," Corbie said. "Only be a minute—It's about a singer that used to work here, a lassie named Inga."

He regarded the Scotsman for a moment, tilted his head to the side and grimaced, "Mister Garvin ain't receiving today."

"Dinnae be haver with me, fella," Corbie said. "He's receiving me."

The door guard squared his shoulders so that he stood six inches taller than the Scotsman and said, "Not today."

Corbie smiled then moved between eyeblinks. Suddenly he had an object in right hand which he pressed up against the throat of the guard.

"What ye feel pressing on your carotid artery is a wee ceramic blade with a razor-sharp edge. I prick ye with this little pinfeather and you'll bleed out in two shakes, laddie. So why don't we agree that ye did your job and ye can take a rest now. Aye?"

The guard, who had done hard time knew there was no equivocation in the Scotsman's voice.

"Okay," the guard whispered with apparently no bluster left in him.

"Good choice," Corbie said. He stepped away from the man and returned the slim black blade up his sleeve. The moment he did the guard threw a punch all the way from the hip.

The Raven had sensed it was coming so leaned away from the uppercut and snapped out a savate kick that landed exactly on the man's jaw. The guard's head snapped back and he was unconscious and snoring before Corbie stepped over him to open the office door and enter.

"I told ye to take a rest."

The interior of the office was done up in a more conventional décor than the rest of the club with wood paneled walls, bookcases and an old-fashioned desk behind which sat the boss.

"What is it—" Bill Garvin said then he looked from the celebrity magazine he was reading and saw the Scotsman. His lean face registered shock but he recovered quickly. "Come in, Corbie."

"You know me—aye?"

"Who hasn't heard of the famous Raven?"

"I'm flattered."

"Don't be, bloke," Garvin said in a Liverpool accent. The pale blond sat back in his chair, putting down the magazine he had been reading and lit up a cigar. He focused his pale blue eyes on Corbie as if were a Judge at the docket. "Most of the word on you ain't good. You sent a lot of guys up the river."

"And across the Styxx too," Corbie said.

"That a threat?" Garvin puffed out a cloud of smoke and leaned forward.

"Think of it as just away to avoid any fankie—any confusion-- in this discussion."

"I'm assuming you uh—removed Alphonse."

Corbie had a hard time not snickering. "Alphonse will be back on duty—with a wee bit of a headache—in no time at all."

"So, since we're to just two immigrant blokes in search of the American dream, eh," Garvin said. "What do you want with me?"

"Ach, it's just a wee bit of an inquiry, actually."

"Okay," he said. "What do you want to know?"

"You had a lassie work for you as singer," Corbie said. "Inga. Married A guy named Norstrum. I just want to know about when she worked here. Did she make any enemies? Any particular friends?"

Garvin sat back and leaned his head on the back of his chair, looking off at the ceiling through a cloud of smoke. "She didn't make enemies, I can tell you that. Charmed everyone she met, anyone who heard her sing. Especially that real estate guy?"

"So can you think of no one who would want to harm her?"

"No."

"How about when she left?" Corbie asked. "What did you think of that?"

"Dumbest thing the songbird could ever do was go with him," Garvin said. "She could have been a real immortal of cabaret. What a voice that songbird has." His eyes got a dreamy look to them for just a hint of a moment, Corbie suspected he was not just talking about her voice.

"So, ye dinnae approve?"

He laughed. "Well, I lost my best act, boyo, she kept the house packed, so yeah, I didn't approve when she set her eyes on him that night. It was clear to anyone with a brain that she lost it for him. And a straight, upstanding citizen like him? Really, those mixed things never work."

"You're saying she wasn't on the up and up?"

Gavin laughed. "Oh, she was a 'good girl,' don't get me wrong and even though she looked like royalty she came up the hard way, yeah know? Worked for what she got- but she has moxie. But he was—well, for all his money he was a sort of bloke you don't turn your back on him—pretty cutthroat with his land deals—I know, had to dodge him trying to buy this place at one point."

"She met him here?"

"Yes," Gavin puffed a cloud that surrounded him. "I remember the night. Place was full to the brim and this big Viking looking bloke comes in with this older, brown-haired frail, wearing glasses, no less." He laughed, "You could see the look on his date's face when he heard Inga's first set. You could tell she knew her time on his arm was done. He swooped in Inga after that, courted her hard; she was dazzled by him. She was gone just weeks after that."

Corbie considered for a moment. "Thank you for your time, Mister Gavin."

"That's it?"

"Aye."

"You just wanted to know about the songbird's dating habits?"

"Aye," Corbie said. "That's it."

"Nothing to do with getting a reward for getting her back for that husband of hers, eh?"

"You don't seem very upset about her being taken."

"Oh, I worry about the kid, sure," Gavin protested. "But nothing I can do about it. And I'm sure Norstrum can pay up anything they ask of him. She'll be fine; she's a survivor."

"Let's hope so," Corbie said, "In any case, thank you for your time." He turned to leave but a chuckle from the club owner stopped him.

"Righteous, eh?" Gavin said. "Awful toff of you considering you've been dancing on the edge of the law in a couple of countries."

"I like dancing," Corbie said with a wry smile. "Goodnight, Mister Gavin."

"Tell that sack of human waste out there to get me a tea, that is, if he's awake."

CHAPTER 4

When Corbie walked into The Rook a jazz chanteuse was just beginning her early set. Claude waved him over the bar.

"Miss Lenore is in the office," the bartender said. "Something important—seems you forgot your cell phone again."

Corbie laughed as it was an open joke that he was always leaving his cell phone when he didn't want to be bothered.

"Don't take off your coat, ma chere," the Haitian said when he stepped into their office. She had glasses perched on the end of her slim nose. "A Miss Datlow called the club when you didn't answer your cell—she sounded distraught. She wanted you to at the Norstrum mansion but wouldn't say why."

"I have a bad feeling about it, Quinee. Best not plan on waiting dinner for me later."

"I'll keep everything warm," she smiled coyly. "Just in case."

"Thank you for coming, Mister Corbie," Arwyn Datlow said when she met The Raven at the door to the mansion. Her tight bun of hair and her attitude were both askew. It looked like she had been crying.

"What happened, lassie?"

"This came," she held up a that had been cut out from magazine and newspaper letters. "Bring 50,000 dollars to The Overlook Fort and place it under the barrel of the ceremonial cannon or you'll never see your songbird again."

Corbie took it in with not much sign of surprise. "That's a stramash," he said. "When did this come?"

"Just before I called your nightclub," she said. "Then Mister Norstrum drove to the fort."

He studied the note. "Why the hell would the kidnappers suddenly drop their price to a bargain basement deal?"

The distraught woman leaned against the sarcophagus in the great room as if she had no strength to stand.

"The Overlook is on the west side," he said thinking aloud, "barely ten blocks from Club Diamond."

"I, uh, yes," she said, "why would that matter?"

"It might mean nothing, Miss Datlow, but tell me—you leaked about the kidnapping, didn't you?"

Her eyes went wide with what appeared to be sudden animal fear.

"Dinnae deny it, lassie, I'm sure we can get record of the call you made."

"All right," she broke down in full tears now. "I couldn't stand her—he never looked at me again after she sang."

"Yet you stayed on—as his secretary?"

"To be near him." She was in full melt down mode now. "But—but if he finds out I leaked the news—and if he loses her because of me, he'll never speak to me again."

"Stay here and don't do anything," Cobie said. "I'll see if I can sort this out."

Then he was off again, full speed toward The Overlook Fort.

The fort had been part of a defensive line set up during the War of 1812 to command Arling's port on Lake Champlain. Long decommissioned it was a historical museum now with an old Civil War era cannon set up in the center of the quadrangle, near the flagpole.

Corbie arrived just in time to observe the burly figure of Norstrum walking away from the cannon and flagpole.

The Raven kept to the shadows and remained unseen as the mogul let the fort and drove off. He considered calling the police—he had remembered to bring his cell phone with him this time but decided they could no arrive in time to do any good.

In a few moments a figure detached itself from shadows on the other side of the quadrangle, went to the cannon and retrieved the package with the money.

It was Alphonse.

He paused to look around, then he took off again at a run.

Can't say I'm surprised, though Garvin must trust you more than a wee bit to let you do the pick-up.

The Raven followed him leisurely, as there was in no hurry. Corbie knew exactly where the messenger was going.

When Corbie got to the Diamond Club he skipped the main entrance and went straight to the roof via a back fire escape. It was an easy entrance as no one was crazy enough to think of breaking into a mob run night spot. Except, of course, The Raven.

The roof door's lock was elementary, and Corbie descended the stairwell to enter it, went on down to the second floor and emerged into an empty hallway.

He found he was in the back-of-house by the kitchen. It meant he could move to Garvins' office unobserved, eventually rounding a corner to see Alphonse standing outside the boss' office.

Before the guard could react to the sudden appearance Corbie launched forward with a straight right cross that hit the man on the chin, snapping his head around so he dropped like a stone.

"With that glass jaw, laddie, ye need to change professions."

Corbie grabbed the doorknob, jumped the snoring Alphonse and burst into the office.

The cockney crime boss was sitting behind his desk with a pile of bonds piled spread out before him.

"Hold it right there, Gavin."

"How—" he stammered.

"Ye were a wee bit obvious, laddie," Corbie said. "So don't be surprised." He closed the door behind and clicked the lock.

"No," Garvin said. "You can't pin anything on me. I didn't snatch Inga."

"Don't you mean your songbird," Corbie said, "That's how you called her in the second note. And yes, I figured you didn't write the first one—that was typed. But I noticed some of those letters on the second one were from that magazine you were reading before. And ye low balled the ransom demand; pretty penny anty."

"I ain't no petty anty clown," Gavin protested.

Corbie laughed, "That ship has sailed, laddie. Stop wasting my time. Why did you think you could cash in on the kidnapping?"

"My songbird was fed up with that jerk she fell for," he said. He lit up a cigar and puffed away. "She used to slip away and stop by here now and then, you know for 'old times sake.' Seems that bloke of hers was treating her like a possession. Not a way to treat that frail. And he was rough about it, I saw bruises on her arm."

He hung his head with a sudden sadness. "Inga told me months ago she thought the only way to get away from her bloke was to run away and pretend to be kidnapped so he wouldn't chase her. I thought she was joking."

"So, when you read she'd been kidnapped--"

"I figured she finally did it," he finished. "And good for her."

"But when it was leaked to the papers you figured you could make a little on the deal yourself."

"She was my star attraction. I figured she'd never actually collect any drop since she was gone, so I deserved to make A little on it. He owns enough."

Corbie picked up the phone on and dialed Detective O'Brian. While waiting to be connected he stared down Garvin and had a sudden inspiration, "Maybe Norstrum does own enough," he said. "Maybe he owns it all."

CHAPTER 5

"**M**ister Norstrum is not at home to you," the rent-a-cop at the front gate of the mansion.

"Well, here' just give him my card," The Scotsman said, pulling a black business card out of his pocket. It had a silhouette of a raven on it.

When the guard reached for it The Raven moved to lock the guard's wrist and delivered a stunning blow to the man's temple. The guard dropped unconscious.

"Sorry, lad," Corbie said, "I hope you've got good medical to deal with the headache."

The Raven raced to the house and rang the bell. He was met by a subdued Miss Datlow who looked confused.

"What—"

"Where is he?"

"In his office," she said, "He doesn't know I told-"

"It won't matter, lassie," Corbie said. "In fact, I think he's happy word leaked."

"But—"

"Just stand back."

When The Raven entered the museum office he found Norstrum sitting at his desk, back to the door and staring up at the painting of his wife.

"Where do you have her?" Corbie called. Norstrum spun to face the Scotsman.

"What are you doing here?"

"I came to see your wife." Corbie looked up at that portrait and once more felt myself captured by the eyes of the woman.

"My Inga is gone," Norstrum said. "They took her from me."

"I don't think so."

"Get out of my house." His eyes flared with anger.

"So, what was it, Norstrum," I asked, "You suspected her of writing the kidnap note?"

The redhaired realtor seemed to deflate, his bluster of a moment ago now gone. His shoulders hunched and his chin dropped to his chest. "I—I found her typing it."

Corbie was surprised by that confession. Behind him he heard Datlow gasp but pushed on, not letting Norstrum regain his bluster.

"Yet you allowed the whole thing to go forward?"

"Leave me alone; she is mine." Norstrum's voice was low whisper. He was shaking his head and his hands were balled int o fists, shaking with how tight he had clenched them.

"Not till I see your wife," The Raven said. "It's clear you agreed to the second ransom just to have someone to throw blame on later to keep you all looking for her elsewhere. Where are you keeping her prisoner?"

Suddenly the burley billionaire launched himself at Corbie and sucker punched him across the jaw.

"She's mine!" Norstrum yelled.

Datlow screamed.

Fortunately, the Scotsman managed to ride the punch to avoid the full force of it, so he staggered back but didn't go down.

Norstrum grabbed a golden inlaid antique Viking axe off the wall and came for The Raven.

Corbie dodged the first hacking cut, then took off his leather trenchcoat and used it like a cape to fend off a constant barrage of attacks. Datlow began to cry hysterically as the pair moved through the display cases, knocking many of them over.

Norstrum slashed at Corbie's head and shoulders, while mumbling incoherently.

"Stop it, stop it," Datlow screamed.

Norstrum drove Corbie backward with the Scotsman only able to use the heavy leather coat to deflect the assault but with no time to react or strike back for the fury of the attack. They blundered into and knocked over more of precious items in glass cases, a bronze statue of a shepherd boy and others until finally, the mad husband backed The Raven up against the sarcophagus.

"No one will take her from me, no one!" Norstrum screamed in a mad rage, hacking at Corbie with an overhead cut that The Raven dodged but when the axe hit the edge of the sarcophagus it bit deep. That gave Corbie a split second to be able to draw and throw one of his ceramic 'pinfeather' knives.

The blade sliced into Norstrum's throat in a fount of blood.

This last act occurred at the same moment that O'Brian and his squad burst into the room. They and Miss Datlow had a front row seat to witness the death of the millionaire.

As Norstrum dropped the ground, his blood flowing out of his throat, the sarcophagus he'd struck with the axe fell open and everyone found themselves looking at the corpse of his wife Inga.

Bruise marks were clear around the songbird's throat, where he'd strangled her.

Miss Datlow raced to the dying tycoon and tried to apply pressure to the wound but it was too late. The tycoon had already gone over the rainbow bridge.

"Looks like you had it pegged right, Raven," O'Brian said with a disgusted tone.

"Sometimes this bird would just as well nae be the all-seeing eye of Odin," the Scotsman said. "We'd best get to all the paperwork, Gordon. I've an appointment back at The Rook and my own wee lassie to tell all the more how I appreciate her."

END

Teel James Glenn has dozens of novels and stories published in over two hundred magazines including Weird Tales, Cirsova, Mystery Magazine, Heroic Fantasy, Tough and Sherlock Holmes Mystery Magazine.

His novel A Cowboy in Carpathia: A Bob Howard Adventure, won best novel 2021 in the Pulp Factory Award.
TheUrbanSwashbuckler.com
Facebook: Teel James Glenn

MOMENT IN TIME

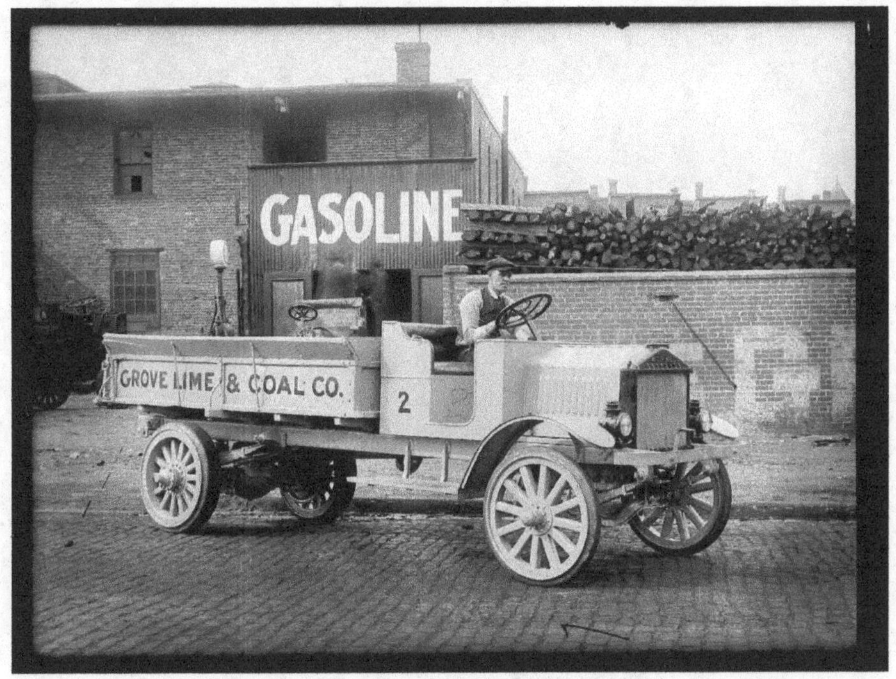

Grove Lime and Coal Company; photo pre 1920.

THE MOST DANGEROUS GAME

BY RICHARD CONNELL

ORIGINALLY PUBLISHED IN 1925

"OFF THERE TO THE RIGHT—SOMEWHERE—IS A LARGE ISLAND," SAID WHITney. "It's rather a mystery."

"What island is it?" Rainsford asked.

"The old charts call it 'Ship-Trap Island,'" Whitney replied. "A suggestive name, isn't it? Sailors have a curious dread of the place. I don't know why. Some superstition——"

"Can't see it," remarked Rainsford, trying to peer through the dank tropical night that was palpable as it pressed its thick warm blackness in upon the yacht.

"You've good eyes," said Whitney, with a laugh, "and I've seen you pick off a moose moving in the brown fall bush at four hundred yards, but even you can't see four miles or so through a moonless Caribbean night."

"Nor four yards," admitted Rainsford. "Ugh! It's like moist black velvet."

"It will be light enough in Rio," promised Whitney. "We should make it in a few days. I hope the jaguar guns have come from Purdey's. We should have some good hunting up the Amazon. Great sport, hunting."

"The best sport in the world," agreed Rainsford.

"For the hunter," amended Whitney. "Not for the jaguar."

"Don't talk rot, Whitney," said Rainsford. "You're a big-game hunter, not a philosopher. Who cares how a jaguar feels?"

"Perhaps the jaguar does," observed Whitney.

"Bah! They've no understanding."

"Even so, I rather think they understand one thing—fear. The fear of pain and the fear of death."

"Nonsense," laughed Rainsford. "This hot weather is making you soft, Whitney. Be a realist. The world is made up of two classes—the hunters and the huntees. Luckily, you and I are hunters. Do you think we've passed that island yet?"

"I can't tell in the dark. I hope so."

"Why?" asked Rainsford.

"The place has a reputation—a bad one."

"Cannibals?" suggested Rainsford.

"Hardly. Even cannibals wouldn't live in such a God-forsaken place. But it's gotten into sailor lore, somehow. Didn't you notice that the crew's nerves seemed a bit jumpy to-day?"

"They were a bit strange, now you mention it. Even Captain Nielsen——"

"Yes, even that tough-minded old Swede, who'd go up to the devil himself and ask him for a light. Those fishy blue eyes held a look I never saw there before. All I could get out of him was: 'This place has an evil name among sea-faring men, sir.' Then he said to me, very gravely: 'Don't you feel anything?'—as if the air about us was actually poisonous. Now, you mustn't laugh when I tell you this—I did feel something like a sudden chill.

"There was no breeze. The sea was as flat as a plate-glass window. We were drawing near the island then. What I felt was a—a mental chill; a sort of sudden dread."

"Pure imagination," said Rainsford. "One superstitious sailor can taint the whole ship's company with his fear."

"Maybe. But sometimes I think sailors have an extra sense that tells them when they are in danger. Sometimes I think evil is a tangible thing—with wave lengths, just as sound and light have. An evil place can, so to speak, broadcast vibrations of evil. Anyhow, I'm glad we're getting out of this zone. Well, I think I'll turn in now, Rainsford."

"I'm not sleepy," said Rainsford. "I'm going to smoke another pipe up on the after deck."

"Good-night, then, Rainsford. See you at breakfast."

"Right. Good-night, Whitney."

There was no sound in the night as Rainsford sat there but the muffled throb of the engine that drove the yacht swiftly through the darkness, and the swish and ripple of the wash of the propeller.

Rainsford, reclining in a steamer chair, indolently puffed on his favourite brier. The sensuous drowsiness of the night was on him. "It's so dark," he thought, "that I could sleep without closing my eyes; the night would be my eyelids——"

An abrupt sound startled him. Off to the right he heard it, and his ears, expert in such matters, could not be mistaken. Again he heard the sound, and again. Somewhere, off in the blackness, someone had fired a gun three times.

Rainsford sprang up and moved quickly to the rail, mystified. He strained his eyes in the direction from which the reports had come, but it was like trying to see through a blanket. He leaped upon the rail and balanced himself there, to get greater elevation; his pipe, striking a rope, was knocked from his mouth. He lunged for it; a short, hoarse cry came from his lips as he realized he had reached too far and had lost his balance. The cry was pinched off short as the blood-warm waters of the Caribbean Sea closed over his head.

He struggled up to the surface and tried to cry out, but the wash from the speeding yacht slapped him in the face and the salt water in his open mouth made him gag and strangle. Desperately he struck out with strong strokes after the receding lights of the yacht, but he stopped before he had swum fifty feet. A certain cool-headedness had come to him; it was not the first time he had been in a tight place. There was a chance that his cries could be heard by someone aboard the yacht, but that chance was slender, and grew more slender as the yacht raced on. He wrestled himself out of his clothes, and shouted with all his power. The lights of the yacht became faint and ever-vanishing fireflies; then they were blotted out entirely by the night.

Rainsford remembered the shots. They had come from the right, and doggedly he swam in that direction, swimming with slow, deliberate strokes, conserving his strength. For a seemingly endless time he fought the sea. He began to count his strokes; he could do possibly a hundred more and then——

Rainsford heard a sound. It came out of the darkness, a high, screaming sound, the sound of an animal in an extremity of anguish and terror.

He did not recognize the animal that made the sound; he did not try to; with fresh vitality he swam toward the sound. He heard it again; then it was cut short by another noise, crisp, staccato.

"Pistol shot," muttered Rainsford, swimming on.

Ten minutes of determined effort brought another sound to his ears—the most welcome he had ever heard—the muttering and growling of the sea breaking on a rocky shore. He was almost on the rocks before he saw them: on a night less calm he would have been shattered against them. With his remaining strength he dragged himself from the swirling waters. Jagged crags appeared to jut up into the opaqueness; he forced himself upward, hand over hand. Gasping, his hands raw, he reached a flat place at the top. Dense jungle came down to the very edge of the cliffs. What perils that tangle of trees and underbrush might hold for him did not concern Rainsford just then. All he knew was that he was safe from his enemy, the sea, and that utter weariness was on him. He flung himself down at the jungle edge and tumbled headlong into the deepest sleep of his life.

When he opened his eyes he knew from the position of the sun that it was late in the afternoon. Sleep had given him new vigour; a sharp hunger was picking at him. He looked about him, almost cheerfully.

"Where there are pistol shots, there are men. Where there are men, there is food," he thought. But what kind of men, he wondered, in so forbidding a place? An unbroken front of snarled and ragged jungle fringed the shore.

He saw no sign of a trail through the closely knit web of weeds and trees; it was easier to go along the shore, and Rainsford floundered along by the water. Not far from where he had landed, he stopped.

Some wounded thing, by the evidence a large animal, had thrashed about in the underbrush; the jungle weeds were crushed down and the moss was lacerated; one patch of weeds was stained crimson. A small, glittering object not far away caught Rainsford's eye and he picked it up. It was an empty cartridge.

"A twenty-two," he remarked. "That's odd. It must have been a fairly large animal, too. The hunter had his nerve with him to tackle it with a light gun. It's clear that the brute put up a fight. I suppose the first three shots I heard was when the hunter flushed his quarry and wounded it. The last shot was when he trailed it here and finished it."

He examined the ground closely and found what he had hoped to find—the print of hunting boots. They pointed along the cliff in the direction he had been going. Eagerly he hurried along, now slipping on a rotten log or a loose stone, but making headway; night was beginning to settle down on the island.

Bleak darkness was blacking out the sea and jungle when Rainsford sighted the lights. He came upon them as he turned a crook in the coast line, and his first thought was that he had come upon a village, for there were many lights. But as he forged along he saw to his great astonishment that all the lights were in one enormous building—a lofty structure with pointed towers plunging upward into the gloom. His eyes made out the shadowy outlines of a palatial château; it was set on a high bluff, and on three sides of it cliffs dived down to where the sea licked greedy lips in the shadows.

"Mirage," thought Rainsford. But it was no mirage, he found, when he opened the tall spiked iron gate. The stone steps were real enough; the massive door with a leering gargoyle for a knocker was real enough; yet about it all hung an air of unreality.

He lifted the knocker, and it creaked up stiffly as if it had never before been used. He let it fall, and it startled him with its booming loudness. He thought he heard steps within; the door remained closed. Again Rainsford lifted the heavy knocker, and let it fall. The door opened then, opened as suddenly as if it were on a spring, and Rainsford stood blinking in the river of glaring gold light that poured out. The first thing Rainsford's eyes discerned was the largest man Rainsford had ever seen—a gigantic creature, solidly made and black-bearded to the waist. In his hand the man held a long-barrelled revolver, and he was pointing it straight at Rainsford's heart.

Out of the snarl of beard two small eyes regarded Rainsford.

"Don't be alarmed," said Rainsford, with a smile which he hoped was disarming. "I'm no robber. I fell off a yacht. My name is Sanger Rainsford of New York City."

The menacing look in the eyes did not change. The revolver pointed as rigidly as if the giant were a statue. He gave no sign that he understood Rainsford's words, or that he had even heard them. He was dressed in uniform, a black uniform trimmed with gray astrakhan.

"I'm Sanger Rainsford of New York," Rainsford began again. "I fell off a yacht. I am hungry."

The man's only answer was to raise with his thumb the hammer of his revolver. Then Rainsford saw the man's free hand go to his forehead in a military salute, and he saw him click his heels together and stand at attention. Another man was coming down the broad marble steps, an erect, slender man in evening clothes. He advanced to Rainsford and held out his hand.

In a cultivated voice marked by a slight accent that gave it added precision and deliberateness, he said: "It is a very great pleasure and honour to welcome Mr. Sanger Rainsford, the celebrated hunter, to my home."

Automatically Rainsford shook the man's hand.

"I've read your book about hunting snow leopards in Tibet, you see," explained the man. "I am General Zaroff."

Rainsford's first impression was that the man was singularly handsome; his second was that there was an original, almost bizarre quality about the general's face. He was a tall man past middle age, for his hair was a vivid white; but his thick eyebrows and pointed military moustache were as black as the night from which Rainsford had come. His eyes, too, were black and very bright. He had high cheek bones, a sharp-cut nose, a spare, dark face, the face of a man used to giving orders, the face of an aristocrat. Turning to the giant in uniform, the general made a sign. The giant put away his pistol, saluted, withdrew.

"Ivan is an incredibly strong fellow," remarked the general, "but he has the misfortune to be deaf and dumb. A simple fellow, but, I'm afraid, like all his race, a bit of a savage."

"Is he Russian?"

"He is a Cossack," said the general, and his smile showed red lips and pointed teeth. "So am I."

"Come," he said, "we shouldn't be chatting here. We can talk later. Now you want clothes, food, rest. You shall have them. This is a most restful spot."

Ivan had reappeared, and the general spoke to him with lips that moved but gave forth no sound.

"Follow Ivan, if you please, Mr. Rainsford," said the general. "I was about to have my dinner when you came. I'll wait for you. You'll find that my clothes will fit you, I think."

It was to a huge, beam-ceilinged bedroom with a canopied bed big enough for six men that Rainsford followed the silent giant. Ivan laid out an evening suit, and Rainsford, as he put it on, noticed that it came from a London tailor who ordinarily cut and sewed for none below the rank of duke.

The dining room to which Ivan conducted him was in many ways remarkable. There was a mediæval magnificence about it; it suggested a baronial hall of feudal times with its oaken panels, its high ceiling, its vast refectory table where two score men could sit down to eat. About the hall were the mounted heads of many animals—lions, tigers, elephants, moose, bears; larger or more perfect specimens Rainsford had never seen. At the great table the general was sitting, alone.

"You'll have a cocktail, Mr. Rainsford," he suggested. The cocktail was surpassingly good, and, Rainsford noted, the table appointments were of the finest—the linen, the crystal, the silver, the china.

They were eating borsch, the rich red soup with whipped cream so dear to Russian palates. Half apologetically General Zaroff said: "We do our best to preserve the amenities of civilization here. Please forgive any lapses. We are well off the beaten track, you know. Do you think the champagne has suffered from its long ocean trip?"

"Not in the least," declared Rainsford. He was finding the general a most thoughtful and affable host, a true cosmopolite. But there was one small trait of the general's that made Rainsford uncomfortable. Whenever he looked up from his plate he found the general studying him, appraising him narrowly.

"Perhaps," said General Zaroff, "you were surprised that I recognized your name. You see, I read all books on hunting published in English, French, and Russian. I have but one passion in my life, Mr. Rainsford, and it is the hunt."

"You have some wonderful heads here," said Rainsford as he ate a particularly well-cooked filet mignon. "That Cape buffalo is the largest I ever saw."

"Oh, that fellow. Yes, he was a monster."

"Did he charge you?"

"Hurled me against a tree," said the general. "Fractured my skull. But I got the brute."

"I've always thought," said Rainsford, "that the Cape buffalo is the most dangerous of all big game."

For a moment the general did not reply; he was smiling his curious red-lipped smile. Then he said slowly: "No. You are wrong, sir. The Cape buffalo is not the most dangerous big game." He sipped his wine. "Here in my preserve on this island," he said, in the same slow tone, "I hunt more dangerous game."

Rainsford expressed his surprise. "Is there big game on this island?"

The general nodded. "The biggest."

"Really?"

"Oh, it isn't here naturally, of course. I have to stock the island."

"What have you imported, General?" Rainsford asked. "Tigers?"

The general smiled. "No," he said. "Hunting tigers ceased to interest me some years ago. I exhausted their possibilities, you see. No thrill left in tigers, no real danger. I live for danger, Mr. Rainsford."

The general took from his pocket a gold cigarette case and offered his guest a long black cigarette with a silver tip; it was perfumed and gave off a smell like incense.

"We will have some capital hunting, you and I," said the general. "I shall be most glad to have your society."

"But what game——" began Rainsford.

"I'll tell you," said the general. "You will be amused, I know. I think I may say, in all modesty, that I have done a rare thing. I have invented a new sensation. May I pour you another glass of port, Mr. Rainsford?"

"Thank you, General."

The general filled both glasses, and said: "God makes some men poets. Some He makes kings, some beggars. Me He made a hunter. My hand was made for the trigger, my father said. He was a very rich man with a quarter of a million acres in the Crimea, and he was an ardent sportsman. When I was only five years old he gave me a little gun, specially made in Moscow for me, to shoot sparrows with. When I shot some of his prize turkeys with it, he did not punish me; he complimented me on my marksmanship. I killed my first bear in the Caucasus when I was ten. My whole life has been one prolonged hunt. I went into the army—it was expected of noblemen's sons—and for a time commanded a division of Cossack cavalry, but my real interest was always the hunt. I have hunted every kind of game in every land. It would be impossible for me to tell you how many animals I have killed."

The general puffed at his cigarette.

"After the debacle in Russia I left the country, for it was imprudent for an officer of the Tsar to stay there. Many noble Russians lost everything. I, luckily, had invested heavily in American securities, so I shall never have to open a tea room in Monte Carlo or drive a taxi in Paris. Naturally, I continued to hunt—grizzlies in your Rockies, crocodiles in the Ganges, rhinoceroses in East Africa. It was in Africa that the Cape buffalo hit me and laid me up for six months. As soon as I recovered I started for the Amazon to hunt jaguars, for I had heard they were unusually cunning. They weren't." The Cossack sighed. "They were no match at all for a hunter with his wits about him, and a high-powered rifle. I was bitterly disappointed. I was lying in my tent with a splitting headache one night when a terrible thought pushed its way into my mind. Hunting was beginning to bore me! And hunting, remember, had been my life. I have heard that in America business men often go to pieces when they give up the business that has been their life."

"Yes, that's so," said Rainsford.

The general smiled. "I had no wish to go to pieces," he said. "I must do something. Now, mine is an analytical mind, Mr. Rainsford. Doubtless that is why I enjoy the problems of the chase."

"No doubt, General Zaroff."

"So," continued the general, "I asked myself why the hunt no longer fascinated me. You are much younger than I am, Mr. Rainsford, and have not hunted as much, but you perhaps can guess the answer."

"What was it?"

"Simply this: hunting had ceased to be what you call 'a sporting proposition.' It had become too easy. I always got my quarry. Always. There is no greater bore than perfection."

The general lit a fresh cigarette.

"No animal had a chance with me any more. That is no boast; it is a mathematical certainty. The animal had nothing but his legs and his instinct. Instinct is no match for reason. When I thought of this it was a tragic moment for me, I can tell you."

Rainsford leaned across the table, absorbed in what his host was saying.

"It came to me as an inspiration what I must do," the general went on.

"And that was?"

The general smiled the quiet smile of one who has faced an obstacle and surmounted it with success. "I had to invent a new animal to hunt," he said.

"A new animal? You're joking."

"Not at all," said the general. "I never joke about hunting. I needed a new animal. I found one. So I bought this island, built this house, and here I do my hunting. The island is perfect for my purposes—there are jungles with a maze of trails in them, hills, swamps——"

"But the animal, General Zaroff?"

"Oh," said the general, "it supplies me with the most exciting hunting in the world. No other hunting compares with it for an instant. Every day I hunt, and I never grow bored now, for I have a quarry with which I can match my wits."

Rainsford's bewilderment showed in his face.

"I wanted the ideal animal to hunt," explained the general. "So I said: 'What are the attributes of an ideal quarry?' And the answer was, of course: 'It must have courage, cunning, and, above all, it must be able to reason.'"

"But no animal can reason," objected Rainsford.

"My dear fellow," said the general, "there is one that can."

"But you can't mean——" gasped Rainsford.

"And why not?"

"I can't believe you are serious, General Zaroff. This is a grisly joke."

"Why should I not be serious? I am speaking of hunting."

"Hunting? Good God, General Zaroff, what you speak of is murder."

The general laughed with entire good nature. He regarded Rainsford quizzically. "I refuse to believe that so modern and civilized a young man as you seem to be harbours romantic ideas about the value of human life. Surely your experiences in the war——"

"Did not make me condone cold-blooded murder," finished Rainsford, stiffly.

Laughter shook the general. "How extraordinarily droll you are!" he said. "One does not expect nowadays to find a young man of the educated class, even in America, with such a naïve, and, if I may say so, mid-Victorian point of view. It's like finding a snuffbox in a limousine. Ah, well, doubtless you had Puritan ancestors. So many Americans appear to have had. I'll wager you'll forget your notions when you go hunting with me. You've a genuine new thrill in store for you, Mr. Rainsford."

"Thank you, I'm a hunter, not a murderer."

"Dear me," said the general, quite unruffled, "again that unpleasant word. But I think I can show you that your scruples are quite ill founded."

"Yes?"

"Life is for the strong, to be lived by the strong, and, if needs be, taken by the strong. The weak of the world were put here to give the strong pleasure. I am strong. Why should I not use my gift? If I wish to hunt, why should I not? I hunt the scum of the earth—sailors from tramp ships—lascars, blacks, Chinese, whites, mongrels—a thoroughbred horse or hound is worth more than a score of them."

"But they are men," said Rainsford, hotly.

"Precisely," said the general. "That is why I use them. It gives me pleasure. They can reason, after a fashion. So they are dangerous."

"But where do you get them?"

The general's left eyelid fluttered down in a wink. "This island is called Ship Trap," he answered. "Sometimes an angry god of the high seas sends them to me. Sometimes, when Providence is not so kind, I help Providence a bit. Come to the window with me."

Rainsford went to the window and looked out toward the sea.

"Watch! Out there!" exclaimed the general, pointing into the night. Rainsford's eyes saw only blackness, and then, as the general pressed a button, far out to sea Rainsford saw the flash of lights.

The general chuckled. "They indicate a channel," he said, "where there's none: giant rocks with razor edges crouch like a sea monster with wide-open jaws. They can crush a ship as easily as I crush this nut." He dropped a walnut on the hardwood floor and brought his heel grinding down on it. "Oh, yes," he said, casually, as if in answer to a question. "I have electricity. We try to be civilized here."

"Civilized? And you shoot down men?"

A trace of anger was in the general's black eyes, but it was there for but a second, and he said, in his most pleasant manner: "Dear me, what a righteous young man you are! I assure you I do not do the thing you suggest. That would be barbarous. I treat these visitors with every consideration. They get plenty of good food and exercise. They get into splendid physical condition. You shall see for yourself tomorrow."

"What do you mean?"

"We'll visit my training school," smiled the general. "It's in the cellar. I have about a dozen pupils down there now. They're from the Spanish bark *Sanlúcar* that had the bad luck to go on the rocks cut there. A very inferior lot, I regret to say. Poor specimens and more accustomed to the deck than to the jungle."

He raised his hand, and Ivan, who served as waiter, brought thick Turkish coffee. Rainsford, with an effort, held his tongue in check.

"It's a game, you see," pursued the general, blandly. "I suggest to one of them that we go hunting. I give him a supply of food and an excellent hunting knife. I give him three hours' start. I am to follow, armed only with a pistol of the smallest calibre and range. If my quarry eludes me for three whole days, he wins the game. If I find him"—the general smiled—"he loses."

"Suppose he refuses to be hunted?"

"Oh," said the general, "I give him his option, of course. He need not play that game if he doesn't wish to. If he does not wish to hunt, I turn him over to Ivan. Ivan once had the honour of serving as official knouter to the Great White Tsar, and he has his own ideas of sport. Invariably, Mr. Rainsford, invariably they choose the hunt."

"And if they win?"

The smile on the general's face widened. "To date I have not lost," he said.

Then he added, hastily: "I don't wish you to think me a braggart, Mr. Rainsford. Many of them afford only the most elementary sort of problem. Occasionally I strike a tartar. One almost did win. I eventually had to use the dogs."

"The dogs?"

"This way, please. I'll show you."

The general steered Rainsford to a window. The lights from the windows sent a flickering illumination that made grotesque patterns on the courtyard below, and Rainsford could see moving about there a dozen or so huge black shapes; as they turned toward him, their eyes glittered greenly.

"A rather good lot, I think," observed the general. "They are let out at seven every night. If any one should try to get into my house—or out of it—something extremely regrettable would occur to him." He hummed a snatch of song from the Folies Bergère.

"And now," said the general, "I want to show you my new collection of heads. Will you come with me to the library?"

"I hope," said Rainsford, "that you will excuse me tonight, General Zaroff. I'm really not feeling at all well."

"Ah, indeed?" the general inquired, solicitously. "Well, I suppose that's only natural, after your long swim. You need a good, restful night's sleep. To-morrow you'll feel like a new man, I'll wager. Then we'll hunt, eh? I've one rather promising prospect——"

Rainsford was hurrying from the room.

"Sorry you can't go with me to-night," called the general. "I expect rather fair sport—a big, strong black. He looks resourceful—— Well, good-night, Mr. Rainsford; I hope you have a good night's rest."

The bed was good, and the pajamas of the softest silk, and he was tired in every fibre of his being, but nevertheless Rainsford could not quiet his brain with the opiate of sleep. He lay, eyes wide open. Once he thought he heard stealthy steps in the corridor outside his room. He sought to throw open the door; it would not open. He went to the window and looked out. His room was high up in one of the towers. The lights of the château were out now, and it was dark and silent, but there was a fragment of sallow moon, and by its wan light he could see, dimly, the courtyard; there, weaving in and out in the pattern of shadow, were black, noiseless forms; the hounds heard him at the window and looked up, expectantly, with their green eyes. Rainsford went back to the bed and lay down. By many methods he tried to put himself to sleep. He had achieved a doze when, just as morning began to come, he heard, far off in the jungle, the faint report of a pistol.

General Zaroff did not appear until luncheon. He was dressed faultlessly in the tweeds of a country squire. He was solicitous about the state of Rainsford's health.

"As for me," sighed the general, "I do not feel so well. I am worried, Mr. Rainsford. Last night I detected traces of my old complaint."

To Rainsford's questioning glance the general said: "Ennui. Boredom."

Then, taking a second helping of Crêpes Suzette, the general explained: "The hunting was not good last night. The fellow lost his head. He made a straight trail that offered no problems at all. That's the trouble with these sailors; they have dull brains to begin with, and they do not know how to get about in the woods. They do excessively stupid and obvious things. It's most annoying. Will you have another glass of Chablis, Mr. Rainsford?"

"General," said Rainsford, firmly, "I wish to leave this island at once."

The general raised his thickets of eyebrows; he seemed hurt. "But, my dear fellow," the general protested, "you've only just come. You've had no hunting——"

"I wish to go to-day," said Rainsford. He saw the dead black eyes of the general on him, studying him. General Zaroff's face suddenly brightened.

He filled Rainsford's glass with venerable Chablis from a dusty bottle.

"To-night," said the general, "we will hunt—you and I."

Rainsford shook his head. "No, General," he said. "I will not hunt."

The general shrugged his shoulders and delicately ate a hothouse grape. "As you wish, my friend," he said. "The choice rests entirely with you. But may I not venture to suggest that you will find my idea of sport more diverting than Ivan's?"

He nodded toward the corner to where the giant stood, scowling, his thick arms crossed on his hogshead of chest.

"You don't mean——" cried Rainsford.

"My dear fellow," said the general, "have I not told you I always mean what I say about hunting? This is really an inspiration. I drink to a foeman worthy of my steel—at last."

The general raised his glass, but Rainsford sat staring at him.

"You'll find this game worth playing," the general said, enthusiastically. "Your brain against mine. Your woodcraft against mine. Your strength and stamina against mine. Outdoor chess! And the stake is not without value, eh?"

"And if I win——" began Rainsford, huskily.

"I'll cheerfully acknowledge myself defeated if I do not find you by midnight of the third day," said General Zaroff. "My sloop will place you on the mainland near a town."

The general read what Rainsford was thinking.

"Oh, you can trust me," said the Cossack. "I will give you my word as a gentleman and a sportsman. Of course, you, in turn, must agree to say nothing of your visit here."

"I'll agree to nothing of the kind," said Rainsford.

"Oh," said the general, "in that case—— But why discuss that now? Three days hence we can discuss it over a bottle of Veuve Cliquot, unless——"

The general sipped his wine.

Then a businesslike air animated him. "Ivan," he said to Rainsford, "will supply you with hunting clothes, food, a knife. I suggest you wear moccasins; they leave a poorer trail. I suggest, too, that you avoid the big swamp in the southeast corner of the island. We call it Death Swamp. There's quicksand there. One foolish fellow tried it. The deplorable part of it was that Lazarus followed him. You can imagine my feelings, Mr. Rainsford. I loved Lazarus; he was the finest hound in my pack. Well, I must beg you to excuse me now. I always take a siesta after lunch. You'll hardly have time for a nap, I fear. You'll want to start, no doubt. I shall not follow till dusk. Hunting at night is so much more exciting than by day, don't you think? Au revoir, Mr. Rainsford, au revoir."

General Zaroff, with a deep, courtly bow, strolled from the room.

From another door came Ivan. Under one arm he carried khaki hunting clothes, a haversack of food, a leather sheath containing a long-bladed hunting knife; his right hand rested on a cocked revolver thrust in the crimson sash about his waist....

Rainsford had fought his way through the bush for two hours. "I must keep my nerve. I must keep my nerve," he said, through tight teeth.

He had not been entirely clear-headed when the château gates snapped shut behind him. His whole idea at first was to put distance between himself and General Zaroff, and, to this end, he had plunged along, spurred on by the sharp rowels of something very like panic. Now he had got a grip on himself, had stopped, and was taking stock of himself and the situation.

He saw that straight flight was futile; inevitably it would bring him face to face with the sea. He was in a picture with a frame of water, and his operations, clearly, must take place within that frame.

"I'll give him a trail to follow," muttered Rainsford, and he struck off from the rude path he had been following into the trackless wilderness. He executed a series of intricate loops; he doubled on his tail again and again, recalling all the lore of the fox hunt, and all the dodges of the fox. Night found him leg-weary, with hands and face lashed by the branches, on a thickly wooded ridge. He knew it would be insane to blunder on through the dark, even if he had the strength. His need for rest was imperative and he thought: "I have played the fox, now I must play the cat of the fable." A big tree with a thick trunk and outspread branches was near by, and, taking care to leave not the slightest mark, he climbed up into the crotch, and stretching out on one of the broad limbs, after a fashion, rested. Rest brought him new confidence and almost a feeling of security. Even so zealous a hunter as General Zaroff could not trace him there, he told himself; only the devil himself could follow that complicated trail through the jungle after dark. But perhaps the general was a devil——

An apprehensive night crawled slowly by like a wounded snake, and sleep did not visit Rainsford, although the silence of a dead world was on the jungle. Toward morning, when a dingy gray was varnishing the sky, the cry of some startled bird focussed Rainsford's attention in that direction. Something was coming through the bush, coming slowly, carefully, coming by the same winding way Rainsford had come. He flattened himself down on the limb, and through a screen of leaves almost as thick as tapestry, he watched. The thing that was approaching was a man.

It was General Zaroff. He made his way along with his eyes fixed in utmost concentration on the ground before him. He paused, almost beneath the tree, dropped to his knees, and studied the ground. Rainsford's impulse was to hurl himself down like a panther, but he saw that the general's right hand held something metallic—a small automatic pistol.

The hunter shook his head several times, as if he were puzzled. Then he straightened up and took from his case one of his black cigarettes; its pungent incense-like smoke floated up to Rainsford's nostrils.

Rainsford held his breath. The general's eyes had left the ground and were travelling inch by inch up the tree. Rainsford froze there, every muscle tensed for a spring. But the sharp eyes of the hunter stopped before they reached the limb where Rainsford lay; a smile spread over his brown face. Very deliberately he blew a smoke ring into the air; then he turned his back on the tree and walked carelessly away, back along the trail he had come. The swish of the underbrush against his hunting boots grew fainter and fainter.

The pent-up air burst hotly from Rainsford's lungs. His first thought made him feel sick and numb. The general could follow a trail through the woods at night; he could follow an extremely difficult trail; he must have uncanny powers; only by the merest chance had the Cossack failed to see his quarry.

Rainsford's second thought was even more terrible. It sent a shudder of cold horror through his whole being. Why had the general smiled? Why had he turned back?

Rainsford did not want to believe what his reason told him was true, but the truth was as evident as the sun that had by now pushed through the morning mists. The general was playing with him! The general was saving him for another day's sport! The Cossack was the cat; he was the mouse. Then it was that Rainsford knew the full meaning of terror.

"I will not lose my nerve. I will not."

He slid down from the tree, and struck off again into the woods. His face was set and he forced the machinery of his mind to function. Three hundred yards from his hiding place he stopped where a huge dead tree leaned precariously on a smaller, living one. Throwing off his sack of food, Rainsford took his knife from its sheath and began to work with all his energy.

The job was finished at last, and he threw himself down behind a fallen log a hundred feet away. He did not have to wait long. The cat was coming again to play with the mouse.

Following the trail with the sureness of a bloodhound came General Zaroff. Nothing escaped those searching black eyes, no crushed blade of grass, no bent twig, no mark, no matter how faint, in the moss. So intent was the Cossack on his stalking that he was upon the thing Rainsford had made before he saw it. His foot touched the protruding bough that was the trigger. Even as he touched it, the general sensed his danger and leaped back with the agility of an ape. But he was not quite quick enough; the dead tree, delicately adjusted to rest on the cut living one, crashed down and struck the general a glancing blow on the shoulder as it fell; but for his alertness, he must have been smashed beneath it. He staggered, but he did not fall; nor did he drop his revolver. He stood there, rubbing his injured shoulder, and Rainsford, with fear again gripping his heart, heard the general's mocking laugh ring through the jungle.

"Rainsford," called the general, "if you are within sound of my voice, as I suppose you are, let me congratulate you. Not many men know how to make a Malay man-catcher. Luckily for me I, too, have hunted in Malacca. You are proving interesting, Mr. Rainsford. I am going now to have my wound dressed; it's only a slight one. But I shall be back. I shall be back."

When the general, nursing his bruised shoulder, had gone, Rainsford took up his flight again. It was flight now, a desperate, hopeless flight, that carried him on for some hours. Dusk came, then darkness, and still he pressed on. The ground grew softer under his moccasins; the vegetation grew ranker, denser; insects bit him savagely. Then, as he stepped forward, his foot sank into the ooze. He tried to wrench it back, but the muck sucked viciously at his foot as if it were a giant leech. With a violent effort he tore his foot loose. He knew where he was now. Death Swamp and its quicksand.

His hands were tight closed as if his nerve were something tangible that someone in the darkness was trying to tear from his grip. The softness of the earth had given him an idea. He stepped back from the quicksand a dozen feet or so and, like some huge prehistoric beaver, he began to dig.

Rainsford had dug himself in in France when a second's delay meant death. That had been a placid pastime compared to his digging now. The pit grew deeper; when it was above his shoulders, he climbed out and from some hard saplings cut stakes and sharpened them to a fine point. These stakes he planted in the bottom of the pit with the points sticking up. With flying fingers he wove a rough carpet of weeds and branches and with it he covered the mouth of the pit. Then, wet with sweat and aching with tiredness, he crouched behind the stump of a lightning-charred tree.

He knew his pursuer was coming; he heard the padding sound of feet on the soft earth, and the night breeze brought him the perfume of the general's cigarette. It seemed to Rainsford that the general was coming with unusual swiftness; he was not feeling his way along, foot by foot. Rainsford, crouching there, could not see the general, nor could he see the pit. He lived a year in a minute. Then he felt an impulse to cry aloud with joy, for he heard the sharp crackle of the breaking branches as the cover of the pit gave way; he heard the sharp scream of pain as the pointed stakes found their mark. He leaped up from his place of concealment. Then he cowered back. Three feet from the pit a man was standing, with an electric torch in his hand.

"You've done well, Rainsford," the voice of the general called. "Your Burmese tiger pit has claimed one of my best dogs. Again you score. I think, Mr. Rainsford, I'll see what you can do against my whole pack. I'm going home for a rest now. Thank you for a most amusing evening."

At daybreak Rainsford, lying near the swamp, was awakened by a sound that made him know that he had new things to learn about fear. It was a distant sound, faint and wavering, but he knew it. It was the baying of a pack of hounds.

Rainsford knew he could do one of two things. He could stay where he was and wait. That was suicide. He could flee. That was postponing the inevitable. For a moment he stood there, thinking. An idea that held a wild chance came to him, and, tightening his belt, he headed away from the swamp.

The baying of the hounds drew nearer, then still nearer, nearer, ever nearer. On a ridge Rainsford climbed a tree. Down a watercourse, not a quarter of a mile away, he could see the bush moving. Straining his eyes, he saw the lean figure of General Zaroff; just ahead of him, Rainsford made out another figure whose wide shoulders surged through the tall jungle weeds; it was the giant Ivan, and he seemed pulled forward by some unseen force; Rainsford knew that Ivan must be holding the pack in leash.

They would be on him any minute now. His mind worked frantically. He thought of a native trick he had learned in Uganda. He slid down the tree. He caught hold of a springy young sapling and to it he fastened his hunting knife, with the blade pointing down the trail; with a bit of wild grapevine he tied back the sapling. Then he ran for his life. The hounds raised their voices as they hit the fresh scent. Rainsford knew now how an animal at bay feels.

He had to stop to get his breath. The baying of the hounds stopped abruptly, and Rainsford's heart stopped, too. They must have reached the knife.

He shinned excitedly up a tree and looked back. His pursuers had stopped. But the hope that was in Rainsford's brain when he climbed died, for he saw in the shallow valley that General Zaroff was still on his feet. But Ivan was not. The knife, driven by the recoil of the springing tree, had not wholly failed.

Rainsford had hardly tumbled to the ground when the pack took up the cry again.

"Nerve, nerve, nerve!" he panted, as he dashed along. A blue gap showed between the trees dead ahead. Ever nearer drew the hounds. Rainsford forced himself on toward that gap. He reached it. It was the shore of the sea. Across a cove he could see the gloomy gray stone of the château. Twenty feet below him the sea rumbled and hissed. Rainsford hesitated. He heard the hounds. Then he leaped far out into the sea....

When the general and his pack reached the place by the sea, the Cossack stopped. For some minutes he stood regarding the blue-green expanse of water. He shrugged his shoulders. Then he sat down, took a drink of brandy from a silver flask, lit a perfumed cigarette, and hummed a bit from "Madama Butterfly."

General Zaroff had an exceedingly good dinner in his great panelled dining hall that evening. With it he had a bottle of Pol Roger and half a bottle of Chambertin. Two slight annoyances kept him from perfect enjoyment. One was the thought that it would be difficult to replace Ivan; the other was that his quarry had escaped him; of course the American hadn't played the game—so thought the general as he tasted his after-dinner liqueur. In his library he read, to soothe himself, from the works of Marcus Aurelius. At ten he went up to his bedroom. He was deliciously tired, he said to himself, as he locked himself in. There was a little moonlight, so before turning on his light he went to the window and looked down at the courtyard. He could see the great hounds, and he called: "Better luck another time," to them. Then he switched on the light.

A man, who had been hiding in the curtains of the bed, was standing there.

"Rainsford!" screamed the general. "How in God's name did you get here?"

"Swam," said Rainsford. "I found it quicker than walking through the jungle."

The general sucked in his breath and smiled. "I congratulate you," he said. "You have won the game."

Rainsford did not smile. "I am still a beast at bay," he said, in a low, hoarse voice. "Get ready, General Zaroff."

The general made one of his deepest bows. "I see," he said. "Splendid! One of us is to furnish a repast for the hounds. The other will sleep in this very excellent bed. On guard, Rainsford...."

He had never slept in a better bed, Rainsford decided.

The End

Thank you for reading!

6	2	9	3	4	7	1	5	8
7	3	8	5	2	1	6	4	9
1	4	5	6	8	9	2	7	3
8	5	7	2	1	3	9	6	4
9	6	3	4	5	8	7	1	2
4	1	2	9	7	6	8	3	5
2	8	6	7	3	4	5	9	1
3	9	1	8	6	5	4	2	7
5	7	4	1	9	2	3	8	6

Winter Issue is next!